THE ERRAND BOY

ALSO BY DON BREDES

The Fifth Season
Cold Comfort
Muldoon
Hard Feelings

THE ERRAND BOY

A NOVEL

Don Bredes

THREE RIVERS PRESS · NEW YORK

Copyright © 2009 by Don Bredes

All rights reserved.
Published in the United States by Three Rivers Press, an imprint of the Crown Publishing Group, a division of Random House, Inc., New York.
www.crownpublishing.com

Three Rivers Press and the Tugboat design are registered trademarks of Random House, Inc.

Grateful acknowledgment is made to Henry Holt and Company, LLC for permission to reprint an excerpt from "Not All There" from *The Poetry of Robert Frost* edited by Edward Connery Lathem, copyright © 1969 by Henry Holt and Company, copyright © 1936 by Robert Frost, copyright © 1964 by Lesley Frost Ballantine. Reprinted by permission of Henry Holt and Company, LLC.

Library of Congress Cataloging-in-Publication Data is available upon request.

ISBN 978-0-307-23743-9

Printed in the United States of America

Design by Phil Mazzone

10 9 8 7 6 5 4 3 2 1

First Edition

For my mother, who taught me the pleasures of storytelling

I turned to speak to God
About the world's despair
But to make bad matters worse
I found God wasn't there.

—Robert Frost, *A Further Range*

THE ERRAND BOY

PROLOGUE

ONE BALMY, GREEN EVENING in June the supper-table conversation turned to brides, a new topic of interest for Myra, our eleven-year-old daughter. Over rhubarb pie she asked Wilma what it had been like to be Daddy's bride, what she wore, what flowers she carried, and all that. Wilma blushed to admit that she *had* been a bride—twice, in fact—but she had never been *Daddy's* bride.

Myra was amazed. "Didn't you want to get married?"

"Oh, sweetheart," she said, "we're married. We just never had a wedding." She laughed and shrugged at me.

"It's a funny story," I said.

"By the time my divorce finally came through," Wilma said, "you were already two months old, and Daddy and I were very busy with you and the farm and everything else, and so we decided to just have a simple little ceremony at the cabin."

"How simple?"

"Oh, you know, nothing fancy." She looked across at me. "Classical guitar, justice of the peace . . ."

"Right," I said. "Good food and a few friends. And no relatives."

"Yes, no relatives," Wilma said. "And no cake and no deities. None of the usual embellishments—except flowers."

"And the Moët et Chandon," I said.

"*Mais oui.*"

"That sounds nice," Myra said. "What did you wear?"

"Nothing!" Wilma said with her arms out. She laughed at Myra's expression. "It never happened."

On a bitter March morning after a big late-season snowstorm, Wilma and I had ventured down to the town hall in Tipton to pick up a marriage license from Esther Nichols, the town clerk. After that, at Esther's suggestion, we headed on out to Fritz Verber's B & B in Shadboro. Verber was an uncle of Esther's and a JP of forty years' standing. "Easygoing, practical-minded old coot," Esther told us. "Man of few words, but he'll do whatever you want. I remember one time—this was years ago now—he married a young couple that wanted to get married underwater, if you can believe that. Scuba wedding. Sign language and bubbles. Old Fritz, he never done any scuba diving before, but he went for it."

We found Fritz Verber out snowblowing his long driveway, a plume of powder sailing over his shoulder. He was about eighty, a little stooped, but ruddy, clear-eyed, and sinewy, with a quarter inch of frosty stubble on his face. He took his machine out of gear when we pulled into his lane. We got out of Wilma's Subaru, leaving Myra asleep in her car seat, and we introduced ourselves. Wilma explained in her breezy, emphatic way that we wanted to get married but with no ceremony—just a perfunctory, no-frills, tie-the-knot kind of deal. Would he be interested? Fritz nodded and asked if we'd secured a license from the clerk. Wilma pulled it out of her canvas tote. We watched him fish his reading glasses from an inside pocket, inspect the document, put away his glasses, take out a pen, lick the tip, and make a scrawl across the bottom. He handed it back to Wilma. "That'll do 'er. Congratulations."

We smiled in wonder at each other and then we kissed. I asked Fritz what he charged.

"Nothin'," he said. "World record, I expect."

Myra was appalled. "But that didn't *count*, did it?"

"Oh, it counted all right," Wilma said. "We loved it. Not too many people get hitched by surprise."

Myra frowned. "OK, but that doesn't mean you couldn't still have a ceremony, right? I mean, you could have a ceremony anytime, couldn't you?"

We saw what was coming.

"And a nice dress, like ivory silk cut on the bias, and a harp player with long hair, and a dozen yellow roses."

"Well, the yellow roses I like," Wilma said.

"How about this summer?"

We looked at each other.

Myra said she would handle the invitations, the caterer, and the musical selections. And she would make a list of questions for us so that she wouldn't forget anything. All we would have to do is pick out the wine. We told her we'd have to think about it, but by the next morning we found the poetry of the idea appealing. If it hadn't been for Myra, we would never have gotten married in the first place. What's more, against the odds, Wilma was pregnant again. And it was June.

It was June in Vermont.

ONE

WEEKS LATER, ON A hot, still Saturday in mid-July, the second day of the Allenburg downtown merchants' Sizzling Sidewalk Super Sale, Wilma and I were headed for Main Street Beverage and Redemption to order the wine for our wedding party. Heavy thunder was rumbling to the north of town. Myra had spent the morning up that way with Hugh Gebbie, a family friend, and because of the way the sky looked in that direction, our thoughts were on the two of them.

With the wedding more than a month away, our mission might have waited, but we'd been up since five, and we wanted an excuse to stretch our legs. We had left the truck and the van at the county fairgrounds, where the farmers' market set up each weekend, and made our way down through Greenleaf Cemetery, crossed the river on the defunct railroad bridge, and turned up the steep, root-buckled sidewalk along Crevecoeur Hill toward Main.

We were happy. We'd sold out of everything, green and wax beans, beet greens, zucchini, broccoli rabe, all our lettuce, peas, salad turnips, onions, raspberries, rhubarb, and herbs. We'd also sold two dozen jars of my sister-in-law's strawberry jam, forty-five pounds of Lance Henault's wildflower honey, and $130 worth of my own fancy garlic, a first this season.

From the top of Crevecoeur where it bisects Main Street, on clear days you could see into Quebec through a gap in the hills, but not today. A leaden curtain of weather hung in between. "They're right in the *teeth* of it," Wilma was saying as we stepped into the crosswalk.

"They're fine. They're indoors—" *eating ice cream and raspberries,* I was about to say, because that had been the plan—feed the alpacas, pick the berries, swim in the pond, and make the ice cream—but I never got the words out.

A revving engine had me twisting the other way to catch a looming, yellow blur. My left hand went to Wilma's chest, and I shoved her back as I pivoted to my right.

My rump glanced hard off the car's fender, though I managed to tuck my head to the side and somersault from my shoulder to my feet again all in one motion.

The yellow car skidded and slammed backwards into the tail end of a camper angled into the curb. It crashed against the bumpers of two more cars before coming to a stop.

Someone was screaming.

Wilma lay still, splayed out in the street. Three blue postal boxes stood on the corner behind her, bolted to concrete slabs. Somebody behind us who'd seen the whole thing later told police Wilma's head had struck the edge of one of those slabs.

She was unconscious, her freckles already faded and her lips gray, her eyelashes gold filaments in the unnatural brightness of the air. I touched her. She was bleeding at the back of her head.

A woman leaned over me and said, "I'm a nurse."

"We'll need a spine board," I said without looking up.

"Are you a doctor?"

"I'm a cop."

"Anybody have a phone?" the woman asked.

"Rescue Squad's on the way," somebody said. And already we could hear the siren.

The nurse dropped to her knee beside me and opened Wilma's eyelid. She felt her chest and her stomach. "She's breathing," she said, "but we'll want to support her jaw—keep her airway open."

"She's four months' pregnant," I said.

The woman glanced at me. She had a tan and short white hair. "I wouldn't worry too much. Nature protects the fetus."

Behind her I could see the flashing lights of the ambulance.

"Take charge here, will you?" I said. "While I check out the driver?"

"Of course. Go."

It was a canary yellow BMW M3 coupe with temporary plates—brand-new. The driver had run the stop sign and swerved hard at the sight of us in the crosswalk, sending the car into a one-eighty.

Two onlookers, an Asian couple, were leaning down and looking in at the driver. I came up behind them.

"Excuse me, please. I'm an officer."

The couple nodded and stepped back.

"You OK in there?"

He looked like a kid—young man—twenty-one, twenty-two, with a wispy triangle of blond beard and a bloody nose. His air bags had deployed. He had an abrasion along his cheekbone, a fat ear, and glass and talc in his hair.

"Hey, in there! *Talk* to me."

"Quit shoutin'!"

"Are you hurt?"

"I'm bleeding, aren't I?" He was dabbing his nose with

the sleeve of his sweatshirt. "Busted my Oakleys. Fucking air bags."

"If you're not hurt, I want you to get out of this vehicle."

He squinted up at me. "That was *you*, wasn't it? I almost took you out."

I pulled on his door. It moved a few inches before the hinges bound up. I yanked on the handle and it sprang wide with a pop.

"Come on, get out."

"Back off, asshole. I just wrecked my brother's car, and I'm not feeling that great, in case you can't tell."

"You drove through a four-way stop—*asshole*—and you hit me in the crosswalk."

"I didn't *hit you*. If I *hit* you, you're dead."

"Are you going to get out of this vehicle or do I have to drag you out?"

"I'm comin'. I *said* I'm comin'."

The kid pulled the key and slid out into the street, groaning. He glared at the bystanders.

"What's your name?" I said.

"Jay Leno. What's yours?"

I reached out and clamped him underneath his jaw and whammed him back into the roof of the car. "You almost *killed* me, wiseass."

He hacked. "Let me go, *fucker*."

I squeezed.

The kid took it, squinching his eyes. Tears came down his cheeks.

"What's your *name*?"

A siren whooped once. I let him have a last shove and let him go.

"All right, all right, all *right*, you guys! Knock it off!" A town cop pushed his way through the few onlookers. Young

and bareheaded, caterpillar mustache, no older than the kid
in front of me. I didn't recognize him.

"Cool your jets, guys, all right?" His tag read BERGERON.

"I'm Hector Bellevance, constable up in Tipton. This kid
ran us down in the crosswalk—me and my wife. She's been
injured. Make sure you Breath-a-lyze him. I'll be filing charges."

"Charges!" The kid coughed. He spat blood into the
street. "I'll sue you for *assault*, asshole."

I grabbed his throat again. "Well, then maybe I should
make it worth my while."

"Hold it! *Hold it!* Jeez, you two!" Officer Bergeron took
me by the arm and drew me away. "Go see about your wife,
Mr. Bellevance. I got it from here."

I WATCHED AS the EMTs put a foam collar on Wilma.
They had stopped the bleeding at the back of her head. I
looked away while they intubated her. The nurse, whose
name I never got, had already left.

At the hospital a gurney was waiting for us outside the
ER. I touched her cheek as they wheeled her inside, thinking
a thousand disconnected things.

I filled out some forms, phoned Hugh Gebbie, then went
out and sat on an orange vinyl couch in the waiting room,
which was unoccupied except for a scraggly-haired young
woman in overalls and the small girl she was holding in her
lap. The girl had a white dressing over her right eye. It looked
like half a softball. Behind them rain was pouring into the
parking lot, silver coins dancing on the roofs of the cars.
When had that started?

Hugh and Myra hurried in, soaked, a few minutes before
the orthopedic surgeon, Julius Kaufman, came out to introduce himself. He ushered us into a room where Wilma lay on
her back, shoulders elevated slightly, plugged into monitors

and an IV. An oxygen mask covered her face. Forehead smooth and eyes closed under her pale gold eyebrows, she looked terribly peaceful.

Dr. Kaufman told us she was probably suffering an episode of transient neurapraxia. "A temporary paralysis caused by the sudden compression of the spinal cord. Any sudden impact that sends the spine into extreme flexion"—he illustrated by dropping his chin to his chest—"is all it takes. It's the sort of thing we see with contact-sport athletes—football players, hockey players. They're usually good as new within forty-eight hours. In Wilma's case, all we know is she's taken a blow to the back of the head and a shock to the brain. She has to heal. I am confident she will."

"What does that mean?" Myra said. "Heal how?" She had been listening, looking down at Wilma, holding her mother's hand loosely in both of hers, her slender, berry-stained thumbs moving over the knuckles. Now she fixed her vivid green eyes on the doctor, and he drew back a little at her expression.

"Well, Myra, there may have been some damage to the tissue caused by her brain's smacking against the interior of the skull. Luckily for us, the brain is *very good* at healing itself. She could regain consciousness anytime. Oh—" He turned to me and Hugh. "Here's good news. The ultrasound says the baby's fine."

"Thank you," I said. "How about the CT scan?"

"To me it looks normal. When the radiologist gets here, he'll have more to say. At this point all we can do is support her and watch her. You know"—he looked back toward Myra—"it's really not all that much different from being asleep."

"It's very different," Myra told him. "Because we can't wake her up."

He smiled and patted her arm.

"I wouldn't want to be asleep if I couldn't wake up," Myra

said after Dr. Kaufman had excused himself. She touched Wilma's hair. Her own wiry red hair, I noticed now, was flecked with raspberry burrs and sticks.

"Dr. Kaufman's right, Myra," I said. "First her brain needs to heal. Then she'll wake up."

"But what if it doesn't heal?"

"It will heal, sweetheart."

"You're just saying that. You don't really *know* that."

On the other side of the bed, Hugh scoffed at her, "You're a tough one, you are."

She faced him. "No, I'm not. I just don't think it makes sense to pretend that something worse can't happen to her when it *could*."

"Myra. You're too young to be so cynical. Don't you believe in the power of positive thinking?"

She frowned. "Not really."

"I do. I believe the mind exerts its own force upon the world."

"So are you saying *negative* thinking could hurt Mom?"

"No, I'm saying good thoughts are healing thoughts."

Myra exhaled, her mouth trembling. Then she crumpled into tears and covered her face with her hands.

Hugh gave me a helpless look.

I went and held her. She pushed her face into my chest.

"She's going to be OK, Myra. 'Transient neurapraxia.' Transient means it's temporary. It goes away."

"Daddy," she said, pulling back to look into my eyes. Her tearful, red face was her four-year-old face the day she crashed her Flexible Flyer headfirst into a bank of frozen snow. "You know what I hate?"

"What?"

"This shouldn't have even happened. You're supposed to *stop* at stop signs."

"The laws aren't foolproof, Myra. Everyone makes mistakes. Some fools make a lot of them."

"Fools abound," Hugh said. He was gazing out the window at the rain. "Foolishness is a fundamental condition of humanity."

"But when fools break the law, you're supposed to *do* something about it," Myra said. "There's supposed to be some punishment, isn't there?"

"That's your dad's department. I'm just an old geomancer."

She almost smiled.

"He'll lose his driver's license," I said, "and his insurance company will be paying Mom's medical bills."

"That's all?"

Hugh chuckled and shook his head.

She turned to me. "Dad, you know what? I wish you wouldn't have had to push her."

I shrugged. "Might have been worse if I hadn't."

"That's not what I mean. I feel *bad* for you."

I knew what she meant—I just wasn't ready to face it. I hadn't been paying attention. For whatever reason, I had escorted my wife into the street without looking. If only I had looked.

Hugh had to get back to his animals. At around five the rain let up, and Myra and I left to find something to eat in the hospital cafeteria. Later, driving through Tipton village on the way home, we saw that one of the twelve giant white pines bordering the village cemetery had come down and flattened thirty yards of wrought-iron fence along with the hearse house, where the cemetery sexton kept his mower and tools. When we arrived at our cabin up in the hills, we were relieved to find we still had power. The tomatoes and leaf crops had taken a beating, but they'd recover. The sky was still pale when we went to bed.

• • •

SUNDAY MORNING we rose with the sun, as usual. The birds' early chorus sounded especially rich, as if they were celebrating having survived the storm. It was going to be a sparkling high summer day.

We ate yogurt and berries, and then I went out to restake the tomatoes. The vines were mostly intact, I was glad to find. All in all, my crops were in pretty good shape. The corn was fine. I had close to a thousand highbush blueberries heavy with red fruit, and they had held up nicely. As Agnes, my mother, used to say, "Healthy plants will always bounce back from ordinary calamities." She was right.

Midmorning, Myra and I drove in to the hospital. Wilma was unchanged. Dr. Kaufman, a nurse told us, would be in sometime after eleven, but I had too much to do to sit there and wait, so I left Myra at Wilma's side and returned to the farm. Around noon, when I went inside for a bite of lunch, the red light on my answering machine was blinking.

I hit PLAY.

"Morning, Mr. Bellevance. Greg Bergeron, Allenburg Police, at about eleven, little after. Hope your wife's doin' OK. Listen, I'm calling in regard to the negligent motor vehicle incident yesterday involving yourself and your wife. You might want to alert your attorney. Ring me back and I'll explain." He left a pager number.

I dialed it, and he phoned back. He asked about Wilma and said he knew Dr. Kaufman—she couldn't be in better hands.

"Good to hear," I said. "So what's this about my needing a lawyer?"

"OK. Guy that ran you down yesterday? He's a Canadian national named Sebastian Tuttle. Vehicle he was operating is registered to his older brother, Jeremy Tuttle. Who you already know, correct?"

"That's right." Jeremy Tuttle and his father, Harold, were

large-scale hog and egg farmers. Jeremy managed the Tipton Egg Works, a recently erected eyesore on King's Knob, a few miles west of the village.

"Vehicle involved, it turns out, wasn't insured, OK? So these three guys, when they left here yesterday—the Tuttles and their lawyer, from Montpelier—these gentlemen were talking like maybe *you* were the one that caused the accident."

"*What?*"

"Right. So, anything you need from us, Mr. Bellevance, just ask. I'm talking photographs, names of witnesses, you name it. Affidavits? You're golden, OK?"

"The little bastard, he's claiming he didn't run that stop sign?"

"What he says is he believes you stepped out in front of him. And he's saying he didn't hit you *or* your wife."

"Bullshit! A dozen people saw what happened! There was a nurse! There was this Asian couple—"

"*I know,* that's what I'm trying to *say.* We got names and numbers, we got skid marks, digital photos. . . . Hey. Sebastian Tuttle's looking at negligent operation injury resulting, plus thirty days' suspension. But as far as the liability issue, this can get ugly. Once you start getting attorneys involved . . . you know what I'm saying?"

"I do. Thanks, Greg, for the heads-up," I said.

"Sure, and the *other* thing is, these two Tuttle brothers? They hate your guts."

I assured him I held their guts in no higher regard.

My anger over this little surprise was not going to subside anytime soon, not as long as Wilma's life was in the balance. But I wasn't about to call an attorney, not before having a serious talk with the Tuttles myself.

I drove down to the hospital at around four. Myra had been keeping vigil and reading to her mother from the *New Yorker.* Dr. Kaufman was "very upbeat," she told me. "*Every-*

body around this place is so upbeat it's sick. But as long as Mom's stable, that's cool. So basically we just have to wait, like he said yesterday." She made a brave smile. Her cheeks were tearstained.

The perfect oval of Wilma's face was untroubled and white, but her freckles were still unlit and her lips looked waxy. I kissed her and whispered that I was here and that I loved her, but after about ten minutes in the room I had to leave. I couldn't look at her and I couldn't gaze anymore out the window. Myra was relieved when I said we should head for home, but it was hard for her to pull herself away.

On the long drive back to Tipton Myra kept quiet. The next morning she was supposed to leave for a two-week summer camp session on the other side of the Green Mountains, where the Audubon Youth Camp had a tenting ground overlooking a wild pond. She had her clothing and other gear already in order, laid out in piles on the daybed in the sunroom. The plan for today—hers and Wilma's—had been to pack the aluminum footlocker.

The path to the cabin was bordered knee-high with daisies, clumps of lilies, red clover, and pasture rose. As we walked, Myra ahead of me on the gravel path, the bumblebees zooming, the swallowtails sailing, the noise of the brook, the warmth of the high sun, the color of the tranquil sky, it all hurt.

"Say, Myra."

"What?"

"Want me to help you pack for Audubon?"

"I'm not going."

We walked up the steps, crossed the porch, and went inside. Myra kicked off her flip-flops.

I watched her go to the fridge and yank open the door.

"I don't mean tomorrow necessarily, but when you're ready. Until Mom's better, I see no reason why you can't—"

"I'm *waiting*, Dad. OK? I'm waiting for *both* of us." She shut the fridge, took a banana from the basket on the counter, and marched to her room, closing the door without a glance at me.

I called in after her. "I think I'm going to drive up to Spud's and let them know what's happened. Want to come?"

"The beans need picking, don't they?" she said through the door.

"I won't be long."

"Right, sure. You start talking and Spud goes, 'How about a Molson?' and pretty soon it's an hour later."

I laughed.

As it happened, though, Spud was in the barn with Harry Thibidoux, the vet, tending to a sick cow, and Brenda and Lyle were out shopping.

I left a note on the kitchen table:

> *Just stopped by to tell you Wilma's in the hospital. She's*
> *going to be OK, but she's in a coma. A car went through a*
> *stop sign in town yesterday afternoon and clipped us in the*
> *crosswalk. The driver, by the way, was Sebastian Tuttle.*
> *Anyway, Myra's distressed, naturally. Give me a call when*
> *you can.*
>
> —H

Later that night after chores, Spud took the time to phone. After I'd described the accident, he asked whether I thought it might have been deliberate. I told him no, Seb didn't even know who I was. I hadn't recognized him either.

"Reason I ask, did you hear about what happened to Doug Henault this morning?" The Henault farm and Tuttles' Tipton Egg Works were neighboring properties.

"No. Tell me."

"Two guys on four-wheelers drove right through Doug's

pumpkin patch, and when Doug started yelling at 'em, they beat the crap out of him."

"Christ. How bad's he hurt?"

"Bad enough. Bunch of stitches, plus they're gonna have to cast his foot soon as the swelling's gone down. But here's the thing. This was a felony—assault and battery, right?"

"I'd say so."

"People go to jail for this kinda shit. But Doug's not pressing charges."

"Why?"

"OK, on *Friday* it seems Doug took his tractor and he went up and invaded the egg farm."

"Did you say *invaded*?"

"Yup. Drove right through the main gate, took a post maul to the front door of the office there, went inside, and I guess he trashed the place."

"That doesn't sound like Doug."

"Guess he lost it."

"So who put the boots to him?"

"He isn't sure who. They had on these full-face helmets, right?"

"He told you this?"

"No, Cindy did—well, actually, she told Brenda. Brenda ran into her this afternoon down to Rite-Aid getting Doug's medicine, and I guess Doug was sitting out in the car. Anyhow, you want to check this out, because if it *was* the Tuttles broke Doug's foot, that *could* be related to what happened to you, like if they're going around taking out the opposition, you know?"

"Thanks, Spud," I told him. "I'll look into it."

TWO

KING'S KNOB, WEST OF the Bailey Plateau, was a symmetrical dumpling of a wooded hill with pasture and fields of hay and corn tumbled all around it. The post-card carousel in Sullivan's Store held a dozen cards featuring the Knob from every angle in all seasons. A little over a year ago some fifty acres on the south shoulder of the Knob were clear-cut for the installation of a steel-roofed laying shed and its attached, two-story egg-sorting, packing, and shipping building. In a letter to the *Allenburg Eagle,* Wilma called the new farm "a grotesque abomination and a perfect travesty in form and function."

According to the writings of Ora Bainbridge, Tipton's first historian, the King's Knob surround was "untouched forest" until 1786, when Vermont, then a sovereign nation, sold the high hill's great stand of white pine to the British Royal Navy. Over the next few decades the hardwood was cut off as well, and the rolling terrain at the foot of the Knob was stumped and settled by the county's earliest farmers, Lemuel Bainbridge (son of Ora) and his Canadian cousin, Roland Gauthier. Their stony, remote farmsteads lay a mile from each other, skirting the Knob to the south and east. The shallow upland soil was mostly poor—shaley or sandy—and neither farm prospered. In the 1930s, the Bainbridge place was lost to a chimney fire and the barns were later sold for the timbers, and in the '50s the last of the ne'er-do-well Gochies finally ran the other farm into the ground. By that time, the top of King's Knob had returned to maple, beech, and ash, with tracts of spruce and hemlock on the north side. The Gochie place stood abandoned until the spring of 1968, when a woman from New York City bought both farmsteads for $22,000. That summer the derelict Gochie place sprang to life in the form of a commune named Mostly Holy Farm. For me, at twelve, what everyone else kept calling the Gochie place (as in "just terrible what happened to the Gochie place") became an enchanted utopia in the most picturesque of country settings, crazy and exotic, swarming with geraniums and cats and industrious hippies, with a sunny white porch, a warped Ping-Pong table in the haybarn, a hookah in the parlor, a Wise Potato Chips van for a henhouse, a shaggy lawn, roaming goats and hens, wind chimes tinkling, and the occasional naked person ambling down to the swimming hole. My mother used to bring me along to the commune for dinners and parties. She was romantically attached for a while to the commune's guiding spirit, a poet and welder named Yuri, whom she'd met at a gathering of recorder players. Through Yuri we got to know the others, most memorably the matriarch, Priscilla Gray, known as Peggy, and Peggy's partner, an exuberant local beauty and free spirit named Annie Laurie Rowell. I had a boy's desperate crush on Annie Laurie. She was in her twenties, wild haired, loose breasted, and breathtakingly careless of male attention.

Peggy, who had taught Latin at a girls' school in Manhattan, adored my mother. A teacher herself, Agnes was once a classics major at Smith College. Through my teens, the

Gochie place was a colorful point of reference, a place I imagined moving to someday. But in the early '80s in the middle of one of the coldest winters ever, after the farm had been without water for six weeks, the core household disbanded once and for all. A year after that, Peggy returned to New York City for leukemia treatments, leaving behind lovely Annie Laurie Rowell and her forty-five Nubian goats.

When Peggy died, the farm went to her one child, Starlyn, who lived in Key West, where he owned a rollicking inn that catered to gays. Starlyn Gray had been homeschooled at the King's Knob commune, which might have been why he was glad to let the old farmhouse and thirty-five acres go to Annie and her partner, Helen Croft, for a small price. Annie and Helen were just starting to do well at the time, marketing Annie Laurie's Chèvre around Boston, and they didn't need the rest of the property, not that they could have afforded it. Within the year Starlyn sold the remaining 480 acres, along with the Knob, to a hog farmer from New Brunswick, Harold Tuttle.

The mention of this transaction that appeared in the *Allenburg Eagle* described Tuttle as "a Canadian businessman." Our town clerk, the incurious Esther Nichols, knew nothing more, and with only this to go on, people in town assumed that Tuttle would do what every other wealthy Canadian who bought land in Vermont had done: build a chalet—some fieldstone monstrosity with an impractical driveway, where he could come to unwind for a couple weeks a year. He had the fieldstone.

In a few months' time a logging operation denuded the crest of the hill and much of the south shoulder. Nobody liked seeing the clear-cut, but the hill had been logged before, and the loggers were local. After that, a construction crew from upstate New York settled in to build a laying house and a processing barn with offices, and the day they were done

Tuttle trucked in a hundred thousand layers and tons of feed. By February the farm was shipping a million eggs a month back across the line to wholesale distributors in Quebec.

Right from the start, the volume of truck traffic irked the neighbors, mostly farmers themselves, and Kevin Blake, our road foreman, was unhappy over the beating the back roads were taking. In the early spring, Blake, Annie Rowell, and Doug and Cindy Henault, who milked 130 Holsteins half a mile downwind of King's Knob, came to me to ask what I could do about all the eighteen-wheelers roaring by day and night. But as long as they had their flaps and obeyed the load limits, the town had no leverage. I did call Tuttle and persuaded him to arrange his pickups and deliveries during the middle of the day, for all the improvement that made. Then, by late April, as the days grew warmer, the truck problem was eclipsed by the stench of TEW's accumulating manure and, soon after that, by the flies.

They appeared in hordes that ranged for more than a mile south and east of the egg factory. They filled the cow barn, milking parlor, and tank room at the Henault farm. At Annie Rowell's, the flies put a halt to her cheesemaking. They were everywhere, by the thousands, in the house, in their food and clothing, landing on their sleeping faces, and on every surface indoors and out. Up at Doug's, they were settling on the backs of his cows in such numbers that the cows took to blowing feed over their backs to get them off. Before long the tormented cows just stopped eating, and Doug's production went off a cliff.

At that time Wilma, Myra, and I happened to be in Belize, snorkling, birding, and wandering through Mayan ruins. My brother Spud's son, Lyle Laclair, was looking after our greenhouse and cold frames. Spud was taking my calls. Annie Laurie Rowell was the first to phone about the fly plague. She was enraged, Spud told me, and a day later, when Doug

Henault called, he sounded desperate—at the end of his rope. Doug had planted his own grain that spring, and in two years he planned to go organic. The fly problem threatened the future of both these wholesome farms, and since I wasn't around, Spud and Doug Henault decided to drive up to the egg farm one afternoon to have it out with Jeremy Tuttle themselves.

They ended up sitting outside the gate beeping their horn for fifteen minutes. No one came out to let them in. So Spud went home, took out a pad of yellow paper, and wrote a three-page letter to the state's commissioner of agriculture, Phil McIntyre, detailing the town's grievances against the Egg Works and demanding the department's intervention. Spud felt sure that McIntyre, a sixth-generation Vermonter and a longtime dairyman, would come down hard on Harold Tuttle, the foreign fat cat with no ties to Vermont.

Spud's answer was in the mail the day I got back from the Yucatan.

> Dear Mr. Laclair:
>
> Thank you for alerting me to the problems that a few of your neighbors have been experiencing up in Tipton. I can assure you that this department has kept itself well informed of Harold Tuttle's Tipton Egg Works, etc., and we are confident that his farm is in compliance with Accepted Agricultural Practices (AAPs).
>
> Before any action can be contemplated by this department, the fly trouble that you describe would have to be researched and documented. All farms have flies, as you know. If it is the case that the Henault and Rowell flies are deriving from the Tipton Egg Works (TEW), in that event there are effective solutions that this department can facilitate for the impacted farmers.
>
> Let me suggest that you ask all parties to keep records to

document any decline in production. In the meantime,
hanging up more fly strips and doing some additional
spraying might make a real difference.

Again, thank you for informing me of your concerns. I
am sure these matters will be resolved to the satisfaction of
all involved.

Most sincerely,
Phil McIntyre, Commissioner

"What kind of jerk is this McIntyre, anyway? I thought he was a *farmer*." Spud was pacing up and down the length of my greenhouse. "First off, that operation up on the Knob, that is no *farm*. It's a factory. Factories are about cranking out one product just as cheap and fast as you can make it. A farm's about a whole lot more than that. Farming's a *life*, not a way to make a living."

This was a sentiment I'd heard him express before. "Well, the state's looking at gross agricultural product, Spud. You know that."

"But that's *meaningless* if you have to trash the community to get your product to market. It's not sustainable. It's not even *cheap*. We are subsidizing this factory-farm bullshit with our *quality of life*."

"I suspect you've caught the commissioner with his pants down. He needs some cover while he pulls them up again."

"We need factory farm regulations like they have over in Maine. That's the reason Tuttle didn't set up over there— because in Maine there's laws to regulate these type of operations."

"There aren't any laws here?"

"That's right. We'll *get* laws—soon as the legislature wakes up—but that'll be too late for Doug Henault and Annie Rowell. Whatever happens now, they're stuck with that fly farm up on the Knob for as long as Tuttle wants to keep it there."

"Doug's filed a lawsuit, you know."

"Yeah, but that's a nuisance case is all that is," Spud said. "Even if he wins it, it's a mosquito bite to the Tuttles."

What I saw for myself when I visited the Henault and Rowell farms moved me to put on a dress shirt and a necktie and drive down to Montpelier for a chat with the commissioner. McIntyre agreed to see me on short notice because I had a reputation in the capital, and he probably thought that a few words and a pat on the shoulder would soothe me.

As it turned out, McIntyre had known all along what Tuttle was planning for King's Knob. Tuttle's attorneys had called his office to inquire about the state's regulations. "Truth is," McIntyre said, "like I told Tuttle, in the state of Vermont a farm is a farm is a farm. Accepted agricultural practices, that's what we go by."

"That's obviously not enough."

"Oh, he'll get the kinks ironed out. Harold Tuttle's a multi-millionaire. When it comes to large farm operations, he knows what he's doing."

"I'm sure. But, come on, Commissioner, you have to admit the state's been blindsided here."

"Mr. Bellevance, when a wealthy international businessman comes to me wanting to construct a state-of-the-art facility on a bony hill farm that's been out of production since Hoover was in the White House, I'm going to pay attention. Harold Tuttle didn't get rich by making stupid investments. Now, that doesn't mean you don't have a problem up there, but if there *is* a problem, we will take care of it, OK? My promise to you."

"Fine. What's the first step?"

"We'll have to have us a look-see. Tuttle's got to get all the glitches worked out before we'll approve any expansion. He knows that."

"What expansion?" I said, the blood rising in my neck.

"What he's got so far, that's preliminary. He plans to erect nine laying sheds. Plus a structure for replacement pullets."

"He wants to throw up *ten more* confinement sheds? For what, *a million chickens*?"

"A million's the optimum number for a medium-size egg farm, according to what I understand. He's a smart man and he's cautious, too. He—"

"Cautious! He's a goddamn pirate!"

McIntyre lowered his chin. "Have you *met* Mr. Tuttle?"

"Not yet. I'm sure looking forward to it, though."

"Truth is, the state could use a few more operations like Tuttle's. Consolidation and expansion—that's the face of modern agriculture, like it or not."

"Commissioner, when Tuttle informed you he wanted to bring all these birds down to Tipton, didn't your department suggest an impact study?"

"That's what we're in the process of doing, Constable."

"I mean *before* you let these people sink their fangs in you."

"Mr. Bellevance, the family farm's been in a death spiral since you were in diapers. I milked a hundred head for thirty-two years, and it just about killed me. These days, *nobody* wants to work that hard if they don't have to. Large-scale operations are the wave of the future. You ever hear of the economy of scale?"

"The economy of scale's a crock of shit! Tuttle's pushing his costs off on the town. Roads, water, ground pollution. All you have to do—"

"*The fact is,* Mr. Bellevance, by *law,* that man has as much right to farm up there as you people do."

"Not at our expense he doesn't."

"Like I said, if there's a problem, we'll fix it. OK? We done?"

"Not until you tell me when you're coming up to Tipton to test the goddamn flies."

"As soon as possible."

"Two days."

"Done."

We shook hands.

Two days later on a picture-perfect May afternoon I met Frank Ianotti, the state entomologist, outside the chain-link gates to the Tipton Egg Works. Taciturn and unsmiling, Ianotti wore thick eyeglasses and a close-cropped black beard that didn't mask his underbite.

He and I followed Jeremy Tuttle into the storage warehouse. Jeremy had sallow skin, a soccer-ball paunch, and an air of exaggerated patience that began to annoy me ten seconds after we'd met.

Thousands of white eggs stacked in trays stood on pallets waiting to be shipped. The shrink-wrapped stacks were seven feet high. We followed Tuttle through the washing, sorting, and packing room, which was quiet, the egg belts unmoving and the inspection stations empty, down a corridor lined with computerized monitoring equipment and into the chicken shed.

Here the smell didn't seem bad, and neither did the flies. The hens were packed so tight in their wire cages I couldn't tell one from another. But they weren't noisy.

"Those birds on drugs?"

"It's the lighting," Jeremy said. "They like it."

Three double rows of cages eight tiers high extended fifty or sixty yards down the length of the building. The aisles were lit by alternating red and white bulbs.

"You think they like this?" I said.

Jeremy shrugged. "If they had a choice, maybe they'd rather be pecking dirt and eating bugs, but they don't know that. They aren't suffering. Look at them. We don't even trim their beaks. We feed 'em and water 'em, and they do what comes naturally, God bless them. Where would we be without eggs, eh?"

"Free-range hens live five times longer," I said, "and they lay more nutritious eggs."

"That's a myth. These birds eat as healthy as any layer on God's acre, and their eggs are the best you can buy. Cheapest, too. You want to pay three-eighty-nine for organic happy-time eggs, be my guest, but you're wasting your money."

A feed trough ran along each tier. Augurs in the troughs drove the feed along. The cage floors were pitched so that the eggs rolled out onto the segmented plastic belts that carried them to the sorting and washing room. Manure and feathers and dust collected underneath on trays, which got scraped into a pit below.

After descending two flights of steel stairs into that dim space below the tiers of hens, we confronted a pond of throat-searing, putty-colored gunk that burbled with maggots. I had to laugh. Ianotti collected his specimens while I waited back in the doorway with Jeremy.

"Without these turbo fans, we could hardly stand it down here," Jeremy was saying. Six tubular fans the size of jet engines had been set into the walls. "They draw out the gases."

"And the flies," I said.

He turned to look at me. "Tell you something about these flies. February, when we got started, you couldn't find a fly on this whole farm. Where did they come from? Don't know, but I nominate Doug Henault's cow barn. Maybe you're unaware, but it was May before Doug got his lagoon cleaned out. He had cow shit running off into Taylor Brook for weeks—you could see it from the road. Think there's any trout left in that watercourse? I haven't caught one. But I haven't gone crying to the state about it either."

After a tour of the Henault farm and half an hour with

Annie Rowell, whose lavish profanity made him nervous, Frank Ianotti had pulled together enough to determine that the plague flies had come from the Egg Works. With that, however, instead of addressing the source, the department sent someone up from Montpelier with a supply of "natural fly suppressant" and spraying equipment—gifts to the affected farmers.

Doug was skeptical. "What's so *natural* about it?" he wanted to know.

"They're pyrethrums," the agent told him. "Made from crysanthemums—safe as the air freshener you spray in your bathroom."

"Call me a pig," Annie Rowell said, "but I don't spray my fucking bathroom, and I'm sure as hell not about to spray my fucking goats. Cancer's natural, too, I hate to inform you."

While his lawsuit was pending, Doug Henault had no choice but to fog his cow barn twice a day. "I been there when he's milking," Spud told me then, "and it's terrible. He's walking around in this *mist*. Don't tell him I said so, but I wouldn't want my kids pouring his milk on their Wheaties."

By early June Doug's flies had mostly expired. So had his mice, a barn cat, and a barred owl, along with some pigeons, swallows, robins, and bats. I took pictures, and Doug's lawyer took depositions. By July the superior court judge had found in Doug's favor and ordered the egg farm to control its flies. The court awarded Doug $50,000 in damages, which didn't cover half his losses.

So Spud's news that Sunday night wasn't particularly surprising. Doug Henault had been holding in his rage for months now, and the court's decision had let the Tuttles off with a slap.

THREE

THE MINISTER BROOK BRIDGE was out, its stone abutments undercut by Saturday's high water, so that Monday morning I had to drive up along the west side of Arrow Lake to approach the Knob from the north, on the Dunstable Road.

Doug Henault was a man usually content to let his wife do the talking for both of them, but if his foot was broken, they'd be shorthanded, and Cindy and Lance would both be out of the house doing chores, so there was a good chance I could get Doug's unvarnished, firsthand account of the two incidents I wanted to get straight before tracking down Seb Tuttle.

I parked in the gravel dooryard beside a circular bed of red, white, and blue petunias that surrounded their hand-painted sign:

CIDOLA FARM
The Henault's
Cindy, Doug, and Lance
Registered Holsteins

The Henaults' queenly Great Dane, Gussie, greeted me at the porch steps. I rubbed her bony head. "Where were you, girl, when your master was getting his ashes hauled?"

They had a nest of baby phoebes above the porch light fixture.

I heard the phone begin ringing just as I knocked, so I opened the screen door and stepped inside. All the fly strips they'd had hanging here in the kitchen the last time I'd stopped by were gone.

"Doug? It's Hector Bellevance."

He was on the phone. "Yeah, OK. Nope, sorry. OK. Yup. Right. 'Bye."

I followed the sound of his voice to his office nook off the dining room and stuck my head in.

"Sorry, Hector. I'm kinda bunged up."

"So I see."

He was wearing work clothes and a sun-faded Purina cap cocked back on his head. Gauzy curtains over the single, deep window let in only a little light. He had a spreadsheet up on his computer screen—it was reflected in the glass of some framed document on the wall behind him.

I'd seen a lot of worked-over faces. Doug's was not that bad—bruised from the swollen orbits on down, stitches in his lower lip and left cheekbone. His right foot, in a blue splint, rested on a folded bath towel up on his computer table.

"Still hurtin', Doug?"

He waved his hand. "How's your wife?"

"She'll be OK. We're not too worried yet."

"And it was Seb Tuttle run you down in the street? Is that what I heard?"

"You talked to Spud."

He nodded. "Was he drunk—Tuttle?"

"Don't think so. He the one who stomped your foot?"

"One of 'em did. Bastards."

"There were two of them?"

"Yeah, two of 'em. One I coulda handled." Doug was about forty, not a large man but broad shouldered and rugged enough.

"What do you think this was about?"

"Spud didn't tell you that story?"

"He said you lost it."

Doug shook his head. "Yeah. You know what *mutagenic* means?"

"Yes."

"OK. Judge Kitzwaller ordered Tuttle to pay damages to Cindy and I—you knew that, right?"

I nodded. "Lost production compensation."

"Yeah, plus Tuttle's supposed to keep his flies under control. OK, Friday I got a call back from Gideon." Gideon Miller was Doug's attorney. "The reason I called him was we been getting this mutagenic gas."

"What mutagenic gas?"

"Coming down off the Knob. Whenever the wind's right and he's spraying this shit, you *smell* it. I didn't know what the hell it was, so I called Gideon and he called Piscopo, Tuttle's lawyer, and Piscopo says it's *Cygon*."

"What's Cygon?"

"Cygon's this insecticide that the EPA classifies as an 'extremely hazardous substance.' This is what Tuttle's treating his chicken shit with. And mister, if you can *smell* this shit, it's getting in your lungs! Now Lance keeps bees—which you know. Hell, you sell his honey!"

I nodded.

"This stuff's *toxic* to bees, Hector. Look." He sat up, found a slip of paper on his desk, and shoved it at me. "That's the label. I downloaded it from their Web site. Says, 'Do not apply if the residue may drift onto weeds or blooming crops.' "

"Sorry to hear that, Doug."

"Gideon says he can get an injunction, but it'll take a couple days, seeing it's Friday. Then he says, 'I'm going to suggest the three of you wear masks when you're working outside. As a precaution. Canister masks, not dust masks.' *Masks?* How the hell do we get masks on Lance's bees?"

"So you went up to the egg farm to put a stop to the spraying."

"Goddamn right."

"What happened?"

"Smashed in the gate. Busted the warehouse door when the kid wouldn't unlock it. Went and hunted up that sprayer and destroyed it."

"Nobody tried to stop you?"

"Nobody was there. Just Toby Elster—poor kid. When I left, I said to him, 'Toby? Tell Tuttle he can bill me for damages. But we're all done with the poison gas. Hear me?' "

"What happened after you left the egg farm?"

"Nothing. Not till Sunday morning."

"All right. Tell me about Sunday morning."

"Well, I'm in the barn and I hear these four-wheelers comin' up, so I come out and damn if they're not cutting donuts in her pumpkins."

"Why didn't you call me? Or the sheriff?"

"Didn't have a chance! They just laid into me." Tears welled in his eyes.

"Why aren't you pressing charges?"

" 'Cause I can't *prove* it was them."

"Give me the details, Doug. Start with Friday."

He took a careful swallow from a cup at his elbow and leaned back in his creaky swivel chair. "Friday. Me and Lance finished getting our square bales picked up, and I'm backing the wagon into the barn, thinking how if the breeze picks up we might not get that storm after all, but then I'm smelling this poison in the air again, and I—" He gritted his teeth. "I couldn't hardly *see* I was so mad. Seems like he don't spray except when the wind's out of the north—on purpose, you know? I unhitched that wagon and I turned uphill and I busted in there and took a hammer to the compressor."

"Who was there at the time?"

"Just Toby, like I said."

"What happened yesterday?"

"Yesterday, Cindy and Lance were at church and I was in the barn, and I hear these two ATVs, and—" He put his hand to his eyes.

"You confronted them?"

"They were wearing full-face helmets and gloves, but I figure one was Sebastian Tuttle. He's runnin' that factory now, you know."

"You recognized him."

"That's the thing, I *didn't* recognize him, but who else would it be? I recognized the *other* one, though. You remember Pie Yandow?"

I nodded. I'd followed the story. Every month or two for twenty years Agnes used to send me envelopes thick with clippings from the local paper to keep me connected, ever hoping to draw me home. My greatest sorrow is that it took her dying to do it. Pie Yandow had been working in his stepdad's milking parlor, which had motorized chains in the gutter to draw the muck out into the pit. The on/off switch was near the doorway of the bulktank room. Pie was on his knees trying to untangle a wad of baling twine from the chain when his stepfather walked in, didn't see him, and flipped the switch. A helicopter flew the boy down to the Dartmouth-Hitchcock Medical Center in Hanover, where a team of doctors spent fifteen hours reattaching the fingers. Because they'd been crushed off and not chopped, however, only the pinkie took. "You think one was Pie Yandow."

He nodded. "He had that hand. Pinned me with it to the side of Lance's truck, and the other guy lit into me."

"Either of them say anything?"

"Just grunts."

"And where was Gussie?"

"Probably hidin' in the back of the barn."

"What kind of machines were they riding?"

"I didn't get a good look."

"What happened after they left?"

"Cindy took me into the ER. Deputy from the courthouse come out, and he wrote down what happened."

"What did he say?"

"Said it sounded like 'mutual affray.' "

"You tell him about Pie Yandow?"

"Yeah."

"What did he say to that?"

"He just said they'd get back to me."

IT WAS NOON when I reached the smashed chain-link gates outside the Tipton Egg Works. A single car and an ATV sat baking in the sun outside the windowless main building.

I pressed the button in the door frame. The steel door was new, the galvanized doorsill still protected by masking tape. Metal filings glittered in the dirt at my feet.

Toby Elster, the son of Shadboro's fire chief, buzzed me through into the narrow vestibule outside the egg farm's office. It was a glass-walled space with a cluttered counter, a rolling stool-chair, and, against the back wall, a cheap, gray desk.

Toby's eyes widened when he recognized me. He hurried out of the office, hugging an aluminum clipboard against his chest.

"Something I can do for you, Mr. Bellevance?"

"Jeremy Tuttle around, Toby?"

"Jeremy don't come down unless there's a problem."

"Doesn't he manage the plant?"

"He used to. Seb does all that now."

"Seb around, then?"

"Nope. He left."

"Not much of a manager, I guess."

"Oh, it don't take all day. He's here early, makes sure the girls is here and all. End of the run, him and the FDA inspector sign papers, then he's done. I'm here ten to six."

"Was he here yesterday?"

"He's here every day."

"Where does Seb live, do you know?"

He shrugged. I was making him uncomfortable.

"Toby, this is important."

"His girlfriend's got a place. I seen her picture, but I don't remember her name."

"Toby. If you ran into a problem here, you'd have to call him, wouldn't you?"

"Nope. I call Jeremy. Lives right over yonder."

"You wouldn't call Seb?"

"Him and Jeremy don't get along."

"You have a cell-phone number for Seb?"

He shook his head. "Seb don't want nobody bothering him. Especially if it ain't work related."

"This is definitely work related." I circled around Toby and entered the office.

He followed me, distressed. "You ain't supposed to be *in* here, Mr. Bellevance."

I started riffling through papers on the desk. "Toby, this is a serious legal matter. I won't be leaving until I find out how to get in touch with Seb Tuttle."

His eyes flew wildly around the little room. "You can try the White Birches. They got an RV there."

"Seb and his girlfriend?"

"No, Seb and Jeremy. Seb stays there when he ain't at his girlfriend's."

"Thanks."

"But, Mr. Bellevance, if you tell them I let you in here, I could get fired."

I took his hand and shook it. "I won't tell anyone, Toby."

THE WHITE BIRCHES was a jewel of an RV park up in the pine trees just across the highway from the sandy beach at the tip of Arrow Lake less than a mile from the boat access. Birches bordered the highway all along this stretch. It was a popular spot for laid-back vacationers shy of the oceanside crowds and traffic and for retired couples pampering the grandkids while the parents slipped away for a week in Quebec City or Prince Edward Island.

The cloudless sky and dry air made this the sort of summer day that north-country people put up with five months of winter to enjoy. I was glad I could pay it that much notice. As I drove up Lake Street, windows rolled down, I felt soothed a bit by how serene the village seemed. The Collins boy was on his plastic trike clattering up and down the sidewalk in front of the library, and a pair of tourists stood on the green preserving their impressions with a video camera.

I passed the town garage, where the view to the northeast opened onto a wedge of the long blue lake. There was nothing on the water but the dazzle of sunshine and patches rasped by the wind and nothing on the far shore but boulders and dark green trees.

Pickups and boat trailers occupied the small lot at the fishing access. At the state beach, there were eight or ten cars in the parking area, but the day was cool for July, in the low 60s.

The White Birches' manager's office, at the top of the long, horseshoe-shaped gravel drive, was one of the two structures Marty Henderson had left in place when he had the rest of the old Lakeview Cabins dismantled about ten years ago. The second structure housed the Laundromat and snack bar. Marty used to coach Nordic skiing at Mount Joseph Academy, where Hugh Gebbie had taught English for twenty years, until the school closed. The Henderson kids were all great skiers.

The campground's shady sites were inviting enough, each ensconced in its own cove among the pines with a pitch-stained picnic table. All the badminton nets, bikes, fishing poles, kayaks, and towel-draped clotheslines made the place feel safe and cozy.

The grounds were quiet. Two boys were at work dragging pine limbs broken in the storm into a pile. Most of the guests had left for the afternoon, off to fish, golf, hike, sail, nap in the shade by the side of a brook.

When I came through the front door, setting a bell tinkling, I was startled to see Marty Henderson's daughter, Kandi, at the registration desk. Kandi looked up, closing the book she'd been reading. Her chestnut hair was tied loosely at the back of her neck, same as always.

"Hector Bellevance! Look at you all nice and tan—and getting gray!"

"I didn't know you were coming back, Kandi." She had just spent two and a half years in the state corrections facility over in Chittenden County.

She shrugged. "It's home."

"You look terrific. You survived."

"Barely."

"How was it?"

"About what I expected. Say, how's Wilma? I heard what happened."

"She's in a coma. She could come around anytime."

Kandi nodded. "You seem pretty relaxed about it."

"Have to trust the experts, don't you?"

"Depends on the experts."

I found myself thinking an old thought, that *Kandi* was a

frivolous name for such a seriously beautiful woman. With her coppery brown hair, high cheekbones, broad forehead, fine nose, and full, down-turned lips, she resembled Katharine Hepburn, an observation more than a few people made during the weeks she was in the news. How old was she now? Thirty-one, thirty-two. She had been teaching PE and coaching the ski team at Allenburg High for three years when she was arrested at her apartment in Shadboro and charged with having unlawful sexual intercourse with a seventeen-year-old student, Evan Spurling. A "concerned neighbor" turned them in to social services. Spurling left the next fall for college in Ohio, and after months of pretrial humiliation, Kandi was convicted and given a three-year sentence.

"Did you want something in particular?" She was leaning across the glossy polyurethaned pine slab of a registration counter.

I'd been staring. "A little information, if you don't mind."

"Sure." She gestured at her book. "Just studying for a test. The Romantic Poets."

"You're back in school?"

She tipped her head to the side. "Kind of. I'm thinking about going for a master's in liberal studies. One course at a time."

"Sounds good. Still swimming?"

Kandi and I had met twelve years earlier at the Allenburg State College pool during lap-swim hours. She had been majoring in secondary ed. It was the middle of my first winter back in Tipton since I'd left for college. My mother had died unexpectedly the summer before, and I was holed up in her hillside cabin, weighing my options after two life-changing reversals in Boston—the overdue split from my wife, Naomi, and the sour finale of my career with the BPD. A relationship was the last thing I was looking for, but Kandi was irresistible. Twice I asked her out for dinner. Twice she said she had other plans. I was grateful for her kindness, and that was as far as it went.

"I swim every day," she said. "Started doing yoga in the slammer. Helped a lot."

"Let me ask you. Do you know someone named Sebastian Tuttle?"

"Yes, in fact. He's the guy that ran into you, isn't he?"

"That's not why I'm looking for him."

She whispered, "*He's a gold-plated jerk.* How come you're looking for him?"

"He and an accomplice may have done a number on Doug Henault yesterday morning."

"What do you mean, 'done a number'?"

"Beat him up. I'd be grateful if you would tell me which RV is his and Jeremy's."

"I believe it. That guy'd kick a puppy into next week for peeing on his tires." She drew out a leatherette registry and opened it. "Twenty-seven and twenty-nine. Booked for the season. New Fleetwood Discovery. Fancy rig—registered to Jeremy Tuttle. His brother." She found a hand-drawn map of the campground in a drawer and circled the sites for me with her ballpoint. "The Fleetwood's his pied-à-terre."

"Seb stay there often?"

"We don't keep tabs on the guests." Her phone rang, and she grimaced. "Good afternoon, White Birches."

I saluted her with my map, leaving her to her work, but she raised a finger.

"Will you hold, please? Thanks so much." She pressed a button on the console. "Hector, before you go tracking down Sebastian Tuttle? Something you should know." She compressed her lips. "Don't tell anybody this came from me, OK? You would not believe all the parole conditions I'm under."

"I won't tell anyone. What is it?"

"This is just speculation, OK?"

"All right."

"I think he's dealing crystal."

"What makes you say that?" As far as I knew, the meth plague hadn't yet reached Vermont, but it had been spreading steadily east since the '70s, and we'd seen enough heroin and crack here in the last decade to know the ice age wasn't far off.

"Day or two after I started working here, this car comes up the loop three times in the same afternoon. Silver Corolla, no hubcaps. Each time they slow down at the end of the loop—looking for somebody. Couple days later I see them come through again, and so I pop out and ask if I can do anything for them, checking them out, OK? Well, these dudes are tweaked to the eyeballs. *Nothin', nothin,'* this one says, the driver, *just looking for a friend.* Later it hit me who this friend was."

"Tuttle."

"Exactly. That's whose RV they were checking out."

"Did you see those guys again after the day you spoke to them?"

She shook her head. "Not those two, but we've been getting lots of other weirdos—bikers, dopers, ravers. . . . Some real marginal characters, Hector. Never used to be like this."

"Any of them have a crippled hand, do you recall?"

"I didn't notice anything like that."

I tore off a corner of the campground map and wrote my number on it. "Next time Seb shows up here, call me right away, Kandi, OK?"

"All right," she said. "But if you bust any of these turd-balls, it did not come from me, remember that. Did *not.*"

FANCY RIG all right.

Most of the other sites were occupied by towable RVs—Dutchmen, Winnebago, Voyager—and a number of pop-up tent campers. Jeremy's motor home straddled two sites at the end of the loop. It was a monster, sleek and yet homely as a brick. No cars nearby. No lawn chairs, no grill, no clothesline, no outdoor amenities. Nothing to suggest that anybody spent much time here.

The Discovery's windows were heavily tinted. It had two slide-outs. I saw no recent tracks in the gravel.

I banged on the door anyway. Nothing.

It was one thirty. I'd left Myra at ten, with Hugh. His having been Agnes's lover for twenty years made him as good as family—but Hugh was eighty-four years old. I was annoyed with myself. How was Wilma doing, and how was my anxious little girl?

I drove the two miles back into Tipton to the public phone on the porch at Sullivan's Store and called the hospital. Myra picked up in Wilma's room.

"Where are you, Dad?" She was not happy.

"I'm at Sullivan's. Mom still unconscious?"

"She's the same. We bathed her and turned her and everything, and I put on her lotion."

"Did Hugh leave?"

"He has *animals,* Dad."

"Right."

"I want to go home."

"Sure, I'm on my way. Give me half an hour."

"Dad—"

"What, sweetheart?"

"She doesn't respond to *anything.*"

"Well, she can't. She's healing. Remember what Dr. Kaufman explained yesterday? All we can do is wait."

"We can *pray.* That's what this nurse told me."

I laughed. Any belief I once had in the prevailing mythology left me when I was about Myra's age, the year my father died. "When we get home, let's take out the canoe, all right? We'll paddle out to the island and dive off the rock."

"OK," she said, brightening.

"It's a beautiful day, Myra."

"I said *OK*."

FOUR

I HAD JUST SLIPPED OUR paddles and vests into the back of the car when Myra stepped out onto the side porch and called, "Da-ad! Phone!"

I jogged across the shaggy lawn and up the steps. Myra had packed the cooler and set it out beside the door with two folded beach towels and some sunblock.

Earlier I'd left a message for Rob Tierney, an old friend and a state police detective assigned to the state's attorney's office in Allenburg. I wanted to see what Rob might have to say about Yandow, Seb Tuttle, and the extent of the meth problem here in Montcalm County. This wasn't Tierney calling back. It was Kandi.

"Hector? He's here."

"Tuttle?" I could hear Myra out by the woodshed, firming up our truck-tire inner tube with the bicycle pump.

"Him and another scuzball I've seen before. They just carried a couple of Price Chopper bags into the RV."

"Thanks. I'll be there in fifteen."

My explanation cut no ice with Myra. "OK," she grumbled, "but I'm coming with you."

"Myra, this is town business. Let me see to the matter, and I'll be back here to get you in thirty minutes."

"That's bull, Dad. You'll take an hour probably, and by the time you get back here it won't even be worth going. Anyway, we're all ready."

Always a force to be reckoned with, Myra was increasingly too smart and assertive to be contradicted. By me, at least.

All I wanted to do now was take Seb's measure in clear light and tell him that if he caused any further harm to any person in my town, I'd make sure he spent the rest of the year in physical therapy and the rest of his life in some other part of the world. "You have your suit?"

Myra flipped up the front of her I ♥ NOVA SCOTIA T-shirt to show me her orange Speedo.

I double-checked the canoe's tie-downs and we headed off toward the lake. The gravel road down off Bellevance Hill followed the brook among the hardwoods and old pasture. When I geared down for the T at the abandoned sawmill on Tug's Corner, Myra grabbed my hand on the shifter.

"Dad!"

There was no one else on the road. I slowed.

"Look." Some fifty yards off beyond a blackberry brake, a reddish doe stood watching us. She took five or six prancing steps and looked back again.

"She has a late fawn," Myra whispered. "Wait."

I stopped. She slipped out.

I watched her hop the bank, a doe herself, then slosh barelegged through a swale choked with sensitive fern, pick her way around a heap of moldering sawlogs, skirting the blackberry canes, until I lost sight of her in the brush.

Five minutes later she was back, legs scratched, ribbons of sweat running down her temples and darkening the curls, eyes dancing. "Twins! Just, oh, *days* old. Two twins snuggled up like this—" She showed me with her hands. "In like this ball. Dad, you should've seen their wet noses. They had these little *leaf flakes* stuck on them!"

She was her mother's child, keen and wondering and tender, with an energetic joy that would ignite in a flash like tungsten. Wilma was going to be fine. I suddenly believed that.

WHEN SHE WAS home from school for the summer, Myra sometimes rode along with me on routine missions, those involving dog ordinance violations, illegal dumping, or kids drinking in the cemetery. She would wait in the truck with a book. Today she read as I drove, so it wasn't until we'd pulled into the campground that she thought to ask what I'd come here for.

"I want to deliver a message," I said. "Shouldn't take long, but . . ." I caught her eye. "No matter what you hear, you stay in the truck, OK?"

"How come? What am I going to hear?"

"Some shouting, maybe some swearing."

"Why? What's it about?"

"I'll tell you later."

"OK, but— Dad?"

"Yeah?"

"Do you have your forty-five?"

I shook my head. "I'll be fine, Myra."

My primary carry when called for was a .45 Colt 1911 A1 semiautomatic. I had a revolver in the safe, too, a Smith & Wesson Model 27 that I practiced with every week or so out of habit. By the time she was nine, Myra had become curious enough about firearms so that, in the face of Wilma's misgivings, I set up a shooting range out behind the cabin, where

Myra could learn gun safety and marksmanship. "No matter how much you may hate it," I told Wilma, "this country's full of handguns, and that isn't about to change. A child who doesn't know the first thing about how to use and respect a handgun will always be in more danger than necessary, and she'll have her parents to blame for that."

At a pawnshop one day I chanced across the classic small-bore target revolver, a fifty-year-old K-22 Masterpiece in good shape, which Myra took to as soon as she held it. The magna stocks fit her hand just right. A natural deadeye, by the end of that summer she was shooting quarter-size groups without a rest at ten yards. Myra's interest in target shooting drew Wilma out to our range now and then, too, but she didn't enjoy it—"I can't get used to the suddenness" was how she put it.

When we reached the top of the loop, Kandi stepped out into the splintered sun on the cabin's low porch step. Myra's eyes went right to her. In shorts and a T-shirt and a yellow fleece vest, her chestnut hair pulled loosely back, Kandi looked like a princess on vacation. I nodded as we passed, and she made a small wave.

"Who's that?"

"Daughter of the owner," I said. "Kandi Henderson. She's an old friend."

"She's pretty."

We passed several sleepy-looking RVs and campers and pulled up opposite the Tuttles' Discovery. Two boys whirred past on bikes. A gray-haired couple on this side of the drive, both overweight, were entertaining a younger couple with two small children. Their motor coach had Virginia plates, and the dingy burgundy Escort beside it was a Vermont-registered car. One of the kids, a toddler, was dragging around a stubby orange Wiffleball bat as big as he was.

Nosed in to Tuttle's site was a late-model black Bonneville—fancy alloy rims, dark glass, Vermont tags. I jotted the number into the notebook I kept in my glovebox.

Myra had returned to her paperback, a fantasy novel two inches thick. I patted her on the knee and slid out.

I gave the side of the RV a few hard pops, then a few more. An intercom hissed on. "Yeah?" The loudspeaker was behind a flush panel beside the door.

"Seb Tuttle?"

"What about him?"

"It's Hector Bellevance. I'd like a few words."

"It's who?"

"Hector Bellevance. I work for the town."

"*Bellevance?*" he piped. Somebody was speaking in the background.

"Two minutes of your time." In the pine canopy overhead a red squirrel chittered at me.

Tuttle didn't respond.

I waited a little longer, then gave the side of the motor home three solid shots with the meat of my fist. "Wrong stage of the game to be making bad choices, Seb. You want to hear me out."

A bolt slid back and the narrow door swung open.

A lean, shaggy-haired young man with a thin beard, dirty jeans, and a chromed wallet chain peered out and spat past me. "So. Talk."

"What's your name, friend?" He wasn't Yandow.

He slitted his eyes at me. The black boot he launched at my face did not come as a surprise—he was no brawler. I hooked his leg with my arm and yanked him horizontal. His head cracked the RV's two steps on the way down, and then, *whump,* he was on his back in the White Birches' riverbed gravel.

I grabbed him by the arm and rolled him over, jamming a knee into the small of his back.

"Ahhgh!" he got out. I had his wrist clamped between his shoulder blades. *"Jee-zus!"* His hairy cheek was mashed into the gravel.

I leaned over him, my weight on his neck. He winced hard. Mucus bubbled out of his nostrils. "You know, it's a shame you're so stupid, but it's lucky you're so clumsy, because this way you get off with a warning. Could've been worse."

"Get offa me!" He'd had the wind knocked out of him.

"Get up, Bellevance. You made your point."

I glanced over my shoulder. Seb Tuttle stood braced in the doorway in baggy, knee-length shorts and high-tech sandals. He had a stainless steel pistol casually dangling at the end of his right arm.

I stood up. "Get that gun out of my sight, Seb, or I will bust you right now for brandishing. You've got ten seconds."

"Don't got a right to protect my home from wackos?"

"Five."

The jerk I'd been straddling groaned and pushed himself up to his knees. He felt the back of his head and found blood on his fingers.

Seb slipped his auto into the cargo pocket of his shorts. "I gotta say, this is only the second time I met you, but you sure seem like a violent individual."

"Good observation. Who is this shithead?"

"That's Ronnie. They call him Raygun."

"Last name?" I tapped his butt with my toe.

"DiGuilio," the guy said.

I nodded and looked back at Seb. We had the rapt attention of the two couples across the road. "Tell me something, Seb. Who were you with yesterday morning out at Doug Henault's farm?"

"What is this about?"

I shook my head. "Come on, it's too nice a day."

"You said *Henault,* right? Henault's the asshole that busted up the egg farm Friday. That's all I know about him."

"Superior court awarded him fifty grand in compensation for losses he incurred because of your flies. A hundred wouldn't have covered it. Now he says the poisons you're spraying are drifting onto his farm."

"I don't know what the fuck I'm spraying, OK? But when stuff like this comes up, there's this thing called the telephone."

"You're hard to find, Seb."

"Call my brother. Have your lawyer call our lawyer, whatever. But no, he goes nuts! You want to talk damages? Front gate, main door plus the frame, plus—"

"That was his mistake, Seb. Yesterday morning somebody went and took it out of his hide. That was a much bigger mistake."

"If they did, it wasn't me. And I have no idea who it was."

"Two guys drove four-wheelers through the Henaults' garden and beat him up when he confronted them. The report I have says one of them was you."

"What report? Why don't you ask *Henault?*" He paused. "They didn't kill him, did they?"

"You mind showing me the backs of your hands?"

He thrust them out at me. I didn't see any scrapes, swelling, or bruises.

"Seb, you ever run into a guy with three fingers missing from one hand?"

"With *what?*"

Ronnie sat back on his haunches and said, "That's Pie."

I leaned over. "Who?"

"Pie Yandow. He's got a hand like that. I used to work with him."

"Where?"

"College Pizza."

"You still work there?"

"Nah, I quit."

"Where do you work now?"

"Coös Furniture."

"Where's Yandow work?"

"Couldn't tell you."

"Do you know Pie Yandow, Seb?"

"I heard the name."

"From?"

"My brother."

"Yeah? How does Jeremy know Yandow?"

"Ask him."

"I'm asking you. What did your brother say about Yandow?"

"I truly don't remember."

"In what context did his name come up?"

"*What context?*" He laughed. "What does that mean, 'context'?"

"What made Jeremy bring him up?"

"I don't remember, I told you. If it was a name like Joe or Bob, I would've forgot it."

I looked at DiGuilio. "Where would I find Yandow?"

He shrugged.

"I'd like to talk to him."

"Good luck."

I turned to Seb. "Somebody hired Yandow to give Doug Henault a tune-up, and nobody had a better reason than you."

"Doesn't mean I did it."

After a moment, I said, "The reason I'm here, Seb, is to give you a message. It has two parts. You ready?"

"Who's it from?"

"Me. First, in this community a man takes responsibility for his mistakes. I want you to tell your attorney it was you who caused the accident that put my wife in the hospital. Second, I recommend—"

He flushed. "No, man, no *way*. Because I never *hit* you! It was my brother's car, and I had never even drove it before. Which was why—"

"Shut up and *listen* to me—"

"*Which was why* I stepped on the gas instead of the brake! My mistake, OK? But I never *hit* you, and we got two witnesses that saw you *shove* your wife. That was *your* mistake. You fucking *own* that one."

My blood rose. I could have throttled the punk if Myra hadn't been here watching. "I have my eye on you, Seb. You're all done spraying that poison. And if you cause any further harm to anyone in this town, I promise you I will run you out of it. You've got no more chances."

"Listen to him, the sheriff from Deadwood."

"I'm the real deal, Seb. Count on it."

I walked back to my truck.

The two couples and the two wide-eyed little kids were standing in front of their picnic table.

"I apologize for the unpleasantness," I told them. "Couldn't be helped."

They had no reaction.

"Dad?" Myra asked when we were out on the highway. "What happened back there with that guy on the ground? I missed it."

"He tried to kick me in the face."

"Why?"

"I'm not sure. A lot of people really don't like the police."

"Only if they're doing something wrong."

"Not always, I'm sad to say."

She said, "Dad? What if Seb Tuttle gets a lawyer? Then we would need a lawyer, too, right?"

"If it comes to that, we'll have an excellent case."

She nodded and asked, "Would we have to sell the island?"

Two or three times a year some Realtor would phone to inquire whether I'd consider letting the property go "for the right price." I wouldn't. The island was better than money in the stock market. Which we didn't have.

"No chance of that. Everything's going to be all right, I promise you."

"What you mean is, whatever happens, we can deal."

"That's right. And we can."

ON THE MAPS it was Buttonwood, but to us it was Granddad's island, because that's what my father and mother had always called our wedge-shaped half acre of rock, grass, black willow, and cedar, where my grandfather and then my father, Reg, had once planned to build a fishing camp—a summer project much discussed and forever postponed. When I told Myra about this, a dream I'd inherited with the island, she was seven and had been camping there with Wilma and me since she was two. She told me then that if she had anything to say about it, the island would never be built upon. "A house would *ruin* it," she said. She had settled the place by then with her own fairy houses made of stones and willow bark. I warned her that she might have to change her mind someday, but whenever we camped there after that, nobody mentioned the prospect of improvements.

We dove from a tongue of red granite that reached out over a glassy, green-blue pool. We ate Wilma's favorite sandwich—sharp cheddar, shaved red onion, sliced cucumber, sardines, Dijon, no mayo, on seeded rye—perched on the sunny rock. Myra drifted around in her tube, head back so her chin pointed up, arms outstretched, legs crossed at the ankles. We tossed a tennis ball back and forth. Myra read her book while I drank a beer and watched the wind.

The sun had dropped behind the mountains by the time

we reached the village again. I stopped at Sullivan's Store for our mail, some cat litter, and a baguette from the new bakery in Shadboro. Myra had received a postcard from a school friend who was traveling in France that summer—the card depicted Matisse's *Basket of Oranges*—but out in the truck, Myra only glanced at the dense message on the back. Fireflies blinked around the gas pump. We decided not to swing by the cabin to check for messages and turned straight onto the state highway south toward Allenburg.

FIVE

"Dad, look at mom's eye. Look at her right eye."

I leaned down. It seemed swollen, the cornea slightly bulging.

I went for help. Andrea, a barrel-chested young nurse we hadn't met, checked her blood pressure, measured Wilma's pupils with a meter and tested their reaction to light, then paged Dr. Kaufman. She asked Myra and me to wait outside the room. They'd be running some tests, maybe getting Wilma on a ventilator. Dr. Kaufman would explain.

We stood waiting at the end of the hallway. We were on the third floor. Outside, beyond the amber parking lot lights, the interstate was a band of white and red beads.

"Something bad's happening, Dad."

I hugged her and stroked her hair, still damp from our swim.

Dr. Kaufman sat us down together in the small common area on the orthopedics floor. "There is a little delayed swelling caused by the bruising Wilma's brain tissue has suffered. The edema—that's the swelling—isn't unusual. Trouble is, the cranium's a closed box, and so it restricts the swelling. But we know how to treat the problem. Her ventilator will help her to relieve the carbon dioxide buildup in her system, and that should take the pressure down. We've also introduced an intracranial pressure monitor." Kaufman addressed Myra. "It's a bolt we've inserted in your mom's skull to allow a small catheter access to the ventricles. Looks weird but works like a charm." He looked at me again. "I don't believe she's in any great danger, Hector. And *this* young lady, I want you to know, is a gem."

THE NEXT MORNING broke clear as the morning before, but the day promised to be warmer. I invested some time in the potatoes, collecting beetles in a coffee can, then dusting the plants with Bt. Later Myra came out carrying two bowls of yogurt and raspberries.

I washed my hands in the greenhouse and we ate out at the picnic table as we often did on fine days, listening to the brook.

"Whale water," I said.

She made a smile. A year ago, Wilma told Myra our brook was whale water because it emptied into the lake, which emptied into the St. Francis, which emptied into the great St. Lawrence, which was where, from the bluffs above a fjord on the Gaspé, the three of us had watched the belugas play one August afternoon.

"Dr. Kaufman called. Mom's stable and the pressure's gone down. And Bruce Davies called." Davies was the Audubon Camp director. "He asked about Mom, and he said they're holding my place in the girls' cabin. They put Pookie up in my bunk." Pookie was the camp's mascot, a plush river otter.

"I'll take you there whenever you want to go, Myra. And soon as Mom wakes up, I'll come back and get you."

"Thanks, Dad, but I can't. I'd just be like I am now the whole time."

"Don't be so sure. The other kids, the activities, the swimming—"

"*Dad.* If I want to go to camp, I'll say *please take me to camp.* You treat me like I'm in kindergarten." She picked up her bowl and headed back toward the house.

Then she paused and turned. "And a detective called. The number's on the pad."

I followed Myra up to the cabin. The number was Rob Tierney's cell. Just as I reached for the receiver it rang.

I took a deep breath. Myra came to her bedroom doorway. It rang again.

"Hector Bellevance." I hadn't answered a phone that way in fifteen years.

"Hector, it's me—Kandi. Something bad just happened."

"What happened? Where?"

"At the campground. I'm at the lake, but I just got off the phone with my dad, and they found a body about half an hour ago up at the campground. I think it's Seb Tuttle."

"Christ. Was he shot?"

"Dad says it looks like he got the living shit kicked out of him. He's up there now waiting for the police."

"At the campground?"

"Yeah. He's all upset. This is going to just *kill* the business."

"All right. I appreciate the call, Kandi. Tell me this, when did you leave work yesterday?"

"About nine."

"Nine. Was anybody occupying Tuttle's RV when you left the grounds, did you notice?"

"Actually, yes. I went out that way when I left, and there was a car there, so they were inside, Seb and whoever."

"All right, Kandi. I'll head over there now."

"No hurry. The state police'll be there, but I thought you should know, too."

Myra followed me as I went upstairs to change out of my work clothes. "So Seb Tuttle, the guy you talked to yesterday, the guy that drove through the stop sign on Main Street— He just got *murdered?*"

"Looks that way."

"Do they know who did it?"

"Nothing's for sure yet, Myra."

"But, so, you're going to go check it out?"

"In a little while."

"What about me?"

"The beans and raspberries need picking, and the onions need weeding."

"Forget that. I'm not staying here alone."

"I'm not taking you to a crime scene, Myra, and that's the end of it. You can ride your bike up to Spud's."

"No way. Whenever I go up there, he makes me *work.*"

"You can stay home and work or go up to Spud's and work. Your choice."

She looked hotly at me, her hands balled into fists. "If we had a cell phone, you could call me, or I could call you. Everybody has a cell phone except *us!*"

Myra knew my feelings on this subject, and I saw no point in reiterating them.

She clomped back down the open stairs. At the bottom she turned and shouted, "Don't you get it that when you really care about people you want to stay *connected* with them?"

BY THE TIME I reached the campground, the Montcalm County Sheriff's Department had each end of the loop blocked off with a white-and-red cruiser. Deputies in the road urged the traffic along. From my truck I could see a few uniformed troopers and bystanders up under the trees, but the state medical examiner's van wasn't here yet and neither was the mobile forensics lab. It was early in the proceedings.

I walked in from the highway, jumped a drainage ditch, and trudged up through the old birch grove to the stand of pines. The police were huddled in front of the Tuttles' monster RV, talking. I scissored over the crime scene tape.

A sandy-haired detective, late thirties, no hat, no necktie, in a rumpled linen sport jacket, was answering reporters' questions. Several of the White Birches' guests clustered under the trees nearby. They were buzzing.

One of them noticed me and said, "That's him, the tall guy. That's him, right?"

The detective glanced at me midsentence as I walked past him. The uniforms turned toward me at the same time. I recognized two of them from the Allenburg barracks—slim, bald Allan Hawley and a trooper in his twenties whose name I'd forgotten. Off behind the RV, beyond a tumbled stone wall, the body lay under a sheet.

None of these guys thought much of me. Their impressions derived from two or three enduring stories about my career in law enforcement—now fifteen years behind me—which were based on what a few people believed they knew about me from stories they'd read or heard somewhere else. The threads of truth running through all that were almost invisible now, even to me. Not that it mattered, except at times like this.

"Gentlemen. Good morning," I said.

Allan Hawley echoed, "Morning," as the others' attention swiveled from me to Kandi Henderson, who was gliding toward us down the piney slope in a white tank top, red nylon running shorts, and hiking sandals.

Kandi was used to men's eyes. She smiled around at everyone and said, "Kandi Henderson. One of you officers wanted to talk to me?"

"That would be me," the sandy-haired detective said behind us. "Sergeant Max Ingersoll." He skirted the rest of us to shake Kandi's hand. I caught two troopers exchanging a look. "Let me ask you to step over to my car—that brown one—if you don't mind."

Kandi favored me with a wry glance. Which Ingersoll didn't miss.

A woman piped up: "Sergeant! That's him—the tall guy I was tellin' you!" The fat grandmother I'd apologized to the afternoon before.

Ingersoll looked me over. "Who'd you say you were?"

Hawley said, "This is Hector Bellevance, Sergeant. He's the local constable."

"Just the man I wanted to talk to. Can you hang for five minutes?"

I nodded.

"What's with him?" I asked Hawley.

Hawley reached around and scratched the back of his head under the brim of his hat, a team player.

The other trooper—with Koslowski on his nameplate—said, "He's out of Middlesex. Good detective. Smart, supposedly. Big on psychology."

"Oh-oh."

Hawley rubbed the corners of his mouth.

"So," I said, "you're waiting for the ME?"

"And forensics," Hawley said.

"Mind if I have a look at the victim?"

"You're the constable. Don't touch anything."

I walked over and squatted and peeled back the sheet.

I looked up into the pine boughs. Repellent a young man as Seb Tuttle was, he'd been given an excessive hammering. Neither eye was visible. Scalp torn back in two jagged places over his skull. Mouth gone. Brains a raspberry bloom in his ear. He had on the same black T-shirt he'd been wearing yesterday afternoon. In my first year in homicide I processed a couple of gangsters who'd been clubbed into jelly and fragments. This wasn't as bad as that. But almost. I replaced the sheet.

No sign of scuffling or struggling, no blood, no real disturbance at all. He'd been carried to this spot under the trees and dumped. More than one person was involved, then, and the murder had taken place somewhere else. Why leave him here?

"Find much inside the motor home?" I asked Koslowski.

"He didn't buy it in there, if that's what you mean."

"Any firearms?"

"Not so far. Had the beans pounded out of him, obviously. But he coulda been shot before that."

"When I saw him here yesterday, he had a small pistol in his pants pocket. Who told you it was Seb Tuttle?"

"He had Sebastian Tuttle's billfold on him. You don't think it's him?"

"No, it's Tuttle. Who found him? And when did you get the call?"

Koslowski looked past me to Corporal Hawley before answering. "Some kid found him. Call came in to the barracks at eight fifty from Marty Henderson, the campground owner."

"You ready, Constable?" Sergeant Ingersoll said. He had a nasally voice.

I nodded at the two troopers. They were already fixed on Kandi, who was jogging back toward the office.

Ingersoll and I strolled down the gravel lane to the Lake Road.

There was no traffic. On the other side of the paved surface, the blue water lapped against a bank of boulders. Until the '50s the only route up this side of the lake used to be across a long causeway out on the ash plain, a route the town closed each winter because the drifting snow was impossible to manage. Over sixty years later, people called this section the new road.

"Girl says she knows you."

"We go back a few years."

"She says you were here yesterday looking for Seb Tuttle."

"That's right."

"Tell me about that."

"I suppose you're aware of the trouble we've been having with Tuttle's egg factory."

"No more than what I read in the papers. Sounds nasty."

I told him about Doug Henault's rampage at the Tipton Egg Works Friday evening and the assault at his farm Sunday morning. He hadn't heard about either incident. He took notes.

"So," he said after a minute. "Henault's been battling the Tuttles in court, and on Friday he goes and busts some equipment at the facility. And then on Sunday Tuttle and somebody else, who Henault says is Pie Yandow, these guys go to his farm and they stomp on his foot."

"He's not sure who it was. They were wearing full-face helmets. That's why he isn't pressing charges."

"But you're saying this Henault might've wanted Seb Tuttle dead."

"Right."

"OK, tell me about when you were here talking to Tuttle. What time was that?"

"Between two and three. Tuttle said he didn't know who put the boots to Doug Henault, and he denied any knowledge of the assault. I left him with a warning."

"What warning?"

"I told him that if he harmed or threatened to harm any resident of my town I'd see him run out of it."

"Witness says you and the men in that RV got into an argument that got physical. Tell me about that."

I described my scuffle with Ronnie DiGuilio and Seb's flashing his pistol.

He didn't like it. "You coulda got yourself killed, going up against two young bucks with no backup and no weapon."

"Luckily, it worked out."

Ingersoll squeezed his nose between his thumb and knuckle. "Ms. Henderson tells me this Seb Tuttle is the same guy that ran down your wife and yourself in the crosswalk Saturday afternoon in Allenburg. True?"

I nodded.

"I heard about that one. And your wife's still in a coma as a result of this incident?"

"That's right."

"Sorry to hear it."

"I'm sure she'll recover."

"So. Negligent operation, injury resulting. But Tuttle, the little shit, he was denying the whole thing. Isn't that right?"

"Right."

"Same as he was denying roughing up Doug Henault. Let me ask you, did it ever cross your mind that Tuttle running you down might have been *intentional?*"

"Yes, but I dismissed it."

"You're the local official that wants to shut down his family business. And here comes Tuttle, he's been pounding beers at the VFW picnic, he sees you crossing the street like a tin duck at the shooting gallery— Boom, he goes for it."

"It was an accident. He hit the wrong pedal. Anyway, he didn't know who I was. Any other questions?"

He paused. "Not at the moment. Got a request, though."

I waited.

"Don't go chasing after Philip Yandow."

"Why? What's with Yandow?"

"Yandow's being watched. Do not screw that up for us, OK?"

"He's being watched, is he? Does whoever you have watching him take Sundays off?"

He smiled and tipped his head uphill toward the office. "You and her ever go out?"

"Why?"

"No reason." He shrugged and said, "Girl's on probation. She's an ephebophile, if you know what that means."

"Somebody with an erotic interest in adolescents. You watching her, too?"

"Sex offender? You bet. You know how that works."

I eyed him for a second. "Let me get you the tag number of that car I saw here yesterday. It's in my truck."

SIX

WHEN I GOT BACK to our hill, Myra was out in the lower garden in a straw sunhat picking haricots verts. We harvested at least twenty pounds of beans a week until first frost, and Myra realized that without Wilma we were going to get behind.

I waved at her and walked up into the kitchen to call Rob Tierney.

I left a short message on his cell. Waiting, I chopped celery and red onion and tarragon for a tuna salad. It rang.

"Rob, thanks."

"Hey, anytime. How's Wilma?"

"Same."

"Hang in there. I hear you dropped by the crime scene at the White Birches."

"Yeah. Tell me, is Max Ingersoll one of those condescending dicks the force likes to promote, or do I have the wrong impression?"

He laughed. "He's military police, so I'd say he's kinda stiff, but *condescending dick* is actually not far off the mark."

"Shame."

"Though, you know, you have that effect on people."

"Do I? Why is that?"

"They can tell you're smarter than they are, and it pisses them off." He laughed. "So, Hector, who we looking for? What's your take?"

"I'd want to talk to a buddy of Seb's named Ronnie DiGuilio. They were together at the scene yesterday afternoon."

"We're on that. We have a BOL out on the Pontiac." He paused. "Come on. Heck, it's me," he prodded.

I was regretting my promise to Kandi, but if Seb really had been dealing crystal, Ingersoll was bound to latch on to better links to that action. "You know Lance Henault?"

"Know the name. Doug's boy?"

"Right. Rugged young man, twenty-two years old. Good, dedicated farmer, solid citizen. But a little edgy, a little inward."

"You didn't mention Lance Henault to Ingersoll."

"Just occurred to me. He could be connected to this."

"You're going to check him out?"

"I might."

"And you wouldn't want Ingersoll to get to him first."

"He has a crime scene to process."

"You're a sly dog. Who else?"

"Seb had a girlfriend. I'd ask his brother for the name."

"Jeremy? I just talked to him. He didn't mention a girlfriend."

"Did you ask specifically?"

"All right. Anybody else?"

"Pie Yandow."

"Forget Yandow."

"Ingersoll tells me they're watching him. What's that about?"

"Couldn't tell you. It's federal, apparently. That badass

goes way back, though. You remember ten, twelve years ago, the Oscar Firman case? . . . river?"

"Vaguely." Our connection was breaking up.

". . . in that town would say anything . . . claiming suicide? . . . er that?"

He was gone.

In the downstairs study I googled Oscar Firman and brought up a few links to local newspaper archives. As I read, the story came back to me. Coös Crossing, winter, 1993. Oscar Firman, a grim-faced grade-school custodian and bus driver, respected but unloved, was reported missing one December morning by his wife. He hadn't come home the night before, a Friday, after the Christmas pageant at the school. Another custodian said he and Firman had left at the same time, ten thirty, and Oscar had locked the building. Because the Firmans' farmhouse was less than a mile from the school, Oscar usually walked home. It had been snowing lightly.

Over the next five days, firemen, sheriff's deputies, and the Allenburg High School basketball team scoured the two routes he might have taken. No one turned up any sign of Firman. One of the firemen went to the trouble of consulting Louise Pinkney, a local medium, who told them Oscar was being held captive in a bread truck. The search didn't end until April, when a fisherman found the body, duct-taped and bound with half-inch nylon rope, in the Connecticut River. Firman's lungs contained water and bits of aspirated grass, and his skull was broken. The medical examiner determined the cause of death to be "asphyxiation from suffocation by means unknown." Probable homicide.

Three months earlier, during the first days of the search, two troopers had collected clumps of fresh silage from the side of the road where a woman driving home from a meeting at the village library on the night Firman disappeared said

she had noticed a pickup with the built-up sides and no tailgate parked cockeyed on the shoulder, fender in the snow-
bank. It had a dusting of snow on the windshield. She had
slowed to a crawl going by, as country people do, to see if
anyone needed help. Painted on one raised side, she recalled,
was the word FIREWOOD and a phone number. The truck had
been empty.

The county sheriff had no trouble concluding that the
pickup must have belonged to Philip I. Yandow, known as Pie,
a local rowdy with an unhappy past and a bad reputation. In
the fall he cut and delivered cordwood in an '86 GMC with
staked sides. Pie had grown up in Coös Crossing, left without
finishing high school, then returned after several seasons on
the carny circuit to take a caretaker's position on Warren Gallagher's horse farm. Yandow told the police right from the beginning that he had not been parked alongside any road at
any time on the night in question, nor had he lent anyone his
vehicle.

Lab analysis of the plant matter in Firman's lungs confirmed a match to the collected samples, which suggested
that what might have been in the bed of Yandow's truck that
night was connected to Oscar Firman's death. The first place
the detectives visited that early spring was Warren Gallagher's farm. Gallagher and his wife were still at their Florida
home for the winter. When forensics found a second match
to the original sample in Gallagher's bunker silo, Pie Yandow
became the lone murder suspect. But he maintained he'd
never met Oscar Firman, didn't even know what he looked
like. What's more, he and his girlfriend had been watching
videos at her apartment in Allenburg that Friday night. The
girlfriend, Mandy Cross, swore this was true—they'd been
watching videos and drinking schnapps. And the video store
clerk remembered them both.

A few others remembered seeing Oscar Firman and Pie

arguing loudly about something on the back porch of the town hall, where some of the men were drinking during the village Holiday Soiree. But by summer their memories had faded, and they no longer had any reliable testimony to offer. As investigators learned later, the Firmans' farmhouse had once been owned by Horace Gagnon, Pie Yandow's stepfather. When Horace Gagnon hanged himself in his barn a month after selling his herd and putting his equipment up for auction, the farm's title passed to Yandow, whose whereabouts no one knew. A few years after that, Oscar Firman picked up the property for back taxes. The soil was played out, but the farm did have a fine maple orchard, and Oscar enjoyed sugaring. He bought a portable sawmill, braced and jacked up the run-down dwelling, replaced the rotting sills, poured a new foundation, then added a porch and a garage. In the lee of the sugarbush he constructed a saphouse built of lumber he'd salvaged from the collapsed barn. The first sunny day in early spring, if he was boiling, the teachers at Coös Crossing Graded marched the kids out to Oscar's for sugar-on-snow. None of this meant anything to Yandow. He didn't care a rat's ass for that farm, he told the police. He'd hated Gagnon's place just about as much as he'd hated Gagnon himself, which was why he'd run off first chance he had.

Every cop who'd talked to Yandow was sure he was behind that homicide, and so was almost everyone in town, but with the girlfriend covering for him and only the silage to implicate him, the state's attorney had no hope of an indictment, and there the case had stood ever since.

THE HENAULTS MILKED after supper. At seven, when I pulled into their dusty drive, the low, white farmhouse was in shadow, though the sun was still gilding the high pasture beyond. After a visit with Wilma, I was happy to be able to leave

Myra in the village at her friend Kirsten's house, where she'd spend the night. Wilma was stable again—though she had a bandaged knot at the top of her head where the bolt had been inserted.

Gussie, the harlequin Dane, greeted me as I slid out of my truck. Cindy Henault waved from the kitchen window, then came out onto the side porch. Her hair had gone entirely gray in the last six months.

"Your peonies look fabulous, Cindy."

"Been a good year," she said.

"You've got the touch. How's Doug doing?"

"Not too terrible. How's Wilma?"

"Same."

She nodded. "I guess you heard Seb Tuttle's no longer among the quick."

"Yes, I did."

"Made my day, Lord forgive me. Any idea who we have to thank?"

"That's going to take a while."

"You know who I jumped to first thing?" she laughed, coloring. *"You!"*

"I can understand that."

Doug had his barn lit with bare fluorescent bulbs, two rows of stubby coils. Underneath ran the milk lines. He still had fifty or sixty heavily studded fly strips dangling down the length of the building, enemy corpses on display. Doug sat on a stool in the doorway reading a newspaper, his right foot in a splint, while far down the aisle Lance tended to the pulsators.

Doug cracked a grin at the sight of me, which I read as embarrassment over my finding him in the barn despite his being banged up and no possible help. He had to keep an eye on things.

We exchanged nods.

"Had it coming, the creep," Doug said.

"How'd you hear?"

"TV. Say, I didn't know Kandi Henderson was back. Girl's got guts, coming back here after what she went through."

"It's her home."

"Most people that stir up a small community like she did, when they get out of jail, they start over someplace else."

"Kandi isn't like most people, I guess," I said. These hills and fields had drawn me back as well, more than a dozen years ago. I had no idea where I'd be if they hadn't.

"The kid's gone, isn't he? The one she was screwing?"

I looked away to let this thread wither, and said, "I talked to Seb Tuttle yesterday."

"Yeah, you did?"

"He told me he hadn't laid a finger on you. Any chance you could have been mistaken about him?"

"Sure, but who else woulda done it? Him and that friggin' Yandow. Unless somebody else is walking around here with a crippled-up hand."

"They had on gloves, you said, gloves and helmets."

"Yandow didn't have gloves. But yeah."

"Doug, I need you to tell me if there was anything specific that made you decide one of them was Seb Tuttle."

"Just he's the hotheaded one of them two Tuttle brothers."

"Yo, Pop?"

Lance had come up behind me. Burly at well over two hundred pounds, Lance stood six or seven inches taller than his dad. He was as rangy and hard as a linebacker.

I turned to him. "Hello, Lance."

"Teat dip's wicked dirty. Where'd you put them new containers?" He didn't acknowledge me, or ask anyone's pardon. That was Lance, sober and blunt past the point of rudeness and committed to farming in a way few young men were anymore. The transition to organic was a plan he'd talked his father into—or he wouldn't have come back to the farm after ag school. He wore loose denim overalls without a shirt. He had an iPod's earbuds around his thick neck. His hairy shoulders were flecked with sawdust. The knuckles of his right hand looked raw and swollen.

Doug eyed him for what seemed a long moment. "Check in the bin next to the tubing."

"Lance," I said, before he could move away. "How'd you hurt your hand?"

He glanced down and shrugged. "Hayin'."

He turned again.

"Lance, wait."

He kept walking. I followed.

"Lance. Hold on a second, will you?"

He crouched and found a mixing bottle.

"State police are going be stopping by here to give you a look, probably some time tomorrow. Do you think *hayin'* is going to make them happy? I don't."

He didn't say anything.

"Hell, Lance."

"You want me to tell you somethin' different?" he asked. I could barely hear him.

"Just tell me whether you went and found Seb Tuttle last night and beat the shit out of him."

"I did not." He straightened and leveled his gaze at me for the first time. "Been right to home since Sunday noon."

"And naturally you have your mom and dad to back you up on that."

He nodded. "Good thing, sounds like."

"Yeah, although if the detectives start giving you a hard time, you call Gideon Miller. You don't have to say anything without an attorney present."

He hefted his jug of concentrate with a jerk that meant our conversation was over. I watched him walk away.

Max Ingersoll would be on Lance like a duck on a bug. If

Lance had punched Seb's ticket, we'd know in a day or two. No danger, anyway, to the people of Tipton.

Outside again, I decided that since I was in the neighborhood I might as well stop by Annie Laurie Rowell's place to see what light she could shed on things. Her farm was just to the east, at the turnoff to the Henaults' place and the egg farm. Some weekends she put in her time at the natural foods co-op, but otherwise she seldom left her place, and since her pasture and goat sheds were just off the road, she might have noticed any passing vehicles—ATVs in particular.

I was backing my truck around in the Henaults' dooryard, admiring Cindy's perennials again, when I happened to catch through my rear window a glint of light bouncing off some vehicle backed into the narrow, leafy lane leading to Doug's woodlot. I hadn't noticed it there when I'd driven by earlier.

I turned in that direction and cruised by. Forest-green Blazer, New Hampshire tags, someone's silhouette behind the wheel. Reading a newspaper.

I pulled to the side of the road and got out.

He rolled down his window at my approach. Red Sox cap, aviator shades, broken nose, black stubble. That and the angle of his head and the cast of his mouth said *cop*.

Then I recognized him. "Byron?"

He laughed, embarrassed.

"What the hell are you doing up here?" Byron Goldstein, last time I had seen him, had been an agent for the Border Patrol. Used to live in North Allenburg. But, last I heard, he'd turned in his badge years ago and moved across the river to sell life insurance.

"Just catchin' up on all the local shit. You seen this here about these bastards poaching deer?" He folded the newspaper and pushed it out the window for me to see.

I had already read the brief story he was tapping with his finger.

TIPTON WOMEN FIND DEER SNARE

Two Tipton women in the woods last Sunday hunting ginseng stumbled on a trap set for the purpose of
taking deer, according to Montcalm County Deputy
Sheriff Neal Cady.

Margaret Wheeler and Dorathea St. Onge, both of
Tipton, last Wednesday called the sheriff to report
finding a snare fashioned of heavy-test monofila-
ment fishing line that someone had strung across a
deer trail less than a mile east of the town reservoir.

"If they're gonna jack deer," Deputy Cady said,
"they might as well just shoot 'em. This kind of thing
burns my butt. Big buck deer's trucking along and all
of a sudden he's got his rack tangled in the fishing
line and he panics. If he breaks his neck, he's lucky. If
he don't, he dies from exhaustion."

The state's investigation is being handled by Vermont State Game Wardens Matthew Curtis and Don
Peck of Allenburg.

"As a hunter," Byron said, "you hate to see this shit. Must
still be some hard-up characters in this town." He chuckled.
"Remember the Gochie brothers? They still livin' up on the
Plateau?"

I knew why he was blathering. "Byron. You're sniffing
around on me, aren't you, Byron?"

"I'm not sniffin'. Nor would I admit it if I was."

"You make one clumsy dick. Why don't you tell whoever
hired you he's wasting his money?"

"How do you know it's a *he*?"

"You tell him, whatever he wants to know, he should try
asking me. This crap is absurd."

"I'll be sure and do that, Hector, I surely will."

. . .

ANNIE LAURIE ROWELL'S long, low goat barn was on the Knob road just after the turn toward the Henault farm and the Egg Works compound above them both. Aside from their allegiance of necessity in the fight with the Tuttles, even though they farmed adjoining properties, Annie Laurie and the Henaults weren't neighborly. Their worldviews clashed. Doug and Cindy were Evangelicals. Annie Laure was a freethinking pagan who celebrated the solstice instead of Christmas. As a teen, Cindy Henault had picketed the Planned Parenthood offices in Allenburg. Annie Laurie had served on PP's board.

Curious goats bounded to the pasture fence when I turned into the farm lane. Two brown-and-white Nubian sentries atop the glacial erratics out in the field *naahhhed* when Annie Laurie's screen door squeaked open. Annie came out, tying her wild gray hair back behind her head. She had on green coveralls and sandals.

"Seen you go by a lot lately, Hector. Been waitin' for you to stop and say hi."

"Busy time, Annie."

"Well, no kiddin'. Say, how's Wilma?"

"Getting there. It's going to take time, but she'll be herself again."

"That's a big relief. She home now?"

"Oh, no, she's— She's still unconscious, Annie."

"She *is*? Shoot. Guess I should stick some zinnias in a jelly jar and get my ass down to the medical center, huh? Say, Heck, while I got you could I ask a question?"

"Go ahead."

"I almost did a jig when I heard Seb Tuttle got whacked. But just from what they said on the radio, that was some vicious murder. Somebody musta got goin' and couldn't quit."

"That could be," I said. "Did you hear about the incident Sunday up at Doug's?"

"Sure didn't. What was that about?"

I explained and asked if she remembered any unusual traffic passing by on Sunday morning.

"Wasn't any traffic at all, and I'll tell you why. Minister Brook Bridge was out south of the Knob from that storm we had Saturday night, and"—she came down the warped porch steps and pointed—"that half-dead granddaddy of a pine tree down by the old springhouse blew right across the road. Took out the power and the phone. Road crew didn't get that mess cleaned up until Sunday afternoon."

"So you mean the Knob was cut off all that morning."

"Yup."

"Must be a field road you could take to get around that blowdown—if you had, say, a four-wheeler."

"I suppose."

"You recall hearing any four-wheelers?"

"Sure don't. 'Course, if it was the Tuttles that went off on Doug Henault, they coulda come over the top of the Knob. Road bein' out wouldn't matter."

"That's true."

"Hey, Heck, I hate to run you off, but I got chores. Tell Wilma she's a champ, will ya? And you come by any day around five for a drink. Me and Helen, that's our cocktail hour."

"Sure thing."

Annie Laurie Rowell, without a shred of maternal sensibility, had no thought at all for Myra.

SEVEN

W HEN I GOT HOME, on the front porch I
found two warm, foil-covered casseroles, a loaf of fresh olive
bread, a green-bean salad, and a bottle of California zinfandel. I had four messages: Maggie Cruikshank at Sullivan's
Store in the village requesting twenty-four quarts of raspberries, Ollie at the food co-op "checking in," Hugh Gebbie asking me to call, and Spud's wife, Brenda, inviting us up to the
farm for strawberry shortcake with fresh whipped cream.

The cabin's emptiness felt oppressive. I fed our cat, Nicole,
poured the rest of that evening's cabernet into a tumbler, and
walked outside to the brow of the hill. The moon hadn't
risen. To the south I picked out Cygnus, Draco, and the Co-
rona. Jupiter hung low over the trees, an incandescent bead.
A jetliner blinked across, bound overseas.

A few miles north, somewhere on the lake road, a motorcycle was winding through the gears. That open stretch of
pavement on the east side of the lake was the place to let it
out—no police, no cars, no risk of transfixed deer in the road.

Seb's corpse had been pretty disturbing. Who could have
done that? A couple of tweakers? Maybe. But if Seb had been

killed elsewhere, then whoever dumped him at the campground, instead of dropping him in the lake or burying him in the woods, had done so for a reason. To implicate someone. Then again, with tweakers, there was no point looking for reasons. Could have been anything, like a hankering for his cute handgun. As for Lance, with a few hundred acres and a big tractor at his disposal, he could have deposited Seb someplace where he'd never be found.

Myra hadn't brought in a quarter of the beans. Eighty feet of spinach needed cutting or it would bolt. The early raspberries would be dropping off the canes in another downpour. I had a round of deliveries to make tomorrow—the beans and lettuces and spinach, plus trays of arugula, mesclun, basil, broccoli, dill, beet greens, and chard, none of them picked. And the raspberries. I had tomatoes to mulch, and asparagus, beets, leeks, onions, cabbages, and carrots to weed.

I had to find help.

When my glass was empty, I drifted back across my shaggy lawn and up the warped steps into the kitchen, where only the twenty-five-watt bulb under the range hood was lit. The cat came halfway down the stairs and made a moan of confusion.

"I know, Nicole, poor kitty," I said. "Where are the ladies?"

I checked the answering machine. Then, though it was past ten, I punched in Hugh's number.

"Still up?" I said.

"Beautiful night," he said.

"Yeah. Myra should be at Audubon camp singing 'My Darlin' Clementine' around a campfire."

"You feel worse about her missing out on that camp than she does."

"That's true."

"Any change in Wilma's status?"

"No. It's a tough one."

"I want you to know I mounted an inquiry here this morning with a blue quartz crystal, a fresh beeswax candle, and the snapshot I have of the three of you from Thanksgiving."

"And?"

"She's going to be fine, Hector. No doubt at all."

"Good to hear. I have the same feeling."

"It wouldn't hurt to let Myra in on my findings. Even though she has me pegged as an octogenarian cornflake." A past chapter president of the American Society of Dowsers, Hugh enjoyed what he'd describe as a certain extrasensory access to a wide array of energy forms and pathways.

"I'll give her the word. You hear about Seb Tuttle?"

"Yes, and I was freaking out here for about an hour or so afterward."

"How's that?"

"Well, I couldn't help thinking that if Wilma had . . . not made it, you'd have every reason to pulverize the guy."

"Your crystal exonerated me?"

He ignored that. "Any idea who killed him?"

"Not yet. But here's the reason I called. Do you have the names of the three high school boys you had stacking cordwood for you last week?"

"Sure. Sleepy, Dopey, and Grumpy."

"They that bad?"

"You're up against it, aren't you?"

"I could use a hand."

"Forget those boys. Turn your back for five seconds and they're text-messaging their girlfriends. I'll be there eight o'clock sharp."

"I appreciate that, Hugh, but there's no need for you to come all the way out to Tipton—"

"Stop! Hey, I finished worming the 'pacas yesterday. If I couldn't do this, I wouldn't offer. Come on now."

I thanked him. If there was a better man on this lonely pebble of a planet, I didn't know him. By the time she was forty-five and in her prime, after having been with my father for twelve years and with Spud's father for ten more, Agnes had found a solid partner in Hugh. The two of them spent twenty years together—plenty of time and, of course, not near enough.

WILMA'S CONDITION was unchanged the next morning. Having slept poorly at Kirsten's house, Myra wasn't able to draw on the reserves of willfulness and hope she needed to keep company with her comatose mother in that overbright room with the dispiriting rooftop view. After half an hour she left with me, in tears.

Hugh was pulling quackgrass and bindweed out of the asparagus beds. The chest-high stalks were all ferning out, and he was hidden in there, warbling one Broadway show tune after another. He had been a trouper in Allenburg's community theater for decades, and his repertoire was bottomless. Over in the raspberries, wearing an open wicker creel for a berrying basket (Wilma's invention), Myra seemed entertained—in contrast to her mother, who, after twenty minutes of this, would have hollered, "OK, Ezio, put a cork in it!"

When we broke for lunch, I had eight messages on the machine—two reporters, Mary at the co-op, Rob Tierney, Vic Parkhurst (Wilma's ex), Esther Nichols, Spud, and Bill Desotel, the chair of the select board. I didn't return any of them.

After making deliveries to the co-op, the health food outlet in East Allenburg, and three village stores in the afternoon, which I rushed through, no chitchat, I got back home under a lowering sky to find Max Ingersoll's unmarked Chevy in my spot in the turnout. I had to squeeze the van in between our pickup and the alyssum bed. I wasn't pleased to

have company. It was just half past four—I had three hours of
good light left, and I needed all of it.

They'd just sat down to iced tea and my leftover raspberry
tart out on the sunporch when I came through the front door,
Hugh, Myra, Max Ingersoll, and that young, swarthy uniformed trooper from the day before, whose name I'd forgotten again.

I washed my hands at the kitchen sink, took a glass from
the drainboard, and went to join them. Myra's face—my eyes
went first to her—looked tense and subdued at the same time.

Ingersoll half rose in his seat. I waved for him not to
stand.

I nodded at Ingersoll and the trooper—*Koslowski.*

"Any news?" I asked Myra.

She shook her head. Hugh was serving slices of tart.

I removed the trooper's campaign hat from the stool
where he'd left it and pulled the stool up to the table.

"Sorry about that," Koslowski said.

"Greetings, gentlemen," I said. "To what do we owe the
pleasure?"

"Pleasure's ours," said Ingersoll. "Your daughter was gra-
cious enough to offer the fruit of her labors, which, as you
can see, we accepted. And I gotta say that's looking like a
very smart move." He winked at Myra.

Hugh's glance reflected my irritation.

Myra had gone to the trouble of getting out Wilma's
heavy amber Depression-glass pitcher for the tea, and she'd
sliced two lemons. I poured myself a glass.

"I'm not sure what you need from me," I said, "but I can
give you five minutes. I have a lot to get done outdoors before
it rains."

"That's fine. I only have a couple questions. Though I hate
to trample on a social occasion . . ."

"Never mind. I figure you want me to tell you why I drove out to Doug Henault's farm last night."

He was savoring his first bite, his eyes half closed. "This is delectable. Us single guys always appreciate a woman's touch in the kitchen. Isn't that true, Mike?"

"Absolutely," Koslowski said. "This is the equivalent of a professional product. What do you call it?" he asked Myra.

"It's a raspberry-almond lattice tart," she told them. "My dad made it."

Ingersoll drew himself straight. "Just proves what people say, doesn't it? The best chefs are men." He took another bite. "OK, Mr. Bellevance, my question is a little more basic than yours, but I'll accept the suggestion. Why did you go out to the Henaults?"

"To find out whether they had anything to do with Seb Tuttle's homicide."

"Did they?"

"They told me they didn't."

"They told us the same thing, right, Mike?"

The trooper made a firm nod.

"We have our doubts and concerns, however," Ingersoll said. "Sure wish you wouldn't have jumped in there ahead of us, Mr. Bellevance."

"Yes, well, I have my own doubts and concerns."

"Is one of them the possibility that your neighbor's son could go down behind the kind of local extermination job you wished you could have taken care of personally?"

"Not a chance. If the Henaults had anything to do with Seb Tuttle's murder, they deserve prosecution and punishment. But I don't see it. Did you find Ronnie DiGuilio?"

"We did indeed. You didn't inform us that you had tangled with this particular individual."

"Actually, I believe I did. What did he have to say for himself?"

"DiGuilio wasn't involved," he said flatly.

"OK. You have a cause of death?"

"What it looked like. Multiple blunt force wounds to the head and face. Boots, baseball bat, ax handle. . . . We'll have a better idea when the ME's done with him."

"Any indication of where it went down?"

He shook his head. "My five minutes. All right, Constable?"

"Sure, go ahead."

"What did you tell the Henaults about the Tuttle murder?"

"Nothing. I said you'd be dropping by with a few questions."

"Did you advise young Lance to come up with some plausible story for how he busted up his knuckles?"

"He told me he hurt himself haying. I didn't pursue it."

"Same as what he told us. Barely. Guy doesn't talk much. I asked him, 'How, haying?' He goes, 'The baler.' Now, myself not being a farmer, I had to ask how a baler could cut and bruise the backs of the hands but not cut his fingers up at the same time."

"Maybe he was wearing gloves."

"Henault said the same thing. He didn't get that from you, did he?"

I looked around the table. Hugh's freighted gaze said he was ready to bolt at the first chance. The fresh wind stirring the bee balm and monkshood just beyond the sunporch windows was urging me outside. "The Henaults didn't kill Seb Tuttle, Sergeant."

"Yeah? See, here's what I don't get. After I tell the two of them that I'd like to take a look at these particular gloves? Why do they tell me they don't have the time to go and hunt for 'em?"

"Get a court order. They'll cooperate soon as they realize you're not just jerking them around."

"That's what I mean. Why do they want to make me go to the judge?"

"Since they have nothing to hide, they see any time spent humoring you as time wasted."

The phone rang.

Myra darted around the end of the small table and into the kitchen. We all waited. She returned to the doorway holding the cordless to her stomach.

"Dad, it's Spud. He says we should come up for supper. Brenda's making lasagna."

"You want to?"

She shrugged.

"Let's do it."

Myra confirmed with Spud and set the phone in the charger. Rather than return to the table, she slipped into her room and shut the door.

"We all done here?" I asked.

Ingersoll drained his tea, tipping a couple of ice cubes into his mouth. He pushed back from the table. "One more question?" He crunched his ice.

"Sure."

"Monday night. Where were you?"

"Here. We got back from the hospital around seven, I guess."

"You and the girl . . ." He nodded toward Myra's room.

"Right."

"What time does she usually sack out?"

"She's in bed by nine thirty and asleep by ten."

He nodded. "Sound sleeper?"

"Usually. There's nothing that would persuade me to leave her here by herself at night, Sergeant, not even for ten minutes."

"That's just what your friend here said." He smiled at

Hugh. "OK," he sighed. "We're outa here. Appreciate your time."

I nodded. "No trouble."

We all got up, and I walked them out to the porch and down the steps.

Hugh followed. No one spoke as we crossed the lawn.

Hugh and I stopped at the lip of the incline and watched the two troopers descend the path to the turnout. I could smell the rain.

"You realize you're not done with this," Hugh said.

"I'm not?"

"According to the state police, Pie Yandow was grilling sausages at the annual Coös Crossing Fire Department Fishing Derby pancake breakfast on Sunday morning."

"That checks out?"

"I guess."

"And Doug Henault is sticking to his story?"

"Apparently."

I waited. "You think I should resolve this contradiction?"

"That's not what I said, Hector."

"With everything I have going on—Myra, Wilma, the farm—do you really think I can't let this one go?"

"That's closer to it."

ALTHOUGH BRENDA WOULD drive a truck when she had to, any other farm chore disgusted or bored her, yet for most of their marriage, as much as Spud tried to spare her the everyday drudgery, he couldn't do it all himself. After a few years, for Brenda, staying on the farm with Spud became a month-to-month proposition. Then, when Lyle turned three, she moved with him into an apartment down in Barre, where she took an office job with Peabody and Sons Memorials. Eight grim and rocky months passed for Spud before he could coax her back to the farm, and even then the marriage remained touch-and-go for a long time.

Lately they'd been doing better. Now that the Amazing Maze had caught on and Lyle had come into his own (at fourteen the boy was already taller than his dad and a willing worker), Brenda was finally free to spend her days in her favorite places, the garden and kitchen, and with the maze drawing tourists in droves Spud found himself making up a bit for the abysmal price of milk.

Everything—the rich lasagna, garlic bread, green olive tapinade, and garden salad—was exceptional. We all relaxed. Spud and Lyle were elated that the Sox had won six straight from Seattle and Detroit, knowing that the scuffling Royals were on their way to Fenway for four more. We all had more lasagna. I had to laugh when Myra said, mimicking Koslowski, "I think this is the equivalent of a professional product."

After Brenda's lemon sorbet, Lyle took Myra out to the barn to show her the new calf, leaving the adults to their herbal tea. As soon as they were out of earshot Brenda asked how Myra was handling Wilma's situation.

I said something about that, and then changed the subject, asking Spud and Brenda what they remembered about the Oscar Firman murder.

Brenda sat back. "Not much. I was over in Winooski cutting hair back then, but it was a big deal in the papers."

Spud said, "The interesting thing about the Oscar Firman case was Firman's farm was the same farm where Pie Yandow got his hand mangled in the gutter cleaner. You remember that, Hector?"

"I remember. Mom sent me all the clippings."

He laughed. " 'Course she did."

"The way I heard it from you," Brenda said to Spud, "Pie

Yandow and two, three others waylaid poor Oscar one night on his way home from work. Got on him so bad they wound up killing him, and they dumped the body in the river. Didn't turn up till fishing season."

"Right," Spud said. "These guys tied him up and drove him out to Warren Gallagher's farm in the Crossing. The way they figured this out was exactly like on *CSI*, you know? From the autopsy. So the troopers *knew* Yandow was the guy—hell, everybody in the *county* knew he was the guy—only they couldn't get one person in that town to testify in court. So they couldn't prove nothing. I'm tellin' you, that case is a prime example of small-town Vermont at its worst."

Brenda laughed through her nose.

Spud got up from the table to let the dog out. Myra's musical voice floated in from the yard. A june bug drummed fuzzily against the screen door.

"Couple summers ago," Spud said, "I was at the fair one time and I see Yandow coming—him and his posse of beered-up jokers with their leather and chains and all this crap hanging off them so you can't miss how *bad* they are. Cruising the midway, right? Mister, you shoulda seen how everybody quick stepped aside, you know?"

"Hasn't happened yet, thank God," Brenda said, "but if Yandow and them was to show up here wanting to get into the maze, I wouldn't know what to do. I'd be too scared to let 'em in and too scared to keep 'em out."

"That ever happens," Spud said, "what you do is you let 'em in, and then you call the sheriff."

The phone rang, and Brenda got up to answer it.

"So," I said, "you think Yandow was working at the pancake breakfast on Sunday or is that his cover?"

He shrugged. "Sounds like the troopers are satisfied."

"They don't know the history."

"Sure they do. You mean the whole witness intimidation thing?"

"I wonder. Everybody who worked that case must be retired by now."

"Are you saying somebody that *does* know the history's gonna have to start poking around?"

I looked at Spud. "You and Hugh. Both of you think I can't walk away from this one."

"You brought it up."

"So?"

"So you *love* it."

"I loved it once. Or I thought I did. Now it seems as if it's a lot more about what I *hate.*"

After a pause, Spud said, "That why you quit?"

"I never quit." The job got easier, in fact, after I allowed hate to govern procedure. The rest of my life got harder, though.

"*Retired,* I mean."

"Spud, I don't care who killed Seb Tuttle. Maybe he scammed some cranked-up bikers, maybe Lance Henault took a tire iron to him, maybe something he got into in Canada caught up with him, but the troopers are all *over* it. I'm not needed, and my pregnant wife is in a coma, and my daughter is mad at me and struggling with her anxiety. I also have a farm to manage."

After a moment, he said, "You wanna bet?"

"On what?"

"You keeping out of this."

"Sure. A million dollars."

Spud nodded. "I'll take it in blueberries."

Myra banged through the door. "*Guys!* Come outside! There's northern lights!"

EIGHT

THE PHONE RANG AT a quarter past six the next morning. I was at the stove cooking down some sliced rhubarb with maple syrup and lemon zest, a compote for our pancakes.

"Top of the morning, Mr. Bellevance. Not waking you, I trust."

"Not at all. Who's calling?"

"It's Harold Tuttle. Are you free to speak?"

"What's the topic, Mr. Tuttle?"

"I have a proposal to make."

From her room, Myra yelled, "Is it about Mom?"

I put the phone to my chest. "No, sweetheart."

I switched off the gas under my saucepan. "I'm sorry for the loss of your son, Mr. Tuttle."

"I appreciate that. The police informed me that your wife was injured as a result of the car accident Sebastian was involved in on Saturday. How is she?"

"Still in a coma. But she's in good hands. She could regain consciousness anytime."

"Ah, well, that's very good, good to know. May she enjoy a full and complete recovery."

"Thanks. What's your proposal?"

"I would like to instruct my attorneys to ensure that all of the costs of your wife's hospital and home care be absorbed by my son's estate."

"What are the conditions?"

He hesitated. "Your answers to three easy questions."

"Anything else?"

"I would like them to be in the affirmative."

"Ask your questions. No guarantees on the responses."

"From what I've learned about you, Mr. Bellevance, I'm going to assume you aren't one of the monsters who beat my son to a pulp. Is that a safe assumption?"

"Yes, though I wouldn't trust the judgment of that so-called detective you invested your money in."

"In twenty-four hours that detective gathered quite a lot of intelligence about your . . . your crime-fighting exploits, Mr. Bellevance."

"Whatever he's gathered, I suspect it's far from intelligence."

Tuttle made a chuffing sound. "These people—these *animals*—who murdered my son, I want them to pay for what they've done."

"The state police—"

"I have no confidence in your state police. That's why I'm talking to you. Here we are, two days after the savage murder of an area businessman, and these people have *nothing*! Two days of interviews, searches, lab work, autopsy results, and all the rest, and they have *no* suspects and *no* leads. Nothing!"

"A case like this can take months to clear, Mr. Tuttle, as I'm sure you know."

"Yes, but as *you* know, Mr. Bellevance, the longer these cases take, the less likely they are to clear—ever."

"Statistically, maybe, but every case is unique, and you can't simply—"

"My son was beaten to death in this community by people who know their way around your town. Do you agree?"

"That seems likely."

"Which leads me to my third question. I need an investigator, somebody smart, somebody who can navigate this backwater without—"

"I'm sorry, Mr. Tuttle. It's the height of the growing season. I haven't got two hours to spare."

"Let me finish. I'm offering a three-thousand-dollar retainer plus three hundred dollars a day, Canadian. In *addition* to every cent of your wife's medical care. Will you think about it?"

I said nothing.

"I hear you thinking already. In the meantime, I'll have the agreement put in writing and faxed to the office at the Egg Works. Meet me there at noon. No later, if you don't mind— I have a flight to catch out of Burlington."

"You're here in Tipton, Mr. Tuttle?"

"We flew down on Tuesday. The Mounties appeared at my door that morning. It was the most—" He coughed and paused for several seconds. "Before we left home, I made detailed arrangements with a funeral director in St. John. We were told by the coroner that we could bring him home with us for the memorial service and funeral. But since I arrived, I've— He's not . . ." His voice cracked. "His face is *gone!* They destroyed his *face!* I—" He muffled the phone.

I waited. His words brought back the broken voice of a young woman named Brigid Haskell, whose eight-year-old daughter had been kidnapped off the T by a child killer named Clarence Wilmot. Taken, bound, and abused over the course of two or three days in a furnace room in Dorchester, then burned. Long before we knew any of that, it was Brigid

Haskell's squeaky voice, the bewildered grief in it, that kept me going as the months went by and everything we could find took us nowhere.

"Noon, then, Mr. Bellevance?" he said.

"At the Egg Works," I said. "I'll be there."

I called Hugh.

He was amused. "Well, well. Here's a wrinkle I didn't foresee. One minor problem, though—you don't have a PI's license."

"I'm calling because I'm going to need your help. I'll give you the three hundred a day to stay on top of things here at the farm. Three to four hours, tops. And I'll pitch in all I can."

"I'm in and happily, but I don't want your money, Hector. I'm almost eighty-five years old. What do I want with money?"

"It's Harold Tuttle's money," I said. "You pay Jennifer, don't you?" Jennifer Cochrane was his full-time hand. She'd been looking after the alpacas for ten years.

"Put it toward Myra's college fund."

"You're a good man, Hugh."

"A friend's a friend. And a killer's a killer."

Hugh had the grace not to needle me for my reversal in the matter. Myra made up for that, however, in her disgust over my sellout.

"He *bribed* you, Dad!"

"No, Myra. He made a proposal and I accepted it."

"Oh, sure. Yesterday you told Spud you didn't care *who* killed that jerk. Now all of a sudden you *do* care, and the only thing that's different is the jerk's father said he would *pay* you."

"That doesn't make it a bribe, sweetheart. I changed my mind."

"Because of *money*!"

"Money's only part of it. Seb Tuttle was no paragon of

virtue, but nobody should have to die the way he did. And no parent should have to endure his child's brutal murder."

"Well, you know what they say, Dad. Shit happens. Especially to sketchy dorks like Seb Tuttle." She had finished her pancakes, and she was chasing the last of the syrup and rhubarb around her plate with the tip of her finger. "So does this mean you're a detective again?"

"Not officially. How do you know what I said to Spud?"

"I heard you. We were just out there on the glider." She paused and added, "Lyle tried to kiss me."

"He did? What was that like?"

"Embarrassing. I don't even *like* him or anything." She shook her head. "Did you ever try and kiss a girl when you were a boy?"

"Oh, once or twice. I was pretty shy."

"Did you, like, *lunge* at them?"

I laughed. "No. As I recall, I kind of tipped myself into her."

"Oh." She thought for a moment. "I guess this means you're not going to be around home too much, are you?"

"In the morning and at night I'll be here. Hugh'll be around most of the time when I'm not, and Spud and Brenda are a mile up the road."

"What about Mom?"

"Mom will be well again, Myra, I promise you. She'll be herself again. Did I tell you Hugh's sources say we should definitely not worry? He wanted you to know that."

"Great. So, then I guess I'm still the designated bedside person."

"I'll drive you over to Audubon Camp whenever you're ready to go."

"Dad!" She banged the table. The plates jumped. "You don't *get* it! All the doctors and nurses, they *all* say you need to have somebody in the *room*, somebody who can talk to her and touch her and everything—for stimulation and, like, *love*. Why isn't that person ever *you*? How come it's always me?"

I didn't have an answer.

She pushed up, annoyed. "I guess this is why Mom says you're so exasperating."

"She says I'm exasperating?"

"Yes. Because no matter what, you're going to do what you're going to do, and *that,* thank you very much, is *that.*"

AT THE WHITE BIRCHES office I waited outside the door while Marty Henderson soothed someone he had on the telephone. "I understand—no, I understand completely, Mrs. Miller. No, indeed. No hard feelings. You, too."

When he was off, he motioned me inside.

"One more cancellation. Lost half of my campers in two days. I'm refunding deposits from people who've been camping here ever since we first opened."

"That's a shame."

"Thing of it is, I can't say I blame 'em. You know what we're getting now? We're getting these people that think they have the right to cruise through a private campground just for the jollies. What is the appeal?" In his sixties, trim and fit as his daughter but craggy and hard-edged, Marty was a self-assured businessman. He got up at four each morning to manipulate his investments online. He had two or three million, according to Esther. During the camping season he lived in one of the five elegant bootleggers' cottages a few miles up the lake on the cove at Westlook. His wife owned Sophie's, an antiques and gift shop in the heart of Allenburg. They were estranged. Sophie, the word was, had never set foot on the campground. Marty played a lot of golf in the afternoons. "Seriously," he said, "where's the thrill in *driving by*? Myself, I'd *avoid* a place where somebody just got his face bashed in."

I shrugged. "It's natural." The first few years on the job I'd been just as irritated by the human compulsion to gawk at tragedy, but over time I came to see it as primal and almost touching. "So do I hear some kid found the body and reported it to you? That what happened?"

"Yeah. I didn't believe it at first. Never had anybody *die* on the premises before, not even from natural causes."

"You know this kid?"

"Jimmy Lussier? Sure, he mows the grass for me."

"Last name's Lussier?"

"Yeah. His stepdad's Nick Verlander—Nick's Small Engine."

Nick Verlander ran a repair shop out on the highway a mile south of the village. He also managed the Mr. Sud's Car Wash in Allenburg, a business he'd inherited from his dad. "Marty, what time do you get here in the morning?"

"Varies. Six thirty, seven."

"Do you recall what time it was when Jimmy told you he'd found a body?"

He sighed. "I been through this three times now, twice here on Tuesday, then once more at the barracks in Allenburg, which they videotaped."

"Investigations are always redundant, Marty. What time was it when Jimmy told you about the body?"

He sighed again. "About eight. I don't wear a watch, so I can't say exactly."

"Thank you. And what did the boy say? Can you remember his words?"

"Kid comes charging in the office here all sweaty and bug-eyed—*Mr. Henderson, Mr. Henderson!* and I'm thinking—" He stopped.

"What?"

"He couldn't get the words out. He never says too much anyhow, Jimmy—at least not to me—but here he is leading me down the lane and I'm going, *Jimmy, what? What is it?* Finally—I don't know how long it took—probably wasn't all that long in retrospect, less than a minute—finally he says it's a *body*, a dead body, and I'm thinking OK, OK, somebody drowned, somebody had a heart attack and bought it in the lake. Because he fishes off the rocks there—Jimmy. But we go partway down the lane and at the dip there he stops and points, which—like I say, not much of a talker. So I go in under the trees and Christ almighty, it's a body all right. Or a bunch of clothes shaped like a body, you know—*bloody* clothes, because . . ."

"Did you realize who it was?"

"I didn't get that close. No, I had Jimmy stand guard so nobody else would find it, you know, and I ran back here and called nine-one-one."

"Who IDed the body?"

"Actually, Kandi did."

"Kandi? She came here?"

"No, no, no. She was home, but after I called the state police I called her. And she goes, *Where is it? What kind of shoes?* and all this, so I tell her, and she's like, *Oh, Christ, it's Seb! It's Seb Tuttle!*"

"That's what you told the police, that Kandi said it was Seb Tuttle?"

"Yeah. Jimmy said it was him, too, come to think of it. Jimmy knows everybody in the park. He's got a thing where he runs errands for people."

"You had no direct dealings with Seb Tuttle yourself?"

"Not really. His brother I know—Jeremy. Runs the Tipton Egg Works—which, I know you're down on that deal, but as far as I'm concerned, Jeremy's OK. Polite, et cetera. Pays up front. Wish I could say the same for his brother."

"You said you didn't know his brother."

"I didn't. I just didn't like the type of people he had coming in here. Last month we even had a couple bikers—gang members—cruise the loop looking for him. I didn't like that at all."

"You talk to these bikers?"

He shook his head. "Kandi saw 'em. I'm outa here before lunch. Regular one o'clock tee time."

"Seb and his acquaintances showed up only in the afternoons?"

"Or nights. I figured he was using his brother's RV to get laid, right? I did see quite the buxom little filly coming out of there two or three mornings."

"You know a guy named Pie Yandow?"

"I heard that name."

Marty remembered the Oscar Firman murder, too, but he couldn't recall ever seeing anyone with a crippled hand. When I asked where Kandi was staying these days, he told me he'd wangled summer accommodations for her in a shack on the lakeshore that its owner had refurbished as a guesthouse.

I knew the place. It was a shelter built for the canoes that used to belong to the Arrow-Wind Camp for Girls. Casper Knowlton, the property's latest owner, a golfing buddy of Marty's, was letting her stay in the old canoe shed as a favor. Knowlton had a lot of money, Marty said, so he didn't need rent, and Kandi was hoping to save enough by fall to buy herself some wheels. In the meantime, she was riding her bike everywhere.

Why Marty couldn't unbend enough to liquidate a small fraction of his holdings to lend his daughter the cash to buy herself a used Civic was between the two of them, of course, but I didn't feel kindly disposed to Marty Henderson. "That's neighborly of Dr. Knowlton," I said.

"It is," Marty agreed, "though I don't know about that shack. I mean, no power, no phone, no plumbing, no lock on the damn door." He chuckled. "Girl loves it down there, though—the mists, the loons, the view, the little lapping waves at night. Rides her bike to work, cooks her oatmeal on her propane stove. . . ." He sighed. "Good to see her so happy again."

THE MANSION at the heart of the old two-hundred-acre camp was a huge, many-windowed Victorian-style retreat—three floors with twelve fireplaces, each with a distinct marble façade, and twelve tiled bathrooms. Its two towers, east and west, one rectangular, one cylindrical, rose against the backdrop of Mount Joseph's granite cliffs. In the 1880s, when it was built, it was the centerpiece of a New York hotelier's country estate, which at the time included an attached billiards hall, a carriage barn and stable, a greenhouse, four formal gardens, a tennis court, even its own railroad spur. Soon after the heirs sold the property, in the '20s, it became the Arrow-Wind Camp for Girls. The main house became the dining hall, infirmary, and administrative offices, and the carriage barn became studios for dance, sculpture, and painting. In the '50s, with the demise of passenger rail, the camp petered out. After that, the carriage barn and stable were leveled for the beams and slate and the gardens succumbed to weeds. Pigeons and squirrels nested in the billiards hall. The mansion itself stood empty for over a decade until a Canadian couple took it on, refurbished it, and turned it into a B & B they called the Arrow Lake Lodge, which never did enough business to break even. After the lodge went under, a local Realtor leased the building to a film producer who shot porn upstairs and ran a seedy nightclub in the old infirmary. Today the estate was a gentlemen's retreat again. Casper Knowlton, a congenial patron of the arts, sometimes hosted summer concerts in the restored rose and peony gardens. The billiards hall had become the orchid house.

When I drove in, I saw no one about. A blue Mercedes station wagon with the windows down stood parked in the shade just past the carriageway. I continued on around the oval rose garden to the peastone lot on the north side of the house and parked my truck at the far end. The only other vehicle I could see was an electrician's van, its sliding door open, near the service entry.

I strolled across the dense grass to the shore. Islands of birches and blue spruce and rare piney specimens I couldn't name were enclosed by borders of yellow azaleas, pink begonias, and ageratum. The canoe shed was east of the open beach among the trees at the end of a small sandy cove near a spring, if I remembered accurately. It was a hazy morning, fragrant and warm and still, and the lake held a glassy reflection of the mountain and the bland sky. On the other side of the water, tendrils of mist drifted past Mount Joe's sinewy façade. Nothing else moved. I could hear ducks nattering somewhere up the bouldery shoreline.

As I approached the beach, voices floated up through the quiet air from the direction of the shed—a man's and a woman's. They were hidden from me by the cedars near the water's edge. The tension between them seemed plain, though I could make out only scraps of their conversation: ". . . *my* life . . ." ". . . you go right ahead!" ". . . im*poss*ible!"

Not to intrude, I walked over to one of the teak benches Knowlton had set along the shore to wait. Soon a flicker of orange appeared through the screen of boughs and then someone—Knowlton, in a peach T-shirt and teal nylon wind pants—emerged from the trees, striding toward the house. If he'd glanced my way he would have spotted me, but he was caught up in himself. I watched him until he'd crested the lawn and passed out of sight at the white cedar windbreak behind the house.

Kandi, in shorts and a blue tank top, was sitting cross-legged on a smooth spit of granite that formed the pocket cove at the canoe shed. Doing yoga.

She swiveled around, her eyes widening. "Hector! You scared me."

"I apologize for showing up unannounced, Kandi, but I need your help. Your dad said I might find you here." My eyes went to a bed of vibrant lobelia along the west side of the shed—it was the same shade of blue as her tank top. Or was it the top of a swimsuit? "This is a great spot."

She smiled. "My own corner of paradise." She rose with the self-conscious poise of a dancer. "I was going to have some tea. Join me?"

"Sure. Thanks."

She walked ahead of me. I looked at the ground.

The shed stood on eight squat concrete piers a foot above the stone ledge. Someone had recently sheathed the structure with lapped cedar boards and closed in the north side with large windows, tall, sturdy, eight-over-eight panels with narrow steel mullions, like factory windows. The interior was cool, a spacious single room without direct light. The north wall framed an Ansel Adams view—the soothing span of the lake from the shadowy cliffs of Mount Joe to the bluffs on the west side. It could have been an illuminated diorama in a natural history museum—the Northwoods Lake Biome.

At the near end of the room were a gas stove and refrigerator and a round porcelain washbasin set in a slab of pine, an oak pedestal table with a dozen candlesticks and a bouquet of black-eyed Susans at the center, and two ladder-back chairs. In the middle of the room were a mission oak love seat, a library desk and a swivel chair, and a double-globed antique kerosene lamp on a marble-topped stand. At the far end were a full-size spindle bed, neatly made, a chiffonier piled with books, and a brass-trimmed, humpbacked steamer trunk.

She lit a burner with a flint igniter. "Like my view?"

"It's magical."

"Every morning when I wake up here, I can't imagine anything more I will ever need."

"Soon as the snow flies, a woodstove may prove a welcome addition."

She laughed. "Flying snow seems a long way off on a day like this."

I walked to the window. "How have things been for you here, Kandi?"

"You have any particular things in mind?"

"A lot of people are surprised you came home."

"Tell me about it. My dad said if he were in my shoes, he'd head for California." She sighed. "I'm no degenerate, Hector. This is *home*. This is where I grew up and went to school."

"Still, it's always a risk, coming back. I did the same thing. First two years I thought I'd made a mistake."

She nodded. "I broke the law, and I accept that. If society wants to call what I did a crime, that's society's right. But I have *paid* for it. What do you accomplish by—" She stopped and blinked back tears.

"That was another kind of risk. You knew that, too."

"Yeah." She laughed, letting the tears spill down her face. "That was the thrill of it." She wiped her cheeks with her fingers. "Shit. I'm not as tough as I look, am I?"

"You don't look tough at all."

"*It's home.*" She sighed and glanced away. "You said that to me one time. Do you remember?"

I shook my head. But it was coming back to me.

"The first time you and I actually sat and talked, that afternoon at the pool. You don't remember this? I sprained my toe on that water polo thing, and you went and got some ice for me."

"What I remember is blurting out something about your

being the most beautiful woman I'd ever seen, or something as blunt as that."

"And I blushed like a Key West sunset."

"I'm sorry."

"Don't apologize! I loved it. But you did come on like a steam locomotive."

"I remember that. We'd been talking for a few minutes, and nobody else was there—nobody in the pool—and the sun was streaming in, reflecting off the snow outside. And you glowed. It was a breathtaking moment."

"You were smitten, weren't you? I was old enough to've heard it all before, you know, but—" She paused and her smile faded. "I'm going to tell you something. Until I met you, I never met anybody as . . . not *powerful*, but, I guess, *deep*, deep in character, if you know what I mean—and it was just . . . I don't know."

"I was deep, all right. I was scraping bottom in those days."

"That was part of it, too. I asked if you'd come back to Tipton for a visit, and you said you weren't sure. Remember that? Then you were telling me about how you'd been forced to retire and your wife had walked out on you, and you had no job and no money. I already knew that your *mother*—who was my first-grade teacher—had passed away the summer before, and everybody who read a newspaper knew how you, well—that whole story. So, I mean, talk about damaged goods. Yikes. But I don't know, you got to me." She laughed. "Now look who's damaged goods."

"You never let on."

"Well, because I was engaged at the time."

"I only wish . . ." I shook my head. Nothing to gain by finishing that one.

I gazed at the silvery breadth of the lake and the green-fringed horizon, while Kandi poured the tea.

"Wilma the same?"

"She's stable. Myra's with her."

"It must be so *hard* for her." Kandi motioned me toward the door. She held a tray with our mugs, a jar of honey, and two small dark muffins in a wooden bowl. "Still, you know, life's full of hard knocks. Learn it when you're young, I say. How old is she?"

"She'll be twelve in October."

We made our way out onto the slab of quartz-veined rock, where we sat in the sun. A great blue heron glided in close, then veered away at the sight of us.

She handed me my tea. I could smell the sunscreen on her shoulders. "So," she said, "you need my help?"

I took a sip. "Kandi, when your dad called Tuesday morning to tell you about the murder, how did you know that was Seb's body he'd found?"

"He found it?"

"Sorry. Your dad says Jimmy found it. Do you know Jimmy?"

"Yeah, he's— OK, Jimmy. Right."

"And Jimmy went to your dad, and your dad called you, and he said that you realized it was Seb who'd been killed. How was that?"

"Because I asked him where it was and what it looked like, and he said it had black jeans and a black shirt, and—" She stopped. "I already told you I figured he was probably running a drive-in pharmacy in there and, who knows, maybe he fucked somebody over. . . ."

"Kandi, did you ever buy drugs from Seb Tuttle?"

The color drained from around her eyes. "Where are you coming from?"

"It's just a question."

"But why are you *asking* it?"

"Because there's more to you and Seb Tuttle than you've let on."

"Is that right?"

"Come on, Kandi."

She rolled her head back on her shoulders. "I will not go back inside. I'll shoot myself first, I swear to you."

"This has nothing to do with the state. Anything you tell me now stays with me."

"Until you get subpoenaed."

"No, Kandi, I keep my promises. I need you to tell me everything you can remember about Seb Tuttle and his acquaintances."

"See, no. You know why? Because I was not *involved* with those dipshits. All I—" She shook her head. "No. No. Forget it."

"A man's been murdered, Kandi."

"Good fucking riddance."

"His body was dumped at your dad's campground. I'd like to know why somebody would go to the trouble to do that."

She shook her head. "I don't know why I ever said anything to you about him dealing crystal."

"I do. He had his hooks in you somehow, and when I showed up asking about him, you figured you could use me to make him go away."

She rose to her feet. "Seb Tuttle thought he was the hot-shit cock of the walk. When really he was scum. But to answer your question, no, I did not buy drugs from him. All I ever did was *talk* to him."

"Did you talk to the bikers who came through looking for him?"

"What bikers?"

"Do you remember telling Marty about the Canadian motorcycle guys who came looking for Seb?"

"OK, yeah."

"Help me out here, Kandi. I need details—what they looked like, what they drove, all that. And I need anything you can remember about Monday night."

She threw her head back. "I'm on probation! I'm a registered goddamn *sex offender*. I cannot get *involved* in this shit!"

"Too late, Kandi."

"No. No!" She untied the drawstring, stepped out of her
shorts, and stood facing me in her royal blue racing suit, both
hands behind her head fastening her hair back with a band.
"Leave me alone, Hector. *Please*, please leave me alone." She
whirled around, took three long strides, and flew out over the
water.

I watched the underwater blur of her legs until the sun's
glare blotted her out. A good minute passed before she finally
blipped to the surface like a loon and began to swim, one
bent white arm and then the other rhythmically catching the
slanting, early rays of the sun.

Among the papers on her little writing table (bank state-
ments, coupons, an application to the health club in Allenburg, a calendar, a new fishing license) I found nothing
helpful. Her night table drawer contained a *Book of Common
Prayer*, a packet of gum stimulators, a Timex watch, hair
clips, a tin of Advil, a prescription pill bottle—Valium, 5 mg—
several foil-wrapped condoms, and a brass pot pipe. I smelled
the pipe's tarry bowl. The pot was here, too, finely screened,
in a black plastic film can.

I sat on the love seat and went through her scuffed leather
handbag. No drugs, no weapons except for a canister of pepper spray, no address book, and no cell phone. She'd called
me from here, hadn't she? Isn't that what she'd said?

No. *I'm at the lake.* Those were her words.

Knowlton's would have been the nearest landline.

What kind of relationship were they caught up in? Knowlton was married—although his wife, an administrator at Bryn
Mawr, spent most of her time in Philly. The condoms said she
was sleeping with somebody, which bothered me in more
ways than I was comfortable thinking about.

I wanted to buttonhole Jeremy Tuttle before his father could get to the egg factory ahead of me, but when I rounded the corner of the reglazed greenhouse and saw Knowlton, now in wraparound sunglasses, leaning against the fender of my pickup with his arms folded, my curiosity sharpened. He was wearing a fat gold wristwatch with a shimmery mother-of-pearl dial.

"Constable. Hope you're not here on official business."

"Why is that?"

"Because I would be alarmed to think we have a town officer who presumes he can traipse across my property anytime he likes without asking my permission."

"I was paying a call on a tenant of yours, Kandi Henderson."

"Ms. Henderson's a houseguest. Is this about the body at the White Birches?"

"That's right. Terrible thing," I said. "Terrible for her, terrible for Marty, terrible for the town."

"Terrible for the victim above all. Though I've seen worse in the ER."

"Worse than what?"

"Quite grisly, from what I hear. I wouldn't want to parse the brutalities. Thankfully, such violence is rare in these tranquil hamlets."

"That's only because these tranquil hamlets have fewer people."

"Score one for the cynical detective."

I shook my head. He was welcome to his prejudices, but not his condescension.

"Did Kandi have anything useful to tell you?" he asked.

"Why do you want to know?"

"She's been through a rough patch, and she's trying to transition back into a normal life. This situation just makes it harder."

"You and Kandi are friends, Dr. Knowlton?"

"Of course."

"Before the murder, did Kandi ever happen to mention Seb Tuttle?"

"Yes, in fact. She told me he was making a pest of himself."

"He was? How so?"

"At the campground, I mean."

"How was he making a pest of himself?"

He shrugged. "She didn't say. I assume he was hitting on her. She's . . . Kandi's in a fragile condition right now."

"So whatever happened between her and Tuttle, she didn't discuss that with you?"

He shook his head. "She didn't discuss it with you either, it would seem."

"She has concerns for her safety. Look, Dr. Knowlton, I'm sure it's generous of you to be looking out for her as you have been, but if any trouble should come up out here, call me at home, all right? I can be here in five minutes."

"Yes, sir. I will."

His salute didn't faze me. Knowlton was smart enough to recognize serious trouble when he saw it. I hoped he was also prudent enough to steer clear of it—though he'd call the troopers before he'd call me. Which was fine, just as long as he didn't try to play hero in the meantime.

NINE

WHEN I REACHED THE Egg Works compound near the crest of the Knob, two men were at work setting new gateposts. A pickup, a car, and two mud-splattered ATVs were parked in the lot. It was well before noon. I made note of the ATVs' tags. The car was a white Camry with New York plates, possibly Jeremy's rental, since his new BMW had to be in the shop. The pickup belonged to the fence menders. I pressed the buzzer and waited.

I pressed again.

Jeremy had on a short-sleeved khaki jumpsuit and black, dust-coated work boots. He'd recently cultivated a goatee like his brother's, but brown. With his sloping shoulders, narrow head, and pursed mouth, he looked a little chickenlike. The fussy whiskers weren't helping.

"We're at the end of the day's run here, Constable. There something I can do for you?"

"Your father phoned me this morning. He's asked me to meet him here."

"What for?"

"He wants my help in finding whoever killed your brother. You two aren't on the same page with this?"

"Does he give a damn what I think?"

"Does he?"

He shook his head. "Never mind. Have you met Dinah Lynn?"

"I don't think I have."

"Dinah Lynn is Harold's assistant. She makes twice what I make for tending to his BlackBerry, checking his blood sugar, and applying her lips wherever requested."

"Thanks for the introduction. While you're in a candid mood here, what are your impressions about what happened to Seb?"

"Impressions. I'm impressed somebody considered him worth killing."

"You didn't think much of your brother?"

"I loved Seb. But he was a worthless human being."

"In what respects?"

"All of them."

"Could you be more specific?"

"He was the prodigal son." Jeremy shook his head. "The inspector—Ingersoll—he's the one you want to talk to."

"Thanks. Ingersoll thinks the Henaults may have something to do with Seb's death. What're your thoughts on that?"

"Doug Henault's a bullheaded clod. His son's worse. Are they capable of brutally beating a man to death? It wouldn't surprise me."

"After he broke in here and took a maul to your sprayer, why didn't you report the incident to the police?"

"Seb was managing the facility. That's his responsibility."

"Why didn't he follow through?"

"What makes you think he didn't?"

"Did you send him down the hill to give Doug a tune-up?"

He shot a glance behind him. "If you really want to pursue this, you'll have to come with me."

I followed Tuttle down a short wide hallway to the sorting room. Water splashed. Two Hispanic women in aprons and rubber gloves were washing and packing eggs as fast as the red, corrugated plastic belts delivered them. They didn't look up. Jeremy said something to them that I couldn't hear over the noise of the work.

"Hiring illegals now, Jeremy?"

"I'm damned lucky to have them."

"You had two local women working for you last time I was here."

"They quit on Tuesday."

"They give a reason?"

"I know the reason. First some raging nutcase breaks into the facility. Then their supervisor turns up bludgeoned to death."

"Did you let Seb borrow your new BMW last Saturday or did he take it without asking?"

"Both."

"What do you mean by that?"

"His Jeep was in the shop awaiting a new transmission. Or was it his girlfriend's Jeep? I was never clear on that."

"And?"

"He had someplace he had to go after work Saturday, and he called my house and asked my wife if he could borrow my new car. Now, to Genevieve, a car is a car. The fact that I had just taken delivery of a new M-three with less than a hundred kilometers on it, which I had not even *insured*, did not give her a second's pause. 'Why, of course, Sebastian. Key's in the ignition.' Technically, we let him borrow the car. He also took it."

"And wrecked it."

"He wasn't used to a stick shift. The car got away from him."

"What's his girlfriend's name?"

"Melissa something."

"Was Seb living with her?"

"I have no idea. He had the keys to the motor home, but he didn't like it there."

"Why did you give him the keys to your motor home?"

"Because I didn't need it anymore. And he is my *brother*."

"Where was he trying to get to last Saturday afternoon?"

"He told Genevieve he got a tip from somebody that his girlfriend was prancing around up at the nude beach, and he was upset."

"Melissa something."

"Exactly."

"You must have been angry with him."

"What is this about, Mr. Bellevance? You want me to confess? My brother was a psychotic playboy, so I had him exterminated for the good of mankind?"

I just looked at him.

He shook his head. "You bastard. You'll do just about *any*thing to drive me off this hill."

"Right now I'm trying to find Seb's killers. There's every reason for you to help me, but I'm not about to force you." Yet.

"Good."

"Did you recruit Pie Yandow to help your brother teach Doug Henault a lesson?"

"Who's Pie Yandow?"

"You don't know Pie Yandow?"

"Yandow . . . No, I'm sorry."

"How about Ronnie DiGuilio?"

"No. As I told Inspector Ingersoll, I'm sure Seb was here working last Sunday morning. He'd spent the night before with us, because he was without a car. As you know."

"Any idea how I might learn Melissa's last name?"

"Can't help you there. I believe she works as a teacher's aide."

"Where does she live?"

"No idea."

"You have a phone number for Seb?"

"Just his cell. Again"—he smiled—"I suggest you get in touch with Inspector Ingersoll. He's a professional, and he's hot on the case."

A buzzer sounded in the vestibule behind us.

"That'll be Prince Hal," he said. "Excuse me, will you?"

I watched the egg washing. The Hispanic women worked like automatons, nervous about me. Many good-sized dairy operations up here depended on illegals these days. Local people wouldn't do the work—long hours, little money, and no benefits. This was better than milking, at least—just wash and pack eggs for a few hours and then hang out in a trailer behind the main building watching Mexican TV until it was time to come back over here to wash and pack eggs again.

"You're early, Mr. Bellevance." Harold Tuttle filled the doorway. His bulk was a surprise—he resembled neither of his sons. The way he wore his trousers low on his slender hips made his trunk into a barrel. He had small eyes and, on second thought, Jeremy's small chin. "But I'm glad to see you. I was afraid you might change your mind."

His hand in mine was a hot, meaty lump. His hair was thin on the crown and silver above the ears, his expression calm and direct, if flushed. He wore a pale blue blazer and an open-collared, white dress shirt that bulged like a sail.

Entering the cramped office ahead of him, I saw a tall, broad-shouldered woman, about forty, with her ash-blond hair in a French roll, standing opposite the simple desk. She wore a fitted gray suit, a rose silk blouse, and sandals with heels. Her legs were bare.

"You must be Dinah," I said. "Hector Bellevance, Tipton town constable."

She gave me her hand. "Dinah Lynn Doncaster. I'm Mr. Tuttle's assistant."

"Lovely manicure," I heard myself say. Each of her fingernails was a two-inch lozenge painted white, lavender, and pink in diagonal sections. She wore three gold rings and a gold watch with diamonds.

"One of my vanities," Dinah said. "Harmless, I hope."

We smiled, and I glanced around for Jeremy, but he'd taken himself to another part of the factory.

Tuttle sat behind the desk, but carefully, just on the edge of the chair. Dinah unclasped the lid of a black briefcase on the computer table, lifted out a check register, and placed it before him.

"I have a question, Mr. Tuttle, if I may," I said.

"Let's wait until the paperwork comes through, shall we?" He was filling out my check.

"Were you and Seb on good terms when he was killed?"

He stopped writing. "What do you mean?"

"When Seb was killed, he was managing this facility. Were you pleased with his work?"

"He was learning the ropes, as the saying goes."

"How was he doing?"

"You'll have to ask Jeremy."

"Jeremy has described Seb as 'worthless.' He also called him a 'psychotic playboy.' "

Tuttle closed his eyes. "Let us not speak ill of the dead."

"My apologies for passing that along, Mr. Tuttle, but I can't help wondering how Jeremy comes by his low opinion."

He took a deep breath. "Sebastian is—*was*—not a businessman. Jeremy's the one with the marketing degree from McGill. Seb dropped out of college after half a semester. Bummed around out in BC for a couple years—got mixed up with the wrong crowd for a while. . . . We thought, get him out of the country, set him up in a quiet place, and he'll settle down, but I suspect he was restless."

"This might not have been the best community for a restless young man."

His jaw twitched. "What happened to Sebastian was not his fault. As for this *community*, this community has done nothing for me, nothing—" He stopped abruptly, red-faced.

Dinah's eyes hadn't left his. "Hal?" she said softly. "Breathe. Now. Breathe."

His gaze slid to the side.

"Shall I give Robothem and Clement a poke?"

He nodded. "Yes, get the— Yes. Excuse me, please, if you will." He pushed up and entered a small washroom behind the desk, closing the door behind him.

Dinah offered me an apologetic smile, then drew a cell phone from the briefcase and pressed a couple keys.

"Marion? Yes, we are. Thank you, Marion." She waited. "Good morning, George. Of course. I certainly will. He is. You too. Bye-bye."

After a moment there was a beep and the fax machine began whirring. Dinah took up the open check register, then set it down and finished writing out the check, which she separated carefully from the blank ones, then paper-clipped it to the two sheets of fax paper, which she signed and handed to me, all with those extravagantly encumbered fingers. I was impressed.

"You arrived here on Tuesday, Dinah?"

"Wednesday."

"And have you been staying at Jeremy's?" Jeremy Tuttle and his wife had built a luxurious house over on the west shoulder of the Knob. They had no children as far as I knew.

"Harold wouldn't dream of imposing. We found accommodations elsewhere."

Tuttle emerged from the washroom, combed and freshened. "Pardon me," he said and coughed. "My health is not all it might be."

I said I was sorry to hear that.

Dinah made photocopies of our agreement and we all signed it, Dinah Lynn as notary and witness.

"If there's anything more you need," Tuttle said, shaking my hand again, "you have my office number. Just call."

"I'll need to see his phone and credit card bills, any recent correspondence, his checkbook, his cell-phone records, his personal calendar if he kept one, anything along those lines, along with his computer, if he owned one."

Tuttle looked in Dinah's direction. "Most of his belongings were seized as evidence by the Vermont State Police. There's an inventory, but I haven't seen a copy of it."

I said I would look into that, and I promised to call when I had progress to report—something I could not guarantee, I added. The state was more likely to break the case than I was.

"The State of Vermont has its own agenda," Tuttle said. "That's the reason I'm putting my faith in you, Mr. Bellevance."

HUGH HAD BEEN harvesting and washing the marketable produce and packing it in the shade of the porch, while Myra had weeded the tomatoes, vacuumed, done the dishes, and changed the cat's litter. When I stopped by the cabin for a quick lunch, they were just about to head out in the van for a round of deliveries and then maybe stop for a dip at the pools in Fern Brook.

"Any word?" I asked Myra.

She only pursed her lips. "Did you find out who killed that guy?"

"Not yet," I said.

"We shot a video for Mom. It's me talking and then Hugh

playing the banjo and us singing 'She'll Be Comin' Round the Mountain.' "

"A nurse made the suggestion," Hugh said. "We're going to go drop it off down there now—unless you'd like to add something . . ."

"Thanks, but I'm just going to grab a bite and go see if I can—"

"Told you," Myra said. She hopped into the van and slammed the door. "There's a message for you on the machine," she reported through the open window.

"Thanks. Thanks." I couldn't think of what else to say.

As they drove off, Hugh's left hand, trailing out of his side window, made a wagging so-so gesture.

I understood her anger, and no one was safer for her to be angry at than her father.

"Hector, Rob Tierney. Look, I'm on my way to South Carolina to pick up a car. Hate to be leaving right in the middle of all this ugliness, but what can I say—I drew the assignment. Should be a couple, three days anyway, but you call me if there's anything I can do at a distance. So, hope all's well. Be strong."

I had been counting on Rob to pass along whatever the state had gleaned from Seb Tuttle's cell phone—stored numbers, mainly—and maybe get me the full name of his girlfriend.

I looked up Gosselin's Jeep-Chrysler down on the strip south of Allenburg and called and asked for Chip Ohlman. Chip and I had been on the Allenburg High Student Council together for two years. Chip told me he was real-real glad to hear from me and what was I up to lately besides farming? Not much, I told him. He laughed as if this had been the most amusing thing he'd heard all day and then asked whether I was in the market for a new vehicle, because if I was, I had called at an *incredibly* opportune time.

I said, "I'm trying to get an angle on a criminal matter up here in Tipton, and I could use your help."

"Ah. This about that murder?"

"Possibly."

"Anything I can do, buddy. What is it?"

I told him if he would ask at the service desk whether a Jeep had recently come in with a blown transmission, I'd be grateful.

"What kind of Jeep?"

"Not sure. Any Jeep that may have come in for a new transmission. I need to find out who owns it."

After a minute he returned to the line. "Bingo, baby! Nineteen ninety-nine Wrangler, belongs to a Melissa Harris. Car came in last week on a triple-A flatbed, been here on the lot ever since. Still want that phone number? Lenny says she's an eyeful."

I thanked him.

Melissa's phone was on auto-answer. "This is me. I'll call you back." That I doubted. "Leave a message if you want."

"Ms. Harris, this is Lenny at Gosselin's, the Jeep dealership? Little problem. I got a question about your Wrangler. Try me at this number soon as you get a chance."

I waited. In just a minute or two my phone rang.

"Service. This is Lenny."

"Hi, did you just call me? This is Melissa Harris?"

"Melissa! Yes, ma'am, thanks for calling back. Listen, I hate to bug you with this, but do you have a spare key to your Wrangler?"

"A spare key? No, I gave it to you. How come, did you lose it?"

"Not totally. But if that proves to be the case, we will definitely replace it. In the meantime, however, if you have another key, we're gonna need it. Listen, Ms. Harris, I will *gladly* come by your place myself and pick it up. Just put it in an envelope and leave it outside your door. Under the mat, or something."

"Do you know where I live? Because what it says on my registration, that on there is old."

"Well, then, I guess that would help."

"Three-twenty-three Ridgeway Drive. It's off North Pine, if you know where that is, up behind the college? I'm house-sitting for some people while they're away. So, if you come, I'll leave the key taped to the mailbox."

I apologized again for the trouble.

TEN

Coös Crossing, a plain town about twice the size of Tipton, lay along the west side of the Connecticut River, one of the few settled outposts between Allenburg and the great northern forest, which stretched through New Hampshire and the woodsy heart of Maine all the way to the coast. The village of Coös Crossing lined a half-mile stretch of the old truck route that followed the river. Not much to it—a blinking yellow light at the Bridge Street intersection, a Rite-way gas station and car wash, a Laundromat, a diner called the Woodsman, Nanette's Stylerie, Joe's College Pizza, Cavanaugh's Auto and Truck Repair, a tiny library, a post office, and a historical society all in the same brick cube, a treeless village common with a limestone obelisk memorializing the Civil War dead and a softball backstop, and, on the river, a long, unpainted, ramshackle building, once a stagecoach stable, home to Coös New and Used Furniture since before I was born. Across from the Baptist church on Bridge Street were the town hall, the firehouse, and the highway equipment yard.

I turned off the highway at the light and swung into the

gravel lot in front of the side door to the clerk's office. I had no expectation that dour Yvonne Linder, the Coös Crossing clerk, would offer me a crumb of information. She was about sixty, obese, arthritic, never married. A lifelong resident of the Crossing, Yvonne was tuned to every social undercurrent—which was what she lived for, the local whirl, granting little favors and, even better, withholding them.

According to yellow flyers still tacked to bulletin boards all over the county, the Coös Crossing Fishing Derby's pancake breakfast had been held here at the town hall. It was the finest building in a shabby town, a stately, somber, wood-frame meeting house with twin front entries, constructed just after the turn of the century.

Cigarette filters littered the weedy gravel near the side door, which had been propped open by a push broom wedged under its knob. The vestibule was occupied by a paper-recycling bin and three stainless coffee urns. A pink stickie note on one of them read, in black marker, TAKE EM. I could hear a country singer warbling inside.

Yvonne had had her office moved up from the basement to the enclosed back porch for the summer, so she wouldn't have to negotiate the long wheelchair ramps each day. Her knees, hips, shoulders—all her joints—were shot. From the exposed porch rafters she'd suspended a few scraggly potted ivies and philodendrons in crocheted hangers, and outside the door she'd set up a folding table for her evangelical pamphlets, "Are You Ready for the Rapture?" "Healing the Hurt in Your Marriage," "When a Loved One Says 'I'm Gay.' "

Though she'd surely heard me pull up and stop at the side of the building, I had to rap hard on the door frame before she would look up from whatever she was trying to seem engrossed in at her steel desk.

"Good morning, Yvonne. I do hope I'm not bothering you."

"Not yet," she said. The sunlight bouncing in off the cedar

hedge at the back of the building lent her complexion a sickly tinge.

"I'll keep it brief. Were you at the pancake breakfast on Sunday?"

"I don't eat breakfast."

"So then you weren't here?"

"You nailed that one."

"Maybe you can give me the names of a few of the volunteers who did come in here to work that morning."

"Why should I?"

"Just figured you'd know. It's your building."

"Why am I getting these questions from you again?"

"I'm trying to resolve a discrepancy on behalf of a friend."

"Right. This have anything to do with Doug Henault?"

"You've spoken to the police, I take it?"

"Yeah, they come around looking for Pie Yandow. Who I don't know a thing about."

"So what did you tell them?"

"Talk to Corey Murphy."

"Murphy was here Sunday morning?" I'd seen Murphy's name often enough in the local newspaper, though I'd never met the man. He owned Murphy's Marine and Recreation, the lone boat dealership in the county. He was also a Coös Crossing selectman and a member of Kiwanis and the Elks and the Sapients, a men's society for intellectuals.

"Like I say, I wasn't here, but Mr. Murphy's been running the derby since they started it." She folded her arms across her belly and sat back. "I got one for you. You're a farmer— don't you know shit stinks worse when you start stirring it up?"

"If that bothered me, I'd get out of the business."

"I'd like to know what kind of business you think you got here."

"Just looking after my townspeople's welfare."

"Well, I got no concern for the people of Tipton, bless their little hearts."

Her computer screen was dark. With arthritic fingers she was peeling printed address labels from a sheet and applying them to envelopes.

"Yvonne, what's the easiest way to get in touch with Pie Yandow?"

"The easiest way? Gosh, I'm stumped."

"Do you know who he works for?"

"Nope. Used to plow driveways."

"Where does he live?"

She shook her head.

"That's all right, I'll find him, Yvonne. I'm sorry you're in no position to help."

"Me, too. You have fun."

I wished her a peaceful afternoon. I figured I'd stripped out enough line to float the word on down to wherever Yandow might have been idling. He knew who I was. All I had to do now was wait.

FOLLOWING THE TWISTING highway north toward Murphy's Marine, five miles up the river on the Vermont side, I passed a pair of touring cyclists, a couple having an adventure. Wilma and I bought mountain bikes the summer before Myra was born, and in those days we'd get out on the back roads once a week at least, even in the cold weather. So far this summer I hadn't even carried the bikes up from the basement. These days it seemed that work was all we could make time for. That would change. That would change as soon as I had Wilma back.

The yard at Murphy's Marine was crowded with watercraft and trailers, but there were no customers.

The salesman who bounded out to greet me said no, he

hadn't seen the boss that day, but he was sure he could help. "Matt Podlowicz," he said, and we shook hands.

He was a jovial, chubby, rusty-haired young man in a white-collared polo shirt, gray slacks, and deck shoes.

"Maybe you can, Matt. Were you at the pancake breakfast in Coös Crossing Sunday morning?"

"I surely was." He laughed and shook his head. "Got off to a rocky start, though."

"How do you mean?"

"Well, because the power was still out! Remember that? From the storm? They had to quick scare up a couple of diesel generators to run the coffeemakers and all. Had a gas grill, though. Worked out good in the end."

"Do you remember who was serving the breakfast?"

"Nah, I'm new up here. Nice people, though."

"Did you happen to notice whether any of the folks serving pancakes had a physical deformity of some kind?"

"A deformity? Not that I recall. Why?"

I told Matt who I was and explained that I was looking into an assault that had taken place on the morning of the breakfast. With two fingers, he produced his card from his shirt pocket. I took it. He asked whether I owned a pleasure boat. Only a canoe, I said. He told me that was *great,* canoes were neat, so were kayaks, and so were Jet Skis! Next time I was in the market for an upgrade in the water sports department he was the man to see. I didn't doubt it.

THE ODDS OF FINDING Jimmy Lussier at home on a fine summer afternoon seemed poor, but his stepdad's place of business was less than a mile out of my way, and Nick Verlander himself might have something to tell me. Once a selectman, he had been a fixture in town for years. He donated mowers to maintain the ball fields, the cemetery, and the common.

Nick's Small Engine Repair occupied a ledgy, fenced-in compound hard by the state highway opposite a bog and the raised, trackless railroad bed, now a snowmobile trail, south of Tipton village. A nondescript cedar-shingled structure built into the steep hillside contained the shop and the residence both. The driveway and the dooryard were crowded by rows of push mowers, lawn tractors, rototillers, and snowblowers. Potted geraniums and planters brimming with pansies and petunias fringed the house itself. Several neat stacks of firewood, staked and covered, stood outside the open shop.

Nick Verlander was a small man, maybe five-six, 140. He'd been quite a womanizer in his day. Used to work for Sears, installing and servicing home appliances and sharking after housewives. Spud believed Nick was sleeping with Brenda during those months they'd lived apart—though Brenda denied it. Colleen, Nick's wife, had lost her first husband to suicide a year or two ago. Colleen's son, Jimmy Lussier, at around fifteen, was a year or so older than Lyle. Nick had no kids of his own.

"Hello?"

The dim, cluttered shop was quiet. I wove my way among machines, boxes, tools, parts, and rapped on the door to the house at the back of the shop.

"Come in!" a woman's voice sang out.

I opened the door to what proved to be a pantry and passed through into a spare kitchen as shiny and uncluttered as the repair shop was grimy and disarrayed.

"Colleen?" I'd seen her a few times at town meetings, at Sullivan's, and at the farmers' market, so we knew each other in a glancing, small-town way, although we hadn't been introduced.

"Nick's out doing pickups," she called from another room. "He say he'd be here?"

"It's Hector Bellevance, Colleen. I'm looking for Jimmy, in fact. He around?"

I heard her footsteps on the hardwood. She stopped in the doorway, a small woman with dull, straight hair to her earlobes, a concave chest, and soft, hurt-seeming, bovine eyes. "This about that murder?" she said in a low voice.

"Yes. Why, what's the matter?"

"Jimmy's not doing too great on that. You know he found the body."

"That's what I hear."

"And he *knew* the man. That's the awful thing."

"Jimmy knew Seb Tuttle?"

"Jimmy knows everybody down at the Birches."

"He must be pretty upset."

"I never liked seeing him spend time down there. I told him, you want to earn a little money you can work for Nick. But no way."

"He and Nick don't get along?"

"They're workin' on it."

She marched past me and went to the sink, where she washed her hands and dried them with a folded paper towel, then used the towel to mop out the sink and dab at the droplets, saying, "These two policemen came by yesterday— detectives, with their shoulder holsters and their slitty eyes, the whole nine yards. They had me go wake him up. I didn't want to, but . . ."

"He's a witness to a homicide, Colleen."

She turned to me, leaning back against the Formica. "Jimmy's been dealing with a lot of hard stuff around his dad, which, I don't know if you know, but he passed away suddenly two years ago. After that, him and I moved in here— after I married Nick—and that's been . . . that's been quite hard. Nick's such a *good* man, but this here's his shop. Plus, even before Jimmy's dad died, there was a lot of . . . rebellious behavior, which is better now." She shivered. "Look, I'm his mother. I know there's sharper knives in the drawer. But Jimmy has been so disturbed— Or no, not *disturbed,* I don't want to use that word. I don't know what the word is, but he can't *sleep* at night, and these detectives, they bust in here, and you know what it reminded me of? You know those nature programs on TV where they show hyenas taking down a baby antelope, like one on one side and one on the other? That's what it was like."

"I'm sorry. What did they want to know?"

"That's the thing! They never said!"

"What did they ask him?"

"Oh, who did he see there, why he was hanging out there, what he was doing wandering around up there at eight o'clock in the morning. *Wandering around?* He *works* there. He mows the grass. He runs errands. You want a quart of milk, box of detergent, he'll bike down to Sullivan's and fifteen minutes later here's your milk."

"Colleen, is he here?"

She looked surprised. After a moment, she said, "He's in bed. Like I said, he isn't sleeping too good since this happened."

"I'd like to have a word with him. Just a few minutes."

"Promise you'll go easy on him."

"I'll try."

She turned away and washed her hands again, drying them with a paper towel. She carefully wiped out the sink. I watched her leave the room, slow on her feet despite her slight frame.

Attached by magnets to the Kenmore fridge were prayer cards, a gold cross, the Ten Commandments in an Old English font, a few detailed felt-tip drawings of muscle cars and drag racers, wheels smoking and spewing dirt, several photos of Jimmy—Jimmy at about Myra's age, asleep with a puppy on his chest, and a more recent shot of a husky, grinning Jimmy in a blue football jersey, number 81, astride a tricked-out Freestyle bike, fists in the air, and Jimmy kneeling in the snow under an apple tree with the neck of a four-point buck across his thigh, and, much younger again, Jimmy holding a cone of cotton candy and sitting on the shoulders of a tall, grinning, snaggletoothed man with a trimmed red beard— the father who'd killed himself. I wondered if Jimmy had been the one to find him. Hung on the side of the fridge was a John Deere wall calendar where Colleen was keeping track of events and appointments. "Elsie recital, 4p." "Chch supper, 2 pies." "Linda M. yard sl." "Clauddette's 6." In every box, in the Tuesday column, the same entry appeared: "Dr. Mackey 4:30p." I flipped back to June, May, April, March. Every Tuesday afternoon. Evelyn Mackey was a child psychologist with a practice in Allenburg. Wilma and I knew her.

Jimmy shuffled in, rolling his wide shoulders. He was wearing a gray T-shirt with the patch pocket hanging loose like a tongue, knee-length cargo shorts low on his tan, slim hips, no underwear, and untied basketball shoes. His eyes were puffy, his lips feminine, wet and full. He had his mother's wavy, dark brown hair, and her sorrowful eyes and lashes—along with her defeated carriage, unless it was an adolescent slouch. He was a rangy kid, over six feet tall and half again Colleen's weight, with long, smooth arms and legs that were just starting to muscle up. His yawn exposed white teeth. At his age I'd been about his size. I stood six-six now.

The hand he offered me was tentative and soft.

"Have a seat." I pulled out a chair for him at the breakfast table.

He slid in and laid his head on his arms, breathing evenly through his loose mouth.

"What grade are you going into this fall, Jimmy?"

"Ninth."

"Sit up now," his mother whispered from the doorway behind him.

Grudgingly, he pushed himself up.

"High school!" I said. "That's great. Bet you're glad you've
seen the last of Tipton Academy."

He nodded and started cracking his knuckles.

"You like hoops?"

He shrugged.

"You're pretty tall for your age."

"So?"

"You know why I'm here, Jimmy, don't you?"

He shook his head.

"Yes, you do!" Colleen said. "I just told you."

"I'm hoping you can help me," I said. "Will you answer a
few questions for me?"

"I don't know. I get nauseous whenever I . . . if I even just
think about it."

"That must have been a shock for you, a sight like that."

"Yeah. You couldn't tell it was him."

"Jimmy, I'm here because I want to make sure the people
who did what they did to Seb Tuttle don't get away with it.
Anything you can remember may help me find them."

He nodded.

"What brought you to the campground so early that
morning?"

"The Emersons. I walk their dog if it ain't rainin'."

"*Isn't* raining," Colleen said.

He clenched his jaw.

"OK," I said. "You were on your way to the Emersons' RV?"

He nodded.

"And what happened?"

"I found him. Out in the middle, under the trees."

"You found Seb Tuttle."

"Yeah."

"Were you on your bike?"

He nodded.

"How come you didn't keep to the road? What drew you out under the pine trees?"

"Ravens."

"You saw ravens?"

"Four or five of 'em. They're big. They're like black eagles."

"You scared 'em off."

"They were *grunting* at me, and I was like—" He blinked. "I was focusing on *them,* you know? That's why."

"That's why what?"

He glanced back at his mother. "Why I got so close. I didn't know he was there. I didn't know what it was."

"When did you realize what it was?"

He shook his head. "I didn't."

"You did too!" Colleen said.

"Why do you keep *sayin'* that? I was just—"

"Because you *did*! You called him the *egg* man."

He rolled his eyes. "Dude, if you would *just* let me finish. That's who he *was,* except I didn't *know* that was who he was when I saw him layin' there."

"Don't call me *dude.*"

"Colleen," I said, "if you don't mind, I'd like you to leave us alone here for a few minutes—me and Jimmy?"

She spun on her heel and left.

"Bitch," Jimmy said.

"Tell me what you know about the egg man."

He hesitated. "*I* never called him the egg man. *They* called him the egg man."

"Who called him the egg man?"

He looked up. "These two guys."

"What two guys?"

"These biker guys. From Canada."

"Tell me about the bikers from Canada."

"They asked me about him."

"About Seb."

"Yeah."

"When did you meet these bikers?"

"I don't know. Few weeks ago."

"Tell me about that."

"I was out mowing over along the side where it slopes down to the brook, and this car pulls up on the road, the loop, and this guy waves me over, so I go over and he asks me if I work here. Then he goes, 'You know which one's the egg man's camper?' "

"And you told him."

He paused. "My mom don't want me talkin' about this with anybody."

"Why?"

"Because you'll make me be a witness."

"Jimmy, if you're a witness, you're a witness. There's no getting around it. You say they were in a car?"

He nodded. "Mustang. A red GT with a Harley-Davidson decal in the back window."

"Was this the only time you saw these two?"

"Yeah."

"How do you know they were bikers? The Harley decal?"

He shrugged. "I guess, and plus they had tattoos and all this biker bling, like chains and patches and stuff?"

"Did you tell the guy what he wanted to know?"

"Well, first I had to go and ask Kandi. Because 'the egg man' . . . I didn't know who they meant."

"And did you tell Seb these bikers were looking for him?"

He shook his head.

"What else do you remember about them?"

"They had these bandannas on and shades, and one of 'em had this tattoo of a snake that went around his whole arm."

"What else?"

"He had this gi-normous Bowie knife and he had a chain."

"Did you tell the state police about these guys?"

"Yeah."

"How did they react?"

"Nothing. They wrote it down."

"How well did you know Seb Tuttle?"

"Not too."

"OK, tell me everything you can remember about him."

But Jimmy didn't want to venture an answer to such an open-ended question.

Sometimes with kids it helped to speak softly and stand close to them but looking in a neutral direction, as if your thoughts were elsewhere. And use the silence. I leaned back against the table to the side of the boy's chair, facing the back window, where, outside, the wall of exposed rock was patchy with seepage. I said, "People like to say kids today don't respect authority, but I've learned that it isn't true. Most kids naturally *do* respect authority—their parents, teachers, the police. They'll do whatever a reasonable adult asks them to do. That's what makes kids vulnerable, because there are too many adults who'll take advantage of a kid's respect for their own bad purposes. Do you understand what I mean?"

"Yeah."

"Is that what happened to you?"

He paused. "Maybe."

"Tell me about it."

He said, "You think them bikers killed him? Because if they did, I'm the one that told 'em where he lived."

"What happened to Seb was his fault, Jimmy. None of it's on you, OK?" I reached over and squeezed his forearm. "Tell me about Seb Tuttle. How did you get to know him?"

Jimmy rocked his head side to side. "I do stuff for the campers. They pay me five bucks and I go get their mail and stuff."

"You do stuff for Seb?"

He nodded.

"Often?"

"See, the way it started, this one time he came out and he wanted me to go get him some Advil, and the next time I got him some burger patties and buns, and he give me a five-dollar tip. That's how it started."

"What?"

"OK. We had this thing where he would give me a rolled-up newspaper and I would take it down to the fishing access. And when somebody would drive up and ask me how was the fishing, I would give them the newspaper."

"Did you know why you were doing this?"

"Seb told me it was gambling tips."

"Did you believe him?"

"I don't know. I just thought it was cool, and I was makin' good money."

"How many times did you do this?"

"I don't know."

"Five times? Fifty?"

"Not fifty. Ten maybe?"

"These people you met at the fishing access, what were they like?"

"I don't know."

"Anybody stand out?"

"Not really."

"How about their cars? Remember any cars?"

He shrugged.

"What cars do you remember?"

"Chrysler 300. Gray."

"You were muling methamphetamines, Jimmy."

"Maybe, yeah."

"When did you figure that out?"

"When this girl told me."

"What girl?"

"This blond girl that hung out with him sometimes. She told me I should quit before my life got ruined."

"She was doing you a favor."

"But then what happened was one time I'm at the mall with Nick, and this geek I don't even know? He recognizes me and he comes up to me right there in the mall and he says he wants me to get him some glass."

"Some glass?"

"Yeah, and I'm like *Out of my face, dirtbag.*"

"What did Nick say about this?"

"Nothin'. He was over in Payless."

"What did this geek look like?"

"Long black hair. Beard, kinda." He shrugged. "So like when that happened I quit, which, basically, I just didn't go down to the Birches for a while."

"Then what happened?"

"Nothing."

"Nothing? I can't buy that, Jimmy. You were in too deep. You knew what Seb had going down. He wouldn't just let you—"

He shoved himself back from the table. Before he could get away, I took him by the shoulders and fixed him in his chair. He resisted, just for show. "Calm down, Jimmy. It's OK."

"Fuck, man, you're abusing me!"

"I'm only restraining you. I wouldn't abuse you."

He slowly unclenched himself.

"Give it to me straight, Jimmy."

"I *told* you, he said they were buying gambling tips. That's what he said, and I believed him."

"Let me explain your options, Jimmy. You can either clam up and get your parents to hire you a good lawyer—that's the hard-ass legal route, which I do not recommend—or . . . *Or* you can come clean with me. That's the right thing to do. Easy choice."

"You don't need nothin' from me. Go find them bikers."

"Here it is, Jimmy. Even if you didn't know what you were doing, you'll be charged with felony distribution of a controlled substance. You're going to be cutting deals to just stay out of prison. Give me some names. I'll protect you when this thing blows to pieces."

I let him wrench himself free. He jumped up, knocking over his chair. *"Ma?"*

"Wrong choice, Jimmy."

"MA!"

Colleen reappeared in the doorway, clenching either side of the frame. Jimmy backed toward her, his cheeks red and his eyes burning.

"I'm real disappointed in you, Mr. Bellevance," Colleen said. The boy pushed past her and disappeared down the hall.

"Me too," I said. "I'm usually pretty good with young people."

"What's so *good* about forcing an innocent child to rat out some vicious, murdering drug dealers?"

"Who's he afraid of?"

"I honest to God don't know."

"Do you know Pie Yandow?"

"Rings a bell."

"That's all?"

"Listen. Whatever's goin' on, my son is not part of it! You hear me? He's fifteen years old!"

"You don't want to defend these people, Colleen."

"I'm defending my *child!*"

"Let the police do that. All you have to worry about—"

"The police? Those two *clowns*? God in heaven!"

"I wish you would trust me, Colleen."

"Why should I? I want those guys locked up as bad as you do, but I am not about to put my son's life on the line to make it happen."

I had no good answer to that one. His life was already on the line, but she didn't want to hear that.

ELEVEN

THE MESSAGE LIGHT WAS flashing, and on the pine secretary in the kitchen a note in Myra's hand read:

> *Mom's AWAKE!!! Yay-hoo!!! I would of called you if only you had a cell you dummy. We need to be there. Kirsten's mom is driving me in. It's 4:30.*
>
> *Love, M*

The recording was Dr. Kaufman's. "Hello, Hector and Myra. Julius Kaufman calling at about two with some wonderful news. Wilma has opened her eyes just now, and she's begun responding to language just a bit. Very positive stuff. So do try and come by soon as you can. Take care!"

More than relief welled up in my chest. I felt a profound gratitude for the mercies of the world, fickle as they were. And for luck. Sure as snow, harder days lay ahead, but this day, at least, wasn't one of them. To feel grateful for that, I decided, was a mark of my years.

I picked up the phone but put it down when I realized that the motorcycles I'd been hearing a few miles off were gearing down for the turn at Tug's Corner, where the road up into our hollow abutted the Common Road.

I stepped outside onto the porch.

The sky was a vivid blue and the air was still and sweet. The lowering sun shot golden rays through the crowns of Spud's sugar maples high on the rise. A perfect summer evening. Far down below my terraced herb beds, the road cut funneled the noise and the yellow dust of the climbing bikes—heavy road machines. Harleys. Nothing else sounded like a Harley. Two of them. Headed here.

I went inside and took my 1911 from the gun safe in our bedroom closet, pushed in a magazine of 230-grain hollow points, and racked the slide. Groping along back behind my sweaters, I managed to find its nylon shoulder rig. I strapped that on and holstered the pistol cocked and locked. Everyday carry was a practice I'd given up long ago, but at times like this the extra two and a half pounds of precision steel against my ribs felt like a spare heart. I slipped on my canvas barn jacket.

From the bedroom dormer I watched through my bird-glasses as two big bikes appeared on the bluff overlooking the road. The riders stopped and dismounted. Both wore matte-black skullcap helmets, wraparound shades, and jeans. One of them, with a tattered mane of black hair and a full beard, was wearing his colors—*Hells Angels Quebec.*

Years ago, sometimes one of Canada's outlaw motorcycle gangs would come rumbling down the interstate. There were a lot of them back then—Rockers, Outlaws, Bandidos, No-mads, Hells Angels—but if they pulled off in Montcalm County it was only to gas up. A few years ago, in the wake of a prolonged turf war for control of Quebec's drug trade, the Canadian parliament passed an antigang law, which resulted in a series of police raids. Today the hard-core bikers up across were either doing time or they'd patched over into the

Hells Angels' organization. The Hells, as they were known in Quebec, had the field to themselves.

They didn't follow the stone path up to the cabin nor, in fact, did they even glance in my direction but strolled off instead toward my lower gardens. They knew I'd have sense enough to come to them, especially if Myra was at home. I was glad she wasn't.

First I ambled down for a closer look at the two chopped Harleys with ape-hangers and blue and white "Je me souviens" motorcycle tags. I took down the numbers, then, skirting the herb beds, walked over to my mother's highbush blueberry plantation, eight 30-yard rows of glossy five-foot-high bushes mulched in pine bark and crowded with pink-red fruit. In two weeks we'd be picking. My visitors were moving slowly down the first row of bushes, helping themselves to any berries that were almost ripe.

"Something I can do for you boys?"

"You Bellevance?" The hairy one with the Hells rocker on his vest took me in.

The other one kept picking. He was wearing fingerless black leather gloves.

I stopped at the beginning of the first row. "That's me. What might your name be?"

"I go by Mad Dog." He had a broken nose and coarse eyebrows that spiked out over his shades like thatch.

"Thanks, Mad Dog. Who's your friend?"

"That's Greaseball." Greaseball had on a purple headwrap and a denim vest with a yellow "1%-er" patch. His long arms were sleeved out in a muddy jumble of ink. Mad Dog was not as fat as Greaseball, but he was probably ten years younger and a lot bigger, almost my height and easily half again my weight. Greaseball was the one with the snake tattoo—Jimmy had made up none of this—and he had a heavy chain through his belt. Mad Dog was wearing the fighting knife, a thick, black Kabar. Adorning his black T-shirt was the image of a bald, screaming, bare-breasted woman with targets instead of eyes.

"You both ride with the red and white?" I asked.

"Mad Dog's a charter officer in the Sherbrooke chapter," Greaseball said. "I'm an associate of the club."

"Well, Mad Dog, Greaseball, I'm glad you dropped by. I have some questions for you."

Greaseball snorted. "That ain't why we're here. You know why we're here?"

"Let me guess. You boys are enforcers, right?" The Hells Angels had confined themselves in recent years to recruiting and administration. They kept themselves insulated by setting up functionaries and mules—getting them growing, cooking, smuggling—while they maintained an arm's-length hold on both ends of the operation, supply and wholesale distribution, keeping their distance from messy day-to-day concerns.

Mad Dog shook his head irritably, looking down at his steel-capped toes.

Greaseball emerged from between the first two rows, squared his bulk, and took a few steps toward me. "Little advice," he said. "When Mad Dog's respecting you, you respect him."

"Shut the fuck up," Mad Dog said. "You want to know why I'm here?" he asked me.

"Better not be to threaten my life. That would be a class D felony. Could get you five years."

"I come by to check out where you live." He hooked his thumbs in his wide belt and made a show of appraisal, which seemed comical and unsettling all the same. "Nice setup. Peaceful. Cozy. Very isolated." He gazed off toward the roof of the cabin visible above the rise, then back at me. "Nice, low-key lifestyle. Wife and kid, too, right? Little girl? Curly red hair? Ten, eleven?"

I went cold.

He nodded slowly. "Friend of mine used to say, 'The more you got, the more you got to lose.' "

I'd had enough. "Get off my land. Before you say something that gets you hurt."

"I'm glad you brought that up, because that's what this is about, is everybody stayin' healthy and minding their own business. Can you get behind that?"

"I'm already behind it."

"Cool. So if there's shit going down and it don't *concern* you, you don't want to get yourself fucking *concerned,* eh? It ain't worth it."

"When scumbags like you start thinking they have business in my town, that fucking *concerns* me. That's how it is."

He took a step toward me. "You don't know shit."

I loosened my shoulders. "Somebody down here's cooking crystal. Popular product these days. Only the ingredients are very hard to come by, at least in this country. That's your line, though, isn't it? No risk to you moving the precursor chemicals, and the return is excellent."

Mad Dog snorted.

Greaseball started circling to my left.

Mad Dog grinned at him. "Our gentleman farmer is—"

I drew out my .45 and thumbed off the safety. "Stop where you are."

They did.

"Thanks. Now I want you off my land."

"You dumb *fuck,*" Mad Dog spat. We had ten feet between us. "You want to do me? Go ahead, motherfucker. *Do* me." He spread his arms.

I was half tempted. Any story would fly in the circumstances, and hell, he had a pair of bull's-eyes on his chest. "I want you off my land," I said. "And I want you out of the country. If you don't make it across the line in thirty minutes, I will have you detained at Customs, arrested, and booked on this side for trespass and criminal threatening. You don't want that to happen, so you'll have to move fast. Don't be slipping back across any time soon, either. Same deal if you do."

Mad Dog turned to Greaseball and urged him along with his gloved hands. "See what we get for trying to do a dickhead a favor?" Greaseball sauntered up across the slope, watching us over his shoulder. Mad Dog and I followed.

"I feel sorry for you, man," Mad Dog said without turning. "This thing didn't have to fall out like this."

"You're lucky it did. This way I'm doing *you* the favor."

He laughed.

"Who sent you here? Yandow?"

"You don't know shit, man. And you would be doing *yourself* a favor to keep it that way."

Greaseball mounted his Harley. It was a banged-up, balky, vintage soft tail, and he kicked and cursed at the thing for a minute before managing to fire it up. He blatted off down the field road, spraying clots of dirt.

Mad Dog slouched in his saddle watching his partner, then turned to stare at me through the oily iridescence of his shades. "Nobody sent me here, man. Do I look like somebody's messenger service?"

What he looked like, with the Hells vest and the fighting knife on his hip and all that grizzled hair bunched out under his soup-bowl headpiece and his red, wind-chapped arms hanging like hams from the handlebars, was the baddest badass outlaw I'd ever run into. Which was the idea. He wouldn't show up here again. Somebody else would get that assignment, some prospect looking to make his bones. Somebody like Greaseball. He'd already scoped the terrain.

"Did you stomp Seb Tuttle?"

"I don't know no Seb Tuttle."

"The egg man. Had an RV in a campground down by the lake."

He kicked his machine to life. "Like I said before," he shouted, "you don't know shit."

In the kitchen I uncapped a bottle of beer and put in a call to a Canada Border Services agent up in Iceville. They knew me up there. He took down the Hells' tag numbers and assured me that anyone on duty would record their names and addresses—no matter where they rode across. He'd put out the request as soon as he got off the line. I thanked him. That much, at least, seemed easy.

"HERE'S DADDY!" Myra announced.

Wilma turned her face to me.

Her skin was like ivory and her eyes looked bright and weary at the same time, but it was so wonderful just to see her smiling again that I cried.

"She can't really speak yet," Myra told me, wiping her own eyes with the heels of her hands. "And she can't come home with us, not until she can walk and eat and do stuff by herself. She's trying to pull everything back together bit by bit by bit, and that'll take time. We don't know how long. Days."

I was holding Wilma's limp, dry hand in my two, rubbing her fingers. "I can't tell you how wonderful it is . . . wonderful to see you breathing on your own. We have really missed you, Wil."

Her smile didn't change. The bolt in her skull had been removed.

Myra came around to stand beside me, taking my arm. "Dr. Kaufman says she probably *wants* to respond, and talk? But her mental landscape is in this, like, *fog*, so she's confused.

But she'll get there. 'One little thing at a time.' That's what the nurse told me."

We sat with her while she rested. Her patch of white ghost pumpkins was looking terrific, I told her, some of them soccer-ball size and apple-green, and we were keeping up with the berries and beans and everything else. Myra told her about how she'd found the fawns and *finally* got to see the aurora borealis. After a time, Irma, one of the second-shift nurses who'd been caring for Wilma since the accident, drew us out into the hallway. There was a lot no one could predict, she told us, but depending on the extent of damage, Wilma could be ready to leave the hospital in less than a week. After that her progress might be halting. For most patients with brain trauma, recovering their balance—physical and emotional—took months. Wilma might continue to experience pain, dizziness, attention deficits, and anxiety. "And," Irma said, "some disabilities can last a long while. You need to know that. But the main thing right now is Wilma's back with us, and the signs could not be better."

"And the baby?"

"The baby's cruising," she said.

As we were leaving, after I kissed her, Wilma's eyes fluttered open, and she whispered something I didn't catch.

I touched her hair. "What did you say, sweetheart?"

She didn't respond.

Myra looked at me. "I think she said, 'My dreams are missing.'"

" 'My dreams are missing'?"

"I think so. What does she mean?"

"Just that, I suppose."

ON OUR WAY HOME Myra announced that beginning tomorrow she would be staying there at the medical center "twenty-four, seven" until her mom could leave and come home with her. I said I wasn't sure that was a good idea, and I asked if she remembered what Dr. Kaufman had told us.

"You can't talk me out of it," she declared, "so don't try. I know what I want to do."

"Myra—" I began, but stopped.

After a minute or so, she glanced at me. "How are you coming with the murder?"

"Hard to say. Still gathering information."

"What information?"

"*Trying* to gather information. It's a slow process."

"So, like, who'd you talk to?"

"Well, earlier today I went to see Nick Verlander's stepson, Jimmy Lussier. You know who I mean, don't you? Eighth grader at the Academy? He was new last year."

"You talked to Jimmy Lussier?"

"Yeah. What do you think of him?"

"He's OK, I guess. Except he hangs out with Kurt Mooney and them. But not anymore, because Kurt Mooney goes to Whetstone now."

The Whetstone Brook School out in East Allenburg was for troubled teens. Kurt was Pearl Mooney's son. Last I knew, they were living in an apartment over a crossroads convenience store out on the Bailey Plateau. Some years back Pearl had done a stretch for heroin possession, plea-bargained down from trafficking.

"You like Jimmy?"

"He's kind of a show-off. You know—he thinks he's cool and smart, but really he's just a jerk. Plus he's mean. Last fall he told Mrs. Timmerman he could smell her underpants." Bertha Timmerman was one of the cafeteria ladies at the village academy.

"No kidding."

"Yeah. Somebody dared him. A lot of people thought that was cool when he did that. Even Lyle."

"Lyle thought that was cool? Really?"

"Lyle's a little dense, Dad."

"He's immature. So what happened?"

"Mrs. Timmerman told Mr. Quintillian, and after that Jimmy had to eat his lunch in the office for a week."

"Does he get in trouble much?"

"Not too. Not as much as Kurt Mooney. How come you wanted to talk to Jimmy Lussier?"

"He's the one who found Seb Tuttle's body."

"Wow, he did? *How?*"

"He hangs around down at Birches. Cuts the grass, runs errands for people."

"So what about the other guy—Yandow? Did you call him back?"

"Yandow called?"

"Yeah, you didn't see it? I wrote down the number."

"I missed that. What did he have to say?"

"Just if you were still looking for him, you should give him a call."

It was after nine when we pulled into the turnout at the foot of our hill, but not quite dark. My pace up the path to the unlit cabin had Myra glancing back impatiently. She was hungry.

"Wait up a second, sweetheart. Please."

She slowed. "What's wrong?"

"The doors are locked anyway."

"How come?"

"Just a precaution."

"How come? What are we afraid of?"

We left our doors unlocked except when we were planning to be away overnight. My mother had never locked her doors either, or her car. She did keep her father's double-barreled shotgun inside the hall closet—"for peace of mind."

As I paused on the porch steps to flip through my seldom-used keys, I smelled gasoline. It was bad. Hugh must have left a gas can on the porch somewhere. But I didn't see one, and he wouldn't have done something like that anyway. We kept the gas cans on apple crates in the utility shed.

"Wait right here, Myra, all right?"

"Are we locked out?"

"Something's not right. I'm going to go around to the sunporch."

"But why? What's wrong?"

"Sweetie, please, you'll have to wait now. Go look for meteors in Aquarius. I'm going to be a few minutes."

I unholstered my Colt and walked around the cabin. On the north side, even in the half-light, two deep gouges in the sill under Myra's desk window testified starkly to a basic sixty-second, B and E. Slice the screen, pry off the thumb-latch, scissor inside.

I entered the cabin through the sunporch door. The front hall was dense with gasoline fumes. A sheet of gas covered the floor.

All we had to do was shove our front door open. A dozen strike-anywhere matches taped head-down along the inside of the door's kick rail would have scraped across the quarry tiles and ignited the vapor, engulfing us instantly in a fifteen-thousand-degree fireball. We would have been roasted alive.

Mad Dog was evidently more determined than I'd given him credit for. I put my gun away.

Myra started thumping on the door. "Come on, Dad, open up! What are you *doing* in there?"

"You can't come inside yet, Myra. Just wait. There's been a little trouble."

"What do you mean? What trouble?"

"You'll have to be patient, Myra, please."

Grabbing a flashlight out of the drawer in the phone table, I headed down into the basement to throw the master breaker.

Then I started opening windows. Wilma's handwoven Persian wool rug, a bequest from her father, was ruined. My blue five-gallon gas can lay on the floor beside the couch, empty. I called for the cat. She was hiding somewhere—unless she'd escaped through Myra's window.

This damn stench would last for weeks.

My anger made concentrating on the moment more difficult than it should have been. I did not want to start thinking about what I'd have to do tomorrow. I spilled a pan of cold water over the matches and stripped the tape from the wood, then carried the cat's food and water dishes upstairs and left them in the bathroom. I pulled together a change of clothes for each of us and our toothbrushes and stuffed them into a carryall. We'd have to stay the night at the farm.

Myra was astounded. "You mean somebody actually tried to *kill* us?" We were walking back down to the truck, the stars all jangling overhead. When I didn't reply, she said, "Do you know who it was?"

"No."

"You have no *clue*?"

"Oh, there're plenty of clues."

"How long do we have to stay at Spud and Brenda's?"

"A day or two. We need to let the cabin air out for a while."

After a pause she said, "Dad, you know, this is really *serious*. Getting burned alive—that's the worst thing that could ever happen to you." She shuddered. "Did you call the police?"

"Not yet. They're not going to be happy with me."

"Who cares? They have to come out and collect the evidence, don't they? Fingerprints and all that. I mean, *you* can't do that."

"I'll call tomorrow. I'll want to be here when they come."

"But— So you mean you're going to keep going with this investigation?"

"I think I have to, Myra."

"What if I said I don't want you to?"

"I would ask you to consider my position."

"What about *my* position? I'm practically an orphan."

We had paused at the lip of the incline where my mother's stone steps curved down to the turnout. In the starlight the roofs of my pickup and the white van were two grainy slabs, like boulders under black water, and across the road the beaver pond held faint, bluish glints. Down in the village a dog woofed.

"Myra. I realize Mom's not out of the woods yet, and now you've got me to worry about besides. But—"

"You know what *Mom* would say? She'd say back off and let the police take care of it."

"I don't think she would, Myra."

"Anyway, you don't even *care* who killed that stupid jerk. You're just doing it for the money."

"We've been through this. I really think you're—"

"Wait here," she said. "I'll be right back." She spun around and bolted back toward the cabin.

"Myra! Hold on a minute!"

She was fast as a squirrel. I started after her, then stopped.

She bounded up the porch steps, hesitated for a second in the doorway, then disappeared inside. The screen door clicked shut.

I waited on the spangled lawn. A motorboat was crossing the lake, and lightning bugs were carrying on in all directions. They seemed as distant as the stars.

"The air in there's totally *polluted*," she said on the exhale a moment later. She jumped the steps. "Poor Nicole's totally freaked! She's under your bed. Even when you pull her out, she goes right back." She was wearing her canary-yellow L.L. Bean daypack.

The farmhouse appeared dark when we pulled in under the yardlight, but Brenda was up watching TV, waiting for her applesauce bread to come out of the oven. Myra and I left our gasoline-soaked shoes and socks outside on the porch.

Brenda broke into tears at the news about Wilma and seemed dumbfounded when we explained why we'd showed up so late on her doorstep. No one spoke while we made up the futon on the sleeping porch for Myra, who immediately shooed us out and switched off the lamp.

Brenda and I retired to the kitchen, where she put on some water for tea. "Red zinger?"

I said, "You know, Bren, if you had some whiskey, I'd take a shot."

"I bet you would. Ice?"

"No, no ice. Thanks."

She rummaged around in the pantry for a bottle of Jim Beam, poured me half a juice glass, and set them both on the table. "Has to be somebody local," she said. "You realize that, right?"

"How local's local?"

"You're the detective."

"More's the pity."

"Because who's gonna just walk into your cabin and start splashing gas around unless they know you're not there, number one, and number two, they had to be sure they could get out again before you came back and boxed 'em in."

"Anybody who'd seen us heading toward Allenburg could've counted on having an hour at least."

"Still, though, you'd have to know the roads."

I said nothing.

"Well, it's gotta be whoever killed Seb Tuttle, right? Maybe it was Lance Henault." She shook her head. "But I can't see Lance setting you up that way. How about Seb's brother—Jeremy Tuttle? Or Pie Yandow, like you were saying before—if Jeremy hired him to do his dirty work. Hell, if he got away with it once, what's to keep him from getting away with it again?"

"I don't know, Brenda."

"He was one sketchy little shit, though, that Sebastian Tuttle." She was pouring water into her mug. "On the news they said he might've been offed as payback for some garbage he was into up across. Unless they're putting that out for deception purposes."

"That's possible."

She sipped, holding her mug of tea in both hands. "You look *wiped out,* Hector."

"I'm sure." My eyes were raw from the gasoline.

"Jeez. You're getting too old for this crap. You really are, you know?"

"Yeah," I said. For all the difference that made.

TWELVE

THE NEXT MORNING I left Myra at the hospital and came home without stopping at the state police barracks to report the break-in. Ingersoll's reaction was bound to be—as Myra might put it—*harsh*. I wanted to handle the preliminaries on my own.

I found Hugh out tending my irrigation hoses when I walked up the hill. He turned off the water.

"What in holy hell's wrong with you?"

"You've been up to the cabin?"

"Of course! Why didn't you *phone* me, Hector? Christ, I go up there and I find the house wide open and *gasoline* all over the floor. . . . Luckily, I called the hospital before I panicked and called the police. Your eleven-year-old daughter has twice as much consideration as her father, if you don't mind my saying so."

"It didn't occur to me, Hugh. I'm sorry."

He shook his head and then brightened. "Hey! That's just great news about Wilma!"

"It's wonderful. Be a while before they let her come home, though."

"It's a good thing you still have a home for her to come back to."

"And a family." The wide rows of young carrots were looking fine, I noted deliberately, their tops all feathering together into deep green quilts.

He nodded. "You think we're safe here?"

"For the time being."

"I've been having visions of hit men with sniper rifles blowing my brains into a pink mist."

"No chance of that. I'm the one they're after."

"That's not reassuring, frankly."

"If you'd rather go home to your place, it's fine with me, Hugh. I'll be all right for the day."

"No, no, I'll stay." He scanned the shadowy tree line beyond the cabin. "But I will say I'd rather be a victim of murder than a witness to one."

I took him by the shoulder. "I'm going up to the house to make some phone calls. Will you be all right down here by yourself?"

"I have no idea. You think I should be armed?"

"Up to you. You can have Agnes's 12-gauge. I've got a box of double-ought buck."

Hugh was no hunter. He thought for a moment, tight-lipped, then nodded, but by the time we got to the cabin he'd changed his mind. I didn't ask why. We took the time to roll up the hallway runner and the Persian living-room rug along with their soggy liners and drag them outdoors.

"Go make your calls," Hugh said. "I'll drape these things over a fence someplace. They'll kill the grass otherwise."

The agent I reached at Canada Border Services on the north end of the lake recognized my name. He confirmed that the Hells Angels gang members I had asked about had entered the Quebec sector sixty miles to the west of Tipton at Highgate at 9:25 P.M. Their names were Gilbert N. Houle, of 2555 Templeton Avenue, Fredericton, New Brunswick, and Bernard Moscowicz, of Sherbrooke, Quebec. Moscowicz's address, 830 Boulevard DePaul, he added, was the address of the Hells' chapter headquarters in that old city. I took it all down and thanked him.

Amid the clutter on the pine secretary under the phone and inside the drawer where we kept the phone book, I wasn't able to find any note with Yandow's phone number on it, so I called Wilma's room at the hospital.

Myra picked it up. Her voice sounded a little too chipper somehow. Mom was communicating in whispers, but not a lot. She was able to smile and nod and move and sit up and eat. Her color was better, and she was asking about me—when could I get there?

"Soon as I can get free. Myra, I can't find anything here with Yandow's number on it. Where did you leave it?"

"On the— You know, on the thing under the phone. I wrote it on the edge of the newspaper."

"I don't see any newspaper."

"It's there someplace."

"Upstairs or downstairs?"

"In the kitchen."

"OK, I'll just keep looking."

"Are the police there?"

"Not yet."

"You haven't even *called* them, have you, Dad? All you care about is your—"

"*I haven't had the chance,* sweetie. Don't scold me, all right? I know what I'm doing. Anything new from Dr. Kaufman?"

"No. Mom's doing great, and I'm a candidate for sainthood."

"Congratulations."

"Really."

"You want to go swimming later?"

"Swimming? You're kidding, right?"

"Not at all. Don't you think Mom would like to know that you and I were going swimming?"

"I already told her what you were *really* doing. I don't know if she got it or not."

"Don't be troubling her mind with too much detail, all right?"

"Don't worry, I didn't tell her somebody tried to fry us."

"I hope not. You have enough money for lunch?"

"The nurses are taking care of me. I already had tea and a chocolate scone."

I told her I'd be reachable at home for the next hour or two, if anything should come up.

"Dad . . . for my birthday?"

"Yeah?"

"Can we get a *cell* phone? Like, for the family?"

"I've been thinking about that."

"Yeah—for about ten years. It's time to *get* one."

"We'll see what Mom says."

"Yeah, yeah," she said. "So are you gonna come here for lunch?"

"I don't think so, Myra. There's a lot I have to do here. Please understand why this is so—" Was she there? "Myra?"

She'd hung up on me.

THE DAYS' OLD ISSUE of the *Allenburg Eagle* with Myra's squarish printing along the top edge of the front page ("YANDOW 273-0150") finally came to light inside the chrome trash can next to the fridge. Hugh had used the newspaper to bundle up the paper towels with which he had mopped up the cat's puke. I went to find Nicole. She lay balled in the middle of our bed and seemed all right, apart from her distress and confusion at the state of the first floor, where she ordinarily preferred to be.

I didn't recognize the three-digit prefix. I punched it in.

"Leave a message," a gravelly voice said, "and I'll buzz you back."

I phoned the barracks in Allenburg and described what had happened to me and Myra to the dispatcher, a Sergeant Pete Tulley. I said the suspects were two associates of the Quebec chapter of the Hells Angels, and I explained why. I gave him their names and addresses and asked him to call in a BOL to Customs, although I doubted they'd cross again soon. Tulley thanked me and said he'd have a trooper out here right away.

Through a window I spotted Hugh. Far to the rear of the cabin, clear against the inky green tree line, he was walking toward the east, a copper L-rod in each hand, dowsing for information. Hugh was still in demand now and then as a remote locater. His business card read, TREASURE, WATER, PERSONS, AND NOXIOUS FIELDS DETECTED, HARMFUL ENERGIES DISPERSED, SUNDRY MYSTERIES RESOLVED, services that Wilma considered "a lot of hooey." She liked to tease me for my credulity, but it wasn't credulity so much as that I believed in the potential significance of the least likely thing. Count nothing out.

"What's the question?" I called through the screen. He had to shape his paranormal inquiries by articulating them somehow.

He didn't answer.

By the time I got outside, he was almost beyond hailing distance, plodding off toward the edge of the mowed sidehill, his L-rods out before him like a pirate's pistols, searching, I suspected, for Hartmann lines, a grid of underground energy currents that could ostensibly help a tuned-in healer diagnose patterns of geopathology. I let him go.

Under Myra's window on the east side of the cabin, the twiggy, flowering potentillas and the hostas had been—no surprise—crushed by whoever had broken the window latch. The exterior sill bore two half-inch-deep grooves left by the pry bar.

In the soft soil under the shrubs I noted two indistinct sets of heel prints, both narrower than mine. Could these have been left by steel-toed biker boots? Not likely.

I knelt and inspected the ground. They had entered and left by the same route.

I looked off toward the trees. Not hard to imagine the bikers taking cover somewhere off the Common Road and waiting until I'd driven off, then slipping back here to set us up. They might have guessed I'd be leaving to get Myra. They had the time, motivation, and know-how. Mad Dog would have had to speak with someone first, but—

The increasing rubber-on-gravel roar I was hearing meant a heavy car was tearing up the incline from the T.

I walked around to the front of the house. The car braked smoothly and abruptly at the turnout. Police cruiser.

As the officer crested the rise, for a startling second I thought I was seeing Wilma in a trooper's campaign hat, but it was just the red hair. This woman was shorter, stockier, younger, and she had a duller, frizzier look about her.

She was Trooper Meredith Gibbs. "And your name, sir?"

I told her, and we shook hands. She was twenty-two or twenty-three. Her rabbity incisors had me wondering if the state's medical plan covered orthodonture. Probably not.

"You called in a break-in?"

"That's right."

I led her around to Myra's window, and we examined the tool marks and footprints. We agreed on two perps, probably amateurs. The screen in its warped frame had been propped beside the window. She snapped some pictures with a digital camera.

"They steal any of your stuff?"

"Just some gasoline." Either the dispatcher had relayed none of what I'd told him on the phone, or she wanted to hear it for herself. I explained what we were dealing with as we walked back around to the front of the cabin. Then I described the incident with the two bikers, mentioned their connection to Seb Tuttle, and told her I had given their names and addresses to Tulley.

"And you're speculating that the reason these two people tried to fireball you is because you're getting close to whoever wasted Sebastian Tuttle? And it might be them, the Hells Angels?"

"They told me if I didn't back off I'd get hurt."

"So you're working the Tuttle case? Is that correct, sir?"

"I'm the constable in this town, Officer."

"So is that a *yes?*"

"It is."

Trooper Gibbs sniffed the air in the hallway and asked if she could have a look at the "incendiary device."

It lay folded on the kitchen counter. She poked at it with her pen.

"I touched it only on the corners."

"And you say you have the gas can?"

"That's right. You're dusting for prints, aren't you?"

She nodded vacantly. "I left my kit in the car." She started off, then paused. "I'm gonna have to roll off a set of yours, too, OK, sir? For standards."

"Mine are already on file."

"OK, great."

Out on the porch Hugh stepped aside as the trooper charged around him with barely a glance. I wondered what had her so preoccupied.

"She leaving already?"

"Just getting started, I hope. Came up the hill to investigate a B and E and didn't bring along her print kit."

Hugh pursed his lips. "Looks like they arrived here by way of your woodlot, Hector. On foot."

"On foot? You sure?"

Hugh led me up through the apple orchard and out along the fieldstone wall skirting the unmowed slope northeast of the cabin. At a certain point he stopped and made a nod toward the traces of a furrow in the waist-high field weeds and brush. He was right. Two good-sized animals had passed through, and it looked as though they'd taken the same path coming and going, something no bear or moose would do.

The woodlot to the north consisted of mixed-age hardwood—maple, birch, beech, and ash—rolling up to a quartzy shelf. From there the view out toward Prentiss Point, a prominent overlook halfway up the west shore of the lake, was spectacular. Below the shelf and farther north, the bluff dropped more steeply away into dense softwoods and a basin strewn with glacial boulders. Past all that were a broad marsh, a reservoir owned by the town, and the municipal forest. Bushwhacking up to my knoll from that direction would require a familiarity with the terrain. Not to mention time and stamina.

"Somebody didn't want to chance being seen, Hector."

"They picked a pretty challenging route, though."

"Well, there you go."

"You know, I think I'd better do a little nose work here before the sign deteriorates. Will you head back and keep an eye on Miss Marple for me?"

He nodded. "I expect you'll be a while. Anything special need doing?"

"You'll figure it out." I paused. "There is one thing. If Pie Yandow calls, set me up with him. Any time, any place."

"Sure thing. Don't you need a bloodhound or a magnifying glass or something?"

"I'm not trying to catch them. I just want to find out where they came from."

The path through the field was plain enough. I stayed to the side to watch for traces—fibers, cigarette butts, hair—and found nothing, although the directness of their path was something in itself. They knew the way.

The air in the woodlot was cool. The wind made a watery rush in the beeches. The inch of leaf litter and duff that carpeted the woods road made their passage easy to follow. On the high spots where the weather had exposed pads of moss and soil I found scrapes and curving indentations: two people, to judge by the contrasting heel arcs. They'd walked side by side for much of the way—strollers more than hikers. I patted my shirt pockets for my reading glasses, but I'd left them on the kitchen table. I measured the prints against my open pocketknife and sketched them into my notebook. These two walkers were not my outlaw bikers from Quebec.

They were locals, Brenda was right—people I knew, and who probably knew me. In rural communities crime often took on an intimate complexity. Whatever it was about, odds were you knew who, where, when, how, and usually (sooner or later) why. My mother used to say that small-town life enhances a person's understanding of what it means to be human, though seldom for the better.

The crest of the land looked out over the Bailey Plateau, now a sea of corn and alfalfa, to Prentiss Point and the lake's keyhole gap against the sky. To the west, the game trail up this pitch was long, skirting the marsh. These guys had come zigzagging up the loose stone, using a few runty trees for handholds and leaving V-shaped gouges in the scree.

I tried to protect their traces but the slope was too unstable, and I ended up sliding and hopping to the bottom. An apron of fallen rock reached out onto ferns and hemlock.

They'd stood here in the shade on the wet ground, resting, talking. One had a hard-edged shoe, the other a rounder one—a sneaker maybe, but not a running shoe. I poked around for a few minutes. Neither was a tobacco user. Deerflies began to find me.

A series of fresh scuffs along the bank of a shallow streambed led me down to a watercourse, probably Burn Brook. They were following a game trail, which was trending in the direction of the municipal forest between the reservoir and the village.

After a time I halted in my tracks at the marvelous sight of a colony of egg-yolk-yellow chanterelles winding for several yards in among the firs. I should have brought a bag. When would I ever get back this way? I stopped to make a record of the find in my notebook. I stretched. My tricky back would not take another night on that sleeper sofa in Spud's den.

Just as I started walking again I caught a flash off to my right. A blip of light.

I scanned the trees on the opposite bank of the brook, but I couldn't see anything. Something had definitely flashed. In two quick splashes I bounded through the water. A moment later I spotted a camo-colored box fastened by clear plastic ties to a basswood tree at head height. I hadn't seen one of these except in magazine ads, but the two mismatched portholes told me what it was—an infrared trail camera. They were common nowadays, set out by hunters to record the movements of game animals.

Damn, this really was a lucky little find. If the device was charged and functioning, chances were good that it had captured an image of my bad guys. *Outrageous,* as we used to say. I wasn't about to leave without that camera, but the box had been secured to the tree with a cable gun-lock. Who owned this thing? On the underside I found a small black label with three lines of gold print. Without my reading glasses, I couldn't make out a word. Hugh was right—I did need a magnifying glass. Or bolt cutters.

I had bolt cutters at home in the shed, but couldn't walk away from this one. I took out my Colt.

BOOM.

Missed. From about two inches. I'd had my eyes averted. Myra would be laughing at me.

My ears were ringing. I lined it up once more, using both hands, fired, and saw the cable swing loose through wisps of burned powder.

I retrieved my brass, took out my pocketknife, and sliced through the plastic straps.

I decided against plodding on through toward municipal forest. Instead, if I could make my way straight out of the woods to the town highway by skirting the marsh west of the reservoir, I'd save half an hour's hiking. On the highway I could hitch a ride into the village and phone Brenda for a lift home. But soon after I'd started off to the north, the terrain turned marshy, with black spruce thick as field corn and a lot of squish underfoot. By the time I had looped back around the wetlands and picked my way back down another game path to the lip of the town dam it was close to noon, judging by the sun. Myra was going to be upset with me.

"Hold it right there, big fella!"

I stopped.

A stocky, round-faced young man—olive shirt and a dark cap—emerged from a stand of popple near the outlet at the foot of the dam. Game warden. He was wearing a pistol in a custom leather cross-draw holster on his duty belt, along with his magazine pouches, cuffs, flashlight, sheath knife, and radio. I didn't recognize him.

"I'm Hector Bellevance. Tipton town constable."

He didn't respond.

"Is everything OK, Warden?"

"I been waiting for you for an hour. Warden Matthew Curtis, State Fish and Wildlife. Would you come down off the dam, sir?"

"Why? Is there a problem?"

"Please respect my request, sir, and come down off the dam."

"Look, Curtis, if this is about a couple of gunshots, I'll be glad to explain that."

"Please, sir. I don't want to have to ask you again."

I descended the brushy incline in a few hops.

"Are you armed, sir?" the warden asked.

"Yes, I am. I've been out here tracking two suspects in an attempted homicide—"

"Without touching it, please show me your weapon."

His own hand went across to the butt of his autoloader as I opened my barn jacket so he could see the .45 along my rib cage.

He nodded. "Thank you. Using two fingers, slowly remove it from the holster and place it on the ground."

I complied. "Curtis, let me say this is uncalled for. The two shots you heard—"

"That your only carry?"

"That's right. I have—"

"Now. What the hell do you think you're doing with that trail camera?"

"It doesn't belong to me, but I believe—"

"You wanna know who it belongs to? It belongs to the State of Vermont. Please set it on the ground next to your weapon."

"Will you kindly let me finish a goddamn sentence?"

He met my glare.

"Thank you. This camera may contain an image of the

two people who hiked up to my farm yesterday with a plan to kill me and my eleven-year-old daughter."

He inhaled, moving his hand again to the butt of his auto. "Sir. Listen to me now. Put the camera on the ground. Now, sir."

I did as I was told.

"Where's your vehicle?"

"Home."

"Where's that at?"

"I'd say about three or four miles to the southeast."

"OK. Now I want you to start walking out of here ahead of me, same direction you were headed, out to the road."

"Happy to. First, how about telling me what's got you so worked up and why you think I have anything to do with it?"

He squinted and gestured at me with his chin. "What's that blood from?"

I just looked at him.

"On your face, your head there—the side of your head."

I had scratched myself above the ear, but I hadn't realized it. I touched the spot. It stung, and I could feel a ribbon of blood, like chalk, to my earlobe and jaw.

I rubbed my fingers together. "Curtis, you know, you and I are on the same side."

"Yeah? So what in the hell were you shooting at? And don't tell me coyotes."

"I had to kill the lock to liberate the trail camera."

"Little extreme, wasn't it?"

"I'll pay for the lock."

He considered me for a second or two. "I bet you that camera's probably got a picture of *you* on there, huh?"

"That's not why I took it."

"OK, let me ask you what you know about the deerjackers that have been operating up there under that ledgy ridge."

"I saw something in the paper about it."

"Know what? I got the feeling you're one of these constables don't think deerjacking's too terrible. One of these local officers believes in *selective* enforcement." He made quotation marks with his fingers.

I said nothing. I'd been known to truck a road-killed moose out to a needy family's trailer without bothering to get the state's approval beforehand, but that was about as selective as I got.

"As a game warden, you hate to entertain suspicions like that, 'cause like you say, we're supposed to be on the same team. And the wildlife belongs to *all* the people, right? Not just a few inbred Frenchmen."

I was pretty sure the wildlife didn't belong to anybody, although this wasn't the time for that discussion. "You know, fella, your insults say less about the people of Tipton than they say about you."

"I'm insulting the poachers—*fella*—not the people."

Butting heads over this was pointless. "Listen. How about we go to a lab someplace where we can find out what we have in that box, OK?"

"Just start walking," he said. "Just walk."

THIRTEEN

WE PICKED OUR WAY in silence down along the brambly foot of the dam to the maintenance road and then out to the town highway. He had stuck my unloaded .45 into the back pocket of his burr-studded Carhartt's. It bothered me to see my ebony grip panels exposed that way, but I didn't bother to object. He had the camera case clamped under his arm.

In the gravel turnout at the gate, beside the twin hydrants for the town's pumper, we came upon two vehicles, Curtis's drab pickup and a state police green and gold Chevrolet. Waiting in the cruiser were Detective Ingersoll and Corporal Allan Hawley, the long-limbed, hatchet-faced trooper I'd spoken to at the murder scene. They popped out at the sight of us.

"Yo, Warden Curtis!" Ingersoll drawled. "Hope you're not about to tell me this guy's your deerjacker!"

"You know each other?" Curtis said.

I nodded at Ingersoll. "Sergeant, I believe that Warden Curtis here has trail cam photos of the two people who tried to kill me last night."

Ingersoll cocked his head. "No shit."

"And I believe they're connected to the Tuttle homicide."

"These people wouldn't be a couple of outlaw bikers from Sherbrooke, by any chance?" Hawley said.

"Wait one second!" Curtis said. "Tuttle homicide? You didn't say anything about the Tuttle homicide."

I turned to him. "You weren't in a listening mood."

His sweaty face was rigid through the jaw. "You know why, wiseass? You ripped off my camera!"

"Hold it!" Ingersoll said. He frowned at Curtis. "OK, now, Bellevance. Quick question, why do you think these biker outlaws want you dead?"

"They figure if they don't stop me, I'll nail whoever killed Seb Tuttle."

"*You're* gonna nail the bastards, Bellevance?"

"*You* nail 'em, I don't care who nails 'em. Doesn't matter to me."

"How about if ATF nails 'em. That OK with you?"

I glanced at Hawley and back to Ingersoll. "The feds are in this?"

"Constable . . ." he said. He crossed his arms. "We already had this discussion. You remember me alluding to the fact that certain things may not be what they may seem?"

"Be a little more explicit, will you? I'm a man of reason, but you aren't giving me any."

"ATF. That explicit enough?"

"Undercover? Are you saying some special agent may be connected to my almost getting firebombed?"

He nodded at Curtis. "Give Bellevance back his gun, will you, Warden?"

Curtis stared at him.

"It's OK, Curtis. Your deerjackers live around here. These bikers Bellevance is looking for are foreign nationals belong-

ing to a known criminal organization. Completely unre-
lated."

Curtis thrust my pistol at me by the barrel, then tossed
me the magazine. I loaded and reholstered it.

"Come on over here a second, Mr. Bellevance." Ingersoll
beckoned me around to the back of his cruiser. "I commend
your motives, Bellevance. You're an upright citizen. But in
this type of situation there's all kinds of stuff that you not
only *don't* know, but you *can't* know it. OK? You're out here
doing your Lone Ranger thing, which I don't have a problem
with that normally. But in situations like this, what you do
not know could get you dead. OK? Do not keep sniffing
around Yandow. It's bad enough you putting your near and
dear in harm's way. But between the ATF, the Border Patrol,
Customs, and us troopers, there's *thousands* of man-hours invested in this operation. Now, taking all that into account,
whether Seb Tuttle's murder is a related issue or not—which
I don't happen to think it is—or whether your farmer friends
are still on the hook or not, bottom line is these matters are
for the *state* to pursue, *not you.* OK?" He lifted his cap and
smoothed his hair back. "Because we know the difference between who we can dick with and who we can't. You don't.
Comprenez?"

"So who's undercover? One of my bikers?" He wasn't
about to tell me, but I wanted to read in his reaction.

He just looked at me, rubbing his teeth with his tongue.
"Leave. It. Alone."

Was Securite Quebec in on this? I had to believe they
were. If they were out of the loop, however, that wouldn't be
a great surprise. U.S. government agents didn't go freely infil-
trating crime syndicates in other countries. Was there any
chance that Greaseball, say, was a Canadian agent on loan to
BATF?

An engine turned over. I glanced up to see Warden Curtis yanking his official pickup around toward the gate, spewing gravel.

"Hey, Curtis!" I shouted. *"Hold on! Curtis!"* I ran a few yards, but he wasn't stopping.

"Guy feels humiliated," Ingersoll said.

"He took the damn *film*."

"It's his, ain't it?" Hawley said.

"I *backtracked* these two people from my farm through three miles of woods and straight down to the game trail where he had that thing mounted. I'm telling you they're *on* that camera."

"Bellevance, I listened to your nine-one-one, and I got news for you. No bikers are gonna leave their hogs here and hoof it through that swamp to firebomb your farm. If that's your scenario, I would love a hit of whatever you're smoking."

"The Hells were a guess. Turns out whoever broke into my house wasn't wearing boots, and they hiked in, which means they knew when I'd be gone. Take a look."

I opened my notebook to my sketches and measurements. Hawley came to look over Ingersoll's shoulder.

"The people who hiked all the way to my place to plant a bomb in my hallway want me off the Seb Tuttle thing, OK? My bad guys are your bad guys."

"Hold it, hold it, hold it. How do you know that?"

"There's no better explanation."

"*No better explanation?* I'm disappointed in you, Bellevance. What about you, Hawley? You disappointed in this analysis?"

"What analysis?"

"When you get your hands on those pictures," I said, "you'll have your killers."

"You know I have the highest admiration for your on-the-job experience, Bellevance, I really do, but there's not that many guys that could actually track two men through three miles of forest primeval. What are you, the last of the Mohicans?"

I gave up and started walking.

Ingersoll followed on my heels. "You know what, Constable? It's highly possible that somebody Tuttle was close to thinks it was *you* that killed him. To me, this firebomb shit looks more like an act of retribution than a tactic."

"Just get the pictures."

"I'll get the pictures, Bellevance. On one condition."

I stopped.

"You pull your nose out of this thing and keep it out."

"You mean Yandow?"

"That's it, yeah."

"A resident of my town *recognized* Pie Yandow as one of the two men who showed up in his dooryard last Sunday morning—"

"That *never happened*, Bellevance. I told you that. Yandow's the scum of the earth, but he had *nothing* to do with Henault getting stomped *or* with the Tuttle homicide. So you leave the fucker alone. Do that for me and you will get your pictures."

"When?"

"Soon as I can have somebody track down Warden Curtis."

"And you'll get right on that? Before something else happens?"

"Like what, Bellevance?"

"Somebody else could get killed, Sergeant. Look, I'll back away from Yandow, but you need to get me that trail cam today."

He laughed. "No wonder they pushed you off the force down in Mass. You make a real decent constable, though, I'll say that."

I shook my head and walked away. Which I regretted a minute later when the two of them sped by me without a glance, leaving me to hike into the village on my own along the shoulder of the town road, parched, angry, and sore in the legs.

It was a beautiful day.

AS SOON AS I got to the pay phone on the porch at Sullivan's, I called the farm. "You just sit tight for a few," Brenda told me. "I got about ten more pints to seal, and I'm outa here."

Maggie Cruikshank was at the register selling lottery tickets to a dark-skinned couple who had just bought two folding beach chairs, a six-pack of Sam Adams, and two of Maggie's ready-made subs. The snazzy blue Mini Cooper outside, with the Connecticut plates, must have been theirs.

Maggie nodded at me as I passed by. "Think we might see a couple trays of raspberries sometime today? Hopefully?"

"Today or tomorrow. You're at the top of the list, Maggie."

"I better be."

The tourists took the chance to stare at me. I had done my best to comb the spruce needles out of my hair with my fingers.

Maggie counted out their change. "Wilma's coming around, I hear."

"She is. Myra's been there the whole time, nursing her along."

"Well, God bless that girl. I swear, if they ever ran a contest for all-around greatest kid, she'd win it every damn year."

I took a shopping basket. What did we need? Milk, bread, and dish detergent. The eternal verities.

The first of Sullivan's three interior aisles was L-shaped. The dairy case was in the back beside a floor-to-ceiling honeycomb of brass postboxes. When I rounded the end of the first aisle, I came upon Kandi Henderson checking for her mail, crouching with her back to me in blue cycling shorts, cleated shoes, and a sleeveless T-shirt, wraparound shades up in her wind-tangled hair. Her brown swimmer's calves and shoulders were perfect. She stood up and grinned at me, a little forcefully—in apology, perhaps, for her rudeness at the lake the other day. Her plastic handbasket held a brick of sharp cheddar, red grapes, a loaf of French bread, a tomato, and a bottle of zinfandel.

"You have the day off?" Like a schoolboy, I couldn't help trying to stake a brief claim on her attention.

"Sort of."

I nodded. Her sunglasses had left red ovals right at the bridge of—

"Are you OK, Hector?"

"I'm fine."

"You don't look fine. You look kind of crazed. Is Wilma OK?"

"Yes, everything's fine. Someone played a trick on me last night. I'm still feeling the effects."

"They did?" She glanced toward the front of the store, letting me know she had no interest in chatting.

"I don't want to keep you, Kandi, but as long as I have the chance there's something I want to ask you."

She stiffened. "If it's connected to the murder, I won't go there."

"What are you afraid of, Kandi?"

"What difference does it make? Shit, Hector, you're an open book. All you're after . . ." She stopped herself, shaking her head.

"Tell me what the threats are. I can *protect* you."

"I don't *want* your protection—or anybody else's!" She headed off toward the register.

I caught up with her. "Kandi, come on, this isn't about you and you alone. It's about all of us. It's about this town."

"You know what?" She spun on me, white-faced. "Fuck this town. *Fuck* this fucking town!"

Her fury froze me.

Kandi slammed her basket on the checkout belt and charged out of the store. By the time I'd reached the porch steps, she was vaulting onto her silver road bike. She had no helmet. She never looked back.

I watched her pump away past the town hall and the Presbyterian church, standing off her seat and canted over her handlebars like a sprinter, her hair riffling behind her. She was the only thing moving—rocking, bobbing, flickering under the rich, green maples, and plunging out of sight down the incline toward the boat access, the state beach, the campground, and the girls' camp.

Overhead some invisible airliner inched toward Labrador, unspooling strands of vapor.

"Yo! Hector!"

Brenda was at the gas pump behind me, getting ready to fill the tank of her Subaru. We traded waves and I returned to the store.

I pushed Kandi's basket toward Maggie. "Ring these things up and put it on my tab, will you, Mag?" I wasn't carrying my wallet.

"I cannot *believe* you're flirtin' with that trashy thing. Your wife's in the friggin' hospital fightin' for her life and you're out on the town chasin' steel-trap pussy!"

"Oh, come on, Maggie—"

She thumped the wine bottle on the belt. "Don't give me that *come on* stuff, mister. You know *exactly* what I'm talking about."

"You're too hard on her. What happened to Kandi could happen to any healthy young woman."

"That woman robbed the cradle!" she said. "She was the goddamn *gym* teacher! Peepin' in the boys' shower room."

"He was seventeen."

"Ever hear of the age of consent? Sure ain't seventeen."

"When it comes to boys and sex, the age of consent's a gray area."

"Well, that's the whole thing right there! Wasn't *him,* it was her! Kid didn't know no better. That woman's *sick,* Hector."

I shook my head, wondering if this kind of condemnation would be less vehement if Kandi weren't such a beauty.

The screen door clapped behind me. "Uh-oh," Brenda sang. "Sounds like Hector's talking sex again."

Nobody laughed. Brenda gave me a look and handed Maggie her debit card. Maggie nestled the tomato in on top of the cheddar and shoved the bag at me.

"Do you have to get back home?" I asked Brenda once we were outside again, getting into the car.

"Not right off. Got a bunch of summer camp kids coming up to the maze at two."

"You do? That corn's not five feet high yet, is it?" Spud never opened the maze to the public before the first week in August.

"Oh, it's real close. This one's a freebie, and anyhow they're just little guys." She cranked the starter. "Where to?"

"The ash plain."

"You don't think Kandi Henderson's part of all this, do you?"

I said I wasn't sure what I thought.

"You know, Heck—"

"What?"

"I wouldn't bring this up, but it's something Mercy Petrow told me, and we both know Mercy's no scandalmonger."

"That's true." Mercy Petrow was the village librarian. Her mother, Eliza, and my father, Reg, had been sweethearts in high school. Mercy and her older sister had owned Upper Valley Books in Allenburg for many years.

"This was a few weeks ago. Mercy was over to Home Depot in Littleton, looking for these special lightbulbs you can get now, and she was walking back to her car, and she walked right by this other car, and who does she see inside it but Kandi Henderson and Casper Knowlton, 'smooching it up.' Her words."

I shook my head. "Knowlton? What does she see in him?"

"You're asking me? What did she see in that high school kid, Evan Spurling? I never figured that one out."

"I guess it's hard to say what anybody sees in anybody. But that never stopped people from pondering the subject."

"You got that right."

"Has to be something, doesn't it?"

"Buncha things, usually."

"I'm not so sure."

She eyed me. "What, you think she's a gold digger?"

"Something like that."

We cruised past the town garage and down toward the ash plain. Approaching us on the other side of the highway were maybe twenty cyclists, a tour out of Quebec ankling up the long incline, each bike with an orange pennant fluttering from a rod attached to the rack in back. Soon I picked out the sliding blue dot that was Kandi, still flying along and leaning into the long descending curve that swept out onto the level causeway. Already beyond the entry to the White Birches, she wasn't on her way to work. As we watched, she passed the turn into the girls' camp, too. After that, unless she was headed for Iceville, in Quebec, her destination could only be Westlook, where her father leased one of the old summer cottages there on the shingle cove.

We closed the distance between us quickly as the grade steepened under the façade of Mount Joseph. Not to overtake her, we pulled into a stark rest area with two uninviting picnic tables—concrete slabs set on vertical lengths of galvanized culvert—and a trash can chained to a NO LITTERING sign. We could see up the empty highway past the break in the guardrail at the mouth of the switchback lane down to the cove at Westlook.

Kandi swerved across the road, dipped through, and winked out of sight.

We followed slowly, allowing her the time to reach the shady parking area above the camps, dismount, and make her way through the cedars to the carpenter-gothic cottages on the shore.

Six cars were in the lot, none of them Casper Knowlton's blue Mercedes wagon—and Kandi must have wheeled her silver bicycle down the root-laced path. Five hand-painted signs nailed one above the other on the trunk of a limbed-up fir read, BUDWIG, MITCHELL, REED, ST. ONGE, DRACHMAN. Nearby, a formal message had been bolted to a steel post:

WESTLOOK PROPERTY OWNERS ASSN.
PRIVATE
RESIDENTS AND GUESTS ONLY
POLICE TAKE NOTICE

"Any idea where she's headed?" Brenda said.

"Marty took a lease on one of these places same time as he bought the campground—Liam Budwig's, if I remember." Feed and grain dealers in Allenburg for more than a century, the Budwigs had let the business go when illness forced Liam to retire back in the '90s. All his heirs had left Vermont. "I'll check it out."

"What should I do?"

I handed her my notebook. "Make a record of these vehicles for me, will you? Make, model, and tag number."

"Sure."

At the end of the path, I paused to survey a bare, sunny stretch of ground between the trees and the shore, a ledgy area no good for gardening or touch football or croquet or much of anything besides stacking firewood. The scene was tranquil—no breeze, no people anywhere in sight, kids hooting and splashing out on a raft in the cove. The shingled cottages with black willows between them blocked a view of the water. Chickadees and purple finches chittered at a hanging feeder. Towels and T-shirts hung on a line behind the Reeds' place. An inboard motor chugged somewhere on the water. Someone in one of the camps was noodling on an acoustic guitar. A chain saw whined in the distance.

Old Glory swooned at half-mast on a white, wooden flagpole behind the Budwig place, the camp closest to the shore. Marty had painted the cottage's once-white trim a pretty pale yellow. To the side of the spindle back-porch rail I noted Kandi's Cannondale with the blue paniers alongside a limp truck inner tube, a steel dog crate, and a couple of kids' bikes leaning against the yellow latticework.

I stood close to the back porch and listened for a minute. Besides the laughing children in the lake and the motorboat in the distance, all I could hear was the person playing around on that guitar. Picking out the strains of an old Beatles song. "Blackbird."

I crossed the porch and rapped on the screen-door frame. The guitar stopped.

I rapped again.

Kandi appeared, silhouetted against the lakeside windows behind her. "What are you doing here?" she said through the screen.

"I came to say I'm sorry for accosting you in public. I have your groceries." I raised the bag.

"You fuck. What do you *want* from me?"

"Details. Anything you recall—"

"You *followed* me here."

"With the best of intentions."

"Stick your intentions up your ass. You're fucking *pathetic*. If you—" She exhaled through her nostrils. "You know what? Go away. Go away. Any decent person would respect my wishes and leave me the fuck alone."

She shoved the inside door shut, sending a gust of air past my damp forehead, and threw the bolt.

I stood there in the heat wondering if I should wait a few minutes and try again. Persistence often paid off in surprising ways. What might happen if I forced my way in? What did I really want to find out? Should it matter to me, or to anyone, whether Knowlton was here with her?

I set the groceries down next to the door and walked away.

Melissa Harris was the young woman I ought to be chasing down. Ronnie DiGuilio. Jeremy. And his wife, Genevieve. Annie Rowell. Jimmy Lussier—that kid had more to give me. Evelyn? Evelyn Mackey, Jimmy's psychologist, happened to be a farmers' market customer of ours, big asparagus fan. Nothing to lose by putting in a call to her.

BRENDA DROPPED ME OFF at the turnout below the cabin. Hugh's Saab was gone. In the kitchen I found a note on the pine secretary:

> *Heck—*
> *Had to go home to check on a few things.*
> *Trooper Gibbs lifted some prints, I think, but she suspects*
> *the perps wore gloves. She also says you better watch your*

back, because (bet you didn't think of this) the malefactors
are sure to know their scheme went awry.

No word from Myra, but your man called. You've got a
meet this eve at 7. Call me between five and six and I'll fill
you in.

—H

Yandow had the confidence to come straight at me, along
with enough curiosity to risk exposing himself, even if on his
own terms. Not that it mattered now.

The lone message on the machine, from Myra, was a single word: "Phooey."

I ate a banana and some broccoli, showered, and changed
into a loose cotton shirt and light khakis, then cut some del-
phiniums and coral bells for Wilma. I decided to swap my
heavy .45 for Wilma's pocketbook pistol, a smaller, flatter
Walther .380—which Wilma never carried and hardly ever
shot. I had an inside-the-waistband holster for it, so it could
ride on my right hip, covered by the shirt.

Inside the closet, I was alarmed to see the gun-safe door
hanging ajar. Had the break-in artists jimmied it somehow?
No. My .357 Smith and Wilma's Walther PPK lay undisturbed
on the padded shelf, along with four .380 magazines, several
stacked boxes of .38 wadcutters and .45 ACP—

The K-22 was gone. And a plastic box of cartridges. That
explained Myra's running back in here last night. Hell. She'd
really crossed the line now. Besides Alaska, our state was the
only state in the country with no restrictions on concealed
carry—but eleven-year-olds packing iron was taking gun
rights a little too far, even in Vermont.

I picked up our bedside phone and dialed the hospital, but
then hung up before it could ring. Better take some time to
collect myself. Besides, this was an issue to handle in person.

Myra was fundamentally sensible, if impulsive. There was no rush.

I found a directory in the nightstand drawer and looked up Evelyn Mackey's office number. Her recording said that during office hours, if she didn't pick up, she was probably with a patient, but she checked her messages on the hour and if the matter was urgent she would return the call right away.

I hesitated. Until now, Evelyn and I had done no more than banter across my display stands.

"Dr. Mackey. This is Hector Bellevance up in Tipton. I'm in need of help with a delicate situation. If you can spare a moment to discuss it, I'll be grateful. It's, it's one fifty." I left the number.

By ten after two, I gave up. Probably this was another request better handled face-to-face. I left the radio playing Haydn and locked the door behind me.

FOURTEEN

MELISSA HARRIS'S HOUSE-SIT WAS a shabby, two-bedroom dwelling in the development that had gone up one cheap structure at a time through the '60s and '70s in a rocky sheep pasture west of Allenburg State College. The yard trees—blue spruce, Japanese maple, flowering crab—had matured quite a bit since the last time I'd been out this way.

Three-twenty-three Ridgeway was set back on one of maybe eight high, sloping lots with southeasterly views across the Connecticut River valley, story-and-a-half, particleboard boxes all without backyards because they had been built hard against the narrow stand of fir and spruce that screened them from the interstate just twenty yards to the west.

The place wanted some attention. The driveway's concrete retaining walls were crumbling at the top, and the peeling eaves and shutters needed to be scraped and painted. The lawn was a nitrogen-starved blend of crabgrass, hawkweed, and ground ivy. It surprised me, on such a fine summer afternoon, to see a television pulsing in the living room's picture window—somebody was actually in there.

Carrying my notebook and my reading glasses in their case, I climbed the steps to a small deck. Here were four white resin chairs and a dry, oblong, plastic planter with straggly petunias hanging out of it. I pressed the doorbell.

The quizzical face of a young blonde peered through the smudged slot window. I was glad I looked presentable. She shook her head. "If you're looking for the people that live here, they're away, and I don't know when they'll be back."

"Melissa Harris?"

She frowned. "Who are you?"

I told her I was a local constable hired to work for the Tuttle family, and I asked if she might have just a few minutes to talk.

She opened the door a foot or so to appraise me, one hand on the door frame and the other shading her eyes. She was *an eyeful,* all right, in spite of the streaky straw-colored hair, plucked eyebrows, bunchy little face, and silver lip stud. She was voluptuous and pale skinned.

"What's this about?"

"I'm looking into the murder of Seb Tuttle. I understand you two were close friends."

"You a reporter?"

"Private investigator."

She seemed intrigued. "I already talked to the state police. You have any identification?"

"Sorry, no—but you can call Seb's brother, Jeremy. He'll vouch for me. I'll wait."

"I wouldn't call Jeremy if I was dying and he had the cure."

"How do you know Jeremy?"

"I met him a couple times."

"He gave me the impression he didn't know who you were."

"Huh. Ask him if he remembers what happened New Year's."

"What happened New Year's?"

"He disrespected me." She reached up to smooth her hair behind one of her ears, then the other.

"What do you mean?"

She sighed. "Jeremy's the type of guy figures as long as you're drinking his Stoli and it's New Year's Eve, he can grope your tits, and you're just gonna let him."

"Jeremy groped you and you smacked him?"

"You got it. Plus I told his wife. She took off after him with a tennis racket."

"She catch him?"

"You know, I never did find that out."

"Is it all right if I come in and sit down?"

She glanced behind her. Some movie was playing on the television. "You don't wanna come in this shit hole."

"Well, would you like to come out here?" I nodded toward the dirt-mottled resin chairs at the porch railing.

She shrugged and stepped out, wincing at the brightness of the day. She was wearing frayed cutoffs and black thick-soled flip-flops. She had purple toenails and a red lightning bolt through a gold horseshoe tattooed on one calf. Through her baby-blue knit jersey I noticed she had a miniature barbell through each nipple. She pulled a chair around and sat, tugging modestly at her cutoffs. One smooth kneecap showed a raised white scar from some childhood accident.

"You're after the people that killed Seb?"

"That's right," I said. "When was the last time you saw him?"

"I don't know. Last week. Week ago Sunday."

"Under what circumstances?"

"He brought me a thing of strawberries."

"Here?"

"Yeah."

"You two were living together, weren't you?"

"No. We broke up."

"When did that happen?"

"I don't know—weeks ago."

"Why did you break up?"

"We had a lot of issues. I don't want to get into it."

"Could you put a name to the chief issue?"

"OK. Maturity."

"How do you mean?"

"As in he didn't have any."

"But you two did live together, didn't you?"

"Not if you mean when you have the same address. If you mean when you sleep over sometimes, OK, yeah, we cohabitated."

"Here? Or at the White Birches?"

"Neither. Mostly it was at some camp."

"Whose camp?"

"Some guy, I don't know. It was his friend's uncle's, something like that."

"Can you tell me where it is?"

"Blacksmith Pond."

"Did you break up with Seb or did he break up with you?"

"Does it matter?"

"Where were you last Saturday afternoon?"

"Last Saturday? How come?"

"Jeremy told me that Seb wrecked his new BMW last Saturday afternoon because Seb was in a hurry. He was in a hurry because somebody told him you were prancing around up at the nude beach."

"Jeremy said that?" She shook her head, disgusted. "That's his whack-off fantasy—me at the nude beach."

"So where were you last Saturday afternoon?"

"Probably in bed. I sleep weekends."

"Did you know Seb was dealing crystal?"

She stared at me in disbelief. "Who says he was dealing crystal?"

"This is news to you?"

"*News?* It's *crap*! Seriously, where you getting this?"

"Why's it crap?"

"Because! Seb? Seb wouldn't even do *ecstasy*. If you knew him, he was very health-conscious. He ate seaweed and fish oil."

"How long did you go out with him?"

"Long enough."

"Six months? A year?"

"About."

"Who you going out with now?"

"Who says I'm going out with anybody?"

"Any girl as pretty as you always has a boyfriend."

She smiled thinly.

I let it go. "Tell me, who were Seb's friends?"

"Seb didn't have friends. He barely had a family."

"He didn't even have you, it seems."

She said nothing.

"Do you know Ronnie DiGuilio?"

"Who?"

"Ronnie DiGuilio. Friend of Seb's."

"Nope, not that I remember."

"Can you recall Seb's mentioning any conflicts or any disputes he was having with anybody?"

"Yeah, his brother. Plus the local yokels up there where the egg farm's located. And once last winter he bought a Glock from some guy that had something wrong with it. But the guy ended up taking it back."

"Did he ever say anything to you about the Hells Angels?"

She hesitated. "Why?"

"Two of them drove through the campground last month asking for him. He must have told you about that, didn't he?"

"They were looking for *Jeremy*, not him."

"Seb told you that?"

"Yeah. How'd you hear about it? And who's making him for a dealer, anyway?"

I shook my head. "Come on, he had tweakers cruising the campground looking for him. He even had a local kid running speedy deliveries for him."

"OK. OK, I get it." She put her hands together and rested her chin on her knuckles. "Henderson. Owns the RV park. Old Semper Fi. Him and his perverted daughter. This is from them, isn't it?"

"So you don't think Seb's dealing meth had any connection to his getting killed?"

"No, I don't, and I'll tell you why. Because they *made that shit up.*" She shook her head. "You really working for the Tuttles?"

"Yes."

"I just realized who you are. You're that constable that got the farmers to sue Seb's egg farm. Shit, if you're looking for suspects, you should go look at them."

"I have looked at them."

"And?"

"I'm still looking."

"You know what's weird to me as I'm sitting here? You been trying to run the Tuttles off their property since May. And suddenly here you are with all these questions about who killed Seb. Like you care."

"I care, Melissa."

"Sure." She stood up. "Sorry if I sound rude, but I really got no more to say to you." I watched her glance down the short sloping lawn to the roadway, taking in a dark blue Taurus as it glided past my truck. She was a wary thing.

MY EYES FILLED to see Wilma's weak smile. When I took her warm, dry hands and kissed her, she was able to squeeze my fingers and whisper, "Hi," which seemed natural and miraculous, like a daffodil in the snow. Her red-gold hair, which Myra had brushed out for her, glistened in the sun reflecting off the roof outside.

Myra wasn't in the room. Nor was her yellow daypack. An aide at the nurses' station said she'd left the floor about an hour or two earlier to grab a bite of lunch.

I told Wilma about how Hugh had been helping pick, wash, and pack, how I was pleased with Myra's steadfastness, and how glorious the weather had been all week. We were keeping up with wholesale orders, although I was afraid we'd have to skip Saturday's farmers' market, unless Brenda wanted to try her hand at sales.

If my news reassured her, nothing in her face confirmed it. She lay there, eyes closed, listening to me, then without opening them she tried to say something I didn't catch, except for the last word: *camp*. Something about Myra's summer camp.

"It's all right, Wil. She'll go next year." After that, with nothing on my mind that wasn't too disturbing to talk about, I said I was going to see if I could find Myra, and we'd be back. She squeezed my fingers again.

The brightly lit cafeteria on the first floor opened onto a hot, graveled interior courtyard, where a trio of crabapple trees sorely in need of pruning watched over a pair of redwood benches. Nice a day as it was, no one was sitting outside, though a few hospital workers sat eating at the tables in the cafeteria. Myra wasn't among them.

I approached the heavily rouged, yellow-haired woman perched on a stool behind the cash register reading a soap opera magazine. Would she tell me whether she had seen a girl, eleven and a half years old, with ginger-colored hair and a dark green—

"You mean Myra? You her dad?"

I nodded. "Hector Bellevance."

"Super kid. Nope, haven't seen her, not today. You supposed to meet her?"

"Someone upstairs told me she'd gone to get something to eat. Have you been here for the last hour?"

"Been here since seven in the A of M. But you know what? It's pretty out—maybe she walked down to Subway."

"Not by herself. She knows better." Then again, she knew better than to run off into the world armed with a handgun. Headstrong as her mother.

She shrugged. "Go get her an iced tea and a nice oatmeal cookie. She'll be along."

Every parent's fear was roiling in my chest like hot smoke. I told the yellow-haired woman I was going to check the gift shop. She shrugged again.

Down the hall inside the corner emporium off the lobby, among the floral arrangements, paperbacks, and banks of candy, I found no one. The clerk smiled inquiringly at me over the register. I gave a little headshake.

I went out to the covered walkway at the main entrance and peered down Hospital Drive to the highway, but except for litter pickers in orange vests off in the distance, there were no people in sight, only cars crawling along under the brassy blue sky.

I SCANNED THE CAFETERIA once more and got back on the elevator, telling myself she had already returned to Wilma's room. But she hadn't, and again no one at the nurses' station had seen her, not for an hour, maybe two. Did I want to leave a message? Just call home, I said. Call home, that's all.

I breezed into Wilma's room to let her know I had a number of things that needed doing, and she made her faint smile again and said, "No worries."

I nodded and laughed. *No worries.*

As if, Myra would say.

Burger King, Subway, KFC, and Thai Delight were the four chow palaces within walking distance—half a mile from the hospital lot along the state highway near the last Allenburg interstate exit. It was conceivable that Myra had decided to stroll down the hill for a dose of sunshine and a break from the soggy wraps and quiches in the hospital cafeteria. But wherever I asked, no one could recall having seen her.

Another possibility, however slim, was she'd run into Hugh, maybe in the lobby, and she'd been upset and he'd taken her out to his farm. But Hugh wouldn't come to the hospital only to leave without paying a call on Wilma, and Myra wouldn't have taken off without leaving a message for me. Unless this disappearance was her way of demonstrating our need for a cell phone. If so, it was working.

I sat in the KFC lot trying to plan my next moves and doing a poor job of it. Go back and wait at the hospital? Head out to Hugh's place? Go home? Stop by the barracks to nudge Ingersoll about Curtis's trail cam? Something else?

My first impulse was to keep moving, but I could not convince myself there was any further use in looking for Myra. She could be anywhere. For her to go missing like this was a seriously bad turn, a bad turn that I should have forestalled by reining the girl in a little. By being a father.

HOME SEEMED BEST. Go home, check for messages, regroup. Kirsten's mom might have driven her back to the cabin, and she'd be outdoors in her straw hat, picking berries. If not, maybe she'd left a message explaining what she'd done, gone to Hugh's or to a friend's.

I called to her from the porch and as soon as I entered the kitchen. "Myra? *Myra!*"

Three messages. I hit PLAY.

Bill Desotel, chair of the select board, "trying to catch you up on a few things." I'd missed the last board meeting. A hang-up. And Rob Tierney. "Hello there, big guy. Having myself a cup of lousy coffee and a Baby Ruth at a rest area north of Richmond. I've been all day long in the state's old Ford flatbed, which is a real POS. Steers like a toboggan. Buzz me when you get a chance."

I called Wilma's floor. No one had seen Myra, sorry, but they would have her call as soon as she showed up. No answer at Hugh's farm.

I punched in Tierney's number.

"Yo, Hector! What's the haps?"

"Not sure at the moment. You have a minute?"

"Absolutely. How's Wilma?"

"Better. Thanks. She's conscious. She's a little fuzzy, but these things take time."

"That's good, that's good. I'm not telling you anything you don't know, but these brain injuries, sometimes it takes a week to come back around. At *least* a week. So what can I do for you?"

I explained where I was with Seb Tuttle, told him about the Hells and the firebomb, and asked him whether I was off base or did he see a connection between the attempt on my life and my interest in Pie Yandow.

After a pause, he said, "Speaking frankly? If I was the individual in receipt of that particular message, I'd definitely take it to heart."

"You'd back off?"

"In a heartbeat."

"Is Yandow behind this or not?"

"No idea. But if I had to guess, I'd say not."

"Is he cooking or selling?"

He paused again. "All I know is that meth eats people alive. From the inside out. The total *willingness* of these morons to destroy themselves with this garbage, maybe you need a PhD to comprehend it, but I gotta say, it sure shoots a hole in my hopes for the future of humanity."

"Forget your hopes for humanity. In your line of work, you're obliged to take the short view."

"Yeah, and in *your* line of work you're obliged to hoe the corn and pick the lettuce."

Ingersoll had gotten to him. "Myra's missing, Rob."

"She's *missing*? What the hell does that mean?"

"She left Wilma's room at the hospital after telling the nurse she was going to get some lunch. That was around one. It's after five now, and she hasn't come back. I hoped I'd find her here at home, but— I think someone has her, Rob, that's what I think."

Rob was close to his three kids, twin boys in college and a girl, Olivia, who was a year older than Myra. Olivia lived with Rob's second wife down in Bellows Falls, where Sara taught school. He got down there every chance he could. "You report this?"

"Not yet."

"For Christ's sake! The longer you wait on a thing like this, the worse it gets. Listen, you call the barracks and get a BOL out *right now.*"

He was right.

"Do it. Meanwhile, I'll see if I can't find out where Ingersoll's at with the trail cam pix. Deal?"

"All right. Whatever he says, call me back."

I explained my concerns to the dry-voiced dispatcher, Tulley, at the desk down at the Allenburg barracks. He asked me if my daughter and I had had an argument. No, I said, not anything out of the ordinary. Had I checked my daughter's room? I was embarrassed to admit I hadn't. He told me he'd wait. I half expected to find her there sleeping, curled up on her side with her hands pressed together under her cheek.

But I didn't.

He asked me if I'd telephoned the homes of all her friends. I hadn't done that either. "Sounds to me like you're in a panicky state, sir," Sergeant Tulley declared. He advised me to call all the likely friends and neighbors, then sit tight and wait for the girl to get in touch. In most of these cases, innocuous circumstances usually were—

I told him there was nothing "innocuous" about these circumstances. "Two people went to extreme lengths to incinerate me last night, and I have to believe my survival is a disappointment to them."

"You know, Mr. Bellevance, considering the ramifications of that particular incident, I'm surprised you didn't keep a closer eye on your daughter."

I thanked him for his assistance and hung up.

I tried Hugh's place once more and then Kirsten's house in the village. She wasn't at Kirsten's. I called Wilma's floor again just in case she'd tried to get through while the phone had been busy. They hadn't seen her.

I squeezed my head with both hands. This thing would overwhelm me if didn't keep myself occupied. The greenhouse. I hadn't looked there. I was out on the porch hollering, "Myra!" when the phone rang. I hurried back inside.

"I got news." It was Tierney.

"You reached Ingersoll?"

"I did. Did you call the barracks?"

"Yeah. I'm an overanxious parent."

"Yeah, well, with missing teenagers, that's typical—they like to wait at least twenty-four hours. And hey, Ingersoll's skeptical, I hate to tell you."

"About what?"

"Everything. The Hells threatening you, the bomb in your hallway, Doug Henault claiming it was Yandow that jumped him. He's betting it was the Henault kid that took out Tuttle, and you're in denial."

"Does he think I'm covering for the Henaults? I'm making this stuff up?"

"You could be monkey-wrenching the state's investigation. He doesn't know why—unless it's because you want to protect your neighbors in the matter of who aced a punk who you were happy to see aced because he had put your wife in the hospital. And Yandow, because he's a local individual with a history of beating the shit out of people, is obviously the best candidate for a fall. So for you it's two birds with one stone."

"That's ridiculous."

"Sorry. The trooper that investigated your incident didn't lift any prints except yours. And the tool marks in the frame were made by a Stanley crowbar which your friend, Hugh Gebbie, has identified as belonging to you. You also contaminated the scene the night before by tromping all around the point of entry. So, as a result, the state's conclusions are inconclusive."

"Why the hell would I want to fake a crime scene at my own home?"

"Like I say, you could be purposely gumming up the works. You're the Tuttles' number one adversary in town. You want them gone in the worst way. And, as a cop, you have a certain roguish reputation."

"Thanks for reminding me. Here's a question. If Lance Henault *had* gone and beaten Seb Tuttle to death in a rage, why would he risk dumping him at a public campground?"

"Because that was the place where he did it."

"There's nothing to support that. Seb was dead when they dumped him there."

"You want something to support it? Lance Henault has a history of pounding on people. Did you know that?"

"What history?"

"He was booked on aggravated assault down in Randolph

a couple years back. Two separate incidents. Busted up his college roommate and took a mop handle to the brother of his girlfriend. Second assault got him a suspended sentence and a fine, plus he had to drop out and complete a course in anger management. Which didn't do much good, because last week he went and smashed his tractor through the gate of the Tuttles' egg farm and busted the front door in with a maul."

"That wasn't Lance. That was Lance's *father.*"

"It was Lance, Hector. The kid that was working there *saw* him."

"So why did Doug tell me it was him?" But I knew before he spoke.

"He doesn't take the fall, his son goes to jail."

I felt my scalp begin to tingle.

"And, as far as your other question, Ingersoll checked out the trail cam images."

"That's good."

"Yeah, well, you're not gonna like this. Seems Fish and Wildlife set up that camera to catch deer poachers, and deer poachers is what they got."

"What poachers? How does he know that? You have names?"

"No names. I guess the resolution isn't that great. Anyhow, Ingersoll's leaving that one up to the wardens."

"You get a time stamp?"

"Didn't ask, Heck. Sorry. You could call the warden."

"Have you met him? Curtis?"

"I've met him."

"Real piece of work."

"You know what?" he said with a sigh. "Forget this stuff, Hector. Really. I'm serious, man. Right now you need to find your little girl."

I didn't say anything.

"You hear me?"

"I hear you," I said. I wasn't about to try asking a favor of Warden Curtis. He'd tell me I'd lost the bad guys' trail and taken up the poachers' instead, could happen to anybody. It was Ingersoll I had to get to.

"Let's hope she's just trying to stress you out—punish you, you know, for what happened to Wilma. It's a tactic I'm familiar with, unfortunately."

"Yeah," I said. But I couldn't see it.

Rob told me to call as soon as I heard something—anything.

"You got it," I said.

I sat hunched on the stool beside the phone for a while, listening to the wind and a nuthatch tooting out by one of Wilma's feeders.

It didn't ring again.

FIFTEEN

I FORCED MYSELF OUT TO the garden to pick beans until my back began to cramp up. I had the cordless balanced on the porch rail so that I could reach it on the run before the machine intercepted the call. It didn't ring.

By seven, aching, restless, half dizzy from thinking in circles, I went inside, cleaned up, changed shirts, and gave Hugh's farm another try.

This time he picked up, and no, Myra wasn't there. He hadn't heard from her all day. Why? After I'd filled him in, I couldn't stand hearing him trying to keep a lid on his own anxiety. "Hugh, I'm going to get off now, all right? I think I should keep the line open."

"Right, sure, absolutely. Hey, call me when you hear from her, will you?"

"Yep."

"Wait—first, real quick, did you find anything out in the woods? Because that trooper . . . She was just going through the motions."

"I didn't find much."

"You lost them?"

"Yeah."

"You saw my note, didn't you? Yandow wants you to meet him at the health club at seven—'in the sauna,' is what he specified. But it's too late for that now."

"Health club's closed, Hugh. It closes at four in the summertime."

"He made the suggestion, not me. I actually think you should go see the guy, Hector."

"Why?"

"I don't know if he's connected to the Tuttles or what's been happening up around your place, but he's a player, and if he wants to see you, that means something."

Maybe. Unless it was like in tenth grade when the tough kid invites you to meet him after school out behind the auto shop. "You could be right, Hugh. You free to come out here again and hold down the fort while I pursue this?"

"Didn't I already commit myself to that? Give me twenty minutes."

After a brief disagreement with myself, I took a bottle of cognac out of the cupboard, poured a glass, took it out to the porch, and drank it.

The phone started ringing. I walked inside and stared at it.

This would be Myra.

I picked it up and pressed TALK. "Hello?"

"Hello, Dad?"

"Myra! My God, Myra. Where *are* you?"

"I'm OK, Dad, but I have to tell you something." Her voice trembled.

"Where *are* you, sweetheart?"

"Dad, Dad, this is important. You have to call the owner—the egg farm owner, Seb Tuttle's father. Who hired you. Call him and tell him you quit, Dad. Tell him you have to go back to farming."

I went cold and clenched the receiver. "Who are you with, Myra? Tell me the name. Just say the name."

"*Please,* Dad. You have to do it. Just quit. Then I can come home."

My heart sagged in my chest. "All right, sweetheart."

"OK? 'Bye."

"No, Myra—wait a second! Myra!" She was gone.

I punched in *69. The number was blocked. I tried *57. "We're sorry. Call Trace cannot be activated at this time." I hung up.

She was OK, though. She was OK. I was covered in sweat.

Whoever they were, they wanted me off the Tuttle case because I was close, that was clear enough. How was I close? I knew nothing, or nothing that I knew I knew. Now I was going to just quit? Was I going to call Harold Tuttle and back away? Could I do that?

I had to.

But how would they be sure I'd cut ties with Tuttle? Did the demand even make sense?

Did it matter?

I flailed through the receipts, old mail, and other papers on the pine secretary—a Thai take-out menu, the recycling center's summer hours, Esther's minutes from the last select board's meeting, the Allenburg Arts Center summer readings schedule—before I found the two-page document Harold Tuttle's attorneys had faxed for our signatures. Near the top was the phone number in Burtts Corner, New Brunswick. Country Valley Foods Ltd. It was after hours, but I had no other number. If I did quit and back off, would they deliver her? Would they just let her go? She had to know who'd snatched her. If they had any smarts at all, they had to realize they were good as fried now, no matter what I did. Unless they killed us. They had that option.

"You have reached the Country Valley Foods Canada home office executive suite. If you know your party's three-digit extension, enter it now. For a personnel directory, press one, or else hold the line for an operator." I waited an empty minute before the system dumped me, hit REDIAL, opted for the directory, and jotted down Tuttle's extension.

I recognized Dinah Lynn's musical inflection. "Harold Tuttle's office. Mr. Tuttle is not presently available. You may leave a message at the tone. Please be sure to include your name and call-back information."

"This is Hector Bellevance. It's Friday evening. Please phone me here at home. It's urgent."

WHEN I DROVE into the Henaults' dooryard, Cindy Henault was kneeling among her peonies, pulling witch grass and purslane. She had her gray hair held off her face by a blue bandanna. I could hear the milking machine after I shut off my motor. Gussie pranced up the lane, woofing tentatively, as I got out of the truck.

Cindy rose, shading her eyes against the lowering sun. She held a three-pronged hand cultivator in her fist. "Evening, Hector. Men are in the barn."

I stood there looking at her.

"Everything OK? Is Wilma . . ."

Gussie shoved a shoulder against my thigh. I rubbed her neck. "Wilma's improving, Cindy, thanks. I'd like to ask you a couple of questions."

"Me? About that murder?"

"Yes. First—"

"Now *you're* gonna start? The police been up one side of Lance and down the other, the fools. Can you believe it?"

"That was to be expected, Cindy."

"But they been here *three times* now. Last time they had a

search warrant. I told 'em, all you had to do was *ask!* We don't have nothing we're trying to hide."

"They find anything?"

She shook her head. "Ever since they bulldozed the Knob, it's been one mess after another and it just gets *worse.* I never thought I'd see our own government officials takin' sides against the family farm. Doug's people go back four generations in this county, and we—"

"Cindy— Ease up a second." I'd heard this rant five or six times. "I need to ask you about last Sunday."

"Why?"

"Last Sunday morning when Doug got his foot broken, you were here, isn't that right?"

She looked away. "Sundays we celebrate the risen Lord down to the Church of the Incarnation."

"Yes, you do as a rule, but last Sunday was an exception. Last Sunday you weren't able to leave the farm. Were you?"

She didn't answer. Her small mouth was a tight seam cross-stitched with fine lines.

"That storm Saturday took out the Minister Brook Bridge. And Annie tells me a blowdown had the King's Knob road blocked off all day."

"All day?"

"That's right."

A manure-sharpened breeze set Cindy's pink peonies nodding. Barn swallows swooped and soared overhead. "Who would've ever expected that Tuttle boy would get himself *killed?*"

"Got trapped by your story, didn't you?"

"Wasn't my story. He's the one been all hot about keepin' the pressure on the Tuttles."

"Doug, you mean."

She nodded. "Him and Lance been buttin' heads for twenty

years. Usually with them it's just words, but . . ." She stopped, blinking.

"Doug was mad at Lance for losing it on Friday."

"I'll say he was mad."

"And Lance got physical," I said.

"We were at supper, middle of the storm, and out of nowhere Doug says to him—because he just *could not* leave it alone—he says, 'Guess what, the cost of the damages is coming out of your savings,' and he just— Lance, he . . ." She began to cry.

"And afterwards Doug thought he could keep Lance out of more trouble if he could pin the beating on Seb Tuttle. Is that right?"

"He *had* to," she squeaked. "Otherwise, what if they took Lance away and locked him up? That's what the judge said last time, and if they done that, who was gonna do the work?"

"Why did Doug pick Pie Yandow for Seb's accomplice?"

She shook her head. "I don't know. Just popped out, I guess."

"Somebody hunting for me?" Doug planted his crutches beyond the granite slab under the open door to the bulk tank room and swung himself out onto the gravel path. His cast was stained with urea. He could see I was making his wife uncomfortable. "There a problem?"

Behind him, Lance, shirtless, filled the doorway, dust motes glittering around him in the shadows.

I said, "I'm disappointed in you, Doug."

"Is that right?"

"You've been lying to me. And to the state police."

"Been fighting to protect my farm just like always. No shame in that."

"What made you link Pie Yandow with Seb Tuttle? Tuttle told me he'd never met the guy."

"You believe him?"

"I'm asking you why you put the two of them together."
He shrugged.

"What's *he* here for?" Lance demanded.

Doug lifted a hand. "Ease off, Lance. I got this."

"If you're tryin' to interrogate us, you can move your ass down the road. People here got work to do."

Doug spun around. "You hear what I just said? Keep *out* of this!"

"Doug, now . . ." Cindy said.

"I'm trying to get a few things straight, Lance," I explained mildly. "I'll be grateful for your cooperation."

"Some things is best left crooked."

"This isn't one of them."

"Get back in there and finish up," Doug told him. "I can work this out."

"Ain't nothin' to work out!"

"Listen to me, Lance," I said. "The police aren't going to leave you alone until they get a line on Seb Tuttle's killer. That's why—"

"*I* didn't kill nobody!" Lance said.

"I'm not the one you need to convince."

"Yeah? Well, I don't give a shit what any of you smart-ass cops think as long as you leave us the hell alone."

"Lance!" his mother scolded.

I spread out my arms to calm everybody down. "You folks want to keep your troubles in the family, that's all right with me. But I need to know what made you drag Pie Yandow into this."

Doug cast his eyes toward the ground, then glanced up at Lance. "He's scum. He killed Oscar Firman, and everybody knows it."

"That was a long time ago," I said.

Lance snorted and folded his beefy arms.

"He just sprung to mind, is all," Doug said. "We were at the hospital, and I had to tell 'em something."

"You could've told them you didn't know who jumped you. That would have been the end of it."

Lance laughed. "Not Pop! If he's gonna make up a story, might's well be a whopper."

"Seb I can understand," I said. "But you put him together with Yandow, and the reason you did that was something more specific than his reputation. What was it?"

"I don't *know*, all right?"

"Has he been threatening you?"

"Why would he threaten me?"

"That's my next question."

"I ain't scared of that son of a bitch," Lance said softly.

"Lance . . ." Doug said through his teeth.

"He won't find out it came from you, Lance," I said.

"Don't," Doug said.

I waited.

The burly young man looked at me over his father's head. "It's 'cause I found out him and the Tuttles are already acquainted."

"And how did you find that out?"

Cindy tossed her gloves and hand weeder into the grass and headed across the gravel toward the kitchen entry. The two men watched her.

Lance jerked his thumb in the direction of the Knob. "I seen him up there—up at Tuttle's place. Him and his truck."

"Yandow."

"Weekends he delivers sofas and shit for Coös Furniture. But if I had Tuttle's money, I wouldn't be too interested in that cheap-ass Chinese crap."

"How did you happen to see Yandow at Jeremy's place?"

"This was end of April, when the flies started getting bad—"

"Don't be a damn *fool!*" Doug said.

Lance ignored him. "Pop kept trying to call the fly factory, but they never call back. You can't drive in there either, 'cause if they don't want to talk to you, they don't open the gate. So, one time after chores, I thought to myself why don't I go straight up to his friggin' house. Well, the goddamn Canuck, didn't he put a gate up there, too. But so I walked in, and it's raining, right? Well, time I get there I'm soaked. And this lady in this long black dress, cocktail dress, who, come to find out, is Tuttle's *wife,* she answers the doorbell, in this gown. And she says, 'Please come in,' so I do. And she goes and gets me a towel to dry off with. Well, I look around and here's Tuttle and these two guys standing in the front room there with their coats on like they just got there or they're just about to leave. Pretty obvious I'm interrupting something, because Tuttle for sure is not too pleased to see me. 'Who's this?' he goes, and she goes—the wife—'I thought he was with them,' and them guys just stare at each other because none of 'em knew who the hell I was, so I said my name, and Jeremy gives her this look and he tells her to have me wait someplace else. She takes me into this other room with these houseplants and a big stage piano in it. She was kinda nerved up, you could tell." He shook his head. "And then she asks me do I want a cup of coffee."

"Go on."

"So a few minutes later Tuttle comes into this other room, right? And now he's all 'What can I do for you?' So I told him he could do something about his friggin' fly problem. Well, 'course he's not aware of a fly problem, but he will surely look into it. Which— Well, you know that whole story."

"Right. How did you know one of these delivery guys was Yandow?"

"I didn't." He gestured toward his father with his chin. "Told him what happened when I got home and he says, 'That was Pie Yandow.' I heard of him, but I never seen him before. Ain't seen him since, either."

"What about the other one? What do you remember about him?"

He shook his head. "That hand's what grabs your attention, if you know what I mean."

Doug was draped like a scarecrow between his crutches, deflated.

"Doug, tell me now. What's Yandow got over you?"

He scowled at me. "You act like he's just some local dickwad. He's a *killer*—son of a bitch ought to be behind bars." He turned on Lance. "And if some killer calls you up on the phone and tells you to keep your damn mouth shut, you listen, by Jesus, unless you want to see your livelihood tore out from underneath you."

"Nobody tells me who I can talk to or what I can talk about," Lance said.

"Yes sir, and that's why you're a damn *fool!*"

"Rather be a damn fool than a damn coward."

"Coward, am I? What happens when he touches off the haybarn? What you gonna do when him and his pals take a machete to the heifers some night? Or they pour arsenic down the well? That bastard wants to hurt us, there's a hundred ways he can do it without nobody stoppin' him or even knowing who did it."

"Listen, Doug," I said, "if there's ever any trouble out here, you call me, all right? I'm five minutes away."

"What good'll you be? He won't leave no calling card. There won't be no proof. What are you gonna do, go put him down like a rabid fox?"

"There's always proof, Doug. It's just a matter of pulling it together."

"You're as bad of a fool as he is."

A HUMID DUSK had settled over the Knob by the time I reached the gate across the mouth of Tuttle's lane, a hinged steel bar suspended by a cable between concrete stanchions. On the other side of the bar the lane curved up through a stony pasture to a house hidden beyond the forested crest of the Knob, Tuttle's ultramodern dream house. I hadn't set eyes on the structure itself, but I'd seen the listers' floor plan in the town files. It wasn't the usual pretentious extravagance builders these days were throwing up all over the country. Some architect in Montreal had designed it. Minimalist and boxy, but costly to build—a lot of blasting for starters, then a frame of steel beams, a copper roof, triple-glazed windows, radiant-floor heating, an indoor pool, and two large outbuildings, not to mention a mile of underground power and an eight-hundred-foot artesian well.

I walked around the gate. Ribbons of mist rose from the gravel. As I neared the house, a dozen motion-sensor floodlights, mounted under the eaves of a detached four-bay garage, burst alight. The paved dooryard was bordered by curbstones and potentilla.

Jeremy's Honda ATV stood in the breezeway. Two fancy mountain bikes leaned against a giant glazed urn. More lights came on, yellow ones in milk-glass sconces. The chesty, ragged bark of a guard dog triggered a pulse of adrenaline that made my hair stand up.

"Is that you, Mr. Bellevance?"

The nickel-trimmed door did not open.

"Yes, it is. Have you got a moment to talk, Jeremy?"

"Do we have anything to talk about?"

"I wouldn't be here if we didn't."

"Just a few minutes. My wife and I are about to sit down to supper."

A bolt clacked, the door swung out on silent hinges, and there stood Jeremy in a rugby shirt, blue jeans, and woven moccasins—with a matte-black assault rifle pointed at the ground.

"Expecting a war?"

"No offense, but until the police catch whoever killed my

brother, I can't take home defense too lightly." He invited me in with his rifle muzzle.

"Where's the pooch?"

"The pooch? Oh. You mean Gunther. Gunther is very well trained."

A recording, probably.

He ushered me into a sitting room with leather club chairs, a grand piano, and an oversized fieldstone fireplace that looked as if it hadn't ever been used. Set inside on the tawny firebrick was an antique crock holding an artful sheaf of dried grasses and peacock feathers. Jeremy laid the assault rifle across a broad leather ottoman, and we took seats.

"So. What's on your mind?"

"Something Seb said to me the day before he died."

"Was that the day you drove out to the White Birches and threatened to rough him up and run him out of town?"

After a moment I said, "I told Seb if he didn't straighten himself out and stop causing trouble, there was no place for him in Tipton."

"How is your wife, by the way?"

"She's improving, thanks." I leaned forward, elbows on my knees. "Jeremy, Seb told me he heard the name *Pie Yandow* from you. How did Yandow come up?"

"No idea. The possibilities are endless."

I took a leap. "Ron DiGuilio told me, 'If Yandow killed Seb, it was Seb's brother set it up.' Why would he say a thing like that?"

"*Excuse me?* Who?"

"Ronnie. Ronnie Raygun. One of your brother's friends."

"Sorry. I don't know that person. Truly."

"But you've met Yandow, haven't you?"

"What's this about Yandow? According to the police, Yandow's in the clear. Unless Sergeant Ingersoll is playing games with me."

"What puts him in the clear?"

"The fact that you can't be in two places at the same time, and Monday night Yandow was at the hospital."

"In Allenburg? The regional hospital? What for?"

"He's a maintenance worker. He runs a waxer on the night shift."

"He works at the hospital? Somebody told me he does deliveries for a furniture business."

Jeremy shrugged.

"Yandow ever deliver anything for you, Jeremy?"

"What kind of question is that?"

"Jeremy—you know, if you make me find out about all this some other way, you will lose this golden opportunity to extricate your balls."

"You're wasting your time," he said, rising to his feet, his fake yawn contradicting him. "Hal put you up to this, didn't he? Family relations—it's all a chess game to him."

"He didn't, but now that you've brought him up, if you can give me his personal number I'd appreciate it."

I figured he'd jump at this chance to toss me a bone. And he did. "I can get that number, but then you really will have to leave. I'm sorry if I seem blunt, but there's nothing I care to talk with you about."

"All right."

The deliberate way he took up his rifle told me he was no firearms enthusiast. He was a man who was afraid for his life. "I have it upstairs in my laptop."

After a moment, I traced his steps into the tiled entry and listened as he climbed the stairs. The scent of olive oil and garlic and the sound of soft music—jazz piano, drums, sax—drew me underneath the staircase in the direction of the kitchen.

The dining room's furnishings were polished aluminum and blond maple, and the air itself seemed to have drawn a grainy luminescence from the dusk outdoors. Two of the room's walls were glass, floor to ceiling. Bands across the sky beyond ranged from orange to rose to salmon, and the mountains made a purple ruffle from Camel's Hump to Owl's Head in Canada.

At the far end of the room the French doors to the kitchen stood open. Water splashed. A piano played a happy riff and the audience laughed and clapped.

A petite dark-haired woman in a checkered apron leaned over an island sink, rinsing cherry tomatoes. Behind her on the sturdy gas range garlic and shrimp sizzled in a copper-clad sauté pan.

"Mrs. Tuttle?"

She gasped. "God in heaven! Where is Jeremy?" She backed away toward a door.

"Please . . . Genevieve." I showed her my hands. "It's all right. I'm Hector Bellevance, a neighbor of yours. Jeremy went upstairs to find something for me, and I'm only admiring your lovely home."

She reached out and flicked off the fat red knob under the shrimp. "I know who you are. You're the village constable— you're the enemy of our business."

"This isn't about the Egg Works, Genevieve. I'm here to talk to Jeremy about Pie Yandow."

"Pie Yandow!"

"That's right. What do you think of Yandow?"

"Of . . . ? Why do you ask me?"

"I respect your opinion. You're a perceptive woman. When he was here, I'm sure you must have gathered some impression of him."

"But I did not speak a *word* to him. Not a single word."

"I see. So you formed no impression at all, not even from his appearance?"

"No impression at all, yes, exactly. I made no opinion. I did not even speak to him!"

"Bellevance!" Jeremy shouted from the dining room. "What are you doing here?"

He brushed past me. "This is a private home! What gives you the right?" He took his wife by the elbows. *"Ma coquette, what is he saying to you?"*

She seemed to go limp, eyelids drooping, her face listing toward her collarbone. *"Je ne l'ai pas dit une chose. Aucune chose."*

"Genevieve," I said, "what you told me was that you didn't speak a word to Yandow."

"It's true!" she cried. *"Dis-lui!"*

"Shh, shh, shh." Jeremy stroked her hair. He found a half-filled wineglass on the butcher block island and placed it in her hands, murmuring something I couldn't hear.

He said over his shoulder, "I don't know what mystery you think you're unraveling here, but my wife has no part in it."

Genevieve moaned and said, "Why won't you let me leave this place? Please. I can stay with Marianne in the house on the harbor."

"Shh, now." Jeremy turned on me. "You can show yourself the door, sir. We've had enough harassment for one night."

I lunged and seized him by the cotton of his shirt—along with a swatch of chest hair by his grimace—lifted him off his feet and jammed his backbone into the doorjamb.

"Arghh," he said, and swung a feeble fist at my head. I caught his forearm and wrenched him around with it. He yelped. I patted him down with one hand. He had nothing on him.

Genevieve slid the patio door open with a bang and dashed off into the dark.

"Who are you afraid of, Jeremy?" I said into his ear. "The Hells or Yandow? Your dad or the police?" I snugged him up short. He slished through his teeth.

"You know *nothing*!" he choked out.

"I know you're the link between Yandow and a gang of

outlaws up across. Whether they forced it on you or not, you're the link."

"You don't know what—"

I wrenched his arm up between his shoulder blades. "There's a lot I don't know. But in case you didn't realize it, I'm an exceptionally determined and inquisitive guy. I want you to communicate that to Pie for me, all right?"

He grunted.

"One more thing. If my daughter is harmed in any way, I will *kill* you. I will kill all of you."

I released him with a shove, and he staggered into the dining-room table. Two candlesticks toppled over and rolled onto the floor. He looked at me sideways, a flush on his cheeks. "I believe you would!" He raked his hair. "For what it's worth, I know nothing about any gang of outlaws, and I know nothing about your daughter!"

"You have that number for me?"

Jeremy straightened his shirt and massaged his sore chest. "In the foyer."

He followed me out into the hall and pointed toward a folded slip of paper in a porcelain bowl on an otherwise bare table.

"Give my best regards to Hal," he said.

THREE MESSAGES: Hugh saying call if you get in before nine, Ingersoll saying nothing ("Max Ingersoll, Vermont State Police, five-fifty-six P.M."), and a woman's voice I didn't recognize at first: "Hello, Hector! It's around six thirty, and I just got in from Ogunquit twenty minutes ago. We escaped to the ocean for a few days. I'm not sure what it is you— Oops! Sorry! This is Evelyn Mackey. Listen, I won't be in the office until Monday, but I'll see you Saturday at the market. We can chat then. Otherwise, feel free to try me at home in the morning."

It was close to nine. The number Jeremy had just given

me produced a robotic recording that repeated the number and invited me to leave a message.

"Hector Bellevance for Harold Tuttle. Please call as soon as possible, whatever the hour. If you don't reach me, leave your number and a time when I may reach you. Thanks."

Sleep would not come. My tension, accented by the insects and hazy, humid darkness outside, seemed connected to the lingering reek of gas in the house. It all made breathing hard and thinking impossible. I got up finally at around eleven, dressed, and without turning on a light went down to the kitchen. There was cold coffee in the carafe. I drank that and ate some leftover green bean salad.

I couldn't stay here. I took up the phone and punched in Hugh's number.

"Hector?"

"Yes."

"Any news?"

"Nothing good. My apologies for waking you, Hugh, but I wanted you to know I'm leaving the cabin."

"More trouble?"

"No. No, but— I have to *move*, that's all. I can't lie in bed here agonizing over everything."

"No word from Myra?"

"I can't discuss it."

"Right, I understand. How may I help?"

"Same. Hold down the fort. I'll make a list for you, all right?"

"Sure, good. I'm half asleep, Heck. Give me a few minutes, so I—"

"No, no, go back to bed, Hugh. Wait till the morning."

"You sure?"

"It's almost midnight, Hugh." It hurt somehow to say the time. Midnight and Myra was gone.

"Anything I should know? Anybody else try to kill you, anything like that?"

I turned my eyes toward the front door, which I couldn't make out in the dimness of the hallway, and in that instant it hit me: *no one* had tried to kill me. That wasn't the plan. They'd used my kitchen matches, my duct tape, my gasoline . . . It had popped into their heads in the moment. All they had come here for was to dramatize the risk I was running in . . . what? In hounding Yandow? If Ingersoll was right and Seb's murder was unconnected to the meth labs and the bikers, then so was Myra's kidnapping. Then again, if Yandow's operation was worth a BATF undercover job and everything that implied, he had good reason to come down on me, whatever it was all about. Had Seb been working for Yandow? Why would Melissa Harris insist that Seb wasn't dealing? Either because he wasn't or because she was part of it, too. Melissa merited another visit. Marty Henderson, too. And young Jimmy Lussier, if—

"Still there, Hector?"

"Sorry, Hugh. Listen, I'll leave Agnes's shotgun in the hall closet downstairs. All right? The shells are on the shelf."

"Very thoughtful of you."

"If the need arises," I told him, "you'll be better off with that old blunderbuss than with a handgun."

"Hector, I am a nonviolent human being. If the need arises, I'm dead meat."

I didn't laugh.

SIXTEEN

Moonless and overcast, the night was velvet-black. The wooded back roads were empty all the way to the bridge across the highway in North Allenburg. A flashing ambulance passed me there. On Myra's third birthday, after a party for her with a few friends, the three of us canoed out to the island to spend the unseasonably warm night under the stars. After we were snuggled in and listening to the music of the water with Myra already asleep between us in our zipped-together mummy bags, a siren sounded somewhere far off. Wilma whispered to me through Myra's curls, "We won't be able to protect her, Heck."

"Where did that come from?"

"I get scared sometimes."

"Of what?"

"That." She swept her hand across the starry spangle. "The indifference of the whole shebang."

"Scared for Myra?"

"For Myra, and for me. Not so much for you," she said with a little laugh.

"But Wil, everything we can do for her we'll do. Let's not worry about what we won't be able to do."

"See," she said, "I can't do that."

"Do what?"

"I can't banish my fears by going *boo.*" She turned away. "Sorry, Hector. It's a pitiless world. Sometimes that fact just sinks its claws in me and drags me off."

I didn't say any more. She could be fairly pitiless herself.

IT WAS ALMOST ONE. Not much action in town at this hour. The lot behind the Red Dog Tavern had three cars in it. I cruised past the high school athletic fields on the plateau and the entrance to the state college campus, onto Poplar, and up the curving grade to Ridgeway. Most of these dingy houses had a single-car garage, if any garage at all, and so the sandy curb was lined with parked vehicles. I squeezed my pickup in behind a Miata, which was low enough to allow me a clear line of sight up the street to Melissa Harris's house-sit.

Every one of these dwellings was dark. Beyond them, through a thin palisade of softwood trees, the meteor glitter of speeding headlights up on the interstate came and went. Through the veil of branches I could make out a row of orange sparks. Cab lights—some long-haul trucker had pulled into the scenic overlook on the rise. From up there, looking east over the treetops you could see Allenburg State's brick-box dorms, the weedy, vacant rail yard on the south end of town, the high-voltage corridor, and the old Fairbanks Dam spanning the river. In my rearview, a peach wash from the tall security lights at the college dulled the more distant street-lights at town center and the blinkers on the two WALG-AM radio antennae on the other side of the dam.

I pushed my seat back as deep in the cab as it would go, slid down, and rested my chin on my chest. If nothing panned out here, in the morning, after checking in with Hugh, I'd pay a call on Evelyn Mackey, then have a heart-to-heart with Max Ingersoll. I was going to need him.

No rest. Not till she was home and home safe.

Stakeouts were never a strength of mine. My churning brain taxed my attention, and worse, I had the temperament of a farmer—I needed to be either in motion or asleep. I recalled other sleepless nights. The time Johnny Uribe got shot during a traffic stop. Took two in the head, his own gun untouched in its holster. Four of us stayed awake for three days straight chasing down tips and leads and tidbits until we finally cornered the gangbanger perpetrators in a Walgreen's parking lot.

The quiet night wore on. Crickets sang. Once in a while a northbound tractor-trailer would lumber up the grade to the divide between the Connecticut and St. Lawrence watersheds, then speed down the other side.

I dozed off over and over, never for long. Before five the eastern sky began to brighten, and soon horizontal sunbeams were clouding my bleary windshield. I dug out my long-billed fishing cap and put it on against the glare.

At about six thirty, two houses down from Melissa's, a stocky young man in jeans and a baseball cap came out through his front door carrying a steel lunch box. His long hair looked wet. He got into a maroon pickup, backed around, and headed down the hill, glancing once and then twice at my truck as he passed. A short while after that, a black Bonneville with its headlights on came up the hill and swung into Melissa's crumbly asphalt driveway.

I leaned up to see better.

The passenger door opened, and Melissa slid out. She was dressed for a rave—red sports bra, gold harem trousers, beads on her wrists and around her neck, hair up in a scraggly bun. She and someone in the car, the driver, exchanged a few words through the open door, and then she laughed, thumped it shut, and ducked into the stairwell slot in the concrete re-taining wall. Before she reached the porch steps, the single-panel garage door under the house pivoted open, and the Bonneville glided inside. The door closed. What was that about? Why not drive in together?

That black Pontiac was the car I'd seen outside the Tut-tles' Discovery the afternoon I'd given Seb his ultimatum. Same shiny alloys and tinted windows. Whose was it? I some-how couldn't see Ronnie DiGuilio owning those wheels. Had there been somebody else that afternoon inside Tuttle's RV?

After a time I began hearing a country-music radio sta-tion somewhere, then a weeks-old baby started to bawl. Blue-jays squawked. An orange tabby crossed the empty street in front of me.

Melissa's windows had their shades drawn unevenly. I could see light inside the living room, but no flicker of activ-ity. She'd gone to bed. With the driver of the Bonneville. Not Ronnie, no chance. Too wired to sleep, they'd be fucking. I reflected on the appeal of pierced nipples. They didn't do any-thing for me.

I hadn't heard about any rave joints up here in the north country, but that didn't mean much. The drug culture moved fast, and the party didn't have to be nearby—hard-core ravers would drive hours for that all-night love-buzz experience.

He wouldn't even do ecstasy. That was Melissa's response to the idea of Seb as a drug merchant. A taste for E was some-thing she didn't mind admitting to. People liked to think their little confessions lent their lies more credibility. Seb was mov-ing meth—if he wasn't, young Jimmy Lussier had a flair for confabulation. And he must have been in business before their relationship went south. Maybe that was the reason.

It was about seven, late enough in the day to begin mak-ing a few phone calls. Too early to roust Jimmy, but I could reach Rob Tierney. And Hugh. Why didn't I leave? I had the lead I'd wanted on whomever else Melissa might be tied in with, and Rob Tierney could get me the name of the Pontiac's owner. Why the inertia? I wasn't done here. While I had the chance, I needed to give myself a closer look at the place.

I popped my door and slipped out of the truck, stiff and sore. I groaned, reaching across to the passenger's seat for my notebook and pen. In khaki pants, canvas barn jacket, and pale green fishing cap, I looked just drab enough to be out on some mundane business for the highway department or the cable company.

I flipped my notebook open and wrote the date and time at the top of a page.

I walked along the curb appraising the utility poles. At 323, I turned onto the slope between Melissa's plain smoke-blue-sided house and 321, a wider and marginally less homely one-and-a-half-story with a dandelion-rich lawn and a splayed antenna strapped to its block chimney. Behind Melissa's and between the debris-strewn patio at the back door and the interstate fence, someone had built four terraced planting beds, but except for a sunshot screen of asparagus ferns in the topmost bed, the garden was all weeds.

The covers over the two lounge chairs on the patio were plastered with a winter's worth of pine needles, and the kettle grill lay on its side. No one had been out here this season. I followed the power line to the corner of the house and inspected the watt-hour meter. To the right of the meter the draperies across two pair of casement windows stood partly open, offering a view of a small dining area and, beyond that, a cluttered kitchen. The dining area was being used for storage, it seemed. The dark oval table and chairs were piled with boxes and shipping cartons. Leaning in a corner was a sheaf of obsolete downhill skis, a few surf-casting rods, a fiberglass kayak paddle, a posthole digger, a stepladder, and a number of galvanized wire tomato cages. The kayak, an orange single, was under the table.

A sudden bump and hum startled me.

I glanced around. The house behind me was quiet, blinds drawn to the sills.

Melissa's garage door was opening.

I hustled down to the curb and made it to the other side before the Bonneville's rear end veered out into the roadway. I stood behind a minivan and watched the garage door swing closed and the Bonneville start down the hill toward town.

AT THE FLASHING LIGHT where the high school's main entrance abutted Breezy Hill, I caught sight of the Bonneville again a quarter mile ahead of me. We had some eight or nine vehicles between us. I watched as he turned left toward the state highway, but the roads were so busy with morning traffic that by the time I'd made the turn myself I'd lost him. Nothing for it but to guess he'd taken the highway north.

So I kept on hard in that direction, pressing through traffic that thinned as the shabby motels, used car lots, and auto parts places gave way to a boarded-up Ames store on the tracks, a dismal mobile home park called Meadowlark Way, and then the long open stretch across the marsh. When I crested the low rise before McPhetres' Sand and Gravel I spotted him again, cruising less than half a mile ahead of me. We had a pickup towing a camper between us.

I passed the camper and closed enough distance before the Y near the lumberyard at Tipton Corner to see the Bonneville angle east toward Shadboro and the Connecticut River instead of continuing northeast toward Tipton village.

He had noticed my truck by now, and if he'd recognized it

he wouldn't like seeing me still on his tail after the turnoff to the village. Just so, as I rounded the next bend, soon as the Bonneville reappeared in my windscreen, he hit the gas and took off.

Now he had two options as long as he didn't scoot off into the woods on some logging road. He could either turn north toward Shadboro and the Mount Joe ski area or head straight into the valley toward Coös Crossing, where he could continue on into New Hampshire or turn onto the river road, a winding highway that only the locals and the tour buses used nowadays. I went with straight.

Descending into the village, I had a long view toward the intersection where the highway abutted the river road. The Bonneville was long gone. I pulled into the Rite-way gas station at the bottom. I knew the grizzle-chinned, watery-eyed attendant, Ned Hasty. He'd worked there forever. Ned rose out of his lawn chair and shuffled up to my window.

"Beauty morning," he said. "Cash or charge?"

"I'm good for gas, Ned. I was wondering if you noticed a black Bonneville go by here a minute or two ago, heading east."

"Ooo, boy. He in trouble?"

"Too soon to say. Should he be?"

"You're the constable."

"Whose car is it?"

He looked thoughtful. "Could be I'm wrong, but if it's the same sedan I got in mind, that would be Maurice Poutre's rig."

"Poutre. Doesn't he own the furniture place?"

"Used to, I know that."

"He live around here?"

"Got a camp on the mountain someplace."

"Thanks, Ned. Happen to see which way he went?"

He shook his head.

I thanked him again, bought a coffee and a banana yogurt from the young woman at the register, and drove on south past the Woodsman Diner, which looked fairly busy, toward the low furniture warehouse occupying the strip of land between the riverbank and the roadway. In the mid-1800s, when Coös Crossing was a stop on the carriage route between Portland and Montreal, this assembly of slate-roofed sheds had been livery stables and smith's shops. Rehabbed and painted the same medium gray, the sheds now made a warren of dim, creaky showrooms for recliners, dining sets, and modular sofas. There was a Bargain Barn for used items.

I drove past. Two cars were parked out in front, a Jetta and a Ford Focus, Vermont tags. The picture windows on either side of the customer entrance had giant letters painted on the glass: "MASSIVE STOREWIDE SALE" and "40–70% OFF ALL ON-PREMISE INVENTORY!"

I pulled over in front of Lazy Jane's Laundromat, which was not yet open, and finished my coffee. During the fishing season I kept two spinning rods wrapped in oilcloth in the bed of my truck, along with a net and a box of hooks and lures, although I hadn't put a line in the water for a few years now, not since Myra decided she disapproved of fishing (it was cruel).

Rod and landing net in hand, I crossed the street and made my way down through a narrow lot overgrown with sumac and chokecherry to the littered bank of the river. I paused to relieve myself. Swallows dove after insects above the rippling green-brown water. Over on the New Hampshire side someone had planted a field of sunflowers. I followed a faint path toward the weedy yard down behind the furniture sheds. A rusty burn barrel, a defunct forklift, a pair of blue Dumpsters against the stone foundation, stacks of pallets and railroad ties. . . . In back, in the shade of a squat, four-legged tower with an old iron-bound water tank on top, stood the Bonneville.

I weighted my line, fixed a bobber to it, and flung it out into the flow. I reeled it in and meandered down to a cottonwood at the edge of the lot. I cast and reeled in again and strolled out into the sunlight. The clapboard siding on this side hadn't been attended to in decades. The small blank door nearest the Bonneville, framed in timbers, probably locked from the inside. There was a set of double doors beside the Dumpsters, but no windows anywhere.

It didn't surprise me to find that Poutre had left the car unlocked with the ignition key on the console—no one came down here but the rubbish collectors. I opened the driver's door, unclipped the garage-door remote from the visor, then took the key and locked the doors. I buttoned the remote into my hip pocket.

The young man in the open first-floor office, manning a high, cracked linoleum-topped desk, was no one I recognized. He had a round, dark face, a delicate nose, and penetrating French eyes. He hadn't shaved. He was clacking away on a grimy keyboard and talking on the phone at the same time—he wore a headset. He said he had a customer and he'd have to call later. "You know I do," he said. He swung the mike wand up to his temple. "Something I can help you with?"

"I'm looking for Maurice Poutre."

He eyed me a moment. "And is he . . . expecting you?"

"Tell him Hector Bellevance is here—Tipton town constable. I need to discuss something with him, if you would give him that message."

"And what might this be concerning?"

"This concerns a motoring infraction and a vehicle registered in his name."

"OK. Well, Mr. Bellevance, Mr. Poutre is not in the building. If you want to leave him a note, or your phone number or whatever, I'll make sure that he gets it."

"May I ask your name?"

"My name? Everett."

"Last name?"

"Murphy. Excuse me, but do you have a problem, Mr. Bellevance?"

I leaned across the cluttered desk. "You're bakin', aren't you, Everett?"

He sneered. "That was you in the Silverado. How'd you find me here?"

"How come you're driving Maurice Poutre's car?"

"I sure don't know what this is about, but whatever it is, I do know it's bullshit, and I have a shitload of work to do this morning. So . . ." He waggled his fingers to shoo me. His red ears and the flutter behind his eyes gave me another message.

His telephone chirped. He flashed me a smile, touched a button, and lowered his mike. "Coös Furniture. How can I help?"

His wide gaze followed me as I rounded the corner of his desk to box him into the office space under the stairs to the second floor. He raised his arms and slid his seat back as I came at him. I feinted toward his gut and then swatted the earphones off his head.

"Jesus!" he yelled. "Ronnie!" He tried to scramble to his feet and fell.

I caught him and shoved him back into his chair.

"Jesus! You— You're fucking out of control!"

"Now that I have your attention, I want an answer. How come you're driving that Bonneville?"

"It's my *uncle's*, OK? Why? Jesus, what do you *want* from me?"

"Maurice is your uncle?"

"Yeah, and he's sick, OK? What do you care?"

"What were you doing out at the White Birches last Monday?"

"At the what?"

"The White Birches Campground—when your friend Ronnie tried to drive his boot through my face."

"I never been to any campground."

"Do you ever let Ronnie take your uncle's car?"

"Why?"

"How did you know Seb Tuttle?"

"Seb Tuttle! Fuck, is *that* what this is about?"

"No, what this is about is crystal, and ecstasy—whatever you're into. And whoever you're buying it from."

He didn't flinch at this. "I'm not buying anything from anybody."

"Melissa says different."

"Now I *know* this is bullshit. *Ron-NIE!*" he hollered.

"Does Pie work for you, Everett, or do you work for Pie?"

"You're really starting to get me irritated."

"Hold IT!"

I looked up. Ronnie DiGuilio had a black long gun pointed down at me over the stair rail. Looked like a military-style pump-action. I shook my head. "Well, if it isn't Raygun! I had a feeling we'd cross paths again, you and I."

He didn't move.

Everett said, "You're on private property, which you are being requested to leave. Right now. Immediately."

"Where is my daughter?"

"Your *daughter*? How the hell should I know?"

"Where do I find Yandow?"

"That's it. OUT. Get the fuck out of my building. *OUT!*"

"I'll get out after you give me the answers I came for, punk—"

A concussive *BLAM* filled the room. The muzzle blast was big as a beach ball. My ears rang. Splinters and dust rained down from the exposed rafters.

My hands were shaking. "That wasn't necessary, Ronnie. I didn't need a demonstration."

"Get OUT!" Everett said. His face was flushed. "You think he won't shoot you?"

"Yeah, I think he won't shoot me. Because if he shoots me, it's game over. But if he watches me walk out of here, he's bought himself some time before the buzzer sounds. A day or so, if I had to guess. You too, Everett."

I turned and left. Out in the daylight, the center of my vision was a blot of white.

LAZY JANE'S WAS OPEN now and empty. A couple of washers were sloshing. I went to the pay phone and called home.

Hugh answered on the fourth ring. "Bellevance farm."

"Hugh, it's Hector. Any calls?"

"Hector, goddamn, where are you?"

"Anything from Myra or the police?"

"Not since I got here. You have two messages, one from Harold Tuttle's assistant and one from Rob Tierney asking you to call him."

"All right. Call Rob and have him reach me here." I recited the number.

In under a minute I had him on the line. "Myra's a hostage, Rob. She called last night. These people who grabbed her want me off the Tuttle murder."

"That's what she said?"

"Then she can come home. That's what she said, yeah."

"Fuck. No trace on the call?"

"No."

"You call the barracks?"

"Not yet."

"You backed away from the Tuttle murder, though, right? And you backed away from the business with Yandow. Right?"

"Yeah, there's a local kidnapping case that's kinda captured my interest."

"If you have backed off and they're watching you, they'll know, and they'll release her. Keeping her does 'em no good."

"Killing her might."

"Shit, Heck."

"If Myra didn't know these people when they grabbed her, she knows them now. Are they going to just let her go?"

"That's how you have to play it. You're not thinking it's Yandow, are you?"

"Myra disappeared from the hospital. Yandow works there."

"He's in the crosshairs, Hector. Soon as the feds have what they need, he's toast."

"Just find out what you can, will you?"

"Look, Hector, I'm just past Stamford. Five hours, five and a half, tops, I'll be there. We'll get her back. My advice? Don't pressure these people. We'll get her back, you hear?"

"Thanks, Rob."

I called the cabin. "Hugh, listen. I'd like you to phone Tuttle's assistant for me—her name's Dinah Lynn. Introduce yourself as *my* assistant and tell her you're calling to inform Mr. Tuttle that I consider my contract with him fulfilled."

"Meaning what? If she asks."

"Just that. But make it clear that I would like to speak directly with Mr. Tuttle, at his convenience."

"Got it. What if Myra calls?"

"Tell Myra I've quit. Tell her my deal with Harold Tuttle is history and she can come home. We'll meet her wherever and whenever she says."

MY BRAIN WAS ROTTEN with fatigue and helpless rage, and I was well aware of that, but I couldn't shake the image of Myra sitting chained to a four-inch drainpipe in the basement of that run-down house up along the interstate. Crazy vision—a dozen other places were no less likely—but something was off about that house. *Majorly off,* Wilma would have said. The boxes and sports junk piled in that dining room said that the basement—where that kind of junk ends up in houses without attics—had been recently put to some other use. Hence the door opener.

The day was turning hot, and the horseshoe loop of working-class homes was fairly quiet, the adults at work, the kids in day care or off at summer jobs. Only a few vehicles remained parked along the curb. At least one of them I hadn't seen earlier, a Verizon repair truck with a cherry picker and two stacks of Day-Glo-pink road cones on the back—just the kind of rig the feds might use to sit on a location for a day or so. As close as I was getting to whatever I was getting close to, if Ingersoll caught on he'd put a quick end to it one way or another. Nothing I could do about that now.

The red Jeep Wrangler in front of 323 was no doubt Melissa's. She would probably sleep most of the day, coming down off her raving. I pulled over across from the Wrangler, got out, put on my hat, took my notebook and my glovebox Maglite, and walked deliberately across the street and right up one side of her short ramp of a driveway.

I paused between the retaining walls to listen, drawing the .380 out of its plastic sleeve. No sounds from the house. I pressed the remote in my pocket and stepped back as the single-panel door shuddered into motion.

SEVENTEEN

THE CONCRETE FLOOR WAS cracked and stained with oil and rust. The smell of rotting garbage from a row of Rubbermaid trash barrels along one side of the room was pungent—yet nothing like the ammoniac stench you'd expect from the residues at a cook site. No propane tanks, no big plastic jugs or containers, none of the telltale by-products of meth manufacture. Not much in the space at all really but an extension ladder on hooks, a stack of snow tires, a shop vacuum cleaner, and an orange snow shovel. The workbench built against the back wall was heaped with old bundled newspapers, magazines, and mail-order catalogs.

Beyond the trash barrels were two doors: one with a mullioned window that opened into the stairwell to the main floor, and another, plain birch veneer, that opened into the utility space. It was locked with a simple through-the-knob tumbler.

I took out the tension wrench and picks I carried in a plastic envelope inside my worn wallet, slipped in the wrench, and raked a pick through the hole a few times until the pins all popped up. The door swung in silently.

I surveyed the room with my Maglite.

Low-ceilinged and windowless, it was bigger than I'd expected. To the left stood a pale green oil burner and a hot-water tank wrapped in foil-covered insulation. There were washer-dryer hookups next to the tank but no machines, only a long, deep fiberglass laundry sink on six legs and a strange-looking sheet-metal tray table—some kind of darkroom setup, I guessed. To my right a large opening in the back wall exposed a set of broad plank steps leading up to a steel bulkhead door. A good portion of the room was filled with more bundled newspapers and, in the middle, a big boxy thing that on first glance I took for a welded stainless-steel evaporator—for syrup making. But that wasn't what it was.

I tucked my .380 back into its waistband holster and walked over for a closer look. Along one side were three lines of inch-high Chinese characters, in red. Underneath those, in smaller letters, were two lines I could read:

Longkou City Jenming Machinery Co., Ltd.
Shandong, China 247701

I copied the address into my notebook. Playing my light around the space, along the far wall in a dim corner beyond the Chinese machine I spotted three rectangular columns of what looked like stone. But they turned out to be made of heavy, gray pulpboard. Egg trays. Head-high pillars of empty egg trays like the ones I'd seen full of eggs stacked and shrink-wrapped on wooden skids at the egg factory.

Right from the first day, Jeremy had been importing his layers, feed, and pullets from New Brunswick and sending the eggs back across daily to distributors in Sherbrooke and elsewhere. Ideal setup for the Hells to exploit, using teamsters to smuggle ingredients and product between Canada's eastern provinces and the innocent hills of northern Vermont. Good cover both ways was all you needed, and the Egg Works was as good as it got.

I picked up one of the trays and turned it over. Nothing to it. Sturdy, rough-textured pulp.

How much of this was the ATF onto? No way to guess. But Seb's murder *had* to be connected to all this. Somehow. If the feds knew who'd killed Seb Tuttle and they were sitting on that, waiting for a bigger takedown, that was over. They had to jump.

Myra trumped everything. Ingersoll would get that. Any cop would get that.

"STOP! YOU STOP RIGHT there!" Melissa—in a high-pitched, quavery voice. "Don't move or I will blow your ass right off."

I stopped. I was in the middle of the empty garage. I could see the sunlight outside glancing off the cars parked on the street and the shimmer of heat rising from the pavement. She stood to my right in the partly open doorway to the garage stairs.

I had decided to take one of the egg trays along with me, though I would not have gone for the Walther even if both of my hands had been free. This was careless. If shaky speedsters were going to keep drawing down on me, sooner or later one of them was going to shoot me.

"Melissa Harris. Just the person I'd been hoping to see."

"You want to see somebody, you ring their fucking doorbell." She wagged the gun barrel. "Get back. Get back against the wall."

I glanced at the locked door behind me.

"Now! Do it!"

I didn't move. "Don't be crazy, Melissa. You have to think a minute—"

"*Shut up!*" she shrilled. "*Move!* Or I'll do it! I swear to God I will. You're a fucking home invader!"

"That would be the mistake of your life, Melissa." I watched her silhouette and the under-lugged rifle barrel she had leveled at my lights, trying to come up with something more. This was no place to get myself derailed.

She shoved the door wide against its closer and stepped into the garage. She wore a fuchsia kimono with a fern pattern worked into the fabric. Her feet were bare, the toenails painted. She hadn't combed out her hair. She cradled a scoped, bolt-action deer rifle, the stock against her ribs and her finger on the trigger. I sought her eyes, but they darted between the sunny morning outside and the closed storage room door beside her, as she tried to decide what to do with me. The girl was still half toasted. She pulled one hand from the rifle and slapped a switch. The garage door began to close, and a fluorescent light flickered on overhead.

"What are you fucking *doing* here?" she piped.

I shook my head. "Everett and I had a talk this morning, and we reached an understanding."

"What understanding?"

"He can explain it better than I can."

"No way! You and Everett? Bullshit."

"He was afraid you wouldn't get it. That's why he didn't want me to wake you up."

She shook her head. "No way." I saw the point of her chin start to tremble. "That's *total* bullshit. What did you *do* to him?"

"Everett? Nothing! He's fine."

"I don't believe you!" She jabbed the rifle at me. "Because Everett, Everett had it all figured out—he *knows* what you did to Seb!"

"I didn't do anything to Seb, and before you get all worked up, why don't we just give Everett a quick call and let him explain? Then we can all get on with our lives."

"You're not going anywhere."

"Fine, I'll wait. Go ahead. Call him."

"No, no. *You* call him. Then let me talk to him."

"I would, but I don't have a cell."

She gritted her teeth. "OK. First thing you're gonna do is put down that tray. Just set it down, set it down right there on the floor."

I did.

"Now," she said, backing away from the stairwell door, "move this way with your hands out beside you. Nice and slow."

"What's the plan, Melissa?"

"Plan is you're goin' upstairs, and me and you are gonna stick around till I get further instructions."

"Fine with me—just be careful with that weapon. If that thing goes off, Everett's going to be very unhappy with you."

"This thing goes off, it won't be *my* fault. OK, you head on up—real slow."

I sidled toward the door, then paused. "There you go! Hear that?"

"What?"

"Out on the street. He's coming."

As she cocked her head, I reached around to my hip pocket and tapped the opener button. The motor hummed. She gasped and turned, stepping to one side.

A quick lunge and I had hold of the barrel. She yelped as I yanked the weapon out of her hands. "Don't hurt me!" she cried.

I worked the action and sent a 30.06 cartridge clattering onto the floor. "You're a lucky girl, Melissa."

Her red face crumpled. "What are you going to do?"

"I'm going to give you some advice. Do you have any family living in the area?"

"What?"

"You heard me."

"No. My— My mom's in White Plains."

"You ever visit her?"

"Just Christmas."

"Melissa, listen. Whatever's going down in the back room there—"

She bolted for the stairwell door. I made a grab for her but she dodged me and hit the stairs, bounding up two at a time.

I just watched her.

She slammed the door at the top. She'd call someone. Probably Everett. What that would set in motion was hard to guess, but things were going to start accelerating, no question about that.

I released the magazine and tossed the rifle butt-first up behind the boxes and newspapers on the workbench. On the way out I stuffed the rifle's magazine into one of the trash cans.

With the egg tray in the passenger footwell beside me, I headed down toward the highway and the state police barracks, telling myself the best thing I could do now—the only thing—was work to stay out in front of the main action, but only a little, like a surfer on a wave.

I had just blown the back end off the feds' show. I'd had good reason, goddamn it. I pounded the steering wheel. The time to dance around with these people was up when they grabbed my daughter. Myra was—

A horn blared at me. At the foot of the hill, where Poplar met Main, I'd just driven right through the damn stop sign. I'd hardly looked.

TWO TROOPERS I didn't recognize and corpulent Sergeant Pete Tulley, the dispatcher, were the only ones in the unpartitioned, overlit front office in the redbrick Troop B barracks along the highway.

They all looked closely at me, taking in my waxy complexion and unshaven face. When I introduced myself to Tulley, he shot a glance at the other two before nodding to me.

"Your daughter ever show up? What's her name again?" He was working a wad of gum.

"Myra. No, she hasn't shown up. You hear anything today from Rob Tierney?"

"Sure haven't, not yet."

"Myra called me yesterday," I said. "She said that if I would quit looking for Seb Tuttle's killers, she could come home."

"That's what she said, just like that?"

"That's what she said. I back off on Seb Tuttle, she comes home."

"So did you?"

"Back off? Yes."

"And so what happened? She didn't come home yet?"

"No, goddamn it, I just told you. She— No, these *scumbags,* these— Whoever's got her—" I stopped and winced. My back was seizing up.

"So you're thinking she's still a hostage of these unknown individuals that whacked Seb Tuttle."

I sighed. "Look, get Max Ingersoll on the line for me, will you, please? And Rob Tierney, too, if it's no trouble."

Tulley eyed me for a few pensive seconds. He'd page them for me right now, he said, if I wouldn't mind waiting out there in the vestibule. Not at all. I was desperate for few minutes' rest and a chance to collect my thoughts.

I slumped into one of half a dozen hard plastic chairs set on each side of the spare, hot, airless vestibule in the red glare of a giant Coke machine. That light, the sputter and drone of Tulley's radio, and the flies above me nuzzling the hot glass in the transom window put me right to sleep.

ONE LATE APRIL day a year or two after Myra was born when Hugh and I were out snowshoeing, hunting for moose antlers on the heights above Spud's farm, Hugh remarked to me out of the blue, "You know, one of the very few things that used to irritate me about your mother was her insistence that the value of longevity was exaggerated. Granted, your Grammy Beryl's MS was a terrible burden for Agnes all those years, and she did work hospice for I don't remember how long, but Agnes herself, as you know, was always, *always* in the absolute *pink* of health. In the absolute pink till the day she dropped dead—which, of course, was *exactly* the way she always said she wanted to go. Funny. She was too sensible to believe in any kind of an afterlife, and yet she didn't mind the idea of dying, not a single bit. Old age. The very thought of it made her queasy. She told me once that if she had a choice between dying young and vigorous or old and sick she'd die young, no doubt in her mind. 'Live long enough,' she used to say, 'and everything you love will be taken from you.' How bleak is that?" He heaved a sigh. "I miss the hell out of her."

So did I. Most men revere their mothers. All mothers deserve reverence, if just in the abstract. But the truth is that Agnes Bellevance was one of those rare persons who embody every wholesome human attribute. We were alike, people often remarked, although it wasn't true. But like Agnes I was not afraid to die.

EIGHTEEN

Ingersoll's driver, the swarthy Koslowski,
brought me back around by massaging my left shoulder with
his paw.

A thread of drool stretched down the front of my shirt.
When I jerked up, I had a searing knot in the small of my
back. A fly was buzzing in my hair. I swiped at it and yelped
with pain.

"Bellevance. Yo, buddy. You compos?"

I tried to focus on the two men, the one who looked like a
rottweiler and the smooth, ruddy, sandy-haired Max Ingersoll. "Sorry, gentlemen. Hard night."

"Do tell. You together enough to pay attention?"

"To what?"

"Sergeant Tierney called me this morning. He's sick, but
we talked a little while. I know what you're going through. I
got a daughter myself. Eight years old and she lives with her
mom, but I see her twice a month." He cleared his throat.
"Bellevance—" He paused. "Can you look at me?"

I forced my head erect.

"OK. Tierney says you like Yandow as the kidnapper of

your daughter on the basis of opportunity—because he works nights at the hospital." He slowly shook his head. "No. N. O. It was not Yandow or his associates that nabbed your little girl, if anybody did. You got me?"

"Did you say, 'if anybody did'?"

"Yes. Meaning only that your daughter is gone and the exact cause of her being gone is still up in the air."

"The hell it is! She told me—"

"I *know* what she told you. Do you know what *she* told Trooper Gibbs when Gibbs was investigating that B and E up at your place?"

"Hold it, hold it. Gibbs talked to *Myra*? When was this?"

"The older gentleman, your friend, Mr. Gebbie, he directed Trooper Gibbs to the orthopedic unit where your wife's at. Your daughter confirms that this firebomb incident apparently occurred. However, at the same time, she told Gibbs that she wants you *out* of this very unofficial private-eye gig that you apparently signed onto."

"Is that right?"

"In the worst way, yeah."

"Christ, you're not really . . ."

They stood staring at me, big men with silvery sunlight radiating from around their ears. Myra had the temerity to arm herself with a revolver, but she would never go so far as to *trick me* into dropping the case by pretending to be a hostage.

Yet it wasn't inconceivable.

A sheriff's deputy came through the front door. "Sergeant—" he said. Then, raising his eyebrows at the tension, he muttered, "Excuse me."

"Let's focus on who killed Seb Tuttle," I said.

"*Let's?*" Koslowski said.

"Bellevance, my friend, thanks to *you*, Lance Henault is buttoned up tighter than the preacher's wife's bloomers."

"You're still wasting time on Lance? *He* didn't kill Tuttle!"

"I like the Hells Angels myself," Koslowski said, grinning.

I looked at Ingersoll. "Nobody you're working with sees any connection between Tuttle and Yandow?"

He tossed his hands in the air and turned around. "I do not *believe* this."

"You people have to *move* on this, Sergeant. My child's *life* is on the line."

"And I am *sorry* about that. But you were warned, buddy, you were *warned*. You know what? *Go home.* Go home, catch some winks, let the A-team do its thing."

"I want my images."

Ingersoll gave Koslowski a look. "He wants what?"

"The pictures. From the trail cam."

"That's Curtis, isn't it? He's spearheading the whole deer-jacking extravaganza."

Koslowski nodded. "All's he ended up with was two probably-male subjects, who you can't see their faces. They're wearing woodland cammies and hats, and they're just basically truckin' along with a gutted doe on a pole during a closed season."

I looked at Ingersoll. "You have my copy?"

"Seriously?"

"We had a deal, Sergeant."

"I know we had a deal," he shot back. "I didn't think you had any interest in poachers."

"Can you get it for me?"

"We don't have it. Have to have somebody grab it off Curtis's computer over at Fish and Wildlife. Write down your email and I'll have 'em send it to you."

I didn't have email. Wilma and Myra did, but I didn't know their addresses. "Have it sent to the Town of Tipton in care of the clerk, Esther Nichols."

"Uh, excuse me, Sergeant Ingersoll." Tulley planted his

bulk at the end of the vestibule, his eyeglasses dangling from one hand. He'd sweated through his underarms. "You have an urgent call. You want to take it out back?"

This, I suspected, would have to do with me. I'd set off the *OOO-gah, OOO-gah* alarm in whatever nest they were watching, and by this time a lot of scurrying had to be going on. So I walked out. Maybe that was a mistake, but the cognitive gears weren't meshing well, and I had to trust my first impulses. If I started second-guessing myself, the whole mechanism could grind to a standstill.

THE MAIN ROADS were jammed with out-of-state cars, RVs, and delivery trucks. Took me fifteen minutes to zigzag across downtown Allenburg to the river and drive out to the state offices' outpost near the dam, a cedar-shake building, the new home to the state forester, the Soil Conservation Agency, and Fish and Wildlife. A few bicycles stood in the rack at the main entrance, which was flanked by yellow marigolds in barrel planters.

Inside, behind a half wall facing the doorway, I found a pixie of a receptionist no older than eighteen. She had a short, feathery haircut and a square diamond on her finger. The name plaque on the counter read BARBARA M. KIPSIS.

I nodded and removed my cap. She didn't like the looks of me.

"Good morning, Barbara. Let me ask, you wouldn't happen to be Carl Kipsis's daughter, would you?"

"Sure am. Why?"

"He and I played basketball together many years ago. I used to know your mom, too. I'm Hector Bellevance."

"You *are*? Ho-*ly*! My dad used to tell *stories* about you. I can probably even remember some of them."

"How's he doing? He still in Puerto Rico?" We'd stayed in touch for a long while. Carl used to try to get me to visit him at the hotel he and his wife owned in Old San Juan, but I never went.

"Still in PR, yep, yep. He loves it. He'll never leave."

"And have you moved back to the home place?"

"My mom's, yeah. But it's temporary. She's remarried."

"I heard that. And it looks like you're engaged."

She wagged her ring at me. "Since last Friday. So what brings you out here?"

"I've come to pick up a copy of the trail cam photo that Matt Curtis has for me."

She blinked. "Pick up the what?"

"It's a digital image of two deer poachers. Should have been emailed to the town clerk's office up in Tipton, but we haven't received it."

"Well, Warden Curtis isn't coming in the office today at all, I don't think," she said.

"That's OK, Barbara, I don't need to see him. All I need is my copy of the image."

"Well, could you, like, come back when he's in the office? Or I could make an appointment with him for you? Because I—"

"I wish I had the time for that, but the truth is, this is a hot-pursuit situation, and I'm going to have to insist on your cooperation."

Her cheeks colored. "I don't know, I—"

"Just point out Warden Curtis's desk for me, Barbara, will you?"

She glanced to her right. "I really think—"

I started off in that direction.

No computer in the first open cubby, just two vinyl armchairs, a pair of disorderly bookcases, a photocopier, and a gray metal desk with a coffeemaker and a microwave on it. The next room looked cramped and dim, its blinds drawn across the one small window. I found a light switch.

"Mr. Bellevance, wait. Wait a second." Barbara was right beside me, agitated as a squirrel. "You can't just go in somebody's office when they're not here."

The desk looked fairly neat—a few reference books between bookends, a green blotter, a Husqvarna coffee mug, a framed portrait of an older couple in a golf cart bedecked with flowers, and a flat-panel monitor.

"Sorry to upset you, Barbara. Look, you can call the state police, if you want—ask for Sergeant Tierney." I switched on the computer. "I'm here because the police sent me here."

She looked out into the bright hallway. "See, no, I'm just filling in while Mrs. Ricotelli's at Lake Winnipesaukee. But, really, I mean, don't you need a warrant or something?"

"To gain access to something that's already mine? Of course not." I pulled out Curtis's chair and invited her to sit in it. "Would you like to handle it, or shall I?"

"Me? Ho, God." She waved off that idea.

In less than a minute I'd found the image file, helpfully labeled "poachers," attached it to an email, and zapped it to tipton.tc@vtlink.net.

I asked Barbara to remember me to her mom and her dad, too, next time she saw them. Relieved to see the back of me, she said she certainly would.

I LEANED DOWN and kissed Wilma's soft, warm mouth. Her bed had been cranked up, and her skin was rich again under her freckles, the gray cast gone. Her hair had been brushed out. Her eyes were clear.

Though I had spruced up in the men's room off the hospital lobby, I had not shaved, and I couldn't do anything about the glittery exhaustion in my eyes. Wilma's distress at all this shone in her own eyes. She squeezed my hands and said, *"Sleep."*

I made an apologetic grin. "You look terrific, Wilma. I can't tell you how wonderful you look."

She smiled. "Myra isn't here," she said carefully.

"She'll be here later," I said.

"I— I— Sorry," she said, sighing. Her eyes brimmed, and mine did, too.

"Come on, Wil! Everything's going to be fine!" I said. I patted her stomach and nodded, and she nodded back, whispering something I didn't catch.

That was about all I could take.

When the elevator doors opened opposite the nurses' station, I exchanged places with the only occupant, the fresh-faced aide I'd spoken with the morning before. She was carrying a food tray.

"We missed seeing Myra this morning," she said.

"Not as much as I did," I told her.

She looked at me blankly. As the brushed steel doors slid closed I noticed a dome of black glass protruding from the ceiling above her head. How had I missed this? Somewhere downstairs there had to be a record of everyone who had passed through the hospital's doors yesterday—probably a series of images taken at short intervals and preserved on videotape or on some hard drive.

A receptionist in the ER laughed when I asked if she would kindly direct me to the head of hospital security. All that was managed out of the maintenance department, she said, and I'd probably want to talk to Calvin.

She leaned toward me and pointed. "Just go down the hall to the end, take a left, keep going past the laundry, then take the stairs to the basement and follow the signs to B-32."

At the end of a fluorescent-lit corridor lined with conduits, I found the gray double doors to B-32 locked. Another simple tumbler—but fiddling with my tools out here in the open was a bad idea, especially since I had no clear notion as to what might be on the other side. Better go back upstairs and ask someone to page security for me, or else phone Rob Tierney and have him call the security chief. It seemed a safe bet Calvin would cooperate more readily with a state police investigator than with a disheveled town constable operating outside his jurisdiction.

In the cafeteria I bought a wedge of warm spinach quiche and a banana and wolfed them down as I made my way to the back row of the parking lot, where I'd left my pickup in a patch of shade. My plan was to drive down the hill to the pay phone at the minimart, put in a call to Tierney, then call Hugh again to see whether he—

I was tossing my banana peel into a weedy drainage ditch on the other side of the curb when I caught sight of a beefy guy, bald, in mirrored shades, coming toward me on my right. At the same time, a large, henna-haired woman in jeans and a gray hoodie was approaching on my left. She had her hands in her hoodie pockets.

I waited for them.

"Bellevance?" the woman said.

I nodded.

"Pie wants to see you." She had a raspy voice and a speed-ster's bad skin and teeth.

"Now?"

"That's what I recommend."

"Your name is?"

"Peggy Sue. I know just what to do."

"How long have you been waiting for me?"

"All my life."

The beefy guy snorted, hooked his thumbs in his belt, and propped his rump against my tailgate. His loose work pants came only to the middle of his huge pink calves.

"I follow you?"

She shook her head. "We're gonna take you there—me and Jumbo."

This was a very bad idea, and I knew it, but I nodded. "All right. Where to?"

She glanced behind her for anyone who might be nearby. There was no one. His jaw muscles were twitching. "Turn around and lean against the side. We gotta pat you down."

"Where is my daughter?"

"What did I just say?" Peggy Sue said.

"Is she all right?"

"Turn the fuck around. We ain't got all afternoon."

I turned around. Jumbo kicked my legs apart. He knew what he was doing. I was glad I'd left the Walther inside my glovebox.

They led me down a walkway to the long-term lot. We stopped at the rear of a plain white GMC panel truck, Vermont TYT 514, and Jumbo opened the back doors for me. He hawked and spat on the ground.

A ribbed partition separated the cargo area from the cab, where I could hear a lively DJ jabbering on the radio. A fiberglass roof vent let in a cone of weak light. One side was lined with built-in steel-mesh shelves. Along the other was a bench cushioned by a folded blanket.

I climbed in and sat. Jumbo hauled himself in next to me, and the rough woman in the hoodie shut the doors behind us as the motor started up. She slid in on the passenger side.

We went north on the state highway and turned onto the interstate access road, but then crossed over the interstate, passed the southbound on-ramp, and kept on, heading out the old quarry road, which was all washboard and dust for a good five miles. Jumbo sat with his elbows on his knees, eyes shut, massaging his paws, humming and nodding along with some music he had in his head. The truck rumbled this way and that for some fifteen minutes out into the rugged hills northwest of town, bouldery woods too dense and uneven to farm. In high school, sometimes we used to roam out in this direction to drink beer and shoot at squirrels.

That was a very long time ago.

THE TRUCK JOUNCED slowly down a rocky lane and stopped.

The doors opened, and Jumbo grunted as he hopped out, leaving a pall of funk in the air. Not only had he ignored my conversational overtures, but he hadn't looked at me once.

We were in a small, brushy clearing surrounded by tall hemlock, spruce, beech—no view at all, only the woods and tattered patches of sky. I heard an ovenbird, and a brook. I had no idea where we were, somebody's deepwoods deer camp, that's all—creosoted board-and-batten, tin roof, rain barrel, prefab chimney, thirty or forty sets of antlers nailed to the eaves of the porch roof.

The tweaker woman ushered me to the steps and motioned for Jumbo to follow. He came up behind me. At her nod, I unlatched the door and pushed it in without knocking, half convinced I'd find Myra sitting at a plank table with Pie Yandow.

Jumbo closed the door.

The cigarette smoke and the half light from two small burlap-curtained windows left most of the interior in shadow, and I had to wait for my eyes to adjust before I could be sure that the only other person in the space was the angular guy standing next to a set of bunk beds without mattresses. He had his arms folded. Toward the back of the room an Ashley woodstove, its sheet-metal cabinet pocked with bulletholes, stood on a pad of loose bricks. The place smelled of mildew, creosote, and smoke.

I waited.

Pie took a long pull on his cigarette, then threw it down and stepped on it. "Something you wanted to ask me?"

"Yes. Did you have Seb Tuttle taken out?"

He looked at me for a moment. "That's it?"

"I'm not interested in the speed factory, Pie. All I want to know is who did Seb Tuttle."

"That's why you're sniffin' after my ass? And jamming up my friends at their place of business?"

"The people who killed Seb tried to kill me. And now they've got my little girl. Whatever I have to do—"

"*Shut up.* You're wicked strung out, I can see that. Back to my question, where do *I* come in?"

"Tell me who to look for."

He sighed. "If I cared, which I don't, I would start by asking myself why did they kill him? Got a theory on that?"

"Speed dealers go down behind all kinds of bad connections."

"OK, the dealer theory. Seb Tuttle was selling meth out of that campground. What's that based on?"

"He wasn't selling meth?"

"In a public location? With tourists all around?"

"He had a kid delivering eight balls to buyers down at the state fishing access."

"Where do you get this? TV?"

I said nothing.

He came toward me, scritching on the gritty linoleum, and stopped. He clenched his hands and shouted in my face, *"I got the urge to SMASH you to pieces!"*

It was the yelling that made me cringe. He was making a show.

He laughed. "Stepdad used to pull that shit. Stand over me with a shovel under my chin, screamin', *I got the urge to smash you to pieces!"*

"He ever hurt you?"

He smiled and looked away. "Once was a time, years back, I used to get that same feeling—that *urge*. But I outgrew it. You get old, right?"

Yandow's eyes and the whistling of Jumbo's nose at the back of my neck told me I was about to take a pounding. I postponed the action before Jumbo could lay his hands on me by sidestepping left and turning to face them with my back to the old Ashley. I had no place to go, but I could use my arms to fend them off, waiting for an angle, unless—

"Sukie!" Pie called out.

The door swung in and the scab-faced tweaker in the hoodie who'd delivered me here, a silhouette against the outdoors, stepped inside. She was holding what I recognized after a moment as a square-nosed, black-and-yellow Taser. So much for a fair fight.

"You know, you fellas start beating on me, and by the time you find out I wasn't your problem, it'll be too late."

"Too late for what?" Pie said.

"To go on living life as a free man."

"Am I missing something?" He looked at Jumbo, who was removing his sunglasses. "He gonna arrest us? Herd us all down to the pokey?"

Jumbo made a chuckle. His eyes were glowing slits.

"Do you want to hear what I have to say?"

"Think you'd be here if I didn't?" Pie glanced back at Sukie. With a flick of his bad hand he beckoned her into the middle of the room. "Keep talkin', brother. I'm listenin'."

"Not here. Outside." Worth a try.

"You want to fucking talk, *talk*!"

"I need to free my daughter. She's only eleven years old."

"You are fucking demented. Guys like you, somebody gives 'em a badge, and they're a danger to society. Comes a point where somebody's got to rein 'em in a little."

"I'm no danger to you, Pie."

"You got that right." He stared at me, then nodded at Sukie. "I'm gonna count. When I get to five, Tase the gentleman."

She painted my chest with the laser sight.

"One," he said.

I stood there.

"Two."

Jumbo chuckled again and coughed.

"It's bigger than me, Pie," I said.

"What is?"

"This mess you're in."

"I have other issues?"

"Government agents are watching your operation. They've been onto you for some time."

"How?"

"From the inside, Pie."

He glanced at Sukie then looked at me again, his face hardening. "Who?"

"I don't know. Somebody on the Quebec end, I'm guessing."

"How do you know this?"

"Ingersoll let me in on it because he was afraid I'd do something stupid and blow the whole operation. Which I've just done."

He paused, suddenly flushed. "You're full of *shit*."

"I'm straight."

"We got a *mole*?" Sukie said. "*Who?* Who's this mole?"

"I don't know."

Pie rubbed his face. "Why should I fucking believe you? What proof do you have?"

"I just traded away the store. If the state finds out I came singing to you, I'll go down like a box of bolts."

Sukie scoffed. "That ain't proof."

"Proof's on the way. You don't want to wait for it."

Sukie squirmed on her feet. "Fuck, Pie. Man, if this is true, this shit? Man, if this is true, this is what Raygun's been all about for two weeks. Fucking *shit*. He fucking *knew* it, dude. I bet it's *him*. You know? I bet it's fucking Raygun."

"Shut up!" Pie said.

The three of them stared at me, and Yandow pulled off his glove so he could fish a cigarette and a butane lighter out of his breast pocket. "All right," he said, "let's just . . ." He lit up.

Sukie rocked her head. "Dude, if he's right on this shit, we got to get back. We got— We got shit to do."

"Shut the fuck up, OK? OK, OK, we'll—" He grimaced, stretching his lips across his gray teeth. "Jesus fucking *shit*."

I eyed the near window. Could I make a break for it? Launch myself through the glass like a dolphin? No chance. I was about to get kicked around a little here. Protect your eyes and your teeth. "You people hurt me or my daughter, and it's just going to go harder on you when the meth lab goes south. Smart thing for you to do is just leave me here."

"That right?" He nodded blankly at me, as his features seemed to relax. He flicked his cigarette past my ear. "Three. Four. Five."

NINETEEN

ELECTROMUSCULAR DISRUPTION WORKS BY brutally jamming the nervous system so the brain can't govern the body and the body collapses within a cocoon of pain. You don't feel yourself coming unstrung, because the pain obliterates any wider awareness. And if it's bad enough, you pass out.

When I could piece the world together again, I was curled on the ground in the dappled sunshine, seared by breezes, swirling in agony, coated in a paste of leaf litter, sweat, and blood. There were flies.

I was alive.

I tried pushing up but crumpled to the ground in an orange haze. My groan crackled with congestion. I had broken ribs. My left hand had something wrong with it. Both orbits were swollen as well, and my vision was off. The flattened ferns under my cheek looked like a bed of seaweed. I couldn't smell anything. I could hear—I could hear crows and the flies and a set of tires tearing along a gravel road somewhere not too far off. My teeth. My teeth seemed intact up and down, and my jaw worked. They could have done a lot worse.

The woods floor was moss and ferns and lycopodium, hemlock scrub, rocks, myrtle. I pushed up again, fighting the dull knives beneath my skin. That I could straighten my spine I counted as a victory.

I gingerly probed at my chest. Kidneys . . . hard to tell. Lungs? Clear. My lips were crusted.

I had to get myself to the hospital. Crawl to the roadway, flag down a car.

I managed to shift to my knees and right hand, hugging my left to my belly. The knuckles were swollen and my wrist throbbed.

I got to my feet and swayed there, wincing. A fall would be hard to take. I felt my face and scalp with my hand. No open wounds—except for a crease and a knot at the back of my head. That one was still wet.

They'd dumped me down a bank off a back road not all that far, probably, from that decrepit deer camp. My wallet and my wristwatch were gone. I shuffled slowly about ten feet through the ferns and duff up to the edge of the gravel. I wobbled there and forced myself to find the sun. It was around two o'clock.

Neither direction looked promising—just sun-splashed ferns and mixed timber on both sides of the road. I couldn't have walked much farther than a hundred yards, anyway. So I waited, swaying on my feet, half nauseated, vaguely listening to the breeze in the crowns of the beeches and a vireo in the distance. Taking short, shallow breaths. The pulse in my torso felt like a function of the beating I'd walked into. When I closed my eyes, as I had to do periodically, the world felt less harsh but more tenuous.

After a while, I started to hear a vehicle coming toward me from the east. I tried brushing the forest debris from my arms and legs but gave up. My vision was improving. A red

Mitsubishi coupe appeared around a bend, trailing dust, and braked abruptly at the sight of the strange person standing by the side of the road. It rolled to a stop beside me. Mass plates.

The driver was a young blond woman with skinny eyebrows and too much green eye shadow. She stared at me through her open sunroof. Another young blonde sat beside her. "You need help?" she said.

"Thank you for stopping," I said, trying to sound reassuring somehow. "Would either of you happen to have a cell phone?"

"Did you have an accident? You have a lot of blood on you."

"I'm afraid I did have an accident. I'm a law enforcement officer, and I need to get myself to the hospital."

"We're not from here. We're looking for Lois and Eric Krassner's? They have Morgans?"

"We are so lost," said the other one.

"Does either of you have a cell phone?" I asked again.

The passenger leaned around the driver and said, "You want us to call an ambulance?"

"That would be good of you, or you could let me use your phone. Either way." I felt light-headed. I steadied myself against the sports car's roof.

The second girl was saying, "Yes, hello? Yes, we're uh . . . I actually have no clue where we are, but there's this guy here on the road and he's had an accident. Yup. Linda Nichols. Uh-huh. Yes, he's talking and walking and everything, but he looks— No. No, he's a law enforcement officer, and we were— OK. Sure." She leaned across the driver's lap to offer me the phone. "Here, you better talk to her."

"Hello, this is Hector Bellevance. I'm out on a back road east of Allenburg in the Hardscrabble Hills area. Can you get a bead on me using this cell signal?"

"We can try. What's your condition?"

"Few broken bones, some blood loss, concussion, may need a few stitches. Possible internal bleeding."

The dispatcher told me to hold the line while she sent a crew in my direction. "You keep your phone on," she said.

I pressed in my home number, intending just to leave a quick message for Hugh, but he picked it up.

"Hugh?"

"Hector! She's back, Hector, she's here."

I had to catch hold of the roof of the car again. "Is she all right?"

"Yes, I think she is—physically, as far as I can tell. She's asleep or I'd put her on. Do you want me to wake her up?"

"No, no, let her sleep. When did she get home?"

"About eleven, eleven thirty. She hasn't said very much. She's pretty discombobulated. You can imagine."

"Did she say who she was with, where she spent last night?"

"No, she didn't."

"How did she get back home?"

"She just appeared at the top of the path while I was picking berries. I ran up and hugged her, but she—well, she responded, but she's depressed. All she said was, 'Where's Dad?' I said I wasn't sure, probably the hospital, and I asked if she wanted me to take her there, but she didn't."

"Did she tell you anything?"

"No. She said not to bother asking her a bunch of questions, because she has promised not to say a word about her abduction."

"Shit, Hugh. She said that?"

"Not in so many words. Her 'experience,' she called it. 'I can't say one single word about my experience.' "

"Tell me, how did she look?"

"Dirty and exhausted. Her eyes were red. Her hair was messy. And she smelled bad."

"My God." Underneath the pain, my relief was turning into something else. Despair. Dread.

"Where are you?" he asked.

"I'm on the road. Anything else?"

"Your man Rob Tierney called this morning. He wants you to know he's sick, and he's at his place in Bellows Falls if you need to reach him. You have that number?"

"Hang on to it. I'll be home soon." I was fading.

A few minutes later Allenburg Rescue came flying up out of the valley, a welcome riot of lights. I thanked my down-country rescuers and surrendered myself to the EMTs.

"YOU SURE that's a smart thing to do?" Hugh said. He had turned, hearing the squeak of a cork being drawn from a bottle of pinot grigio.

"I'm sure it isn't. But I'm on a roll."

He sighed. He was stir-frying green beans with ginger. "Time to rouse the young lady, I guess."

"Better you than me. Let her know what to expect, will you?"

He nodded and placed the lid on the wok. I didn't want my bruised and swollen face to be any more of a shock to her than it had to be. I had a wad of gauze taped to the back of my head and an ice pack fixed to my left arm with a compression wrap. I'd managed to shave and shower, but I looked like I'd been through an earthquake, and every sinew in my back and chest was taut with sawing pain.

After a short time Hugh emerged from Myra's room with a thumbs-up. "She'll be joining us. Give her a few minutes while she hits the head." He winked. "If you'll excuse the expression."

"Don't . . ." I said. I couldn't laugh.

When she appeared in her doorway in shorts and a camp T-shirt, the hardest thing was to keep myself from sweeping her up in my arms and spinning her around. The skin beneath her clear green eyes was discolored, and she had a few bug bites, but otherwise she looked fine—no scrapes or contusions that I could see.

"Oh, Myra," I said, tearing up. I kissed her at arm's length. "I'd hug you if I could."

"God, Dad. Pie Yandow did that to you?"

I nodded.

"How come?"

"I blundered into a criminal operation he's been running, and he took offense."

"He could have *killed* you."

"No doubt." I asked her to come out into the living room where we could sit and talk for a minute before Hugh put supper on the table.

She flopped onto the blue beanbag chair by the fireplace. It seemed a wonder to see her like this—the same! Though nothing was the same. Late-day sunbeams filled the room.

Glass in hand, grimacing, I lowered myself to the arm of the couch and took a swallow of the wine, grateful to be able to taste it.

"You're a hurtin' unit, Dad."

"Looks bad, I know, but I'll recover."

"How could you let that happen?"

I stopped myself from shrugging. "Guess my luck broke the wrong way."

"I mean, what were you even doing *talking* to him—if you were all done working for the egg farm guy?"

"I was looking for you, Myra."

The cat padded across the rug and stepped up carefully into Myra's lap. She had her gaze aimed out the window. "Well," she said, "that was completely useless."

"Hindsight's twenty-twenty."

"What did he say when you said you quit?"

"Who, Tuttle? I don't know. What did he say, Hugh?"

"I never reached him," Hugh said from the other side of the fieldstone chimney. "I spoke with his assistant, a Ms. Doncaster, and I gave her your message."

"Did she say anything?"

"She said that the provisions contained in your written understanding would be suspended, and I said OK, and she thanked me."

Myra sat up. "Does that mean he's not going to pay Mom's medical bills?"

"That's not clear," I said, "but it's nothing for you to worry about. We're just lucky we're all here."

"No kidding."

"I'm going to ask you some questions, Myra."

"That's nice of you, and I totally get why you want to. But I wouldn't bother."

"How do you feel?"

"With my fingers."

"Sweetheart, please."

"I don't *know* how I feel. I am mixed up about a lot of stuff, OK?"

"Did this abduction begin at the hospital?"

"Dad." She shook her head.

"Where's your twenty-two?"

"I lost it."

"They took it from you?"

"I *lost* it."

Only a wheelgun aficionado would see the value in that old rimfire. Still, they'd have to be exceptionally stupid to pawn the thing. Though you never knew. I'd put a trace on it. "Did they abuse you in any way?"

She looked miserable.

"Myra, that is the one question you're going to have to answer."

"They didn't abuse me. They didn't even *touch* me, OK?"

"Would you like to see a doctor?"

"No."

"All right. But I'll be making an appointment for you with a psychologist we know. Evelyn Mackey. Whatever you discuss with her will be entirely between the two of you."

"Don't waste your money."

"Myra—"

"Dad! Stop, OK? Please."

"I'll stop. But first I'm going to tell you something, and I want you to hear me out."

She said nothing.

"These people, the people who kidnapped you and held you hostage, are some of the most despicable people on the planet. They are killers and worse. They deserve no consideration here, Myra. They—"

"I *knew* you'd never get it, and I was right. All you're about is catching the evildoers. Gotta get those bad guys! Woo-hoo! Lock 'em up! Well, you know what? You can't *catch* all the bad guys! It's like catching all the lightning bugs. You can't do it! And you know what else? It's not the number one thing in life! It's not even top ten. Look out there." She threw her arm toward the broad bow window and its eastward view across the tops of the conifers and Tipton's steeples to the dome of the mountain against the sky. "Look at the *good* stuff in the world. Look at your gardens, your blueberry bushes. Look at Mom up there just trying to *talk*. Dad, you know what she would say right now? She'd say—"

"*Enough!* Hold it *right there!*" I grimaced—not good to raise my voice. I said gently, "I admire your point of view. And I realize you've made a promise in exchange for your freedom. I also realize, believe it or not, that I can't catch all the bad guys." I paused. "But whenever some slimeball slips into my orbit I'm going to take notice, Myra, and if whatever he's into threatens anyone I care about, I'm going to put an end to it."

"Did you put an end to Seb Tuttle?"

"No, Myra. The people who kidnapped you did that."

She sighed. "You know what, Dad? If farming's not enough for you, maybe you oughta coach basketball or something."

"Soup's on, kiddos," Hugh said.

She scrambled up, and the cat leaped away.

At the curly maple dining table, at the end of that perfect day in July, over bowls of Hugh's cream of shiitake soup, I raised my glass of wine. Hugh lifted his seltzer and Myra her cranberry juice.

"On this summer evening," I said, "we have much more to be thankful for than we have to be frightened of, so let's praise those good things, our homes and families and friends, and the earth we share with the flora and the fauna. And let's bear in mind that these good things sometimes must be defended. Because they have their enemies, and our devotion to the good things makes us vulnerable to their loss."

"Here's to the good things," Hugh said.

"And to their enemies," I said.

Myra gave me a curious look. "Their enemies?"

I nodded.

Hugh and I watched her.

"To the enemies of the good things," she said finally. "May they burn in hell. Or wherever."

"Here's to Wherever," Hugh said. "May it prove a nice place to hang when eternity rolls around."

After supper I took the phone out onto the porch and called the barracks to tell the dispatcher—not Tulley now, but someone I didn't know—that my daughter, Myra, was no longer missing; she was home safe. "Good news, then!" the officer said. I said, yes, it certainly was.

After that I got Rob Tierney on the line.

"Food poisoning," he told me. "Hit me a couple miles shy of the Putney exit. Sara had to come get me."

"Hell. How are you doing now?"

"All right. I hear Myra came home."

Hugh had relayed this news. "It's frustrating, Rob. She *knows* who these fuckers are, but they made her promise not to talk, and she's holding to it."

"That happens. Give her time. She OK?"

"Physically, yes, I believe she is. For the rest, it's too soon to say."

"Right. How's Wilma?"

"Making progress. She's heard nothing about the kidnapping."

"Hope not. Heck, I have to ask. Are you sure it was a kidnapping?"

"No doubt, none at all."

"OK. So what are you going to do?"

"I'm going to nail them, Rob."

"How can I help?"

"First, what about Pie Yandow and the ATF investigation?"

"Oh, Christ. That's a catastrophe. Somebody tripped up or jumped too soon, I don't know what happened, but you got all the brass up there right now—Bennett, Swindak, Kitchener. . . . They'll get it figured out, I guess, but right at this moment it's insane."

"Anybody hurt?"

"Not that I've heard, but I guess the cock-a-roaches are bookin' big-time."

"They get Yandow?"

"I don't know as they got anybody yet. There is no joy in Mudville, mister, I'll tell you that."

"That's too bad."

"Yeah. So on these kidnappers, you gonna wait for Myra to unbend for you or what's your plan?"

"I'm not about to press her."

"No. What's next?"

"They grabbed her out of the hospital, I believe, and so there should be a record of their entering and leaving that building."

"You looking into that?"

"First thing tomorrow."

"Well, good luck with that. I'll be in the office till about noon if you need anything."

"Good to know."

"Hector, before I let you go. . . . This type situation, when you have strong personal feelings behind what you're trying to do and you're all alone, you want to be sure you don't get too far out ahead of yourself, you know?"

Too late for that. "Thanks," I said.

"What I'm saying, you need a second opinion, backup, whatever, you *call* me. OK?"

"I will," I said.

It was dusk. A muscle spasm jolted me, and the stars blurred. I could hear the slap of Hugh's sandals behind me as he came out onto the porch with two mugs of tea. "Do I take it you're not going to report this second attempt on your life?"

"I can't."

"Because he'll kill you if you do?"

"It's more complicated than that."

"I am not reassured."

I shook my head. "She in bed?"

"Couldn't tell you. Her door's closed."

"What do you think?"

"I think it's good that she'll be seeing a psychologist. The sooner the better."

"Hugh, tell me this: while Myra was missing, did you by chance do any remote locating?" Hugh sometimes dowsed maps as well as physical terrain.

"Is the pope Catholic?"

"And?"

"Inconclusive. All I had was a topo, and the scale just wasn't fine enough. Either she wasn't far from here—roughly a two-mile radius—or maybe my being inside her home warped the emanations I was receiving."

"So either she wasn't far from here, or she was."

"Hey, you asked. If I had any useful information, you know I wouldn't keep it from you."

"Yes, thanks. You're a saint."

"And you're in no condition to be rounding up sinners."

I nodded. "I could use some morphine."

"You could use a testosterone suppressant."

We stood in the twilight as Virgo emerged in the west. A band of coyotes in the slough by the defunct sawmill was trying to teach their pups how to sing. Not far from the spot where Myra had found those two late-season fawns. Was that only Monday?

Hugh tossed the dregs of his tea and said he guessed he'd be back in the morning at about seven. He reached up and rubbed my shoulder. "Go to bed," he said. "Take your pills and go to bed."

TWENTY

THE TOWN HALL'S DREARY basement was cool on this muggy Sunday morning. A veil of dust particles twinkled in the sunbeams angling through the well windows. Esther had explained over the phone how to get into her email's in-box to download the trail cam image, and now I sat upright at the clerk's desk contemplating the crooked, grainy snapshot of two male figures moving away from the camera, briskly, it seemed, as the twilight was seeping fast from the mostly obscured sky. The time stamp read 8:28 P.M. They had another thirty minutes in the darkening woods before they'd make it out to the apron below the dam. I enlarged the image and printed a couple of copies to take with me.

There was no jacked deer on a pole—these two guys weren't carrying anything. This discrepancy wasn't on Koslowski. He had no reason to lie to me. He'd played up the gutted doe only because Curtis had invented that detail to galvanize his case for cutting me off. Small man, that Warden Curtis. Koslowski had the woodland cammies right, or partly right. The stocky figure to the left, the one nearer the camera, had on a camo-mottled poncho, a backwards cap, and a camelback hydration system. The taller, lanky one to the right was wearing a nylon shell in a dark color. You couldn't see their faces or tell their hair color or even distinguish the type of footwear they wore, and yet a few details stood out. The backwards cap belonging to the heavier one had a shield-shaped emblem on it, but, enlarged, it was too fuzzy to read. He wore a sheath knife on his belt. The lankier one in front had on a small bluish or grayish backpack. The weight of it tugged the yoke of his loose jacket down off his shoulders to expose his shirt, which had a row of three white arches across the back.

I pulled up Google and typed in the words I'd copied from the side of the boxy Chinese contraption in the basement of the house on Ridgeway. Several sites popped up. The first took me straight to the Longkou Jenming Machinery Company's colorful Web page, with animated letters against a drawing of towering blue skyscrapers. The site confirmed what I'd guessed—the machine was a small-scale pulp-molding machine—it made egg trays. "An advance technique with international adoption of this machine combines the fulfillment experience that our factory has with much research to tray manufacture but now become, the domestic technique and quantities is the one and only. Have already sold many go toward whole country everyplace, and export many nation." Scrolling down through the tangled descriptions of several models, I found Melissa's: "Our small farm type egg tray machine, number one Traymaker 72, very advance, have won more praise from both overseas buyers and domestic clients in Shandong, Hebei, Dongbei and other provinces."

I called home. Myra answered.

"How are you feeling this morning, sweetheart?"

"Good. Hungry. You're not at the farmers' market, are you?"

"No, I'm in no shape for that this weekend. Is Hugh handy or is he outside somewhere?" I'd left him with a list of chores.

"I guess, I don't know. I'm fixing a bagel."

"OK. As soon as he's got the van loaded, he'll be taking you in and dropping you off with Mom while he makes deliveries. I'm going to meet you at the hospital around noon."

"So where are you now?"

"Town offices."

"How come?"

"Just catching up on some business. Listen, I'm going to get you in to see Evelyn Mackey this afternoon, if I can."

"That psychologist?"

"Yes, you've met her at the market. She's one of our regulars."

"So, hold it, if you're not coming here to get me, what are you going to be doing?"

"Do you want me to come get you?"

She didn't answer at first. I heard the teakettle's whistle die as she lifted it from the burner. "You said you would quit."

"Yes, and I did quit."

"Right. You quit and then you *un*-quit?"

I listened to her pour the water into her tea mug. "Give me their names, Myra."

"What if you got *killed?* What if I told you something, and because of that you got killed?"

"I promise you I will not get killed."

"You can't make promises like that. You can't control the future."

"I'll have lots of help, Myra. I won't be taking these people down by myself."

"That just proves it."

"What?"

"You still can't focus on *us*—me and Mom, or the farm, or

any other consequences. You're just focusing on your own self."

"What other consequences?"

"Say you arrested them, OK? Say they got sentenced to jail. Even if they *did* kill the egg man, which they didn't, they wouldn't get locked up forever, and when they got out, do you know what could happen to whoever put them in there?"

"I'll tell you what *would* happen. Nothing."

"Oh, right. That's another promise?" Her temperament was intact. "Uh-oh. Dad, you know what? Those two detectives are back."

"Ingersoll and Koslowski?"

"Yeah. They're walking up from the greenhouse, it looks like." I could hear her leaning up to the wide window over the kitchen sink. "Dad, are they coming here to *question* me?"

"You mean about the kidnapping?"

"They're not going to arrest me, are they?"

"No, sweetheart, no. They're coming to see me, not you."

"What do they want you for?"

"Information. But listen now. If they ask for me, you don't know where I went and you don't think I'll be back anytime soon, all right?"

"Why? You just told me you were getting *help*. Who are you getting help from? Spud?"

"Myra—"

"They're here," she said. "'Bye."

Evelyn Mackey picked up on the first ring.

"Evelyn. It's Hector Bellevance. Have you got a moment?"

"I was just on my way out the door, but sure. What's up?"

"I won't keep you." As briefly as I could, I described what Myra and I had been through in the last week and ended by saying I hoped she could make some time today to talk with the girl, because she wouldn't talk with me.

"What do you mean?" she asked in a sharper voice. "She won't talk at all?"

"No, no, she's talking, but she can't— She won't answer my questions."

"Is she there, Hector? I would say a word to her now, please, as long as she might feel open to that."

"No, I'm— I'm not home right now. You can reach her up at the cabin if you want to—but not right at this moment. I believe the state police are there."

"Right *now*, you mean? Myra's at home talking to the police and you're not there with her?"

"Right. I was speaking with her just now, and she—"

"Wait. Hector, where *are* you?"

"I'm at the town offices in Tipton."

"Yeesh. OK, tell me if I have this right. Myra just got released yesterday by some kidnappers who are still at large, and you left her at home to deal with the police by herself?"

"No, Hugh Gebbie's there with her. Evelyn, don't scold me. The situation is more complicated than it seems."

"How complicated is looking after your *child*? Sorry—" She reined herself in. "Sorry, Hector. All right, let's do it. How's one o'clock? My office is on Jackson Terrace."

Last, I looked up Nick's Small Engine. Nick answered. I asked him if he'd mind putting Jimmy on the line. *Who is this?* he demanded. Soon as I told him he hung up.

I had to head home. There was a part of Myra I would never quite adjust to, that contrary and obdurate part of her that was all Wilma and then some—Wilma squared. I changed my mind about driving in to Allenburg to show Rob Tierney the trail cam image. I could reach him by phone— and maybe he'd make the time to come out.

Allowing the detectives twenty minutes up at the cabin seemed generous. They had plenty to do elsewhere—Ingersoll wouldn't wait around for me. I parked my truck to the side of Sullivan's Store, out of sight of the road, and went in for our mail. My face drew a few stares.

I had just made myself a cup of coffee when one of the four burly, crew-cut college jocks who had been horsing around in front of the beer cooler backed into me.

I grunted and caught myself against the coffee counter.

The kid turned and grabbed me to keep me from falling over. I grunted again, gritting my teeth.

"What's wrong, buddy? You OK?"

"Let go," I said on the exhale. He had his hand on the square butt of my Walther. I knocked it away.

His eyebrows went up. "Yo, check it, the guy's packin'!" He gave my shoulder a playful punch. "What're you packin' a gun for, old man?"

"Somehow, fella, I don't feel like explaining myself to you."

He put on a hurt look. His sunburned pals were entertained, so he said, "Seriously, man, this is *God's* country. How often do you think people get killed around here?"

"Once," I said. I took up my mail.

As I headed toward the exit, one of his friends said, "Ooo, Kenny. K-O, dude."

AS MUCH as it hurt just to ease myself in and out of my truck, that I could do it at all seemed worth celebrating. Compared to bleeding out in the woods or lying in the ICU unconscious and hooked up to life support, getting away with just three fractured ribs, a badly sprained left hand, a concussion, some scrapes and contusions—that was nothing. I'd get better. My spleen and liver were unharmed and my lungs hadn't been punctured. The two doctors who'd examined me both remarked on my natural sturdiness, but more than my own resilience I figured I had Yandow's prudence and foresight to thank.

Just before our turnout, I met Hugh and Myra in the white delivery van headed in the opposite direction. We stopped beside each other in the road. Hugh rolled down his window. On the other side of him Myra aimed her gaze straight ahead. It troubled her to look at me.

"You two headed in already?"

"Yep. Got my work cut out for me." Hugh picked up my clipboard of order sheets off the seat and waggled it. They were yesterday's deliveries.

"You going to the co-op first?" The Morning Glory Natural Foods Co-op in North Allenburg, my primary wholesale customer, was on the route to the hospital.

"Sullivan's first, then the co-op. Then the young lady and I will drop in on Wilma Strong, and after that I make a swing out—" He looked at the clipboard. "Out the center road to Peabody's and points east."

"Thanks, Hugh."

"Your man Ingersoll stopped by the cabin looking for you."

"So I hear. How did he seem?"

"Oh . . . intense, I'd say. How did he seem, Myra?"

"Ticked off."

I peered across at Myra. "Did the detectives ask where you've been?"

"All he said was he was glad I wasn't still missing."

"Neither one of them asked you about being kidnapped and held hostage by some bad people?"

She didn't answer.

"It was a fairly brisk little encounter," Hugh explained. "Ingersoll said that when I saw you I should tell you to call him immediately and stay put."

"Guess I just missed you, then."

"You must've. Rob Tierney called, too."

"And?"

"Same thing. Get in touch and don't leave your place."

"Sounds like they're on the same page. Listen, I'll join you at noontime at the hospital, all right? And Myra—don't leave Mom's room. You hear me?"

She made an OK sign.

I REACHED ROB TIERNEY at the state's attorney's office on the second floor of the federal building in Allenburg, where he spent most mornings doing paperwork.

"Hector! Where are you, Hector—home?"

"I've got the trail cam images of the two deerjackers. I'd like you to have a look at them, if you've got a spare ten minutes."

"Hector. You didn't mention to me that somebody kicked the shit out of you yesterday."

"No, I guess not, but that'll be hard to miss when you see me. How'd you hear?"

"You didn't file charges, either. You didn't even call it in. How come?"

"What's wrong?"

"Goddamn it, you're not *talking* to me!" He was not happy. "Jesus, I laid it all out for you yesterday about us being *blindsided* in this undercover operation that just blew up in our friggin' faces—I'm talking both sides of the border now—and you don't say *shit* to me about it, when *you're* the clown that lit the fuse!"

"I apologize for that."

He heaved a sigh. "Do you realize what this makes us *look* like up here? Ingersoll wants your *nuts,* buddy!"

"So you grabbed Yandow?"

"Shit, man, Yandow's done. Yandow's dead, Heck."

My scalp buzzed. "How?"

"Ka-boom to the cabeza."

"Who's the shooter?"

"Unknown. They found him in there when they moved on the lab."

"When was this?"

"Early this morning."

"And he was dead when they got there?"

"One hundred percent headless, from the sound of it."

"Any other DOAs?"

"Don't know. It's a work in progress."

"I can imagine. So where is this lab?"

"Where is what?"

"The lab."

"You're kiddin' me. You *invaded* the damn place yesterday morning—*after* you got done casing it."

"Three-twenty-three Ridgeway?"

"What Ridgeway?"

"Or do you mean the furniture barn?"

"You didn't know?"

"Rob, I didn't go in there looking for Yandow. I was looking for the people who killed Tuttle, because they had *my child.*"

"Tuttle! Jesus Christ, Hector, Tuttle was *nothing* to these people. He bought a couple eight balls off one of the stockroom guys that worked there, maybe some pot, but *that was it.* He was nothing but a punk."

"He was also retailing crystal for Yandow, Rob."

"Bullshit. Who told you this?"

"Local kid named Jimmy Lussier. Seb Tuttle had him making bicycle deliveries to buyers down at the fishing access."

"Lussier. That the kid that found the body?"

"That's right, and I interviewed Henderson's daughter. She works in the office there in the afternoon. She had an encounter with a couple of tweakers she saw cruising the RV park more than once. Also a couple of Hells. They said they were looking for Seb."

"This would be Kandi Henderson?"

"Smart woman."

"Kandi Henderson's a troubled individual, Hector, which I'm sure you're aware of."

"Meaning what?"

"Plus she's not exactly a big fan of law enforcement."

"After what law enforcement's put her through, that's not exactly a surprise. She knows a tweaker when she sees one."

"No argument there." He paused. "Listen, man, just in case I didn't already get this across to you, you're in very deep shit."

"For what?"

"For what? For giving up a federal investigation to two of its major targets. Who then took a good look at their situation and concluded it was time to boogie. Which resulted in a number of pieces falling through the cracks—most importantly, Everett Murphy himself."

"So they had a bug in the furniture place?"

"Phone tap. The quality is for shit, but some tech nerd waved a wand over it. It's you."

"You heard it?"

"Yeah, Heck, and I gotta say I am disappointed in you. You go in there to rag on these jokers and you end up shit-canning the whole show."

"After Ronnie DiGuilio busts a load of shot over my head."

"That's an excuse?"

"I don't need an excuse. First time I ran into DiGuilio he was at Seb Tuttle's RV at the White Birches. So he connects Tuttle to Everett. If the feds were sitting on Seb's killers because they had too much invested in a bigger score down the road, my daughter's kidnapping reordered their priorities."

"You're a better detective than that, Hector."

"You think I'm wrong about Tuttle and Everett?"

"You're wrong about who beat the punk to death. Murphy, Yandow, DiGuilio, and them, even if they had a good reason to pop the guy, they're not that stupid."

"Anybody could have paid a couple of tweakers to go wild on the guy."

"Sure they could, but *why*? Why whack Seb Tuttle?"

He was right. "We're still on the same team here, aren't we?"

"Sure we are. But, jeez, man, you really stepped in it this time."

"Do me a favor?"

"Christ. What?"

"Would you put in a call to whoever's managing security today at the regional hospital and tell him I'm on my way there for a look at some of their video records? Tell him I'll be grateful for their cooperation."

After a moment, he said, "Give it a rest, will you, Hector? Your girl's home safe, and both of you are hurtin' . . . Just give it a rest." Then he hung up the phone.

Inside her closet, Myra's laundry hamper was spilling over, and I realized with a pang that no one had done any wash in a week, not since before Wilma's accident. What had she been wearing that morning? These green shorts—the same pair she'd had on the day before—and that lavender T-shirt from the Susan B. Anthony Women's Leadership Center in upstate New York, a gift from an old friend of Wilma's. I carried them into the light.

The hips and seat of her shorts bore patches of worked-in dirt, as if she'd had to sit and lie on a rough floor or on the ground itself. They smelled of wood smoke.

No semen stains. No traces of blood that I could see. Bits of debris—and mineral flecks—and the smudges of a chalky substance on the back of the T-shirt and on both shoulders showed she'd slept in her clothes that night, probably on a rough floor, in some barn or a shed. Inside her waistband and front pockets she'd picked up a few coarse hairs—from live-stock of some kind, or maybe a dog. She hadn't been held in an ordinary house—not in any clean, weatherized shelter. These residues could be analyzed and the hairs and traces identified, something I would arrange for, but for now all I could do was segregate the articles in separate paper bags and push on.

ON MY WAY UP to the farm, I spotted Spud's dark blue Toyota Tundra on the rise above his Christmas tree field, some twenty rolling acres of Fraser firs and balsams. He had a small crew out there pruning the six-foot trees, a seasonal job I knew he wanted to put behind him before the corn maze was ready for business. One of the workers, I saw, was Lyle.

Spud glanced over at the sound of my truck in the lane and walked up to meet me on the rise, carrying a pair of long-handled loppers.

"Detective Ingersoll find you?" he asked.

"Not yet."

"He come up to the barn looking for you, and he was all—" He halted. "*What* in holy hell happened to *you?*"

I gave him the story as succinctly as possible, omitting mention of Myra's kidnapping, and he kept lifting the Massey Ferguson cap off his head and running his sap-stained fingers through his hair, saying, "Jee-zuss!"

We were both waving off the deerflies.

"Man oh man! So what's it like gettin' Tasered?" he wanted to know.

"It's pretty debilitating."

He snorted and said, "I'll just bet. Well, *damn*, ain't some-body gonna go and arrest that son of a bitch?"

I went on to tell him how Yandow had been discovered shot to death last night in a meth lab in Coös Crossing—

"*Goddamn!*" he breathed, wide-eyed. "I just saw that in

the paper! But it didn't say anybody got shot. Wait—" He reached into the cab of his pickup for a copy of the *Eagle,* our slim, inconsequential daily. The front page bore a large, street-level photo of the furniture building down on the river with a dense wedge of smoke ballooning out of its north gable and two fire hoses sending fans of water through a block-and-tackle doorway high under the peak of the roof. I skimmed the story.

HIDDEN METH LAB DISCOVERED
AFTER BUILDING CATCHES FIRE

The Vermont State Police, the Montcalm County Sheriff's Department, and federal agents of the Drug Enforcement Administration were called in late Saturday night after local firefighters responding to a blaze at Coös New and Used Furniture in Coös Crossing found what police say was a clandestine lab for the manufacture of methamphetamines or "crystal."

Alerted by a passing motorist, fire departments from Coös Crossing and Allenburg responded to the call just after 1 A.M. Coös Crossing Fire Chief Danny Masure said the timely cell-phone call and the quick action of his volunteers, along with the town's new class A pumper/tanker, should be credited with saving the commercial structure from total ruin. The cause of the fire is under investigation, according to state police spokesman Sergeant Pete Tulley.

After the fire was suppressed, firemen came across the hazardous chemicals in the stone-walled basement below the showroom and storage barns. The quantity and hazardous nature of the materials caused sheriff's deputies to evacuate two village apartment buildings. Early Sunday morning, police obtained a search warrant, and a hazmat team moved in to clear out the old wooden building.

Several local individuals are facing possible charges of production of methamphetamine and possession for the purpose of trafficking. The building and the furniture business are owned by Maurice Poutre, a longtime resident of the town. Occupants of the two evacuated nearby apartment buildings in the village would be allowed to move back in Sunday morning, according to Sergeant Tulley.

At the scene early this morning along with federal drug agents were Gilman Bennett, State Commissioner of Public Safety, Simon Swindak, Director of the State Police, Medical Examiner Martin Griswold, Lieutenant Tim McDowd, head of the Drug Task Force, Mike Gillingwater, Chief Fire Investigator, and Major Virgil P. Kitchener, Commander of the State Bureau of Criminal Investigation.

About 20 pounds of meth worth more than $500,000 on the street were found on the premises and seized. Chemicals and equipment in place suggested the clandestine lab had been producing substantial quantities of the illegal stimulant for many weeks, Sergeant Tulley said.

"They're not ready to release anything about Yandow," I said. "I'm sure Griswold hadn't even looked at him yet."

"Hold on," Spud said. "I just thought of something. What if Ingersoll thinks it was *you* killed Yandow?"

"He might."

He laughed. "Wow, but this is some hairy-ass shit, Heck! *Goddamn.* Guys cooking up methamphetamines down under that old stable? I mean, *crystal meth*? I can hardly imagine it."

"It's a plague, and that's no exaggeration."

"I hear you, but how many dirtbags do we have around here that actually use that shit? You can't tell me we got enough meth-heads in Montcalm County to support a whole friggin' lab."

"We don't have enough quiche eaters in the county to support the egg factory, either."

"So you're saying these people were cookin' the stuff here and shippin' it up across?"

"I'm betting the Hells put this together. Same kind of thing the Mexican gangs have going out west—deliver the ingredients to some out-of-the-way farmhouse in Indiana or Colorado, then ship the finished product someplace else for distribution. Hard to detect if your channels are secure." I spotted Lyle ambling toward us up the slope.

"So is that who you think did Yandow? The Hells Angels?"

"They're on the list for sure."

Folded into my notebook I had two copies of the trail cam image I'd printed on the best paper I could find in Esther Nichols's supplies closet. I took one out and smoothed it on the hood of my Silverado.

"What do you think?"

"What of? This? It's two guys in the woods."

"Look close. Tell me if anything stands out."

He leaned over and peered at the print. "Well, looks like old-growth hardwoods with a lot of understory, lot of hobblebush. They're walking alongside a trout brook looks like, and one of 'em's wearin' a little pack, and the other one's got one of them waterbags on his back." He shrugged. "Looks like a couple hikers to me."

"Game warden says they're deerjackers. I think they're the two guys who tried to firebomb my cabin."

"No shit. How come?"

I told him how I'd traced their course through my woodlot and down over the ridge and how, by taking the trail cam, I'd foiled Warden Curtis's scheme for trapping his poachers. Unless these two were his poachers after all.

"I never knew you were that good of a tracker, Hector."

Lyle came up beside us, flushed, his long hair flopping like wings on either side of his face.

"Tracking people isn't hard if the sign's fresh," I said. "As long as they aren't lost, people tend to take the easiest route."

"OK, but . . . damn, I mean, you really think this is them?"

"I do."

"Well, hell, it's too bad you didn't get a better picture, you know what I'm sayin'? Like if they were closer."

"Yeah. Though if they'd been closer, they might have seen the camera."

He nodded, staring at the image, while Lyle stared at me. "Damn, did you get in a fight, Hector?"

"Wish I could say I had."

"Why, what happened? And how come you're not down at the farmers' market?" He'd come up to fetch a jug of Gatorade from a cooler in the truck. Deerflies were circling his head like satellites.

"Your dad'll explain."

He turned to Spud. "What're you lookin' at?" He leaned over to inspect the photo. "Who's them guys?"

"Can't tell," Spud said. He was about to say more, but I raised a palm to stay him.

"Know what?" Lyle said. "The big one in back almost looks like Kurt Mooney."

"What makes you say that?" I asked.

He gestured with his chin. "The army jacket. With the hood. That's what he used to always wear, that jacket from Desert Storm with the lightning bolt patch on the sleeve. Plus he has a hat like that, too, with the lightning bolt on it, but you're not allowed to wear a hat when you're in the building."

"You know Kurt Mooney?"

He shrugged. "Just from in school."

"Kind of a tough hombre, from what I hear."

"I don't know how tough he is, but he's been homeless ever since the end of mud season. I guess his mom kicked him out. She's a drug addict."

"He's homeless?" Spud said. "Come off it. Who told you that?"

"He's *homeless,* Dad."

"Who does Kurt Mooney hang out with, Lyle?" I said. "You have any idea?"

He shrugged. "I saw him outside Subway one time with a couple weirdos from the Whetstone School. They're Goths, like."

"Goths?" Spud said. "What's that? You mean like devil worshippers?"

"You are so ignorant, Dad. They're *anarchists.*"

"You know their names, Lyle?"

"No. Well, one of 'em's Mason. Mason Gulick."

I glanced at Spud. "Take another look, Lyle. Tell me what else you see."

He set the Gatorade on the hood of my truck and picked up the photo. Squinting, lips compressed in concentration, he said, "I don't know." Then he said, "Randy Moss!" and he chuckled.

"Who?"

He pointed to the figure in front, the one whose weighty pack had drawn the collar of his windbreaker off his shoulders. With a finger Lyle traced the three white arches across the yoke of the shirt, and then I saw it—they were the tops of three uppercase letters. "You can't see the M," Lyle said, "but see, that's O, S, S. It's Randy Moss!"

Wide receiver for the New England Patriots. "Good eye there, Lyle."

"So what's it about, Kurt Mooney and Randy Moss?" He looked at Spud, then at me.

I said, "Fish and Wildlife thinks these could be the guys who've been jacking deer lately up in the town forest."

"Wow. If that *is* Kurt Mooney, don't go telling him I'm the one said it was him."

"Don't worry, Lyle."

I could feel their eyes on me as I inserted my frame delicately behind the wheel of the Silverado.

Spud frowned. "Your ribs are broke, aren't they?"

"Only three of 'em."

He shook his head. "Friggin' Chuck Yeager. So how's our Myra holding up under all this?"

"Hell, you know Myra."

"Yeah," he said. "Girl takes after her dad. Ironman."

Myra's stoicism was an attribute I hadn't given much thought to, but on my way down the hill toward the village I realized that unless she broke her pledge not to say a word to anyone about her ordeal, I could show no cause for sabotaging the ATF takedown. But she would loosen up. In time. Something more than fear was enforcing her silence. They had engaged her sympathies. She felt *gratitude.* A return of trust. Maybe even some perverse respect, depending on the story they'd spun for her.

Or else she was completely terror-stricken. *Evelyn,* I said to myself. Evelyn would have a way to reach her.

If Rob was right and Seb Tuttle was nothing more than a punk who'd made a couple of drug buys from Ronnie or Everett or maybe Melissa, then Jimmy Lussier's story was not just a fabrication, it was a ploy. Not just some smart-ass kid's load of crap but a smoke screen produced to hide something bigger. What? Hell, he was just a *kid.*

It was close to noon.

Making it to the hospital in time to pick up Myra and get

her to Evelyn's office on Jackson Terrace by one o'clock was not going to happen. The kid, rangy Jimmy Lussier, was now a more immediate concern. In that snapshot stuck by a heart-shaped magnet to his mother's refrigerator, he'd been wearing a blue-and-silver Patriots jersey, number 81 on his chest.

Number 81. Randy Moss.

TWENTY-ONE

I PULLED IN TO THE repair shop yard to find Nick Verlander outside helping a customer unload a venerable Lawn-Boy from her hatchback. I waited in my cab while he attached a red repair tag to the mower's pushbar and handed the owner the stub.

The woman did a double take at the sight of my face. Once she'd left, though, Nick didn't ask about how I'd gotten banged up, wanting not to seem too inquisitive, I hoped. Nope, he said, Jimmy wasn't around. Truth was he hadn't set eyes on the boy for two, three days now. He was camping someplace, him and a couple buddies.

"Any idea where?"

He laughed. "I can't get two words in a row out of that kid—it's like pulling teeth. He's at the age where he don't tell you nothin' and you can't tell him nothing, 'specially me."

"You don't get along?"

"He's at the age, like I say."

"Is Colleen home?"

"She's down to the Good Shepherd, getting ready for the

recital." He looked at me hard. "What do you want to see him about?"

"I have a few questions for him."

"He wouldn't have nothing to say to you, anyhow—trust me. You seen today's paper?"

"Yes, I have."

"Somethin', ain't it? Ten to one they find out Seb Tuttle was tied in with all that nonsense."

"Could be. Let me ask you something, Nick. When Jimmy's dad died, was he the one who found the body?"

"Yup, and it wasn't pretty. Why?"

"Oh, seems he's been through a hell of a lot lately."

"You got that right." The phone had begun ringing in his shop, but he was ignoring it. "What did you want to ask him about?"

"Jimmy knows a lot more about what happened down at the White Birches than he's letting on, Nick."

"So? You think anybody in this town cares who punched that dingleberry's ticket?"

"You've been a town officer, Nick. You know I'm committed to ensuring the welfare of everyone who lives here."

"Forget the civics lesson, Hector. Bottom line is him getting killed had nothing to do with us."

I smiled at that. "These buddies of Jimmy's, you know who they are?"

"Nope."

"Is one of them named Kurt Mooney?"

"*Mooney?*" He frowned, casting his eyes around the yard as if appealing to the gallery of mowers and tillers. "Know what? I'm pret'near a week behind here, and come the first of August I'm gonna be taking her down to Old Orchard whether I'm caught up again or not, so if you wouldn't mind moving yourself along . . ." With his open hands he made as if to shoo me toward my truck.

I stayed where I was. "Where is he, Nick?"

He folded his arms across his chest. "You think I'm lying to you?"

"That boy is in this thing up to his ears, and somebody's got to give him the chance to come clean. If he doesn't, the consequences could be severe."

"By the looks of you, they been severe already."

I nodded. This was hopeless. "Is that all you have to tell me?"

He stared at me for a few seconds. His phone was ringing again. "Yeah. That's all I have to tell you."

"That's a shame," I said.

I HURRIED BACK into the village to use the phone at Sullivan's to call Wilma's room at the hospital. If Hugh hadn't spent too much time visiting with the vendors, he ought to be done with deliveries by now. He'd be glad to accompany Myra to Evelyn Mackey's in my place.

Kurt Mooney and Jimmy Lussier couldn't have taken Myra. She would never have let them—she knew them too well. They simply couldn't have talked her into leaving the hospital, not a chance. Only an adult could have done that, someone she thought she could trust. Someone she respected. Or already knew.

I had to wait for the phone to free up. The covered porch at Sullivan's Store was hopping on a hot Sunday in late July, kids perched on the railing eating ice cream bars, beachgoers waiting at the take-out window for subs and sodas, fishermen replenishing their coolers with bagged ice, jocular tourists on the porch steps taking pictures of one another at this quaint little outpost, a pair of jazzily attired cyclists making a phone call, and me closing in on a thrill killer.

One of the nurses picked it up. Wilma was doing great today, she reported, just great! Couldn't quite *converse* yet, but if I had a message for her she'd be happy to pass it along. No, no message, I told her. I said I'd been hoping to speak with Myra or Hugh, if either of them was nearby.

"Hm," she said. "You know what? If you can hold just one second, I'll go check with Jenny."

My scalp began to burn.

The nurse came back. "Wilma's had no visitors, Hector, not today. We all figured Myra was over at the farmers' market—with you."

"Of course," I said. "Well, I suppose they changed their plans. That's fine—I'll be up there a little later."

At the back of the produce aisle, the display of Bellevance Hill greens and berries said he'd been here. Something bad had gone down somewhere between the village and the hospital. Car trouble. Or worse. Unless they'd gone back to the cabin for some reason.

But the van wasn't parked in the turnout or up at the end of the steep field road beside the greenhouse. They hadn't been back here. I went inside to check my messages in case they'd phoned, but no. I tried Hugh's place. Nothing.

Upstairs in the cool bedroom, I strapped on my .45 auto and an extra magazine and kept the .380 in my waistband for backup. Billows of sunshine spilled across our unmade bed, where Nicole lay watching me through half-closed eyes. I had never felt worse in my life.

THE COUNTY THOROUGHFARE south out of Tipton wound through a gap between the wooded hills and a marsh. The structures on this stretch were few and all hard by the road—a power substation, Nick Verlander's place, Butler's Bait Shop (boarded up for years now), Merriweather Spring (a two-inch iron pipe set in a stone basin), and a pair of derelict trailer homes. After that the road leveled out and paralleled the old railway bed for a few miles before it curved east through river valley farmland outside of North Allenburg, a crossroads village on the interstate with a motel, a truck stop, a shopping plaza, and, in the old Grand Union space, Morning Glory Natural Foods.

The co-op was as crowded and noisy inside as Sullivan's had been. I checked for my beans and broccoli and premium berries in the cases in the back of the store and found nothing of mine. Either they hadn't made it all the way here, to North Allenburg, or they'd decided to go straight to the hospital.

Out on the sidewalk again I paused to stare back north into the wispy blue above the hills. Hip-hop thudded from a car in the crawling traffic between the co-op and the shopping center. I watched two state police cruisers pull out of the big truck stop down the way and turn toward the interstate. They were headed north—that had to be one crazy scene up there at Coös Crossing.

MUCH AS I WANTED to see her, I couldn't show myself to Wilma. She would insist on knowing what had happened to me, and that was a story for another day. From the in-house phone outside the hospital gift and flower shop, I reached the nurses' station on Wilma's floor and learned that Myra and Hugh had not yet made an appearance. This wasn't good.

At the end of the long basement hallway, this time I found the steel double doors to B-32 ajar, and standing at a workbench at the back of the large room, where he was operating a power grinder, a plump, bald guy in goggles looked up toward me. He switched off his machine and moved the goggles to his forehead.

"Lookin' for somethin'?"

"You Calvin?"

"Who wants to know?"

"Hector Bellevance, Tipton town constable. I asked Sergeant Rob Tierney of the VSP to call you."

"Yup, he said you'd be coming by. Something about a little girl maybe getting abducted?"

"Yes, Friday afternoon here at the hospital. I'd like to review the security tapes of that day."

"No problem. You have a car accident or something?"

"Or something, yeah."

He pushed up from his stool, brushing off his denim work apron. "We just installed this thing end of June. Way-cool new digital video surveillance system. Color, too! Old system was black and white." He pulled out a chair and sat down at one of three computer monitors on a long oak library table. "You know what you're looking for? I got, like, thirty-two different camera locations. They're all on five-second intervals. You want a particular floor, main desk, pharmacy, ER? Or, I mean, what are you looking for?"

In minutes Calvin had pulled up one image of Myra entering the elevator on the neuro floor and two consecutive images of Myra walking out through the hospital's sun-filled glass-enclosed vestibule at thirty-five minutes after twelve on Friday. She was by herself. In the last picture it appeared as though she had turned to the right, toward the parking area, rather than left, toward the roadway and the sidewalk.

We reviewed about fifteen minutes' worth of images on either side of twelve thirty. Some two dozen people passed through that busy vestibule in that span of time, and none was Jimmy Lussier or anyone else I recognized.

Except for the silver-haired man in the green, short-sleeved physician's scrubs and pale blue slacks striding out into the glare of day about a minute after Myra. His face was averted. But his gold timepiece with the pearlescent dial looked a lot like the distinctive wristwatch Casper Knowlton wore. What would he be doing here?

I thanked Calvin for his help.

Upstairs at the Emergency Room intake desk, the bright-eyed young woman named Rachel recognized me from my visit the day before. Had I come in for more treatment? Behind me, a boy with a scraped face and a broken arm was whimpering, talking with a young doctor.

I smiled and said no and asked Rachel if I looked like I needed treatment, and she smiled. I explained that, in fact, I was looking for Dr. Casper Knowlton, if by chance he might be available.

"Dr. Knowlton? Gee. As far as I know . . ." She found a book on her desktop and flipped it open. "No, Dr. Knowlton's not scheduled in today, and he's not on call. Maybe someone else could help?"

I gave her a small shake of the head. The doctor was ushering the whimpering boy and his hovering grandmother in for X-rays.

In a setting like this, Myra would have done almost anything the smooth-talking doctor asked her to do. Knowlton wasn't a stranger to her. She had met him a year ago, when he hosted a Democratic Party fund-raiser that she and Wilma and I attended up at the old girls' camp. Any pretext Knowlton could invent might get Myra to leave with him. Where to? The girls' camp? The White Birches? Henderson's cottage out at Westlook?

I didn't think Knowlton would have killed Seb Tuttle. But if he was connected to the murder, the likeliest link would be his neighbor and golfing buddy, Marty Henderson. Wouldn't it? Or Kandi.

"Rachel, will you kindly check and tell me whether Dr. Knowlton was here in the hospital Friday morning?"

She frowned and hesitated. "I don't— Is there some reason you're—"

"Hector? *Hector?*" The hoarse voice came from the open recovery area behind her.

I charged around the intake desk as Rachel rose in protest. "Mr. Bellevance! Please! Just a minute!"

I beat through the green curtains separating one side of the ER treatment area from the waiting room.

In one of the recovery alcoves an old man, his head bandaged, lay back on a gurney with a—

"Hugh! *Christ,* what happened to you? Where's Myra?"

"Oh, Jesus, Hector, I don't know! I don't know." His speech was slurred.

"All right, what happened, Hugh? How long have you been here?"

"An hour? I don't know. We got waylaid, Hector." His voice broke, and he shut his eyes. "Down on the Common Road. Some gal—"

"*Who? Who did this?*"

Rachel and a husky male nurse came hustling up on either side and tried to push between me and Hugh.

"*Sir! Sir! Sir!*" the nurse was barking. He had a canister of pepper spray aimed at my face.

I raised my arms, holding my hands out to the sides to appease him and also to open my jacket so they could see my holstered .45. "Listen up, now, people! This man's the victim of first-degree felony assault! I need to take a statement from him *right now.*"

"Right, right, he's right! That's right!" Hugh said.

The husky nurse and Rachel exchanged a look. Just then somebody's scream and a rising commotion out in the waiting room had Rachel trotting back in that direction.

"Two minutes!" I told the nurse. "That's all I need. Two minutes, and I'm out of here."

Someone screamed again.

Hugh's hands gripped the edges of his mattress as he tried to raise himself. "Some— Some young woman. Flagged me down, asked me— Asked me to look at her radiator. Soon as I leaned over, a guy jumped up and *wham*. Next thing I know I'm down in the weeds covered in blood, and the van's gone. And so is Myra!"

"We'll get her back, Hugh. How are you doing?"

"OK. Got beat on worse than this down in Hattiesburg, freedom summer. You think they thought I was you?"

The nurse said, "Lay back down now, Mr. Gebbie. Come on now."

"They might've," I said. "Where did this happen?"

"Tipton. Just before we got to the Common Road. There was a car angled off the shoulder with the hood up. And— And this dark-haired gal was standing there waving. Naturally, I pulled over. But how did she—"

"What kind of car?"

"Blue. Slate blue."

"The dark-haired gal, was she a striking-looking woman about thirty?"

"Yes. Beautiful."

"And they took the van."

"Somebody did," he said.

Knowlton. Knowlton and Kandi. What could have made them decide that snatching Myra again would improve their situation? Knowlton wasn't that stupid. "Did you see anybody else?"

"All I saw— No. All I saw was twinkling stars and twittering birds. That's not just a metaphor, in case you've ever wondered."

"How did you get here?"

"Dumb luck. Missy Garret was driving by. She and her sister. And they saw me sitting on the side of the road. I couldn't've been unconscious for more than a minute or two, but—"

"Did they report this to the police?"

"I— I don't think so. They were pushing to get to Logan. Flight to Frankfort, I think they said."

"Did *anybody* call the police?"

"The doctor did. I think he did. The doc who stitched me up. Real young guy. Wispy little mustache. Hell, I *told* him I was carjacked. And I said these bastards, whoever they were— They *kid*napped *Myra*." He began to cry. "You think he didn't believe me? You think he thinks I'm some dithering nutjob?"

"No. Trouble is, the police are all tied up with the big meth bust. Look, Hugh, if somebody does show up here, don't tell him you've spoken to me, all right?"

"Got it. What are you going to do?"

I squeezed his shoulder. "I don't know. But I'll sure as hell come up with something."

TWENTY-TWO

I WEDGED MY SILVERADO IN among the pickups and boat trailers parked at the fishing access and made my way along the shore, painfully maneuvering among the alders and willows and straddling waterlogged blowdowns, until I reached the trim grounds of the old girls' camp. The hammered-silver lake was buzzing with motorcraft and dotted with canoes and pedal boats. A few sails gleamed off to the north, where there must have been a breeze, though they didn't appear to be moving.

By the time I'd reached the camp's onetime archery pitch, my workshoes were soggy and my trousers soaked to the knee.

Knowlton's blue Mercedes wagon stood in the porte cochere between the orchid house and the main building. No other vehicles and no people were in sight. Leaning against a side porch pillar was Kandi's silver Cannondale.

I walked up the four broad steps, opened an unlatched screen door, and stepped into a plain, tiled kitchen. The appliances looked like antiques. I heard no voices, no music, only water—a fountain of some sort. I walked through a parlor, a spacious formal living room, and out through a set of wide French doors to a bluestone patio hemmed with azaleas. To one side an artificial streamlet splashed down a set of veined marble slabs. Eight white wrought-iron chairs surrounded a glass-topped table, which was bare except, at one end, for a white lunch plate, a tumbler with a lemon slice in the bottom, and a black Motorola cell phone.

I pocketed the phone. I looked off across the lawn toward the glimmering lake and the façade of Mount Joe, then looked back at the house behind me, a mountain itself.

Myra was somewhere else.

I followed a path lined with granite curbstone to the croquet lawn and headed across the grass toward the canoe shed, hidden among the shoreline cedars.

From behind the screen of boughs, I could see Knowlton and Kandi sitting in the sun on the natural stone pier, cross-legged and bent toward each other, talking earnestly. I was too far away to make out anything they were saying.

If these two took my girl, where would they have stashed her? I slipped through the cedars to the door at one end of the ramshackle shed and looked in through the uncurtained glass. Nobody.

I tried loosening my neck and shoulders, drew the .45 out from under my arm, and racked the slide and locked it. I was close, very close. One way or another, I told myself, this whole ordeal was just about over.

Knowlton's jaw dropped when he glanced up and saw me standing between him and Kandi and the shoreline.

Kandi's head whirled around, and she froze.

"What in God's name are you doing here, Constable?" Knowlton said, putting on an air of bluster.

"Kandi," I said. "Where is my daughter?"

"Well, check it out, Cas," she said. "The tough guy's armed and dangerous."

"Oh, for Christ's sake," he said.

"Looks like you're a little the worse for wear, aren't you, Hector?" Kandi said.

"Where is she, Kandi?"

"What's the gun for? You really think you might have to use it?"

"I hope not. I'm placing you both under arrest for carjacking, felonious assault, and kidnapping in the furtherance of another crime. I'll help you in the days ahead, Kandi, but starting now I'm going to require your close cooperation."

Knowlton looked at her. "What is he *talking* about? You didn't go and grab the kid again! *Please* don't tell me you did that."

"You're hooked into this one, too," I said to him. "You lured the girl out of the hospital."

"The hell I did! I didn't *lure* anybody!"

"*Shut up!*" Kandi barked at him. "What do you think he's gonna do, shoot you?"

"Kandi," I said. "You're a better person than this. You give me my little girl, and I'll see what I can do when—"

"I'm *better*? Is that supposed to *placate* me?" She laughed angrily. "I'm not going back in the fucking can, mister. You best get that straight right now. I'll kill first."

"I don't doubt it."

"Kandi?" Knowlton patted the air in her direction. "Stop. Just calm down." He nodded encouragingly at her and then looked at me. "Mr. Bellevance? You, too. Calm down, OK? You'll be getting your daughter back. But I hope it's clear that you have to leave this young woman alone. She's very brittle. She—"

Kandi reached out and whacked his mouth with the back of her hand. "Didn't I just *tell* you to *shut up*?"

Knowlton scrambled to his feet, cupping his chin. "That's enough," he breathed, "that's more than enough."

Kandi rose swiftly as well, her crossed calves scissoring, her eyes wide and burning.

I said, "Kidnapping and extortion. Class-A felony. You're looking at twenty years, both of you."

"You're looking at grief for *life*, if you don't wise up real fast."

"Kandi, don't make this worse than it is. You didn't kill Seb Tuttle, did you? What're you into? Drugs?"

"Get off my case, *both* of you! You want your girl back? Go home and wait! Go home and *wait*, you hear what I'm saying?"

"Kandi— Listen to me!"

She made an antelope leap from the outcropping into the shallow water and dashed out across the shingle.

"Kandi!"

In seconds she had bounded through the cedars and out of sight.

Knowlton stood and watched her, trembling.

"It's Jimmy," I said. "It's Jimmy, isn't it?"

He nodded. "She's crazy."

"Where are they?"

"I don't know. I don't know."

"They have Myra. Don't they?"

He sighed raggedly and shook his head. "I had *no part* in that, I swear to you! She said she only wanted to *talk* to the girl! Talk, that's all!"

"Why?"

"Why? To get you off her case! Why should you give a shit about Seb Tuttle?"

"Why should she?"

"He was *stalking* her! He was *threatening* her, and she's— Kandi's so brittle." He was weeping now.

"How could Tuttle threaten her? With what?"

"She'd bought drugs from him. And she wouldn't *sleep* with him."

"So he was threatening to rat her out if he didn't get a piece of her?"

"I would have *given* her anything she wanted! Oxycontin! Anything!"

"Did she kill him?"

He spat out a red gob and wiped his lips with his wrist. "I would have given her a *life*! A future!"

"Answer me. Did she kill him or not?"

"I honestly can't imagine it. But she was not going back to prison. Whatever it took, she wasn't going in there again."

"So who did kill him? Jimmy? Somebody else?"

"I don't *know*. I don't know what happened. I truly don't."

"Come off it, Casper! They whacked the guy! You know that much."

"I don't believe Kandi had anything to do with it—not directly, anyway. She's only trying to protect that adolescent."

"She in love with him?"

"*In love?* He's half her age."

And you're twice hers, you moron. "Did you let her take your car this morning?"

"She's been free to use my car all summer, yes. And my hot tub and my laptop and my washer-dryer. Whatever she wants."

"Did she say where she was going?"

He shook his head. "I never even knew the car was gone."

BETWEEN THE STONE PILLARS at the mouth of the girls' camp drive, twin crescents of spewed gravel told me Kandi hadn't sped east on the Lake Road toward her father's campground and Westlook, as I'd expected, but instead had turned west, toward the village. She'd gone to join Jimmy, I could only guess, wherever he was holed up—to warn him. Maybe to run with him. And wherever he was, Myra was there as well, waiting for me.

That was all that mattered. The essential questions now had answers—obvious answers. Naturally, Kandi had fallen for the smooth-faced virgin boy. Sure, she'd dazzled Seb, and Knowlton, and me, and every other red-blooded man who'd laid eyes on her. And Seb had worked his game and played his sleazy angles and paid the price for being the self-engrossed fool that he was.

What was Knowlton's word for her? *Brittle.* Brittle, hell. She was enraged. And desperate. And, yes, more than a little crazy.

She was the motivator and the mind behind this busted scheme to protect her precarious freedom, and now she'd seen just how badly she'd blown it, how freedom's highway had shrunk to a slippery crease in the clay.

PEARL MOONEY'S small apartment was above Bev's Quik-stop, a run-down crossroads convenience store on the west side of the lake between Tipton and the Bailey Plateau. I parked off to one side and walked around a grove of sumac and a small, fenced enclosure for portable propane tanks to a weed-tufted lot, where the hull of a speedboat and a few gutted American cars sat in the sun.

Two flights of covered stairs at the back of the building led to a sloping porch crowded with junk—a plaid recliner, a rust-splotched chest freezer, a rifle shooter's homemade bench rest, and a dish tub of dirty kerosene, dead insects, and engine parts. I knocked on the rattling door-window and waited.

From the porch landing, the long view across the flats, ruffly with green corn, was placid. Apart from the fringe of the Green Mountains, far to the west, the singular feature that stood out was King's Knob, three miles off. On its crest Jeremy Tuttle's fancy house shone like a dull spark. How long would he last up there now? A week?

I knocked again. I could hear someone shuffling toward the door. A fat, jaundiced woman in a sleeveless jersey parted the water-stained curtains and peered out at me.

I smiled and nodded.

She unlatched the lock and opened the door a foot or so. The air inside reeked of gas and cigarette smoke, and the woman smelled of urine and sweat. Her dry colorless lips made her look ill. Her limp hair hung to her jawline. "If you're one of them repo boys, you're shit outa luck."

I shook my head. "Sorry to bother you, Ms. Mooney. I'm Hector Bellevance, Tipton town constable, and I'm looking for Kurt."

"Kurt? Huh. Well, he ain't here." She wiped the corners of her mouth with her fingers. She appeared to have no teeth.

"Do you know where I can find him?"

Pearl Mooney swayed slightly and glanced to the side, then looked back at me. "So, who done that to you? Weren't Kurt, I hope."

"No, I got worked over by a couple of bad guys. It's got nothing to do with why I'm here."

"Bad guys, huh? How come they did that?"

"Long story, Pearl, and I'm in a hurry. I need to locate Kurt as soon as possible."

"Well, he don't live here, and I got no clue where he's at."

She tried to close the door, but I blocked it with my foot. "Please. I'm sorry, but this is an urgent matter, and I believe you can help."

"Why's it urgent? He do somethin' wrong?"

"This is his home, Pearl, isn't it?"

"Not no more it ain't. Landlady kicked him out three, four months ago."

"You mean Bev Hebert?"

She nodded. "See, Rainey—that's her dumb-ass son-in-law—he caught him stealin' stuff, just candy and stuff, and she said he had to go or she wouldn't let me live here no more. Which, what was I gonna do? I got no place else to go."

"When was the last time you saw him?"

"I don't know, long time ago. How come you're askin'? What did he do?"

"Local game warden thinks he's been jacking deer. But I'm afraid it may go deeper than that."

"What's that mean, *deeper*?"

"Pearl. Come on. You know where he is."

"Snagging deer? Shit, that's nothin'. People gotta *eat,* you know."

"You think it's OK to take deer out of season?"

"I think the law's a little *small-minded* sometimes. Lot of people, you know, they don't even got food stamps. You take Kurt—poor kid's out there on his own, livin' off brookies and dandelions."

"That's a shame. Where is he holing up?"

She shrugged. "The woods."

"What woods? Where?"

"Jesus! How do I know *what woods*? The woods!"

"In a tent? Somebody's camp? What?"

She shook her head derisively. "Next time he slides around, I'll sure ax him for you."

I took two steps to the side of the doorway and yanked up the handle on the lid of the rusty Kenmore chest freezer. The gaskets were shot—every wall of the box was furred with two inches of frost—but a quick rummage through the jumble of crystal-coated parcels disclosed several good-sized packages of what appeared to be crudely butchered, coarse-grained venison wrapped in newspaper and plastic. I pulled out a haunch and peeled the newspaper away. "Look at this, Pearl. You've got deer meat in here."

"So? You can't prove nothin' from deer meat. Could be from anywhere."

"I can tell by your face this is Kurt's. And see the date on the newspaper here? April twenty-seven. This meat's *illegal,* Pearl—the evidence is beyond contradiction."

"Shit, what evidence? You can't prove that's his! That could be anybody's!"

I dropped the frozen meat and shut the lid of the freezer. "Look. I don't want to bust Kurt. I want to *talk* to him. I'm requesting your cooperation. But if you won't tell me where I can find him, I'm going to arrest you as an accessory to a game violation. You really want to go through all that?"

She drew her lips tight against her empty gums. "You prick. Jesus. He's up back of the reservoir someplace, all right? Been up there since mud season, tryin' to make it on his own, livin' off the land like a damn hippie. Back of the reservoir, that's all I know."

"So then he hasn't been going to school?"

She scowled at me. "Kurt? Kurt don't need school. He's fifteen goin' on fifty. His loss, poor kid. Thinks he sees the big picture."

TWENTY-THREE

FROM THE END OF the Civil War until 1954, when Tipton became the last village in the country to get electric power, the men of the town spent a few days each February harvesting blocks of ice from the reservoir to store for use in the village iceboxes and the creamery. The blocks were drawn on a sledge into the town's limestone icehouse, an oblong, flat-roofed structure that now stood under the mossy ledge behind the reservoir like a looted crypt, its thick hemlock-timber door long since removed, its slate floor carpeted with leaf litter. Only the squirrels had had any use for it until about ten years ago, when the select board sold the building to a sculptor down in Rhode Island who coveted the stone. But the sculptor died before arranging to have the building dismantled and trucked down to his studio, and since then his family had shown no interest in the material.

It all fit—the two boys' route through my woodlot and down over the ridge skirting the wetland east of the reservoir, the dry dirt and limestone dust worked into Myra's clothing, the shelter Kurt Mooney would have sought on leaving his mother's place, even Myra's reluctance to get any kid she knew in trouble. Especially if she'd bought their story—or Kandi's story. Kandi, with her charms, would have had no problem duping Myra. Or, for a time, anyone else.

The mouth of the old trace that led from the Common Road through the town forest up to the icehouse at the back side of the reservoir was grown in with spruce and popple. Passing by on the paved road, you'd never pick it out—you had to know where it was. I left my truck on the shoulder and lowered myself in short, stiff steps down the bank, gritting my teeth. The absence of sign in the thick roadside brush said no one had used this route in a long while. If my hunch was right then, Jimmy had driven my van in to the dam on the maintenance road and pushed Myra ahead of him on foot around the reservoir to the old icehouse, where Kurt had been keeping himself.

After all the walking I'd done, trudging up through the woods was agony. I was racked with rippling chest pain, pain overbalanced only by the need to see an end to this craziness, which, in a strange way, put Myra's plight to the side. I didn't doubt I would get her back. I didn't doubt I would have her home unharmed at the end of the day as long as I could handle whatever lay ahead. And I could. With everything I had going for me—surprise, experience, firepower—from here on out it would only be a matter of shrewdly applying those advantages.

After twenty minutes of clench-jawed plodding, I reached a rise from which, through the trees, I could see the broad, silver-blue surface of the reservoir. Off to the side and maybe a hundred feet away, in the shadow of a ledgy escarpment fringed by alders and black spruce, I could make out one pale wall of the icehouse, scabby with lichen. The door opening, from this angle, was out of sight.

And that was it—no vehicle in view, no woodpile, no smoking fire pit, no sign of recent human presence—except, on the intermittent breeze that brushed the water, the smell of human dung. That seemed telling enough.

Then from beyond the reservoir, bouncing off the rough ledge that bounded the wetland to the south, I heard a woman's cascading laugh. After another moment she appeared—Kandi, in the turquoise top she had been wearing at the lake, followed by Jimmy in a red T-shirt and low-slung, khaki cargo pants, each of them carrying a dozen pints of raspberries—my raspberries—in a cardboard tray.

I almost felt like laughing myself at the infuriating spectacle they made, two carefree lovers strolling through the tawny grass and black-eyed Susans along the rim of the reservoir. I moved up to a spindly clump of red osier at the edge of the trees and crouched there to watch.

As they got closer, their musical voices wavered in the soft summer air. If I could hear them, anyone inside the icehouse could hear them, too, but no one came out. Hard to believe anyone would stay inside that dank stone box on a day like this.

Kandi and Jimmy reached the small clearing between the icehouse and the quiet water and set their raspberries on the ground. They fed each other a berry and embraced. Then they kissed. I shivered to see it, Jimmy's hand caressing her buttocks, her arching throat. My God.

Then on the path beyond them—my heart froze—I saw my little girl shuffling along with two big trays of green beans. She had a rope around her neck, a mountaineering rope, pinkish in the sun. A few feet behind her with the rope coiled in his right fist was Mooney, a big kid in a backwards cap and desert cammies. In the other hand he held what looked like a bird gun. When they reached the open area, I could see they'd hobbled her with a short length of rope tied between her bare ankles.

My vision left me for a second or two. Given the chance, broken ribs or no, I could have ripped that boy to pieces.

Myra looked back at him. He was speaking to her.

She set down her green beans and then lowered herself on the ground. A few yards off, closer to the water, the two lovers were lolling back, snacking on the damn berries. What the hell could they be thinking? What were they planning to do with themselves? And with Myra? It was like an aphrodisiac, their fierce desperation.

I had no cover between the osier and the icehouse, just brush and weeds and a single stand of alders. They'd spot me before I could close enough distance to separate Myra from Mooney's grip on her, and I didn't know enough yet to charge into the middle of this situation. Jimmy and Kandi I might finesse, but I didn't know Mooney. I couldn't count on his good sense, not with Myra's neck in a noose. I needed to maneuver closer somehow, and I needed to keep Mooney's firearm out of play. Circling around to the west to angle in from the softwoods under the escarpment would have me wading through the tea-colored marsh—bad idea, especially since I was in no shape to swim if I had to.

I needed help. I needed backup. Not that any police officer would have backed me up if I'd made the request, not even Rob. They'd slap on the cuffs and hold me for arraignment on obstruction charges.

Watch. Wait for an opening, that was all I could do. If they left, I'd have to follow.

Mooney must have lain down. I couldn't see him. Myra's cloud of red curls stood out like a poppy above the grasstops. She wasn't moving, just sitting, tethered to that stupid kid. My heart ached for her. She'd seen Hugh attacked and left for dead at the side of the highway. She'd been dragged out here again, knowing what kind of dismal ordeal lay ahead. Holding me partly to blame, too, for violating the bargain I'd made with her captors.

I tried edging around the low screen of osier for a clearer

view of the scene. Kandi and Jimmy, sitting apart from Myra
and her keeper, were wrapped up in each other, talking, caressing, whatever—I couldn't quite see them. None of them
were looking in my direction. They were facing the water. If
they stayed like that, I might manage to belly in closer—but
the going would be difficult and slow. Yet as long as Mooney
remained where he was—

A loud, music-box jingle made me jump. I let out a yell
and jerked around to my left, groaning at the pain. Where the
hell—? The loud jingle came again. I tried sitting up.

Knowlton's *cell phone*—I had the fucking thing in my side
pocket. I fumbled for it as it jangled again, pulled it out, and
flipped it open. It lit up. I tossed the thing into the trees behind me.

They were standing, all four of them, staring toward
where I sat on the ground. They had seen me, seen me moving, even if they weren't sure who—or what—I was.

I pushed to one knee and slowly straightened.

"Dad!" Myra cried out.

Mooney had his bird gun aimed in my direction.

Kandi said something to Jimmy.

"Fuck no!" Jimmy responded. "Fuck no!"

I walked toward them slowly, watching their faces. After
I'd taken maybe half a dozen steps, Mooney said, "You better
halt right there!" He still had the climbing rope wrapped in
his right fist.

I showed him my open palms and kept coming.

"I said *halt!*" Mooney swung the shotgun around and
stuck the muzzle in the small of Myra's back.

She flinched.

"Quit movin' or I'll blow her wide open!"

I stopped. Some ten yards separated us.

"I don't *believe* you!" Kandi squealed. "You don't know
when to quit!"

"You kidnapped my child."

"*Please,* Dad, *don't!*" Myra wailed. "They don't want to hurt me! They're just—"

"That's enough, Myra," I said.

When I looked Jimmy's way again, I saw he'd pulled a handgun from a pocket of his waistband and now assumed a Weaver stance, gripping it with both hands. Myra's K-22.

"The game's over, kids," I said. "It's time for you to do the good and sensible thing. I'm here to help."

"Nice try," Jimmy said in a flat voice. "You can just turn around and hump it back where you came from. Now."

"Shut up!" Kandi barked at him. "We can't let him go! What the hell are you *thinking*?"

"Well, we can't take him with us!"

"I *know* that! Christ." She eyed me. "Where is that pistol you had before?"

"I'm wearing it. Under my left arm."

"OK. With your left hand, open your jacket so I can see it. Real slow."

I did.

"OK, now just stay like that. Don't move. No bullshit, you hear me?" She approached me carefully, reached out, and tugged my auto out of the holster. She backed up a few steps, then popped the magazine. She counted the rounds, shoved it back in, and racked the slide. "Now," she said, "sit on the ground. Do it!"

I sat.

"Dad," Myra said, "you never should've come out here. They're not hurting me, and you can't *do* anything anyway. They just want you to leave them alone—that's really, really all they want!"

"Myra, honey, I'm going to ask you again not to speak, all right? Don't say any more." Her white cheeks were streaked with dirt and tears.

"You don't *get* it, Dad. You didn't get it before, and you still don't get it. They're being *nice* to me, and they don't have to be."

"That's enough now, Myra."

"I just wish you—"

"*Myra!*" It hurt to shout.

She made a breathy sob and covered her face with her hands.

"What you fail to appreciate," Kandi said evenly, "is that Jimmy and me, we have *nothing* to lose. Whatever happens from here on out, we either skate free or we're all done, we're up in smoke."

I shook my head. "Nobody's skating free. This thing has to end right here, because if it doesn't, it's going to get much worse."

"For *you*," Kandi said, "not us. We have nothing to lose, like I said. You, on the other hand, have *everything* to lose."

"Plus," Jimmy said, "it don't exactly look like you're calling the shots."

"No, Kandi's calling the shots. And she's been calling the shots from the beginning. Hasn't she, Jimmy?"

"So what?"

"Don't get sucked in to his bullshit!" Kandi said to him. She was suddenly flustered and angry.

Kurt Mooney's eyes shifted between me and the lovers and back again. Myra stood with her head hanging, looking at her feet.

"Who told you we was out here?" Kurt said suddenly, jabbing his gun at me.

"I'm a detective, Kurt. I figure out stuff like that."

"But how?"

I smiled. "Look, if you don't want my help, that's your decision. Just let Myra go. The rest of it doesn't matter anymore, not to me."

"Fuck that," Kandi said. "If all you wanted was her, you would've gone home like I *told* you to do."

"Hell, Kandi, you didn't really think I'd just go home, did you?"

"I guess not. You're the fuckup the cops ran out of Boston. And here you are, still tryin' to prove you got what it takes to be a hero."

"No, Kandi—"

"Shut up! The girl's our ticket out of this place. Nothing can happen to us as long as we got our magic charm."

"You won't get anywhere with a hostage in tow."

"Why couldn't you just leave us *alone*? The state police don't give two shits who waxed that prick. Why do you?"

"A man was murdered. You don't think—"

"Sebastian Tuttle? Jesus! He was a *rodent*! Anyway, who says he was murdered? Just because he died a violent death, that doesn't make it murder."

"You should have called me, Kandi. Or the police."

"Oh, right, I forgot. When seconds count, the police are only minutes away."

"He was lookin' to *rape* her!" Jimmy said.

"That's what I'm trying to say, Jimmy. You had *cause*. Tell me how it happened."

"He was coming on to her. He was tryin' to get over on her because he knew she was on probation—"

"Jimmy!" Kandi turned on him. "What did I just fucking *say* to you? Don't tell him anything!"

"I think I understand, Jimmy. You were defending this woman's honor. If that's your story, you should stick to it. Right now that's your best chance out of all this."

Kandi shouted, "Bullshit! *Bullshit!*" She turned to Kurt. "You're in this, too, Porky. We're not leaving you behind either. Come on, we gotta make a plan for how we get out of this place with nobody following us."

Kurt's mouth hung open. He was lost for words.

Myra lifted her head. "Dad? You know what?"

I nodded at her.

"Last weekend when Seb Tuttle hit you with his car, he was *trying* to hit you. He wanted to run you over 'cause you were going to shut down the egg farm."

I looked at Kandi. "She getting this from you?"

She sighed. "He stomped on the gas instead of the brake? You buy that?"

"Does it matter whether I buy it or not?"

"I'm curious how gullible you are."

"If what you did to Tuttle was justified, I will do everything I can to help you make that case in a court of law."

"Sorry. I've been there. In the eye of the law I'm cold spit."

Myra was looking at her feet again. Behind her, Kurt Mooney had his 20-gauge leveled at me, the buttstock against his hip. A few iridescent blue dragonflies were making aimless loops above their heads. "Myra, all I want to do is take you home. I don't care anymore what happens to these people, where they go, or what they do. How about it? That sound good to you?"

She nodded.

"How about it, Jimmy?" I looked the boy in the eye. "You go your way, we go ours?"

He glanced at Kandi, lowering the revolver.

"Are you fucking nuts?" she asked me. "You waltzed into this deal. No way are you just waltzing out again."

"*Wait,*" Jimmy said, straining. "Why not? So, I mean, why don't we just take off, like go where you said before, where they won't be lookin' for us?"

"Why not? *Why not?* Wise *up,* babe, will you? You let this guy go, what do you think, he's gonna just say, 'Bye-bye, Jimmy, have a nice life'? He's gonna go home and *forget* about us? Is that what you think?"

"No, I don't know. But we can't just . . . you know . . . We can't just, like, *do* 'em."

"What do you suggest? I'm all ears."

"What I just said. If we go where they can't find us . . . We drive someplace and we get new identities."

"Yeah. And what place would that be? Remember what your friend Kurt told us this morning? Huh?"

Jimmy just looked at her.

"What did you tell us, Kurt?" she demanded, turning to him. "Huh? Come on."

His eyes narrowed. "I don't know what I said. I said a bunch of stuff."

"You *said,* 'Nobody's *ever* gonna find you guys out here in the woods.' Remember that?" She turned to Jimmy. "Am I the only one that sees what we gotta do here? Tell me."

The distant clatter of a passing helicopter had Kurt searching the sky, then Myra.

"Tell me!" she shouted.

"Tell you *what?*"

"Jesus Christ. OK, try this one. What was the big mistake we made with the egg man?"

"I know, but that was because we didn't have a *car.*"

"And now we do."

"So what are you saying?" He paused. "We should just *disappear* these people?"

"Do you see any other way? 'Cause if you see another way, tell me!"

He frowned. "But with *Tuttle* . . . I mean, that guy— That guy was a fucking creep. He woulda sent you back to jail!"

She made a tight smile. "Thought he had all the cards, didn't he? So, yeah, we did what we had to do. Only now there's these unforeseen consequences."

"Like what?"

"Like him!" Kandi gestured at me. "Same deal, see? Same as the egg man. Only thing we can do."

Kurt shook his head. "The thing is, we keep doing what you tell us, and it *don't friggin' work!*"

"What do *you* suggest we do, Kurt? Give up? Is that what *you* want to do? You want to spend the rest of your life eating powdered eggs and gettin' butt-fucked in the graybar motel?"

"*Jeez,* Jimmy," Kurt whined. "Dude, I *told* you we wouldn't get out of this, man! Fucking shit! I ain't killing these people. I ain't no damn hit man!"

"*Dad!*" Myra cried. "What's happening? Are they going to shoot us?"

"Shut up!" Kurt shouted. He jerked the rope. Myra staggered backwards and fell to her knees. She coughed and reached up and unsnugged the nylon noose with her fingers. It wasn't a fixed knot, then. Given the chance, she could free herself.

Jimmy sighed and sauntered over to Kurt's side. "She might be right, dude," he said in a low voice. "I mean, it's not like we got a whole lot of options."

Mooney said something to him.

"We can't just let 'em *go*," Jimmy said. "We let 'em go, they call the cops, and we're fucked. It's *over*, man."

Kandi shifted her weight one foot to the other, watching Jimmy closely, her head nodding spasmodically, almost trembling, the .45 hanging loose in her right hand. She was baked, I realized.

I flexed my shoulders and slipped my right hand under my jacket to make sure the Walther was still riding in the compression holster inside my waistband. It was.

"But with Tuttle," Mooney was saying, "he had a *gun*. This's different. If we just blow these people away or whatever, it's . . . I don't know. It ain't legal. We got no excuse . . ."

"Who's gonna know? Who's gonna find 'em?"

"Kurt's right, Jimmy," I said. "The Tuttle thing by itself, that you can probably beat. But you start executing people in cold blood, and you're done. You're done for life."

"Shut the fuck up!" Kandi yelled, coloring. "Just *shut the fuck up!*"

Myra was doubled over on the ground, weeping.

Jimmy stuck his .22 back into his waistband and returned to Kandi. "Chill, Kandi . . . Hey hey hey. Chill now. Don't get all bent, OK?" He stroked her hair. "We can figure this out, no problem. We're in control—"

"You're an *idiot!*" Kandi screamed at Kurt.

"Fuck *you,* bitch! I'm not takin' shit from you. That's why I'm out here in the puckerbrush. Because I don't take nothin' from *no*body."

"Bullshit. You're out here because nobody gives a fuck if they see your fat ass again. Which actually could work to our advantage." She pointed the .45 at him.

"Jesus!" Kurt yelped, cringing.

"Whoa, whoa, whoa," Jimmy said. "Hey, hey, chill now, chill, OK? Let's get this figured out. OK? We can figure it out."

"Not too much to figure out, Jimmy," I said. "You want to run, you should go for it. Let Kurt sit on us here for a few hours. Plenty of time for you two to make it to Montreal, Boston, hop a jet to Houston, Rio, wherever. Or just keep driving. That's gonna be your best shot, I promise you. It's a big world out there."

He wasn't listening to me. He had his head bent to Kandi's white face. She was speaking to him in soft tones. Her eyes were on me. He nodded slowly. This thing was about to get messy.

Myra sat slumped on the brushy ground, sniffling, eyes downcast, waiting for whatever was coming. A few feet away

Kurt was watching the huddled lovers in sullen silence. The rope between him and Myra hung slack.

I slowly straightened my spine and shuddered at the pain sawing in my trunk. "Myra," I breathed.

She looked up at me, red-faced.

"You OK?"

She only stared at me.

Kurt idly watched me crawl across the weedy ground to where she sat. I caressed her shoulder. She dropped her face into her hands and wept again. Her neck was raw from the chafing.

"Shh," I said, helplessly.

"We're both gonna die," she squeaked. "And Mom will never know."

"No, sweetheart, no. We are not going to die."

"Shut up!" Kurt said.

I glanced at Kandi. They were kissing again.

I bent to Myra's ear. "Listen to me," I whispered. "Can you take off the rope?"

"Only if I have to pee."

"But you can get it off."

She nodded.

"OK, pay attention. I'm going to back up a bit here. As I do that, you take hold of your rope and slowly draw the slack out of it. I'll be watching. When I shout, 'Police!' you yank on it as hard as you can, then slip out of that noose and scoot behind me. OK? Got that?"

"Yup," she said.

Jimmy turned to look at us. He was grim-faced. He pulled the .22 out of his shorts again. I couldn't help but notice his erection. "Kurt," he said.

"What?"

"It's like she said, dude. We got to go the distance."

"What's that supposed to mean?"

"What we just been talking about! It's gonna work. We do this right, and it'll be like they just disappeared."

Kandi rubbed her face, her mouth, her chin, shifting on her feet, her eyes moving from me to Kurt to Jimmy and back, fingers twitching. Myra had both hands on the climbing rope.

Kurt was slowly shaking his head. "This fucking sucks, you know that?"

"It is what it is," Jimmy told him. "We can do it, dude."

I scrabbled away from Myra and yawned, gauging the distances.

Just as Kurt began to say something else, I squared my shoulders and pointed with my left hand toward the trees. "Look! Police!"

Their heads all turned. I flipped my jacket aside and drew the Walther. Myra yanked on her rope.

Kurt grunted and lurched sideways, and the shotgun's muzzle swept the ground. "Shit," he said.

Jimmy yelled, "Hey! Stop!" and he raised the .22.

I put two quick rounds into his gut.

He doubled over, took a step, and fell. "Hooo," he said.

Kandi crouched, swinging the Colt around.

I shot her three times in the chest, *boom, boom, boom.* Her mouth fell open and her eyes dulled for a second. She aimed at me again, wavering, but then turned the other way to shoot at Kurt, who was kneeling now with his arms over his head. The gun wouldn't fire.

I sent my last two rounds into her torso, wrenching her sideways. Either the Colt had jammed or the safety was still on or she never pulled the trigger. She let it fall from her hand and bent to where Jimmy lay rocking and hugging himself. She put her face down to his. "Hhhuh," she said. Blood bloomed and cascaded from her mouth like a magician's scarf.

"Jesus, Jesus, Jesus," Kurt was wailing. He'd lost his hat.

Behind me, Myra lay curled in a ball. I pushed to my feet and went for the Colt, but before I could close the distance between us, Kandi had rocked back and grabbed up the .22.

I stopped. She seemed to look in my direction, but her eyes were empty. She cocked the revolver. I dropped close to the ground.

She placed the muzzle against her temple and fired, collapsing onto Jimmy's shoulder. He was grunting, panting and crying, his cheek and neck painted with her blood. "I don't— Uh. I don't wanna . . ."

Kurt was sprinting off toward the trees now, gripping his 20-gauge in one hand like a relay baton.

My heart was thudding, my mouth dry as paper.

"Dad? Did you get shot?"

"No. No, I'm all right."

"They were going to kill us, weren't they? That's what he meant."

"I believe so, yes."

After a moment she said, "I wish you didn't have to shoot them."

I had no reply. Wishes were for the future, not the past.

"But I'm glad you had Mom's gun."

"Me, too."

"Are they dead?"

"Listen, sweetheart, go back and see if you can find that cell phone, will you?"

I stooped to pick up the two handguns and then knelt beside Kandi.

She had a pulse, and her lungs rattled with her breathing, but she'd bleed out before long. Jimmy was still huffing, his eyes squeezed shut, his forehead sweaty and gray. He might make it if I could get him some attention.

I got down on my hands and knees to vomit. I nearly

passed out. My ears were ringing, and everything seemed gauzy with the tears filming my eyes—but I could hear birds twittering somewhere.

"Dad?"

"Yeah?" I breathed. The pain was crushing.

"I found the phone." I could see Myra's red sneakers and her white cotton socks bunched around her dusty ankles. She dropped down next to me. "You want it?"

"Call nine-one-one for me, Myra, all right? Tell them there's been a shooting here at the reservoir, and we're going to need an ambulance."

She pressed in the numbers.

I listened to her steady voice, which, by wintertime, would be the sweet, sure voice of a twelve-year-old girl whose mind by then would have cushioned this hard incident in layers of reflection one upon the other until she'd turned it into something smooth and valuable, like an oyster its bit of sand.

TWENTY-FOUR

At the request of the state's attorney, Rob Tierney called the cabin to say he would be stopping by on Monday morning to debrief me in the aftermath of the shootings. Myra and I had spent the rest of Sunday afternoon at the hospital, first with Hugh and then with Wilma, who was alert and strong enough to take in the story of all we'd been through. And that night was hard. Myra woke herself screaming, and I was in too much pain to sleep at all.

But in the morning we treated ourselves to a hearty breakfast of Brenda's fresh eggs and home-cured bacon, and now Myra was busy vacuuming the upstairs. Dr. Kaufman had told us there was a good chance Wilma would be released to our care the next day. She was sitting up and speaking clearly, even walking a little on her own—a turn that could not have come at a better time.

I called my retailers in the evening to let them know we'd been contending with a few setbacks but that I expected we'd be resuming regular deliveries by Tuesday afternoon. They all asked after Wilma, assuming her accident was the reason for the trouble, and I told them she was doing great, coming home in a day or two. They'd know the rest of the story soon enough.

I called Hugh to check in with him. He was home at his farm, seeing to his animals. Would he be able to join us at the hospital after lunch? He'd call back and let us know. Last, I put in a call to Harold Tuttle's office, where Dinah Lynn Doncaster's cool voice invited me to leave a message. "Hector Bellevance at about eight fifteen. Harold, I want you to know that the people who took your son's life have been dealt with. The details will be in the news today, but call me if you have any questions."

Rob brought us a box of donut holes, but we'd already eaten, so he and I took a carafe of coffee out onto the lawn and sat in two of Agnes's green Adirondack chairs. The morning sun came and went behind drifting heaps of cumulus, while I described for Rob's digital recorder how the day before had gone. Jimmy Lussier's condition was critical, Rob said, but he would survive. Kurt Mooney had been collared by a deputy sheriff trying to hitch a ride on the interstate ramp down in White River. He was in juvenile detention. Kandi, as I knew already, was dead. I asked how Marty was taking it. Rob didn't know. I gave him my thoughts on Casper Knowlton, and Rob took a few notes.

After I finished, he was silent for a while. I could hear Spud's baler.

"How are you doing?" he asked finally.

"All right."

"Tough to process a shoot as bad as that one all by your lonesome."

"It can be."

"You going to see somebody?"

"I may." I doubted it.

He turned to look at me. "How's Myra? Awful thing for a kid to go through."

"A deranged woman wanted to erase us from the world, and Myra understands that. But you can be sure I'll be getting help for her."

He nodded and sighed. After a moment, he said, "They'll want you in for an inquest. Tuesday or Wednesday; soon as we can set it up. Lot of wild shit going on at the moment."

"I'm sure."

"Man, there is nothing more friggin' complicated than a homicide scene inside a meth lab."

"Any determination yet on Yandow?"

"No. Autopsy's tomorrow, I believe. The fire was set to cover the homicide and destroy the lab. Two more minutes—literally—and it woulda worked. Shock-and-awe time down in Coös Crossing. Took dental records to ID the guy as it was."

"You round up the other players? Yandow's crew? Ronnie DiGuilio? And that guy Everett?"

"Everett, yeah, Everett Murphy. He got intercepted down at Miami International, and the ATF picked up DiGuilio, plus a couple lab rats, on their way to Boston. As far as the Hells and whoever else was in on this—that's all up in the air for the time being. I guess the Hells have their asses covered pretty good."

"So you knew Ronnie and Everett were running this meth lab?"

"Me? No. Ingersoll knew, and the feds knew, of course—but they had no idea of the scale of it. They basically knew the Hells had Ronnie set up in there cooking product. But jeez, man, turns out these people had a gazillion kilos of pharmaceutical pseudoephedrine stashed down in that basement. Along with all this fancy manufacturing gear and whatnot. ATF figures they might have been cranking out upwards of thirty pounds of shit per cycle—that's *huge*. Not to mention an undetermined quantity of MDMA. They had four of these industrial-grade, twenty-two-liter reactor vessels in aluminum cradles with electric heating coils underneath, all hooked up to tubing and gas filters. Just unbelievable. These ATF guys, man, they were blown away—never seen anything like it."

"Do they know where these precursor chemicals came from?"

Tierney nodded. "All legally imported into Canada from Asia—China, India, Myanmar, Hong Kong. . . . Our neighbors to the north weren't monitoring any of this action too closely until just a year or two ago. Obviously the Hells took advantage of that situation."

"And it was the Hells who got the stuff down here to the lab?"

"Yeah, that much we had on a tip. The piece we were waiting on was how the fuckers were moving the garbage back across the line."

"Tipton Egg Works," I said.

"What about it?"

"That was the channel, Tuttle's egg factory."

"Based on what?"

"Two things. Last spring, just by chance, Lance Henault ran into Pie Yandow and another player—DiGuilio, maybe—having a little discussion up at Tuttle's place on King's Knob. Second, when I—"

"Wait. Your source here is young Lance Henault—who already swore up and down it was *Yandow* that put the boots to his old man?"

"Right."

"Pretty flimsy, Heck."

"Come with me," I said. "Let me show you something interesting."

I led him down to the turnout, where our vehicles were parked in the shade of the willows. In the beaver pond across the road, frogs were chirping. I told Rob how I'd bulled into the cellar of Everett Murphy's girlfriend's run-down tract house up on Ridgeway and discovered the ultimate link between Everett's meth lab and Tuttle's factory farm.

I opened the Silverado's passenger-side door, took out the egg tray, and handed it to him.

"What's this?" he said.

"There were a couple hundred of these stacked inside Everett's girlfriend's basement."

"Two hundred egg flats?"

"Yeah. Along with a small, industrial pulp-molding machine, and a healthy supply of paper pulp."

"OK. So?"

"Your guy on the other side of the border saw the ingredients go out, but he didn't see the product coming back. What you have there in your hands is the reason."

"Our guy wasn't on the other side. He was on this side."

"*Here?* Here in Montcalm County?"

"Yup."

"Jesus. Did he get out OK?"

Tierney shook his head. "Actually, he didn't make it."

I went cold. "What happened?"

"He got aced."

"How? By whom?"

"Not real sure."

"Who was this guy?"

"You don't want to know."

"He wasn't with the Hells?"

He sighed and swore under his breath.

"Rob. If I had anything at all to do with this guy getting taken out, I want to know. I need to know."

"It was Pie."

"Yandow? *Yandow was a federal agent?*"

"De facto. He came to us."

"What prompted that? What did he want from you?"

"You remember the Oscar Firman murder. Well, the attorney general was about to reopen the case."

"Somebody came forward?"

"His old girlfriend, Trudy, or whatever, who was his solid alibi at the time, last winter she got herself jammed up on a bunch of drug charges down in Rutland, and she offered to sell out Yandow in exchange for charges dropped."

"And so Yandow cut his own deal with the AG's office?"

"And the U.S. attorney. That's right."

"How long have you known this?"

"About twenty-four hours."

"So you didn't know it until he turned up dead?"

"Nobody knew but the AG and the feds. I guess Ingersoll got pulled in on account of you suddenly sniffing around after Yandow."

"Who did him? DiGuilio?"

"Unclear. Like I said, the ME hasn't weighed in yet."

"Son of a *bitch*."

"I told you you didn't want to know."

"Fuck that, Rob! I wanted to know from the beginning. I *needed* to know—but all Ingersoll would tell me was *back off, back off*."

"You got that right! You think Ingersoll's gonna compromise a federal investigation to some goddamn local constable?"

"What choice did I have? Two crazed boys tried to firebomb my home. Was I supposed to let that stand? Hell, they kidnapped my daughter!"

He didn't say anything.

"You see that, don't you? Some drug-dealing punk gets his face turned into salsa in my little village and it looks to me like the state police are too preoccupied or cynical to mount a halfway-effective investigation, and I'm supposed to back off? Not a chance, Rob. That's not who I am."

After a pause, he said quietly, "I know who you are. Trust me, I'm not blaming you for what happened to Yandow. But with all due respect, Hector, Seb Tuttle was a POS, and we would've gotten around to him eventually."

"Not good enough, Rob. Sorry."

He shook his head in dismissal of the whole thing, or maybe just of his complicity, or maybe of me, and he tossed me the egg tray.

I couldn't come up with anything softening to say. I watched him crank the starter, swing his big beige sedan around, and roar off too fast toward the Common Road.

ON THE BACK of the living room sofa Myra had laid out a couple of tops and pairs of shorts for us to take to the hospital so that Wilma could choose what to wear. She was sitting at the kitchen table with her markers, scissors, glitter, and construction paper, making a "Welcome home, Mom!" poster.

I set the tray beside her and borrowed an X-Acto knife from her crafts box. She had drawn and cut out four silhou-ettes of Mom doing what she liked to do, skiing, driving, swimming, and cycling, and she was arranging them on the poster board.

"That looks really nice, Myra."

"You had seven phone calls," she said.

"I'm a popular guy."

"Five of them were reporters. I wrote down their names. Esther says there's a select board meeting tomorrow at seven thirty. And Hugh called."

"How is Hugh doing?"

"Good, I guess. He says he can meet us at the hospital."

"Great. How about you? How are you feeling?"

"Weird."

"What do you mean?"

She stopped to think. "I keep seeing them. They don't go away."

"Kandi and Jimmy?"

"And Kurt Mooney."

"It's going to take time, sweetheart."

"What if he comes after us?"

"Mooney? I expect he'll be locked up for quite a while."

"I know. I mean when he gets out."

"He won't come after us. Neither will Jimmy. They'll grow up." I hoped.

She shook her head. "Kandi told me they didn't do anything wrong. She said she and Jimmy were like Romeo and Juliet, and if you got her sent to jail over nothing except love, you would have to pay for that. She was going to make sure."

"Myra. Kandi believed that if she could get rid of me, then nobody would ever figure out what they'd done. And she might have been right."

"She said it was the Hells Angels. She said Seb musta cheated them somehow, and nobody *ever* gets over on the Hells Angels."

"Right, and I might have believed that—if Jimmy and Kurt hadn't tried to barbecue us."

"I know. God, that would have been *awful* if they did."

I stroked her arm.

"How come they showed up here that day, those two bikers? Just to scare you off the case, like Jimmy was trying to do?"

"Who told you about that? Hugh?"

"Yeah. The police asked me about it, too."

"Seb's murder was a big problem for them. Kandi and Jimmy both let it out that they'd seen the Hells come through the campground asking about 'the egg man.' Pretty good story. Tough for the Hells if it stuck. But the state and the feds didn't want to come down on them because they weren't ready to pull the trigger on the meth investigation. So the Hells saw *me* as the big threat."

"They didn't care about Seb Tuttle, either?"

"What they cared about was the egg factory. They had their hooks in Jeremy somehow—maybe in Seb, too. They sure didn't want me messing with the Tuttles."

"And the police didn't want you messing with Yandow."

"Right."

"Dad, don't you feel kind of sorry now that you didn't just do what the police told you to do?"

"I feel a lot sorrier that you and I had to go through everything that we went through."

She nodded soberly. "You know what I keep thinking? I keep thinking, OK, so they killed Seb Tuttle. *So?* I mean, if you murder somebody, I know that's the worst. But they only did it to *protect* themselves, you know? Like in self-defense. Because Seb was blackmailing them, because he knew Kandi and Jimmy were in love."

"Doing drugs is a crime, Myra. So is taking sexual advantage of a minor. And killing somebody to cover up those crimes is just about as bad as it gets."

"Yeah," she said. "I guess."

I slid the short blade of the knife carefully around the fused outer edge of the egg tray. The thing separated, biscuit-like, into a top layer and a bottom layer. Prying them apart, I discovered within the cone of each protuberance a hollow containing a compressed ball of crystal about the size of a macadamia nut. I whistled.

"What is it?" she said.

I showed her.

"Ooo, that's drugs? Those nuggety things?"

"Cute, huh?"

"It's *so* weird." She touched one with a fingertip. "So what do you do? Do you eat it?"

"You smoke it. In a special pipe."

"Yuck, really?" She frowned. "I don't even get why people smoke cigarettes. What's so great about drugs, anyway?"

"Do you remember when you and Lyle used to spin around on the lawn and get so dizzy you couldn't walk straight?"

"Yeah, but that's like the Tilt-A-Whirl at the fair. That's nothing you would ever get *addicted* to."

"All I mean is people have a natural urge to distort the way they experience the world, purely for the pleasure it gives them. It's human."

"Yeah, but you take somebody smart, like Kandi. Why would you do drugs when you know already that they could destroy your mind and your body *plus* you would go to jail if you got caught?"

"Some people do crazy things. For all kinds of complicated reasons. That's why we make laws and hire other people to keep the peace."

"So we can be safe from the crazy people."

"And the crazy things, that's right."

MY NOISY NYLON DELTA, a purple, lime-green, and rose pterydactyl with a twelve-foot wingspan, soared and swooped above Spud's high hay piece, ripping the air in figure eights. Wilma leaned back against the pull, arms straight out, dancing, hopping, her heels digging into the hay stubble. The kite's lines joined her to the blue, as she powered the delta toward the ground and up again, out and up, shedding wind.

I sidled along next to her, taking a few snapshots with our old Nikon. Myra was applauding from one of the camp chairs we'd set out on the knoll.

It was another perfect summer afternoon. Wilma had been back with us for three days. She was almost herself, and that alone seemed miraculous. So far she showed none of the signs of confusion, irritability, or depression that we'd been advised to watch for. It was Hugh's belief that Wilma simply possessed too much strength of character for any conk on the noggin to send her askew, and I could only agree.

My preliminary interview on Tuesday afternoon with the state's attorney had been brief. There would be a formal inquest in a few days. I would eventually be charged with obstructing a federal investigation, but by wintertime, after all the complexities had sorted themselves out, the state and the feds would drop all charges. Jeremy and Genevieve Tuttle would quietly slip out of the country. I would receive by registered mail a creamy letter from Adam Robothem, Esq., of Robothem and Clement, Harold Tuttle's lawyers in New Brunswick, thanking me for my services, confirming that "all of the provisions of our original understanding" would be adhered to as agreed, and requesting that I direct "any and all further communication with Mr. Harold Tuttle to the offices of the undersigned."

The state would seize the property and assets belonging to the Tipton Egg Works, but, without Yandow, never would manage to prove that Jeremy Tuttle had a knowing connection to the meth operation. The following spring Jeremy's glass-walled house on the Knob would be on the market for two million dollars, and the onetime Egg Works would be no more than an empty factory temporarily owned by the State of Vermont. Pie Yandow's murder would never be solved.

The cell phone started chiming. It was in Wilma's vest pocket. I had to laugh.

Myra yelled out, *"Mom! Phone!"*

Flushed with exertion, Wilma shot me a glance and hopped closer, so I'd be able to reach into her pocket for her. "You want to answer it?"

"Let it answer itself!" I said.

We had picked it up at the Verizon store the day before on

the way home from a joint checkup the hospital. By evening, Myra had the thing all set up—ringtone, voice mail, call forwarding—and stocked with all the numbers Wilma was likely to need. This was the first time it had gone off.

"It might be Yolanda!" Yolanda was Wilma's midwife.

She tugged the big delta out of one last swoop and then crashed it nose first with a rattling thud.

"Awesome, Mom!" Myra shouted. "You sure stuck your landing!"

"Hi!" said Wilma, out of breath. "Oh! Yes! Hi, Annie! Yes, it sure is. Oh, you bet I am—every minute. Thanks." She looked at me. "Why, sure. Yup, he's right here."

I shook my head. "How the hell did she get that number?"

"Wait—I'll give him to you." Wilma pressed the phone to her stomach and said, "Sorry, Heck. It's Annie Laurie Rowell."

I took it. "Annie! What's up?"

"Victory, Hector! That's what's up! Victory is ours!"

"The egg farm's history."

"Yes! The curse is off the land. Last truckload of wretched creatures just came down off the Knob. They're on their way to some other purgatorium, I guess, but at least we're good and done with that nonsense. Wah-*hoo*."

"Must be time to break out the champagne."

"*Exactly* what I was thinking. I want you and Wilma to come over and pop a cork with us. Say five o'clock? Fine cheese and crackers and *mucho* bubbly!"

"Love to, Annie. Let me talk to Wilma and call you back." I snapped it shut. "Annie's invited us for champagne and Chèvre."

"Me too?" Myra said.

"You can come," Wilma said, "but no alcohol for me and you. I'm pregnant and you're not even twelve years old."

"Hey," Myra said, "don't knock double digits. That's halfway to adulthood."

"Next half's the killer," I said before I could stop myself.

Wilma turned on me with her hands on her hips. "I predict a very happy and responsible adolescence for Myra. She is going to be the perfect model of a big sister."

"I don't know about 'perfect model'," Myra said, "but I really do think the baby will like me. And I know I can teach him lots of neat stuff."

"Did you say *him*?" Wilma asked.

"I just have this weird feeling it's going to be a boy," she said. "Also, hey, don't you think it's about time we figured out what his name's gonna be? I do. We should make a list. Girls' names, too, just in case. OK?"

We looked at each other. Wilma's pale eyebrows rose.

"Guys?"

"OK," we said at the same time.

ACKNOWLEDGMENTS

I owe a great debt of gratitude to my supportive friends and neighbors, as well as to many generous farmers, physicians, educators, writers, and law enforcement officers, for the inspiration and guidance they have given me during the crafting of this novel. Among them are Fran Bessette, Lori Choiniere, Craig Dreisbach, Tony Ganz, Dean W. Gibson, Gary Moore, Howard Mosher, Dick Perry, John Ruttenburg, Amy Shollenberger, and Dorothy Gibson Stevens.

Thanks, too, to my astute and attentive agent, Howard Morhaim; to Shaye Areheart for her invaluable abetment; and to my wonderful editor, Kate Kennedy, who has made this a better work of fiction than it would have been without her. Last, the love and patient encouragement of my wife, Eileen Boland, have made just about everything better.

ABOUT THE AUTHOR

DON BREDES is the author of four other novels, including the two previous Hector Bellevance literary suspense novels *Cold Comfort* and *The Fifth Season*. He lives in northern Vermont with his wife and daughter.

Also by Don Bredes

THE FIFTH SEASON

*A tale of love, betrayal, and
one very strange season*

Hector Bellevance is back in the town of Tipton, Vermont, for *The Fifth Season*, growing vegetables, dating the hotshot reporter for the local paper, and serving as town constable, when road commissioner Marcel Boisvert apparently goes berserk. Hector finds the county sheriff shot dead in Marcel's dooryard and the Tipton town clerk shot dead in her office.

Marcel has disappeared . . .

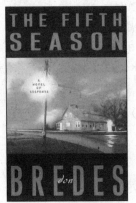

The Fifth Season
$12.00 paper (Canada: $17.00)
978-0-609-60688-9